# BELIEF'S HORIZON

BOOK ONE OF THE LIGHTFEEDER MENACE

I. W. FERGUSON

HAPPEN.NET

This is a book of speculative fiction. Names, characters, events, locales, and crazed notions are either the products of the author's direct telepathic link to a cat who stares at walls, or used in a fictitionish manner.

Furthermore, any resemblance to actual persons, living, pretending to live, undead, or dining with their ancestors; or actual events, or fictional events I don't know about or can't remember, or actual anything else is purely not my fault because I didn't mean to. Seriously, blame the cat.

*For Colsen and Case. May you find all the motivation, discipline, and curiosity within you to live great stories.*

# PART ONE
# THE VISITORS

# ONE
## BIGGER GIANTS

"Hello, little mouse. What are *you* waiting for?"

Lamplight flickered in a shiny black eye; whiskers twitched. Anxious breathing pulsed under slate-gray fur.

"Oh, forgive me. You are not considered little among your people. I can see that you are a fierce and brave mouse." Happen Fell lifted split firewood, fir and hemlock, its bark shaggy with grayish dried moss, and dropped pieces into a wheelbarrow one at a time, trying not to think about the letter, the one he hoped would be waiting for him in the kitchen. A mouse watched from one end of the slowly dwindling stack. Happen rolled the loaded barrow to the drying-porch on the south side of the house, stacked the wood in crossed pairs to allow ventilation, and then returned along the worn dirt path edged with low ferns, mosses, oxalis, lichen-covered rocks, and deepening shadows. The remains of the sunset had finished spilling off the edge of the world, but left the sky glowing as if it had eaten the sun and was digesting it with a slow, blue-violet satisfaction.

Happen soaked up the glow as best he could. It could be the

last sunset he'd see for half a year—unless the letter from his uncle had come while he had been hiking to the healing spring to refill the jug for his father. To check the mail, he first had to finish his chores, yet here he stood, as still as the grand hemlocks surrounding his home. *What if the letter says no?*

"There you are. Not afraid of a squeaky old wheelbarrow." Arriving back at the lamplit east wall of the barn, he took a few more splits from the stack, as far away from his valiant new friend as possible, then saw the edge of a nest built with twigs, strips of cedar bark, and dried moss.

"Not afraid when there's a family and a home to defend." He filled the wheelbarrow from a different part of the stack, then idly rolled it to the drying-porch, imagining what the animal might be thinking. The wood stack's defender might even be Happen's age in mouse years, and preparing for *his* Summering Task. When Happen returned, the mouse streaked across the path on some errand. *Probably checking* his *mail.*

"Swift as falcon shadow you are, little mouse. And as quiet." Happen shook a spider off his elkhide glove, and loaded more wood into the wheelbarrow, exposing another nest.

"I see you have neighbors." He felt the mouse watching from some dark gap between the logs, and kept talking to distract himself from the specter lurking in a hidden corner of his mind —the possibility that he might have to wait another year to leave. "They're like the villagers in the second *Odais Chronicles* book. All their lives led in safety and comfort. But then, without warning, their home is being dismantled, and with autumn rains due any day now. So they've sent you to repel the giant."

It *was* oddly similar to that story from his favorite book series, except this giant was thin, with thick brown hair tufted heedlessly over a high forehead, instead of stout, fat-nosed, and balding. Also, his parents always said he looked curious and interested in everything except his chores, but he pictured the fictional giant's face with a mean and dim-witted expression as he dropped chunks of the castle wall into his gigantic wheelbarrow.

"Fierce and brave you may be, but what can you do against an enemy so large? They didn't even give you a magic sword or anything."

The cozy nest invited him gently in the warm lamplight, lined with dun fur and bits of down bravely scavenged from the feathery remains of a cat's meal. He wanted to curl up all tiny and take a nap in it, not destroy it. Maybe if he left some of the wood against the barn wall that faced away from the house, his father wouldn't notice. Not this year anyway.

Not wanting to leave his smell on the animal's home, he lifted the wood surrounding the first nest and, grunting under the weight of eight split logs, carried them around the corner. He moved the other nest in the same way, and gingerly placed a few pieces on top to hide the exposed nests.

"This might work, my friend, and it might not. There are bigger giants in this world than I."

"Hap!" his father yelled from the back door of the house. "Aren't you done yet?"

Happen quickly tossed a couple of armfuls of wood, *thunk-thunk* into the wheelbarrow, careened through the yard, and called out above the frenetic squeaking, "Almost."

"Bring the lamp in. You've used enough oil as it is without doing your day's work at night. Might even speed you up a bit."

"Yes, sir. That makes sense. I can finish moving that wood tomorrow."

"No, you'll finish tonight after you bring the lamp in. Today's chores today. By thunder, you know this!"

Happen grumbled to himself, extinguished the lamp, and brought it back to the house. He knew there'd be no point in asking about the letter yet. Grateful for the few leaks of gray moonlight that filtered through the trees, he finished moving the firewood, feeling the path through boot soles worn thin.

"We saved you some dinner," his father said as Happen entered the dim kitchen. The flicker and glow from the smudged window of the summer stove illuminated the gray-blue flagstone floor and the rim of the glass in the unlit lamp on the table. "But you'll have to guess what it is in this light."

"Have you heard from Uncle Tinker?" Happen breathed in the aroma of roasted elk, onions, and garlic as his father ladled stew into a bowl. Reginall Fell limped from the stove to the table with a bowl in one hand and a stout maple crutch in the other, while Happen washed his hands in the stone sink and wiped them on his linen shirt.

"The doctor came up from Pury today by the tull trail, all that way to check on my splint and make sure the bone is setting properly. Also, brought us a letter from Tinker." He limped back to the stove, grabbed a bowl from a shelf, and ladled some stew into it. "Might as well have another with you. There's a little left if you want more," he said. A hint of a smile started in his eyes as the firelight kindled bits of gray in his auburn beard.

Happen knew his father would wait, would make him ask. He wasn't sure, though, whether his father knew about the sickly feeling that had been squeezing Happen's gut since the accident had endangered what would be his first trip off this miserable peninsula. But the letter *had* come. He squeezed the ceramic bowl between his hands, trying to stay calm by looking down and following the tight grain pattern in his wooden spoon.

"Yes, sir," he said in a shaky voice. "What did he say?"

"Thanks for asking. He says the bone's setting just fine, but I'll have to stay off it till Longest Night at least. Of course, he doesn't know about the healing spring, but it's still going to take at least a mester—"

"The letter, Father!"

"Oh, you meant what did *Tinker* say! I should have known." He paused to chuckle. "Your uncle approves of the plan, though he says Cortham will be jealous."

"He approves. That means . . . that means I'm going?"

"Yes. Your mother is making new boots for your trip right now."

Happen took a deep breath, and the lurking specter retreated. In two days he'd be on his way to the autumn trade fair —both completing his Summering Task and finally seeing the world beyond the Irelian woods.

Happen hadn't slept well, but was too excited to keep trying, so he crept down to the kitchen early. The sun hadn't yet risen above the forest to the east, but the sky was bright with anticipation and it filled the room with a soft, indirect light. Now that he knew he was leaving, the sights and smells of his home warmed his heart. This time of year, the kitchen smelled of drying apples. The breakfast table, made from sturdy maple slabs rounded with pumice, smoothed with sharkskin, and finished with linseed oil, seemed steeped in warmth, laughter, and love, and had earned a golden hue and scattered nicks and scratches from three generations of refinishing and hard use.

He settled down with a piece of bread to reread the last episode of the *Cravey Mysteries*. The best thing about the autumn trade fair was the stack of *The Sirreltis Seasonal* that his father always brought home. The *Seasonal* was published quarterly and included news from Aeriskenn and elsewhere around the four continents, as well as several serialized fictional works. The *Cravey Mysteries* were his favorite. In each episode, Inspector

Cravey scoured the big city for clues to some outlandish crime, and always found some clever way to catch the villain.

When his mother entered the kitchen, she put her hand on his shoulder and squeezed gently.

"Hap, dear. You don't have time for reading today."

"I'm almost done." He was nearing his favorite part—where Inspector Cravey saved the lovely Miss Mithey from the kidnappers by disguising himself as a chimney sweep.

"No. Put the *Seasonal* down and listen to me."

Happen marked his place with a finger and looked at her. Darlem Barlawine Fell's long brown hair was tied back, and her quick brown eyes squinted with worry as she considered her son. "Your father can't pack the cart this year, or ride tulls, or do anything that puts weight on his leg. After your morning chores, you'll need to ride Abernathy on the gravel again to prepare his hooves. We also need you to get ahead on the firewood and help with autumn cleaning. We're counting on your help. There will only be seven days till the Windy Mester by the time you get back. There's so much to do before you can even start packing."

"Can't we get Osgar to do some of all that?"

"You know Osgar went home after harvest, lazytoes." She ruffled his hair fondly. "He's got his own mother to help get ready for winter. And I've got to prepare for the start of school, dry more apples, and bake bannock for your trip. We also have to jar the rest of the garden harvest. I'll make you a list."

Happen slouched, staring at his boots. A list day.

"Come on. You can get it done if you stick to business. Start with the cow." She pulled the *Sirreltis Seasonal* out of his hand. "Journeys require preparation. This is something you want to do, yes?"

Dinner that night was interrupted by the pounding hoofbeats of a tull cantering toward the house. The tull slowed as it passed the front porch and headed toward the barn. Reginall lifted his splinted leg off the chair, grabbed his crutch, and limped to the back door.

A loud, whiny voice called from out by the stable, and his father responded tersely.

"It's only Osgar," Reginall said, returning through the kitchen.

"He just left two days ago!" Darlem said. She did not like surprises, and she did not like Osgar.

"Says he's got news. Hap, fetch us a couple of pints, would you, lad? And bring me a stool from the kitchen."

Osgar Tallowey had been working for the Fells since he was thirteen. Other employees hadn't lasted more than a year, blaming the dank Irelian weather and moving on. But Osgar always came back, every year for seven years, and for that he was given ale at the table when he arrived, like a guest. He was a skinny man with dark eyes and long limbs, and something about the way he slouched over his mug with his elbows poking out on either side reminded Happen of a spider. Darlem loaded a plate for him, asking after his family. Happen waited, annoyed that Osgar got to sit in *his* old chair, his father's leg suddenly able to rest on a kitchen stool.

"I confess," Reginall said, "I'm mighty curious about what could get you all the way back out here so soon."

Osgar had a habit that vexed Happen immoderately: when he told a person anything, even something obvious like "it's raining out," he'd first look around as if checking to make sure no one else would overhear what he was about to say.

"I heard some rumors at the Crackling Fire about trouble on the roads," Osgar began, his stringy blond hair dragging on the table as he checked the kitchen and the front hall for potential eavesdroppers. "I knew you were planning to send the young master to the fair in your stead, any day now in fact, so I hurried out right away." He always called Happen "young master" in Reginall's presence.

"The inland route especially," he continued. "There's troublesome wanderers on the road, likes of which we haven't seen around here. Old Bahnsen says they must be from very far away. Jocco says we haven't had so many strangers come through since ever."

Happen tensed. He was getting a familiar bad feeling about Osgar's news.

Osgar paused to sample the ale, glanced furtively at Happen, then returned his focus to Reginall. Happen's mind raced. He'd seen that look before. Then it came to him. Osgar was trying to keep him from going. Why else would he ride all the way from Pury with news of trouble on the road, especially the part of the road his father was most concerned about?

"That would be about three strangers then," Happen blurted out sarcastically. Even though he'd never been to Pury, he'd heard about Jocco's reputation for exaggeration.

"Hold your tongue," his father said.

Happen stood and edged toward the pantry. His heart was rushing, and he needed space to breathe and think while keeping an ear on the conversation.

"I don't think it's safe for the young master to be out on the road these days," Osgar said. "Not in these troubled times. Not at his age." Then he added, "With respect, sir."

*Not again.* It was like the first time he went fishing by himself. It was like the first time he'd been allowed to walk to Cor's house from school. He hadn't seen Osgar coming then, either. He stood in the pantry with his fists clenched and his forehead against a shelf, the rough cedar plank impressing its pattern on his skin as he waited for the dizzying sick feeling to fade. His father would listen to his only reliable employee. They spent so much time working together, harvesting and grinding the oats, felling trees, hunting elk . . .

"Well, Osgar, how's about you tell us what you actually know about the nature of these unusual travelers."

Happen heard a trace of skepticism in his father's voice, and returned as far as the doorway, where he could see the two men talking.

"Right, sir, I was getting to that. Bahnsen said he'd seen one guy whose coat shimmered like it was wet, only it wasn't. And it was blue like the summer sky, he said. Miss Jainter saw it too and said it wasn't like any fabric she'd ever seen. Like it was made of wet paint, she said."

"Surely unusual fabric is nothing to be afraid of?"

"Right, sir, but what do you make of this? Rister's cousin, she sold an apple to one of these travelers, and he sliced it open with a shiny knife harder and sharper than knapped flint, she said. He saw her eyeing it, and showed how it could cut right through an elk-bone blade like it was a child's toy. But the strangest thing I heard was about two of them that went through on a wagon in midday. Mr. Fell, they didn't have mouths."

"What?"

"That's just what I said, too. Word is, they looked close enough to regular folks except they didn't have mouths. Their faces were just . . . smooth there. Jocco and Rister swore up and down it was true. I wouldn't believe them, but with all this other stuff going on . . ."

Happen was surprised. Osgar was really piling on the tull dung. His father wasn't the sort to abide ghost stories, though. Osgar should have known this kind of story wouldn't sway him.

Reginall paused and considered for a moment. "Surely it was a trick of the light, or perhaps some of their unusual clothing that made these travelers appear the way they did."

"By thunder, I didn't think about it being unusual clothing. That might explain it—part ways anyhow—I don't know why anyone would want to wear something like that. Still, though, could be folks are overreacting a bit. Been known to do that on occasion at the Crackling Fire. However, I was thinking, considering the unusual circumstances, I'd offer to go in his stead, sir. I could make sure your trade meets your expectations, no lamp oil spilled, if you know what I mean, sir."

Happen started, outraged. What did he mean, "no lamp oil spilled"? He'd used too much lamp oil reading at night, but he hadn't spilled any. He went to the kitchen to fill glasses of water for everybody, and so he could spill Osgar's in his lap. But it took a long time to fill the glasses. Happen's great-grandfather Bartlefen Fell had built an aqueduct to bring water from a nearby spring into the kitchen, and it tended to run low in late summer. This night just a thin trickle sauntered lazily down the carved stone sluice by the sink. Fetching the tray and glasses, he had missed some of his father's response, but waiting for the glasses to fill, he could hear better.

". . . mature enough by now to benefit from a trip like this." Had he been talking about Happen?

"Another option would be for me to escort him myself, sir, to see that he arrives on time and returns safely and all that." Happen cringed at the thought of traveling for six days with Osgar.

"I thank you for the offer, and for coming all the way out here to share the news with us. He'll only be on the inland route alone for a couple of leagues, and my brother will be with him after that, so there's no need to send you as well. Feel free to join us for breakfast before you leave tomorrow morning. Also, if you could please, when you get to Pury, take a message to my brother for me, and tell him that preparations have taken longer than I expected when I wrote him. Happen won't be arriving in Pury till Midluskday, probably by dinnertime."

Osgar thanked Darlem for dinner, and headed out to his room above the barn. He passed through the kitchen, ignoring Happen and taking an apple from the bowl on the table.

Happen breathed again. He'd been wound up tight, like

when they twisted the rope swing at school to make the little kids dizzy. He breathed intentionally a couple more times. A small part of him, he was surprised to discover, was also relieved that he wasn't leaving in the morning, that he had one more day at home.

# TWO
## CLEANING FISH

> Old-timers at the Royal Academy of Aeriskenn say the Irelian peninsula had no recorded history before the Fells arrived to clear land for a farm. The bards of Aeriskenn say the peninsula itself scares people off, with its dark skies, damp weather, and the wildness of isolation.

REILLY, NORA C. (2046). PLANET GRITH:
ALLURING, EXPLOSIVE, AND IMPERILED.
NEW YORK, NY: HARCOLLAN &
MACHUNSTER PUBLISHING

I t took a long time for Happen to fall asleep that night. His mind kept returning to Osgar's visit. Had Osgar really heard strange rumors at the Crackling Fire, or had he made it all up? Father hadn't been swayed by the story. Osgar had come all that way for nothing. Served him right.

In the past, Happen hadn't been so lucky, like the time he went fishing alone.

When he was eight, his father had taught him how to fish, but family fishing trips were rare. When he asked if he could go by himself, his parents answered him with questions of their own. "Do you know how to get to the fishing hole? Do you know how to clean the fish you catch? Can you scare off a cougar?"

He started practicing throwing rocks with a sling right away, but it wasn't until the next summer that he remembered to pay enough attention to learn the way both to and from the bend in the river where the closest fishing hole was. Later that year, he remembered to ask his mother to teach him to clean the fish. Finally, by the end of the summer, he could hit a target from fifty paces, clean fish, and describe the path. His parents said if he took care of everything himself, he could go the very next day. He had been almost too excited to sleep.

That next day he'd awoken with the sun almost over the trees, much too late to make the long walk out to the fishing hole without having to come right back to get his chores done by dark. He had assumed that one of his parents would have woken him in time for fishing and had breakfast ready and a lunch packed.

The next night Happen left his window open, and the chirping of birds woke him in the morning. He dressed quickly and crept down the creaky stairs, keeping close to the wall where the steps were quieter. He made a couple of sandwiches, put some ice in a creel, and found his tackle basket and rod. He fit it all in his backpack with his sling and a tull's horn of angry rocks, and set out for the river. He felt so proud to be heading out alone. The sky glowed in the east, and the cool mists of night retreated from warmer morning breezes carrying the sweet scent of late summer decay. Cedars and hemlocks and groves of knobby old maples with huge leaves covered the path in shadow. A large moss-covered rock with leafy, pale green lichens marked the correct direction at the first fork. An old fallen cedar, nursing a row of skinny saplings in a mossy bed, led the way at the next.

A low fog still floated above the fishing hole as he settled down to eat his sandwich, dangling his boots over the water from his perch on the fallen hemlock log where he fished with his parents. No one chastised him for wasting bait, or talking too loud, or any of the numerous things he usually did wrong, and by midmorning he'd caught a couple of smallish bull trout and was feeling hungry again. He decided to cast one more time before seeing if any late blackberries could be found nearby.

A loud splash in the river to his left startled him. It sounded like something heavier than a fish. It was quiet now; no birds called, and a fear crept over him. Was he going to see a naiad? He gripped a branch on the hemlock, breathless, listening. No, the birds had been quiet for a while, and the sudden noise had just made him aware of the silence. The silence made the noise seem louder than a fish. He breathed deeply to slow his heart rate the way he'd learned from the description of Odais's archery lessons. *Naiads don't get you if you stay out of the river.* That splash meant there was a big bull trout to catch, though.

He edged upstream, scooting along the log. When he stopped to hang his tackle basket and creel on the stub of a branch, another loud splash, a little farther upstream, teased him. He edged farther up, imagining the speckled brown back curving gracefully in his net, until he felt the thinning log bend under his weight and he stopped. There he hung his gear and hurried to bait his hook.

The worm wriggled out of his grasp, shedding bits of cool, dark soil onto Happen's canvas pants. He reached for another one, but his log perch jerked beneath him, and he lost balance, his arms flailing. His fishing line slid through his fingers. The hook pierced his palm and was forced deeper by the log as he tried to grab hold.

Then he was underwater, looking up at dazzling rays of sunlight. He struggled his way to the surface, gasping for breath, and shook the wet hair out of his eyes. He had surfaced out into the pool a ways, the river taking him slowly downstream. He tried to swim, but his boots had filled with water, and the river pressed painfully against the hook in his palm when he paddled.

He reached toward the bank with his good hand again and again with strength fueled by panic. He kept his head up and eyes open, though. He wanted to at least see the beautiful naiad before she drowned him. Instead he saw Osgar, standing on the bank and throwing a coil of rope, which hit the water in front of him with a slap and a hiss and began to sink. He grabbed the rope, held it to his chest, and looked around for the naiad. Maybe he could see her *and* survive.

"Hang on, kid. I got you." Osgar pulled Happen out of the channel to the river's edge, then cut the fishing line and helped him up out of the water.

Happen coughed up some river water, relishing the solid feel of the riverbank and the smell of grass and soil.

Holding a piece of ice from the creel helped dull the ache in his hand, but he was despondent about the accident, thinking it would be years before he'd be allowed to fish alone again. Clouds rolled in from the southwest, darkening the forest as he followed his rescuer on the path.

"Something shook the log I was sitting on."

"Oh? You didn't just lose your balance, or fall asleep?"

"No!"

"I'm just teasing you, kid. I think maybe you got unlucky, sat in a place that bothered a collachin. I've heard they make trouble out here sometimes." Osgar looked about nervously, as if collachine hid behind every tree, listening and plotting to ambush him.

Happen shrugged and went back to watching his feet. "I've never had trouble with collachine before . . ."

"Don't believe me, huh? Think you know everything about collachine. Fine."

They didn't have collachine in Pury; they only lived in forests. Maybe Osgar had lived in a forest before he moved to Pury? Happen didn't know. He did know that collachine slept when the sun was high, but he didn't feel like arguing. He preferred to imagine the cozy collachine dens under the tree roots. He'd never been in one, and was too big to fit now anyway. But he knew enough about them to imagine their dim halls under arching tree roots, carpeted with last year's fir needles, leading to dark tunnels breathing cool dampness that paws at your mouth and nose with the rich smell of soil. A serpentine path would slope gently to a hollow lined with dry leaves and grasses, and lit with a glow worm or two.

He pictured two young collachine, squatting and facing each other with heads down, concentrating on that game they were always playing with roundish pebbles. Without understanding their language—which sounded like a variety of grunts and squishy noises to him—the rules of the game weren't clear, but he had discovered that they value pebbles round enough to roll somewhat predictably, and seemed to use them both as game pieces and currency. Happen sometimes traded ones he'd found for bits of the maple sugar they made each spring. He'd tried trading them other things—once he tried to trade the smallest fish he'd caught, because they're the hardest to clean—but they really only wanted round stones.

"Well, there's one good thing about this accident," Happen said to Osgar, without looking up from his feet.

"What's that?"

"With an injured hand, I probably won't have to clean the fish."

"Ah. You don't like cleaning fish?"

"No, I can't stand it, but I like fishing, and I like eating the fish, so it has to be done," Happen said, echoing the words of his parents. He loved the shimmering scales and colors on the outside of the fish, but the inner organs made his stomach churn.

"Let me teach you a little trick I learned." Osgar stopped and looked around the forest as if he were divulging a great secret he didn't want the squirrels to know. A light rain pattered through gaps in the trees and the coolness of autumn rose from the shadows. "It's about working smarter, not harder. You like to be smart, right?"

"Yes." Happen's ice chunk had melted, so he got another from his creel.

"Okay, here's what you do: insist on cleaning the fish. This trick only works if you act like you want to do it. Then, do a lousy job cleaning the fish. It may take a few times, but keep insisting that you want to clean the fish, and keep doing a lousy job cleaning them. Pretty soon, you won't have to do it anymore."

"Really?"

"Works every time. Now, he won't like you bringing it up, not at all, so I wouldn't say a thing about it if I were you, but have you ever seen your father clean a fish?"

"Sure I have. But . . . I guess, not so much." Happen hadn't thought about it before, but looking back, he realized that, as far as he could tell, it was his mother who cleaned and cooked the fish.

"Exactly. Most likely he wasn't doing it the way she wanted it done."

"But wait, won't they just get angry with me?"

"That's why you have to always act like you want to do it. So long as they don't think you're shirking, you'll be fine. Some folks are just better at things than others."

Something about this plan didn't feel quite right, but Happen would do just about anything to have someone else clean his fish, and it seemed clever, so he decided to give it a try.

After only a couple of fishing trips that next summer, his parents started giving his fish to Osgar, saying that he would take care to clean them properly. Happen started to protest, but then he found he couldn't tell the story without making things worse. Osgar had tricked Happen into making himself seem incompetent, and had been given his fish, too. His nemesis smirked and winked when no one else was looking as he enjoyed fish while Happen had an arrowhead butter sandwich for dinner.

It was two years before he was allowed to fish by himself again, but he always felt like someone was behind him, and fishing lost its appeal. It was several years later, after the ridge ghost incident, when it occurred to Happen to wonder why Osgar had been at the fishing hole at that time of year with a rope. He might be carrying rope in the spring when cutting firewood, but not during harvest. That rope had probably been used to jerk the sitting log.

Happen's father knew no one liked Osgar, but said not having to train a new employee every year was worth a little unpleasantness. Yet even now, as a fifteen-year-old lying in bed trying to sleep, he could feel the hard knob of the scar in his palm, and the loss of what Osgar had taken from him.

But this time? This time would be different. It had to be.

# THREE

# LAUGHING BANDITS

> On the continent of Berythea, rites of passage are complex; critical to the formation of both the identities of individuals, and social relationships; and supported by legal systems. Perhaps the most anticipated of these is the coming of age ritual known as Summering. Older children grow weary of phrases that begin with "When you're Summering. . ." It's a time of life associated with experimentation and discovery. (Reilly, 2046)

―⌐ᵣ―

Happen's murky morning thought-voice allowed him to sleep in for a while, he wasn't leaving until tomorrow, he had one more day at home. *But why?* Today should be the day of his Summering Task. He'd filled the kitchen and dining room boxes with dry firewood, restocked the drying-porch with wood from the seasoning stacks, and split and stacked more firewood to start seasoning. He'd milked the cow, gathered eggs, helped dry and jar apples, cleaned the water closet and the chicken coop, and packed the cart. Everything on his list was done.

Thinking about that list, he almost suspected his father had broken his leg on purpose, knowing Happen would do anything to go on this trip. Maybe he delayed the trip to make Happen do even more chores?

After the Task and the Ceremony, he'd be Summering. People would stop giving him lists of chores and talking to him like a little kid. They said the Summering Task changed a person. *What would that be like?* He found he wasn't falling back asleep after all, so he got up to the sound of fading hoofbeats which meant Osgar had left. Thank goodness he didn't get what he had come for.


After breakfast, his father directed him to take a ladder to a storage closet in the barn. On a high shelf, next to a broken axe handle and some wagon-wheel spokes, sat a large crossbow. Once they'd cleaned off the dust, replaced the string, and lubricated the windlass, the bow looked impressive. Although he'd read about them—Odais used one in the Inirthean War—he'd never seen a crossbow before and hadn't realized how big they were.

"I know Uncle Tinker's strong," he said. "But I don't see how—"

"You always jump straight to the first conclusion that pops into your head, whether it makes sense or not. Try to think it through just a little bit further. This bow is obviously too big and heavy for a man to carry and use, so how might we make it useful?"

Lessons from his father always started like this. First, an insult that made Happen too angry to think logically, then a pedantic tone that ground the anger to a gritty dust and rubbed it in, followed by a question that Happen suspected he could probably reason his way through to learn something if he wasn't feeling so resentful.

"I don't know."

"You don't know. Well, you'll see then." Reginall set down his crutch and crawled under the two-wheeled tull cart, dragging his splinted leg behind him.

"In my younger days, you had to be ready to defend yourself out on the road. Hand me that bow, will you? No, the other way. Yeah, it fires back, you don't want to hit your tull, now do you? Right. Now, there are pegs in here where it fits, but to get it in place, you have to lift one of the sideboards. I'll get the latch, but I'll need you to hold it up from out there."

Something scraped the underside of the cart, and the rear right sideboard dropped about a thumb and swung briefly on leather hinges.

"Push that in and up," his father said. "No, use both hands, like you mean it. That's it, hold it there." One end of the cross-bow's prod stuck out for a moment, then disappeared again. "Okay, let it down." Happen let go of the sideboard, then heard the scraping sound again, but a half-thumb gap remained between the bottom sideboard and the one above it.

"I'm sorry, sir. The latch didn't work right. Should I hold it up again?"

His father grunted, and a thin piece of wood stuck out through the gap.

"It worked just fine. You've made an assumption about a process that you have no experience with and went from there to an erroneous speculation. It's not particularly helpful." He crawled out from under the cart and pushed a leather grip onto the end of the thin piece of wood.

"There, the bow is installed. Now you need to learn how to use it, so pay attention. First, open the back cover, and hook this thing to hold it up. Hopefully, this will be all you need to do to change someone's mind about you. Second, if necessary, load the weapon."

He took six arrows from a shelf and rolled them onto a tray inside the cart through the gap in the sideboards. "Now to the other side. This"—he grabbed the leather grip on the handle poking out the side—"is the trigger, but if you push it back this way, it loads an arrow from the tray. Then to draw the bow you take this"—he pulled a wrench-like tool from a pouch on his belt —"stick the square peg in there and crank it around a few times . . ." Clicking sounds emanated from under the cart. "Don't overdo it now and break the windlass. Soon as it gets hard to turn, stop. There. Now it's drawn. Don't go standing around behind a stranger's tull, and don't go behind this cart when the bow's drawn. Tinker's clever at making things, but they're not always—"

"I understand, sir. Don't go behind the loaded cart. Can I push the trigger?"

"Just a moment. We're still hoping you don't have to, right? In the barn is one thing but out on the road you don't want to push that trigger. This is a composite bow made from yew, ram's horn, and cougar tendons. The drawing mechanism is geared to be easy to draw, but there's plenty of tension in that bowstring, and these arrows are heavier than what we use for elk hunting. Do not push that trigger unless you absolutely have to. Do you understand?"

Happen hesitated. His father continued. "I am quite sure you do not. You think it will make a thundering great sound as it sticks in the barn door, and that's all you're thinking. It does not make a thundering great sound if it hits a person. Here is how to release the tension and unload the weapon." He reinserted the drawing wrench, and pushed in until it clicked, then resisted the wrench handle as he let the crank unwind. He pushed the trigger toward the center of the cart and the arrow fell to the ground.

"Fetch your practice target, and we'll give it a try. We need to test the new bowstring."

Happen wheeled out his archery target from the other side of the barn and placed it by the doors, in line with the crossbow in the cart.

"Not there. Move it about ten steps to the left."

Happen furrowed his brow, but moved the target.

"Good, now reload and draw the bow."

Happen returned to the side of the cart, pushed the trigger back to load an arrow, then turned the wrench to the draw the bow.

"Can I push the trigger now?"

"You're not even pointing at the target! Please try to think about what we're doing."

"Oh, right, sorry. Do I . . . uh . . . turn the cart?"

"Turn the cart!" His father didn't try to hide his exasperation. "No. Go over to the other side of the cart, so I can show you how to aim the bow."

Happen felt a deep unsettling in response to his father's disappointment. It was a familiar feeling, but uncomfortable all the same. When you're tall enough to be Summering, but you're still Springing, that's how people talked to you. It was a difficult time. He reminded himself that Odais's parents had been killed, and that he was lucky to have parents at all. He took a deep breath and started to cross behind the cart, but caught himself and took the long way around the front.

"That's better," his father said. "There's hope for you yet. Here's the lever to change your angle. Standing on the side, you can lift here and slide it back and forth like this, but unless your target's close, it's hard to aim from the side, so you can hop up into the cart and reach down, or kneel under it and reach up."

"Yes, sir."

"Now, aim it at the target, then you can push the trigger."

Happen crawled under the cart, aimed the bow, and then

crawled out on the trigger side. When he pushed the trigger, the cart shivered and made a swishing sound. It seemed like such a whisper compared with the shout of the arrow, which ripped through the edge of the coiled straw target, and thudded deep into the stout barn wallboard behind it. He stared at the bite taken out of his target, and then the arrow stuck in the wall.

"Go see how deep it is," his father said, smiling with his eyes.

When Happen returned, he wanted to draw the bow and shoot again, but his father put a small bag of coins into a wooden box, handed it to him, then set down his crutch and crawled under the cart again.

"You can practice later. This hidden coin box won't fool any serious bandits, but it has fooled some into thinking they'd found what we were hiding. Did I ever tell you about that time?"

"No, sir. You were robbed by bandits?"

"Ah, well. Hand me that box, and grab me the hammer for these pegs. When I was younger, the fair was much smaller. More like an informal gathering of farmers and trappers looking to make trades without having to go all the way into the city market. Pretty soon the city merchants caught on to the fact that they could get a better selection of goods and better prices by coming out to this gathering that happened every fall. And it got bigger and more organized every year.

"One year, when you were just a tiny thing, Tinker and I heard about some farmers who'd had trouble with bandits on the road to the fair. Just in case, Tinker added this box under the cart—we shared the cart then, we'd just started our Harvesting and didn't have much gear yet—and we put some coins in there, about a third of what we had, and hid the rest in an old toolbox. Sure enough, on our way home, they caught up to us on the Rillbane Causeway." He paused for a moment to hammer in a peg.

"The Rillbane has a wide marshy estuary, and the causeway has only one lane, with turnouts every so often for passing. We saw them gaining on us, so we stopped in a turnout to let them pass. Only they didn't."

Happen knew the Rillbane was a river, but he didn't know what an estuary was. He leaned on the cart and tried to imagine his father as a young man in a place with no trees.

"They drew bows on us, and we weren't prepared for it. They didn't want anything too bulky, but they took our whiskey and some of the lighter fabrics we'd bought. What they really wanted of course was the king's solani." He hammered in another peg.

"'You yokels didn't buy much,' they said. 'Must be hiding something . . .' They poked around the cart and found this box, and figured out to move the bean sacks and oil jugs and pull up the floorboard to get in it. 'Aha!' they said. Then, 'This is all you got for the year's trade?' 'My brother likes to gamble,' I said, and Tinker did his best to look sheepish. They laughed at that. 'He looks the type,' they said, and drove off laughing, but with only a third of our money."

Happen helped his father out from under the cart.

"Money was tight that year. But we worked hard, and planned well, and Tinker built the crossbow and modified the cart for it. He found a grove of black locust trees out in the drylands east of Pury, and built some shields for us. The next year, when we saw someone gaining on us on a narrow road, we wouldn't let them pass until we knew who they were. And sure enough, when those bandits came up behind us on the causeway yelling, 'Pull over, yokels!' we had the bow loaded and drawn. That's a good thing about a crossbow, you can draw it a few waves before you need it. It was almost worth the shortage of the year before to see them floundering when we sent an arrow between their tulls and clean through their wagon. The look on their faces when they realized they couldn't turn around or get past us . . . by Grith, that had us laughing so hard we almost didn't have the bow redrawn in time. One of them tried to approach along the edge of the road, but we angled the bow over and put an arrow through his arm. That got them all on the ground till we were out of range. And we didn't have any trouble from them after that." His father inspected the goods packed in the cart.

"Why did you take the crossbow out of the cart?" Happen asked, hoping to distract his father from looking too closely at his packing job.

"As the fair grew it attracted more wealthy merchants, and the bandits became better organized and better armed until the Aeriskenn merchants' guild helped the king finance regular highway patrols. After several years with no sign of trouble, we figured we could carry more goods in the cart if we got rid of the weight of the bow." His father was frowning at a bag of oat flour.

"You think I might need it?"

"Probably not. But things do change, and this being your first trip, I'd rather be safer and sell a bit less flour. I'm glad Osgar's worrying reminded me of it. Make sure you tell Tinker I installed it. And keep your short bow handy. The highway patrol are primarily concerned with protecting the wealthy merchants, they aren't there for you. Sleep near the tulls, and get up and armed if they sound nervous. Abernathy is especially wary of strangers, living up here as he does. He'll let you know if there's trouble about." His father lifted a bushel of antlers to look behind it.

Happen sighed. *Not again.*

His father had explained how to pack the heaviest items, the sacks of oat flour, over the cart's axle, but Happen forgot until he was halfway through, and ended up with bushels of antlers and elk jerky in the front, bushels of wild onions on one side, and sacks of flour on the other side with just a few along the back. He thought it would be close enough, but when his father got a good look at it, he told Happen to repack the whole cart.

"I understand that this isn't exactly what you asked for," Happen said. "But it's done now. Can it be done well enough? Please?" He'd been hoping to have time to reread the first book of

*The Odais Chronicles*, where the young hero sets out on the first of his epic journeys.

"It's not a matter of asking nicely. A cart this poorly balanced will put extra pressure on the tull, and the bearings will wear unevenly; it's liable to get damaged hitting a bump or a hole in the road. It could turn your trip, and our trade for the year, into a disaster. It has to be redone."

Happen sighed. "Yes, sir."

"If you took more of an interest in why things are done the way they are done, we wouldn't have this kind of thing all the time."

"I guess."

"Do we have to have an actual disaster to teach you the value of doing things the right way?"

"No, sir."

"We need a Fell to learn the farm if we are to keep it in the family."

"I know." Happen didn't want to think about that. Not yet.

"I know you don't understand the value of it, because you've always had plenty, but I wish you could . . ." His father paused, considering his son sadly. "I wish you could understand the value of the farm without having to learn everything the hard way."

Happen felt like his father didn't see him at all. "But I'm not just a younger version of you or Tinker. You don't know what I need to learn." An anger welled up inside him, one much older and heavier than could be built in a day. It churned below his surface so intensely that Happen grew frightened, swallowed it down, and looked away.

A light gust of wind whistled through the open barn door, and a passing cloud dimmed the sunlight.

"Hey," his father said. "Did you feel that?"

"Yeah."

"It's here. A day or two late, but here." The breeze had a different feel, cool and damp. Father and son stepped outside to breathe the changing of the season. Happen wondered if his father was going to respond to his outburst, and couldn't decide if he wanted him to or not. High gray clouds reached toward them from the southwest, towing the vast annual stampede of wet ocean air, which, when pushed up against the Irelian mountains, would let loose an extended soaking barrage that dampened the spirits of all but the hardy collachine. The wind picked up a bit more, dashing about through the fir trees in the yard like a puppy exploring a familiar haunt. It still had the dry, dusty smell of late summer as it whooshed along the garden fence, setting the row of dead sunflowers nodding, their sallow, straw-gray heads drooping eastward, rasping and rattling in bloodless song.

"Won't get the smell of it till after I leave, though," Happen said.

"No, but I think I'll go fire up the stove, so you'll have that."

He meant the masonry heater in the dining room. The little summer stove was built into an outside wall of the kitchen to keep it from overheating the house. But the masonry heater was a mountain of brick and stone rising through the middle of the house. Bartholofew Fell, Happen's great-great-grandfather, built most of it long ago, although later generations added to it as the house grew over time.

The bricks of the heater could be seen, and its warmth felt, in almost every room in the house. It took a long time to warm up, but then it provided a comforting, thorough, dry heat after a cold rainy day, and changed the smell in the house in a way that made Happen glad to be home. Toward the end of winter, when he hadn't seen the sun or moons for half a year, the house would feel small and stuffy, and he longed for the end of fires and the spring opening of windows. But at the beginning of autumn, the lighting of the stove was welcomed like an old friend.

# FOUR
## RESTORING EQUILIBRIUM

" One of the core tenets of the Gracarrai religion is the promotion of literacy, and since Gracarrai came to prominence on Grith, technological advances in printing and new forms of publishing have been celebrated with regularity. (Reilly, 2046)

⌐

Happen awoke reluctant to leave his heavy wool Springing blanket. A subtle scent of woodsmoke spiced the air, and the weight of the blanket and the gray light outside encouraged him to close his eyes, and float back into the depths of dream. The moss covering the cedar shake roof silently absorbed the rain, but drops pattered on the packed gravel and puddles by the barn. A gust of wind rattled his window. It was the sudden Irelian autumn, reminding him what day it was. He got up. *This is the day I'm finally getting off the peninsula.*

There would be no accident or illness or bad weather or meddling from Osgar this time. His mother was taking their other tull, Arble, to the schoolhouse with a load of firewood, but even if they couldn't go for some reason, he and Abernathy would still be leaving. He felt fine; Abernathy and the cart were ready. He hopped down the steps and out the door to stand in the rain, looking up, letting it fall on his face and closed eyes. It was good, normal rain. It fell patiently, straight, normal. He was really going this time.

$$\llcorner_{\!\!\!\frown}$$

After cinching up the waxed canvas tarp covering the load strapped to Arble's back, his father put his hand on Happen's shoulder. "We have a family tradition for times like these." He took off his hat and placed it on Happen's head.

"Wear this with good health and fortune. I look forward to your return."

"Thank you, sir." It was a nice leather hat with a wide brim.

"Good. Now, don't let anyone touch this hat when it's on your head. Your mother may want to straighten it or something, that's okay, but nobody else. And don't you touch another man's hat when it's on his head. Be respectful when it's merited, and when it's not, be somewhere else."

"I will, sir."

"Keep covered from the sun. You're lucky to have your mother's dark skin, which helps, but you'll be leaving the forest. Much of the trail has no shade at all, and sunburn hurts. We're counting on you. It's a long winter with no trade."

"I know, sir."

His father squeezed Happen's shoulder fondly, patted it firmly, then turned to his wife. "Darly, have a good trip. I look forward to your return as well, and only partly because I need you to make me a new hat."

Happen and his mother and the two tulls set off, heading east. Happen hadn't been able to find his staff, and felt a familiar anxiety sapping his energy, but his father had cut some new staves that spring, so it only made them a few moments late. Tall evergreens on either side wove thick branches over the cart track, keeping in a gloom that was too dark for reading. Maybe tomorrow morning, when he left his mother at the schoolhouse and set out by himself for Pury, it might be dry and light enough for reading. Besides, his mother probably wouldn't let him read today anyway.

"Oh, the music, Hap, the music! There are whole bands of musicians playing together, and much better than your uncle with his ratty old fiddle. And the food! Try as many different foods as you can. There's so much to experience. And you must see a play while you're there. I do hope the actors' guild sends out a good one for . . ."

He stopped listening and resumed the thread of his own thoughts. His mother was forgetting that she had said all these things to him several times before. He seriously doubted he'd have the time or inclination to see a play or a choir. Those were things Mistine would want to do, not him. In a few waves she'd ramble into some feature that would trigger a shift from what she was excited for him to experience, to what could go wrong.

". . . and it's okay to talk to people, as many people as you can, so long as you don't give them any money. People will say anything and everything, and it's all very interesting, just don't give your money to strangers. And only buy food from carts with signs that have a display showing their prices. Some of those vendors like to charge whatever they think they can get away with. But, oh, the seafood! You'll get to try crab! And lusks! Get the lusks boiled in wine, that's my favorite, though it can be messy, so make sure you have a napkin. And then try the . . ."

Her rambling and the forest gloom began to coat him in a blanket of drowsiness. His stride wavered, and he steadied himself with a hand on Abernathy for a moment that filled him with that uncanny sense like he'd been in this situation before.

Was it some other time he was thinking of, when he was headed to school with his mother, wearing new boots, and . . . were both tulls with them that time? No, just Arble with the firewood. No, the other common factor was Osgar. Or that he was worried about Osgar. He was remembering the first autumn walk to school after the ridge ghost incident. He had new boots that year also, to replace the ones he'd lost in the marsh escaping the fake ghost Osgar and Mistine had rigged up to keep Happen from visiting his cousin in Pury. The humiliation of that experience was still unbearable, and he felt his face flush. He had to use Odais's three-step plan for restoring equilibrium: present, goal, music. First, use the senses to reorient into the present. Second, choose an achievable yet important short-term goal, and work toward that. Third, hum a tune, either internally or out loud if necessary.

Happen breathed in the rich smell of damp forest, listened to the pattern of tull hooves thudding on the duff-covered gravel track, felt the pumiced grip of the new hemlock staff in his hand, and drank in the pale green of the ferns uncurling above the forest floor along the way. His short-term goal would be the schoolhouse, where they expected to arrive that afternoon.

The schoolhouse was about a league from his house, and, depending on the route taken, two or three leagues from Pury. They'd built it when Tinker had moved to Pury to try to save his marriage. Darlem had been educating Happen and his cousin Cortham, and they wanted to continue that instead of sending Cor to the town school in Pury. After some time, a few other families in Pury sent their kids there, too, and it became a small source of income for the Fells.

Happen had always approached the schoolhouse, and the school year, with a complicated mix of feelings. School was more interesting than harvesting arrowhead tubers or cutting and stacking firewood, although he did enjoy hunting in the woods for wild onions, mushrooms, and antler velvet. He also had more free time for reading on the farm. At school, he was assigned books to study with subjects like the development of glass or the use of geometry in architecture. But he preferred to read stories about adventure and mystery, especially ones set in warm, sunny climates. The farther away from Osgar and the farm, the better.

Because of the distance, both students and teacher stayed at the school day and night for three days at a time. At first, when Happen and Cor were the only students, the new school had been fun, but as other kids joined, he and Cor had more chores to do. Then the second year, Osgar and his sister Mistine came to town. Happen's mother told Happen and Cor how the new children's father had left the family: he came into town, rented a room at the inn for them, and then just left. And so, they had to be extra nice to the Talloweys, even if no one liked Osgar.

"You're so quiet, Hap. What are you thinking about?" She had that worried look again.

"School."

"It's the first time in eight years you won't be going. It's a big change."

"Yeah."

"In all the excitement about going to the fair, we haven't talked much about your future lately. Have you been thinking about it?"

"Not really." When he'd graduated, his parents had had a big argument about his future. Darlem wanted him to attend the academy in Aeriskenn, even if they had to sell the farm to pay the tuition. Reginall wanted him to stay and learn to manage the farm. Happen wanted very much to attend the academy, but didn't want them to sell the farm. It had been in the family for four generations, and he loved it. But he didn't want to manage the farm, not yet anyway, and he knew Cor didn't either. Thinking about his conflicting priorities and unable to find any compromise or way forward that honored both, his mind just gradually filled with fog until he didn't even know what he wanted. He wouldn't have any say in the matter until he Summered, so the unmade decision loomed in the corner of his mind, waiting for its chance to torment him. He'd spent the summer reading and hoping that completing his Summering Task would help him decide.

"That's for the best, I suppose," his mother said. "Sometimes it's best to focus on the present. We want you to make your trades and then enjoy the fair. How are your boots feeling?"

"Fine."

His mother sighed and was quiet for a while. Then she told stories about when she was a girl and her parents worked hard so she could get an education even though they didn't have enough to eat and how he should appreciate all they had. He stopped listening because he'd heard the message before and though he probably *should* appreciate all they had, there was a difference between thinking it and feeling it. And he didn't feel it.

It wasn't raining at the school. Though the cloud cover persisted, less rain fell there, as it was farther east and at lower elevation, and so less affected by the climate pattern that afflicted the peninsula. Still, the roofs of the schoolhouse, shed, and outhouse were thickened by heavy green and brown mosses, just like home. But his mother was different. She changed when at the school. Like the shortening of days for winter, she became colder and less patient, and though the change arrived at the same time each year, it always took Happen by surprise.

She made a list. Happen helped sweep, dust, clean the kitchen, and make the beds in the loft. As the sunlight he'd planned to read by slowly dwindled, a frustration churned in his stomach. He'd been looking forward to getting back to the first book of *The Odais Chronicles*.

After dinner his mother wanted to go over the trade list to

make sure Happen could read her handwriting and understood the amounts. She said Tinker would show him how to scout the market to set competitive prices. Also, Tinker would sell the powdered antler velvet for them. It was extremely expensive and there was a specific exporter they sold to each year who would buy all they had.

"We're selling more than usual this year, because"—she paused to clear her throat—"well, because your father missed some work with his accident, and we're going to buy more lamp oil than past years—"

"I said I'm sorry, okay?"

"I know, I know, I'm just explaining why we're doing what we're doing," Darlem said. "You do better work when you understand the reasoning behind it. You might find you like going to the fair and want to do it again, so you should learn the business end of things. Okay?"

"I know." Happen crossed his arms and gripped his elbows. His father had already been through this. Her reminder about learning the farm business added a volatile ingredient to his churning frustration.

"Good. Now start with medicines." She pushed the list across the table at him, reading it upside down so he could see it well. "Chinchona bark to fight the ague is the most important one. Kids at school are always coming in sick because of those marshes near Pury. We always tell their parents to move away from the southeast part of town, but that's where they can afford a house, so they stay there, and we have to have chinchona bark. One eighth of a stone."

"Okay, I understand. I'll make sure to get an eighth of a stone."

"Good. Also, get Tinker's help buying the whiskey. He'll be more than happy to make sure it's good before you buy it."

"And then the food, then lamp oil, and then the fabric and

leather, and last the news and Azmerian stones for Longest Night. I know the order of things."

"Your father didn't think you were listening and wanted me to go over it with you one more time."

"You think I'm going to mess this up."

"It's not that," she said. But Happen could tell it was, and he felt something dark and ugly rising inside him.

She continued, trying to soothe him. "It's just that sometimes you have your own way of doing things, and we think if you understand *why* we do it this way—"

"All you think about is doing things your way." He hadn't raised his voice in anger toward his parents in a long time. Words surged out from him. "Why don't you ever think about asking how I want to do things? You're always giving me lists of things to be done just so, but you don't—Rrrr. I want to make my *own* lists, with my *own* choices." He was yelling now. "I'll bring your damn cart back with tea and cheese and whiskey and everything and then I'm turning right back around to go to Aeriskenn." He stomped up the narrow staircase to the sleeping room. The boys' side had a western-facing window, and as the oldest boy for the last five years, the bunk by the window had been his. He was well accustomed to using every last bit of the fading light for reading.

# FIVE
## SLAYING HIS TROLL ARMY

 The single most impactful limitation on Grithian technological advancement, the dearth of metal can be traced to the "six-foot policy." This core tenet of Gracarrai law prohibits the extraction or use of any resources more than six feet below the planet's surface. The top layer of the planet is considered a gift to the people, but below that is the sacred residence of temporarily incorporeal souls, which must not be disturbed.

Gracarrai's enforcement of this prohibition is aided by widespread legends of harm that came to those who delved too deep. Local ethnographers have documented versions of one popular tale told on all four continents. Each version varies slightly, but the core narrative describes a family moving to a town, building a proper house, but digging their latrine too deep, hoping to avoid the need to dig another in the future. Within a year, every member of the family died of the local equivalent of dysentery. (Reilly, 2046)

*⌐ʄ*

"I**t's just you and me now, bud," Happen said to Abernathy, patting his neck. The tull nuzzled his other hand, checking to see if there might be a carrot or apple hidden there.

"Oh no. Just because it's me alone doesn't mean we throw the rules on the barn roof. No treats before work. Let's get going."

Abernathy waggled his ears sadly, but started the cart down the path, with Happen walking beside him. They left the shed and passed the schoolhouse, where his mother waved from the front steps. He hadn't felt like talking in the morning, so he'd hurried through breakfast, then left with a quick hug.

"I've never been this way before, Aber," he said. He had looked down this track many times, wondering about the day he'd leave the farm. Now, actually walking away from the school and away from his home, he felt something inside him let go, like a boat released from its mooring and floating downstream. Past the school, the trees thinned and weeds crowded the path, encouraged by the increased sunlight. The path sloped gently downhill, but Happen and Abernathy struggled through the overgrowth as it grew denser and taller. He had been hoping to read as he walked once out of sight of the school. Reading would have to wait.

"This section here," his father had said, pointing to the map and tracing with his finger along the ragged line from the schoolhouse south to the inland route. "It's going to give you some trouble. For the spring and summer holidays, Tinker comes up and cuts the woody brush off the track, but by now it'll be fairly overgrown again with the faster-growing weeds. These aren't the skinny ferns and sorrel we get on our paths, so they'll slow you down some."

Soon the trees fell back from the trail and grew no more, replaced with tall bushes that crowded the track, limiting Happen's horizon to the immediate present. The path curved gradually one way, and then the other, so that it revealed little of his future, and was continually disappearing close behind him. When the weeds began to scrape the bottom of the cart, Abernathy slowed, then stopped. Happen took off his father's hat and coat and hacked at the stalks with his staff to clear the path ahead. The chore made him glad for the new staff, heavier and longer than his old one. Wind-borne seeds floated up and northeastward in a long, lingering stream, like a pennant proclaiming Happen's passage.

When they stopped for lunch, he gave Abernathy a carrot and thanked him for his morning's effort. The sky was close, with a low but thin cloud cover that let the heat of the sun in but not out. Happen emptied his first waterskin and started his second before getting back to work.

The low clouds thickened enough to block the sun, and time seemed to have stopped. It felt like late afternoon when he finished his second waterskin, and he still hadn't reached the inland route. *Could I have missed it somehow?* Although the weeds were ornery, it was clear that there had been a path between these bushes, and only one path. Bits of gravel still ground under his boots when he stepped between the weed stalks. He knew his father liked to exaggerate in both directions, enlarging the size of the fish that got away and belittling the length of Happen's list of chores, but this was so much more than "a little trouble." He would certainly give his father the tull's hind hoof about it when he got home.

It was somehow still late afternoon when Happen stopped again, too tired and thirsty to go on. He shared an apple with Abernathy.

"You're a big strong tull; can't you just pull through this stuff?"

Abernathy just looked at him. Didn't even twitch an ear. Happen went to the back of the cart in a huff and looked back at the ragged path he had cut. This had to be a trick. Somebody's idea of a joke, but it wasn't funny. Today was supposed to be the day he was finally going to get off the peninsula. Tomorrow he would see Pury for the first time. But somehow he'd ended up going the wrong way, into an endless forest not even twice his height. Odais defeated an army of trolls, winning glory and admiration. Happen Fell was stuck in morass of weeds. The scornful laughter in his mind belonged to Mistine Tallowey. Ugh. Burning her letters hadn't helped him forget her like he'd hoped. He could still see the eager, loopy handwriting forming the mysterious promise in her words, still recall the way he felt reading them—chosen and special.

He reached for his waterskin, but found it empty. Leaning against the back of the cart, he remembered the crossbow. It wasn't drawn or even loaded, but having it inches away and pointed at his lower back was unnerving, so he stepped away quickly. Mistine laughed again. *Afraid of his own undrawn weapon! Some hero.* Happen cringed. This couldn't be his story. The rough-hewn path leading back to the school was *not* his path. If endless weeds were his troll army, then he would slay them until he could stand no longer.

After about ten more hard-fought steps through the weeds, the air changed. Then his staff, stained green with the blood of his enemy, met less resistance, and he had arrived—somewhere. Very recently, someone had broken the trail from the other direction, but then stopped, as if giving up and deciding not to go this way. He asked Abernathy what it meant, but the tull only waggled his ears in a puzzled sort of way. Happen hacked and stomped a few more weed stalks, and they continued on. After a gradual bend to the east, the path widened and then spilled onto a road.

His boots crunched on gravel spotted with low-growing weeds. Something dark moved on the road in the distance, and Happen's gaze was drawn west, but whatever it was had gone. To

SLAYING HIS TROLL ARMY   43

the south the ground fell away into a wide, marshy lowland, creating the flattest and broadest horizon he had ever seen. Dark low clouds tumbled toward him across the vast marsh that hid the Clementis River, and the cool breeze carried a damp smell he didn't recognize, chilling him through his sweat-soaked shirt.

*This must be the inland route.* He felt like an ant in all the space. He hadn't expected it to be so empty. But then, he didn't have reason to expect anything; they hadn't talked about what it would actually feel like to be here.

"Well, Aber, let's get going," Happen said. The sound of his small voice in all that quiet space exacerbated his uneasiness, so he didn't speak again. After a moment, he stopped his tull with a hand on its shoulder and looked back. The tall bushes along the north side of the road formed a sheer wall, showing no indication of the cart path to the schoolhouse. Thick dark clouds rolled toward him on the southwest wind. Happen shivered, turned, and trudged on, head down. He no longer felt like reading.

Tull, boy, and cart moved quickly on the smooth road, and soon it began to rise. The lowlands to the south and the bushes to the north gave way to shallow rolling grasslands on both sides. After a slight northward bend in the road, a grove of tall trees appeared in the distance. As they drew closer, he could make out large branches that reached up and out giving a rounded shape to the trees. Indistinct cart treads wandered off the road north toward the grove. He'd never seen this kind of tree before. This must be the oak grove where he was supposed to camp. He followed the treads gratefully.


Happen unhitched Abernathy from the cart by the trunk of a large oak, and they headed toward the creek. Abernathy found a sloped bank already marred with tull prints and clambered into the shallow creek to drink. Happen found a steeper bank upstream and filled his waterskins before taking off his boots to soak his feet. Wind rustled the oak leaves in the branches over-head as the sky darkened. There wasn't much time to gather fire-wood, but then he didn't feel up for gathering, and he had some firewood from home. The cool water soothed his feet, but the creek hissed vague warnings and the growing shadows cast rumors of some discarnate threat that made him want to hide, not darken the shadows with a light of his own.

He'd planned to put on clean, dry socks after soaking his feet, but he'd forgotten and left them in the cart, so he had to put his damp, sweaty ones back on to get to the cart. He cursed to the sky, but the sound was swallowed by a gust of wind roaring through the high branches of the trees. Mistine's voice sneered that he was way too upset about socks, out of all proportion, and should just go home to his mother. When she first started sending him notes and they became friends, she would tease him every chance she got, and it was lighthearted and fun. The next year though, teasing that might have sounded similar to the other kids, felt to Happen like it had been carefully calibrated to peck out bits of his broken heart, like a carrion crow enjoying his carcass.

The gusting wind lowered and poured, swirling among the oaks, searching for him. Gnarled branches twisted and reached, menacing the cart huddled under their dubious protection.

It wasn't supposed to be like this. Happen gnawed on some cold elk jerky and one of Abernathy's carrots. Odais's first adven-ture had a stressful beginning, as he was chased from his home by the evil Tormenc, but Happen had expected his would be fun, or at least relaxed. He'd pictured himself by a nice campfire by the river at sunset, turning a spit, roasting a rabbit he'd shot for dinner, confident and happy, in no hurry for anything, just glad to be going to the fair, eating his dinner under the stars at last.

But here the sunset was merely a gray smudge on the edge of darkness. No stars, no fire. Instead, a baseless and humiliating fear spurred him to unpack his sling and rocks to keep them ready and close at hand.

The wind came in great waves rolling high and loud through the tall trees. It came in sudden short gusts rushing low among the trunks, pushing spurts of dead leaves into hurried eddies. It came with a cold dampness that stuck where it landed, then seeped in through cloth, skin, bone, and marrow. When the rain came, he spread his bedroll on the drier ground under the cart and lay down. The cart creaked and shuddered, and only occasionally shielded him from the windblown rain. In so many ways, it wasn't supposed to be like this. He felt like crying, which he hadn't done in ages, but found that he couldn't. Eventually, he fell asleep.

Happen lay on the braided rug in front of the masonry heater, looking up at freshly split and planed cedar planks in the ceiling. The hearth looked different, smaller, and clean: no ashes, no soot stains. He got up and added wood to the fire, but no heat came from it, only a damp fear and a sound like that made by the grindstone when they ground oats at the mill. He fell back onto the rug.

His father sat at the dining room table, and Happen called to him, but he didn't respond. Happen had to warn him about the hearth. He tried to get up so his father would see him, but he couldn't raise himself. He could barely move his limbs at all. The grinding noise and pulsing fear emanating from the hearth intensified, and took shape in words.

"Bartholofew Fell. You dare craft spirit into prison for the ephemeral designs of the flesh."

"That's not me! I'm not Bartholofew, I'm Happen."

"Bartholofew Fell. *You* built this hearth with my bones. You will pay in kind."

It wasn't fair for this fear to be squeezing his heart like this. He yelled again for his father, but he didn't seem to hear anything. The fire roared, chilling the room.

"You may not leave."

"No! That's not me."

"You may not leave."

Something warm and damp pushed his cheek and he was in a different place, dark, cold, and loud. The warm dampness pushed his shoulder then his face again. Abernathy's breath enveloped him with a great sigh, and Happen could move again.

"Oh, Aber, hello," he said. "Oh, thank goodness." He patted the tull's wide nose, and felt his stomach relax. He propped himself up on one elbow and looked around. No light or sound reached through the heavy rain. Abernathy nickered and Happen patted him on the nose again, grabbed the two wide horns that grew along his snout, and pulled gently like he used to when he was a kid. "Did you wake me up because the storm scared you?" Happen asked. He knew this was silly, but the idea soothed him. "It's okay, Abernathy, I'm here. It's okay. You're going to be okay."

# SIX
## CALLING FIRE

      Children are considered to be one of the most dramatic manifestations of Grith's generous nature. As a result, the education of children is a sacred (and expensive) endeavor, paid for by all citizens— not just parents, and methods and styles of teaching are debated constantly. The expense also tends to limit family size, as parents with more than two children are considered to be taking advantage of the community. (Reilly, 2046)

⌐ᵣ

Morning dawned gray and quiet. Remnants of the night's rain dripped from oak leaves above the cart. Abernathy sniffed at a bag of wild onions spilled near a broken ring of rocks surrounding the wet ashes and coals of a recent campfire site nearby. Happen ate an apple, then packed up his things, feeling as if a part of himself hadn't quite woken up yet. He kept his book in his large coat pocket, anticipating a straight stretch of road ahead. They set out for Pury.

The road was void of other travelers again. Happen chuckled, remembering Osgar's concern about strange travelers, especially on the inland route. *The only stranger here is me.* They crossed an old stone bridge that let the creek under the road. It looked just like the bridge where Odais met his first troll, with a shallow arch and knee-high parapets of rough stones held by gray mortar. The creek burbled along well below the bridge, leaving plenty of room for spring floods. But the trolls had either been slain or driven to the mountains hundreds of years ago.

The low clouds burned off in the eastern sky ahead, freeing the full power of the sun's rays. At first Happen enjoyed the dry warmth, but the foreign sense of space overwhelmed him. He was a mouse in the middle of a cleared field, and the sun was a hawk overhead. Wishing for a tree, or a cloud, he remembered his father's hat. Putting it on and lowering the brim against the brightness, he could block out most of the sky and focus on the yellow-gray sandy gravel and the dry, golden grass on either side. He settled into the steady rhythm of Abernathy's pace and listened to the gravelly rolling of the wheels, with an occasional drowsy glance at the road ahead.

After the bridge, the road curved and sloped gently higher till it reached a plateau of stunning flatness. Happen stopped and stared. He could see for leagues in every direction. The world seemed split in two perfect halves: a blue one above, and a yellow one below. The road ahead was as straight as a shinglewood tree with no top, but he'd be lucky to get anywhere because someone had cast a spell on the road. It reflected light as if it were covered with water, but the air above it shimmered and pulsed arrhythmically, as if it were on fire. But water would have evaporated by now, and there were not enough weeds on the road to burn so intensely.

"Do you *see* that, Aber?"

The tull waggled his ears impatiently, took a couple of steps forward, and turned back to look at him. His father had said that tulls could sense danger, and that he should trust his tull when traveling. But if someone could set water on fire, perhaps they could mask danger from a tull, too. He thought about turning back, or trying to go around somehow, but no one would believe him, and he'd been warned not to leave the road.

Abernathy repeated his impatient gestures. It seemed crazy to walk into a wizard's fire on a road in the middle of nowhere, but then he could hear that tone in his parent's voices: an oozing mixture of disappointment and disrespect. Sometimes it just irked him, and sometimes it infuriated him, but it always got worse when he couldn't do something they thought he could do. Much worse.

There seemed no other option than to follow his tull, but the strangeness of the road prevented him from reading as he walked, peering ahead at the unnatural fire, wondering what it would be like when he reached it.

Some time later, a dark shape hovered above the road in the distance, a thing with no legs, seeming like part of the fire in its movement. Surely an apparition, possibly the wizard who had enchanted the road. Whatever it was, it was coming toward them.

"Well, here goes, Aber," Happen said in a quiet voice. "Our first stranger." He stuck his finger into a knot hole, and pulled open the small cabinet door in the side of the cart that covered his bow and a quiver of arrows. His hands shook as he strung his bow, then hung it on a buckle of Abernathy's girth strap. Looking back to the road, he saw the apparition had taken the form of a tull pulling a cart, and a person walking beside.

When he came to a wider place in the road, Happen pulled over and stopped to await the approaching cart. Abernathy's neck muscles tensed under Happen's hand, but he remained still and quiet.

An older man walked alongside the tull pulling the cart. He didn't appear to be armed. As they drew within an easy conversational distance, the man halted his tull, and studied Happen and his cart. Happen couldn't remember what words to say, so he waited in an uncomfortable silence. The man's skin was weathered, and his clothes looked familiar, like those a farmer might wear. Abernathy wasn't comfortable, but he didn't seem alarmed at all. Finally, the man smiled and said, "Good morning to you, young sir!"

"Good morning, sir." He was so relieved to see a farmer instead of a wizard, he blurted out, "I'm heading to visit my uncle near Pury!" with much more enthusiasm than was necessary.

The man chuckled and said, "Well, I've just come from there myself, and I reckon . . ." he looked up at the sky, where the sun neared its apex. "I reckon you'll be on time for dinner." He chuckled again and resumed his journey.

"Thanks, I will, sir," Happen said. "Thank you, sir."

*Maybe the road isn't covered with watery fire after all.* In the long bells of featureless road remaining that day, he replayed this interaction over and over again in his thoughts, chastising himself for acting like an overeager puppy, and determined to make a different impression the next time. In the stories he'd read, all the characters in Aeriskenn and other cities were so confident and self-assured among strangers.


Late that afternoon another dark shape appeared in the distance, but this one grew into a house as Happen drew nearer, a sign that he was close to Pury. More houses appeared up out of the grasslands, and the road became less weedy and more rutted. He took a deep breath and resisted the urge to speed up, not wanting to display his fear. He'd never seen so many houses. *There must be at least forty.*

On a front porch a skinny old man wearing a straw hat rocked in his chair. Happen considered waving, but remembered that he wanted to appear calm and cool, and tried a polite nod. The old man squinted at Happen and spat on the ground, rocking slowly.

At the next house, a woman watched him from a window, but jerked the curtain closed before he could even nod. He'd read that cities could seem unfriendly to country folks, but he hadn't expected to encounter that in Pury. He looked forward to being welcomed at Tinker's.

A cluster of close buildings surrounded the crossroads where the inland route met the Old King's Highway. He turned north and there stood the Crackling Fire, its sign hanging by two knotted ropes tied to a bracket on an old, weather-beaten building. The faded red paint on the flaming log below the carved words had flaked off, revealing gray wood beneath. The two front windows were curtained against the westering sun. A dusty breeze swirled up the road from the south, and the ropes creaked as they rubbed against the bracket.

He'd always wanted to visit this tavern he'd heard so much about, but he felt small and lonely and watched. It wasn't what he'd expected somehow.

A heavily laden but swiftly moving wagon pulled by tulls in a tandem hitch passed through town, raising dust and noise. *On their way to the fair, no doubt.* Watching the wagon pass, Happen felt excited about the fair for the first time on his journey. The Old King's Highway was wider and flatter than the inland route and covered with gray packed gravel. The dust and noise settled over it and Happen followed. He could stop in at the tavern on the way back. Soon he came to the tree with two trunks that marked the turn onto a weedy little cart path, heading west to Tinker's house.

Along the way down the path, the crickets started again. Happen hadn't noticed when they'd stopped in town, but they were nice and loud here and their song comforted him. *I forgot to hum a tune. I never finished restoring my equilibrium. Was that two days ago?*

Happen had never been to his uncle's house before. Once, he'd asked his mother why they never went to Tinker's for holidays, and she said simply, "Tinker prefers it that way." As the house came into view, he saw that it might be less comfortable in the winter. The foundation had settled, causing the house to lean a bit, opening some gaps between the logs in the walls. It had a large covered porch on two sides, and one of the front stairs was missing. A curtain moved in the window by the door, and Happen's cousin Cor burst through the door, leaped over the porch stairs, and ran out to meet him.

Cor spent summers away east, over the mountains, where his mother lived. She left Tinker when Cor was a child, but he'd always spent summers with her, returning in time for school. He was a year younger than Happen, and this would be the first year that Cor would be in school without his cousin. Things had been awkward between them in the spring. Happen had been excited for the future and Cor had been envious. Happen wondered, now, if this visit would be worse, if Cor might resent him for going to the fair with Tinker.

"Oh musical! I wasn't expecting you!" Cor sounded genuinely glad to see him. "Have you seen my father? Did you stop in at the Fire?" The cousins exchanged a clumsy hug.

"No, I didn't stop. I haven't seen Tinker—"

"You haven't been here before, have you? Let me show you around. Come on!" Happen started to follow Cor back toward the house when Abernathy brayed. The boys looked back, and the tull waggled his ears as if to say, "Aren't you forgetting something?"

"Oh, right. I have to get Abernathy out of his harness."

They parked the cart in the barn, gave Abernathy a carrot, and let him out to graze with Hendrin, Tinker's tull.

"Where's your father?" Happen asked.

"I don't know. I got home this afternoon, and there was a note on the door that said, 'Emergency, back soon, could be a day or two.' So I have no idea. But our tull's here, so he can't have gone far. I expect he'll be back tonight. Where's your father?"

"He broke his leg."

"You're going to the fair without him? Is it still your Summering Task?"

"Yes, and yes," Happen said.

Cor was quiet for a moment. "I'll go next year."

Cor was a good friend, and didn't tease him too badly for not knowing what a mirage was. He took Happen up his favorite climbing tree—one he'd talked about many times at school—and showed how much he'd improved with a bow and arrow, after a summer of practicing. He described the girl he liked who lived in the town where he went to visit his mother. Happen interrupted him just enough to ask about dinner and sleeping arrangements, then Cor continued telling of his summer as they made dinner and cleared a couch. Happen tried to listen to Cor's stories, but kept wondering where Tinker was. And he couldn't help but remember that Osgar lived in Pury.

The next morning Tinker still hadn't arrived. Happen worried about being late for the fair. He would have to leave the following morning at the latest, but he'd been hoping to get a good spot to set up. Late arrivals were relegated to remote edges of the fair, which meant less fun and more walking each day to get to the food rows. He would have had his fill of walking by then. They had just closed the cart's back cover over the crossbow and put the arrows away when they heard Osgar calling. He was hurrying into the yard carrying a staff and a backpack.

"Hello, young master," he said, addressing Happen. "I'm glad to find you here." He looked about the yard, as if his news was so secret that even the tulls shouldn't hear it, then continued. "I have a message from your Uncle Tinker. I borrowed his tull several days ago, so I wasn't surprised when he came to me yesterday to borrow mine. He had an urgent need for fast travel and asked for my help. He wants you to start for the fair without him and I'll take his tull and trade goods north with you. He'll catch up with us in a couple of days, at which point I'll ride my tull back home, and he'll continue with you to the fair."

Happen kicked at the packed dirt in front of the barn, his chest tightening. *It's not supposed to be like this. Why can't Tinker be here so we can go together like we'd planned?*

Cor interrupted the awkward silence. "Thank you, Osgar, but that won't be necessary. We've already made other plans. Hap and I will be leaving soon, and I'll return your tull when my father catches up with us."

"You—" said Osgar and Happen simultaneously, but Happen recovered from his surprise first. "You rode tulls all summer, didn't you, Cor."

"That's right. My grandfather said I was quite good with tulls."

Osgar thumped his staff on the ground. "Now, just a thundering moment here, your uncle asked me to do this for him. He wants a man to look after you, not a boy."

"It's good of you to be concerned," Happen said. "But we'd rather not trouble you for this. I'm sure Tinker would have preferred our plan if he'd thought of it. Perhaps he wasn't sure exactly when Cor would be returning from out east. We'll take care of it."

"I've done lots of traveling," Cor said. "And we've got two good tulls to warn us of any danger. Anybody tries to sneak up on us, the tulls will raise the alarm."

"That is true." Osgar mulled it over, pulling on his chin. "Especially Abernathy. He hates strangers, doesn't he? Living out there so far from town." He paused, looking back and forth between the two boys. "It will be less complicated for me this way."

"We'll be sure to explain to Tinker that you offered, but we insisted that we continue with our own plan," Happen said.

"I appreciate that. I wouldn't want Tinker to think I couldn't be relied upon."

As soon as Osgar was gone, Happen let out a huge sigh of relief. "Thank you, thank you, thank you. I did *not* want to travel with him."

"And I'm not so excited about going to back to school without you."

"This will make you late probably."

"The later the better."

While Cor packed, Happen told him about Osgar's last visit to the farm, warning about strangers on the road. Cor hadn't seen anyone unusual, though he'd ridden in a carriage over the pass and back to Pury, and slept a good portion of the three-day ride.

"Seems like he really wants to go to the fair," Cor said.

"Yeah. Before I left he was still trying to convince Father to send him instead of me, or with me. Rode all the way from Pury. I don't understand why he doesn't just go on his own."

"For one thing, you have to buy a stack of script or have something to sell to get in. Plus, even if he had a way in, I don't think he has the entrance fee."

Tinker's gear was already packed, so it didn't take long to prepare. They hitched both Abernathy and Hendrin to Tinker's caravard, and trailed the cart behind it, so they could ride together on the caravard's driving bench. Technically, Happen was supposed to walk, because it was part of his Summering Task, but he decided that so long as he was traveling without Tinker, the rules had already been deviated from. When Tinker caught up, everything would go back to the way it was supposed to be.

Before leaving, Cor wrote a note for his father which read: Went north with Hap, Hendrin, caravard. Harvest Mester 7th to full.

The highway north of Pury was flat and quiet. It plowed through dry golden grasslands, only occasionally passing small groves of trees. The boys repeated old stories their parents had told about the fair, and speculated about what they might have left out. The evening breeze carried occasional currents of autumn coolness as the sun lowered behind the mountains. When the rosy blush faded from the snowcapped peaks of Antler Range to the east, a heavier chill settled over the road, and taller trees adorned the hills more densely ahead.

They stopped to camp at a wide clearing in the thickening trees, dotted with stone fire rings.

"There are rabbits to be hunted around here," Cor said. "I'm sure of it. Can you call up a fire after walking all day?"

"I think so. Go shoot us some dinner. And if I can't get it going, we can build a bow drill when you get back."

Cor headed south, against a gentle wind, with his bow and quiver to hunt. Happen headed north with his hatchet, to find dead branches to burn and some green maple for spits and crotchets. Building and calling the campfire was an honor typically handled by the oldest male in the family. Happen felt mature and independent working on it, much more so when sharing it with Cor than when making one for himself. Also, he felt a curious guilty pride because this was something he could do that Cor couldn't. Cor's voice wasn't deep enough yet to call a fire on his own.

He cleared the stone ring at the site they'd chosen, and scraped away the layer of ash to get access to the soil. With dry kindling from home close at hand, he spread out the Fell family traveling ciorcagnal, making it as round as possible, then poured the water until the circle of rope was fully saturated. His father said any string or rope would do for a ciorcagnal, and any rocks would do for Agnalian stones, but he'd bought two sets from a peddler which worked a little better than most. Not as much better as the peddler had promised, his father always reminded him, but still better. They had one set at home and one for traveling.

He placed sticks of kindling in a triangle over the ciorcagnal and set the Agnalian stones at each point, put some cedar bark tinder into the center of the circle, and began to call the fire up from Grith. He liked to start by humming the tune, like his father did, just to get started, while he built a small pyramid of kindling above the tinder.

The fire song didn't have words, but you had to sing something, you couldn't just hum. Happen got his best results from repeating a "bom" sound. Breathing deeply and slowly to relax, he sat up straight, just outside the circle.

"Bom, bom, bom, bom." He sang the rising notes. "Bom, bom, bom, bom." He sang the falling notes. "Bom, bom, bom, bom-be-bom." He closed his eyes and pictured the heat welling up from Grith's molten soul. By the time he'd started singing it through the third time, a thin wisp of smoke rose from the tinder. He felt the weight as he finished the verse, placing more kindling over the budding fire with heavy arms.

It was nearly dark when Cor returned.

"Hey, you did it!" he said. "Brilliant!"

"Thanks."

"I only got two rabbits. I was hoping for more, but at least we've got dinner. Looks like we'll need more wood, though."

"My energy's starting to come back a little, I can g—"

"Musical! I'll go get more firewood, while you clean the rabbits." Before Happen could argue, Cor dashed out of sight as if he'd been learning from his prey.

That night, working together with Cor to set up camp, care for the tulls, and roast rabbits, Happen felt his worry ease. They were on their way, Osgar was back in Pury, and Tinker would be along in a day or two. They could have slept in Tinker's caravard, which was like a wagon with an enclosed shed on the back. Tinker used it as a mobile workshop, and had built in a folding bed for longer trips. But Happen wanted Tinker to find him following the Summering Task rules if he arrived during the night, and Cor liked the adventure of sleeping out. They built a nice big fire, partly for warmth, and partly to make it easier for Tinker to find them.

Sparks from the fire floated up, hoping to join the stars that shone in the gaps between the dark fir trees.

"I can't wait till next year when I get to come, too," Cor said. "This year I probably won't get past the turnoff for the pass before Father catches up and I have to head back. But maybe he'll be late, and I'll get to see something new."

"Yeah. Going down the cart path from the schoolhouse to the inland route for the first time was exciting."

Cor sighed, and poked at the fire with a stick. "I can't wait till *I* get to leave the schoolhouse for the last time. Did you pee on the wall or something? Like when Seddy left, remember?"

"No," Happen said. "No, it wasn't like that at all. I always thought it would be, but it wasn't. I was thinking about how at the fair I'll be able to do math in my head and speak with decent grammar."

Cor stopped poking the fire and stared rigidly at Happen. "Thunder and lightning, Hap, you're serious."

"Yes, I am. I think it might have been helpful."

"Ugh! If I'm reading the Legend of Happen Fell, I just put the book down. Odais never would have thanked his jailer!"

Happen pointed at Cor with his last rabbit bone. "Yes, but even Odais needed to learn stuff."

"He learned stuff as he needed to. Meanwhile, he slew dragons and saved damsels and sunk pirate ships. He learned to read and write from the monk in the orphanage, and then he was out of there. Odais didn't do rote lessons, hone chalk bits, and sweep the floor. You do remember how tedious those rote lessons were, don't you? I can't wait to be done with it and go traveling."

Happen looked into the fire. He and Cor hadn't talked about the future in a long time. It was different then, back when it still *was* the future, and they chafed at the school's requirements. Cor was still there, in that time and with that way of looking at things.

"It's different now, Cor."

"No. No, it can't be. It just looks that way because you're . . . because you're worrying about stuff. Odais didn't worry about stuff."

"Most of the time, he didn't . . . I mean, he did what he had to do. But *I don't know* what I have to do. You don't understand what it's been like. All summer long I was going to the trade fair and then Father broke his leg . . . what was I going to do then? It hit me—like hiking along a trail that leads right off a cliff or something. All that space in front of me just like that, and it felt like any step would be wrong. Wrong and unfixable. I couldn't even think about it. But at the same time, I couldn't *not* think about it. I was just glad they came up with this plan."

Cor went back to poking the fire thoughtfully.

Happen continued. "Osgar tried to foil it with his story about weird-looking strangers, but Father wouldn't let him."

"Hey. You don't suppose . . . ?" The fire snapped, and a burst of sparks floated up and faded out.

"What?"

"How *did* your father break his leg?"

"The grain hoist broke in the old mill and some sacks of oats swung down against his leg. Osgar brought him home in a wheelbarrow."

"Was anyone else up at the mill with them?"

"Oh, thunder," Happen said quietly. "Oh thunder, thunder, thunder."

# SEVEN

## ROLLING OFF THE ROAD

> Similar to the way early fairy tales (see Grimm, etc.) were told by parents to keep children out of the woods and close to home, Berytheans describe dangerous creatures that inhabit potentially hazardous places in the physical geography. Troll legends are common. Berytheans proudly say of their countryside, "every river running higher than a toddler's head has at least one naiad, and every sea worth its salt—at least one dragon." (Reilly, 2046)

Tinker didn't catch up with them the next day. Happen was worried and wanted to wait, but Cor was having fun seeing new things after they passed the highway that led east over the mountains, so they kept on. Early that evening they crossed over the Davoura Gorge.

Happen remembered seeing the Davoura River on the map. It drained off the foothills west of the Antler Range, collecting tributaries and gathering size on its way through the Anabelis Hills. After a waterfall, it squeezed through a deep and narrow gorge before reaching a gentle passage through plains and emptying into the Sirreltis Sound. At school they'd read a book about the building of the Old King's Highway, which followed as direct a route as possible from the great farming valleys of southwest Berythea to Aeriskenn and other port cities farther north, crossing the Davoura above the gorge by means of a truss bridge made of pegged timbers.

They stopped in the middle of the bridge to look out over the gorge. The weight and power of the water churning through the tight channel felt like twenty times that of the little Irelian River where Happen fished, even from the bridge railing thirty-five feet above the glistening surface. The river was blue in that light, with a greenish milky cast to it. The south wall of the gorge was black granite, covered with a pale green moss in places, and softened by hundreds of small bright green ferns that waved frantically in the misty wind that seemed to be propelled through the gorge by the water's influence. The north wall was less steep, but with more moss and larger ferns.

Cor hopped up on the railing and walked along it, dragging his hands along the beam above his head.

"Come on," Happen said. "Let's go find a camp before dark."

Cor stopped and cupped his hands at his mouth and shouted, "Echo!" but no sound returned. "Hey, the gorge ate my echo!"

Happen rolled his eyes. "I'm so sorry, cousin. Maybe you can grow another one someday."

Cor spun around, grabbing the truss, and glared at Happen. "Never. *That* one was my favorite and there'll never be another like it." He spread his arms wide and stepped along the railing. "I shall forevermore be echoless." He caught his toe on a splinter and lost balance, flailing his arms. Happen jumped at him, grabbed his leg and pulled him roughly onto the bridge.

"Come on, Echoless," Happen said. "Let's go find a camp."

"All right."

Happen jolted awake in darkness. Something pulled him by the ankles. Dragged out of camp and away from the cart before he even knew where he was. Cool, dewy grass rushed by in the pallid glow of a clouded moon.

Cor yelled, not far ahead. A dark shadow skidded along in front of Happen, then melted in the gloom.

"Cor! Aber!" Happen screamed. "Abernathy!"

Happen tried to reach his ankles. Rope, tied in a noose, pinned them together. The pressure tightened with a painful jerk and a blink later something hard scraped his hip. A tree! Too late he reached and bashed the back of his hand as he veered past, changing direction and picking up speed again. *If I had my knife . . .* His knife was in his belt next to his bedroll. *If I could pull on the rope enough to loosen the knot . . .* Bending his knees, he finally got one hand to the rope. A gray band of road appeared in the dim moonlight just before he banged up onto it, losing some skin from his knuckles and his grip on the rope. He rolled to his left, twisting the rope, back to the slippery grass. Cor was yelling, dragging on the gravel road.

"Roll, Cor. Roll off the road!" Happen had to keep rolling to stay off the abrasive gravel. It seemed like the best thing to do until he saw the railing of the truss bridge approaching fast.

"The bridge! Get back on the road!" he shouted, rolling back in a panic, but it was too late. Happen struck the outside edge of the railing, bumped his head on the ground and fell into the gorge. A new pain ripped into his ankles as his drop stopped, and he swung upside down over shadow. The surface of the river told him, in soft slaps and whispers, that it was too far down.

His shaking hands wouldn't reach anymore. His knees and hips felt weak and stretched, and wouldn't bend. His rope rubbed the railing as the swaying slowed. Cor was there, too, closer to the bridge as his rope was shorter. After a moment of numb confusion, he heard the groan of rope chafing on wood, repeating intermittently.

"Hap?" Cor said.

Happen moved his mouth but couldn't connect anything in his thoughts long enough to form a response.

"I'm getting pulled up." Cor said this without emotion, as if he thought Happen couldn't hear him anyway. After a few moments, Happen heard another voice, but couldn't make it out. Then, he was being pulled up also. The slightest motion turned the dull ache in his ankles to a screaming sharpness, but it seemed like going up must be better than not.

"Cor," he said, finding his voice had the same monotone as his cousin's. "I'm coming up, too."

"You should have stayed home, little whelp," the other voice said.

He knew the voice talking to Cor. His cousin was whimpering now.

The familiar voice continued. "But it's better this way. Just get it done all at once."

"Osgar?" It *was* Osgar pulling up the rope. Happen remembered Osgar pulling him out of the river that time. *Saving me* again? Happen's rise stopped when his feet, like Cor's, were almost even with the bottom of the bridge. Osgar's silhouette ducked behind the railing.

"It's okay, Cor! It's Osgar." He couldn't understand how they'd gotten there, or how Osgar was there suddenly pulling them out of the gorge. Nothing made sense, but he couldn't be dreaming. He'd never felt pain like this in a dream.

Osgar's silhouette reappeared. "Ah. The last little elk finds the wolf, eh?" He chuckled. "My father used to say that to me all the time. You okay, kid?"

"I'd be better if—"

"Grubs and maggots," he interrupted. "You were supposed to drag on the road. Would have done you worse, and I could have just let you go. Cor's bleeding enough to draw the naiad's attention." He said this as if Cor had been a good boy and eaten all his vegetables, while Happen had been misbehaving.

"What are you talking about?" Happen asked.

"I couldn't kill you in front of your tulls, I need them to trust me," Osgar said, as if talking to himself. He leaned out over the edge of the bridge with a staff, looking down at the boys and muttering, then disappeared again.

Cor's whimpering grew louder.

"Shut up, I'm trying to think," Osgar barked.

Happen was trying to think also, but found he couldn't get beyond the thought that Osgar had said he couldn't kill them in front of the tulls.

"This ought to work." Osgar seemed to be working on some task while talking. "Anyhow, I've always wanted to see a naiad. Haven't you? I thought I might see one that time I dunked you in the fishing hole, but I have since learned more about their taste for blood."

"Why are you doing this?" Happen asked.

Osgar chuckled again. "Why?" He leaned over the edge of the bridge, his pale forehead glowing in the strengthening moonlight. "I am going to inherit the Fells' farm. Not you shirking whiners."

The pressure on Happen's ankles strained his mind, making him dizzy. Any movement made it worse, especially in the left ankle. He felt an intense need to sit down.

"The clouds are breaking up, so I should have enough light to see her soon. Just have to prepare the bait." He reached his staff over the edge, a knife lashed to the end. Moonlight glinted off the blade before it slashed across Happen's calf. Happen reached toward the pain, but the effort made it worse. Warm blood streamed down his leg.

Osgar looked up and down the road as if to make sure no late-night travelers could catch his final words to Happen. "When you left without Tinker, I followed to make sure you were safe, but I wasn't following close enough, out of politeness. When I got to the bridge, you were climbing around in the trusses playing tag, silly kids. Playing when you should have been working, just like the rest of your coddled lives. But Cortham lost his balance, Happen reached for him, and they both fell in. Before I could save them. Terribly sorry." Osgar had the knife in his hand again. Sawing at the rope.

The pressure released from Happen's ankles, and he dropped.

Happen brought his hands together above his head just before the impact.

# EIGHT

# INVISIBLE FIREWOOD

> Berytheans are very particular about burial. A person who cannot be buried may be burned, or if at sea beyond the sight of land, wrapped carefully with a weighted shroud. Should a body be eaten by an animal, that animal would become a dangerous supernatural threat. (Reilly, 2046)

A FTER THE THUNDERCLAP moment of striking the surface, Happen's ears roared as he tried to get his bearings. It was too dark to see which way was up, and the only direction he felt sure of was the flow of the stream.

He tried to swim to the side, toward what he hoped was the closest shore. He wanted air. He wasn't rising fast enough. Wet clothes and the rope around his ankles weighed him down. He had thought he'd wanted things before, but now he experienced an intensity of desire he hadn't known existed. His chest, then his whole being, ached with wanting air. He pushed frantically at the water, but soon his striving slowed, weakening, and a deathly cold heaviness seeped into him, reaching toward his heart. Thoughts of his mother came unbidden, and the desire for air abated, replaced with sadness. *Why did I have to yell at her? Why did I have to leave in anger?* He kept swimming but felt no progress. *So much easier . . . to just open your mouth and breathe . . .*

A strong arm reached around his chest and lifted him with a great tug. A pause, then another pull upward. One more lift and he broke the surface, gasping, sputtering, dizzy, nauseous. Someone was behind him; a shoulder supported his head. He felt his body try to turn and push down on the shoulder and cough up water at the same time.

"Be calm. Breathe easy now. I have you." The voice in Happen's ear was so calm and melodic that he stopped struggling. He was still dizzy and sick, but he could watch bits of moonlight on the dark water, and breathe.

"Who . . ." He couldn't finish the question without stopping to breathe.

"I am the river Davoura," she sang.

*The naiad!* Panic jolted through him again, and he thrashed to get away, but her arm tightened around his neck. Something like a foot or a fishtail flashed in a moonbeam, breaking the glittering black surface in front of him before disappearing with a splash. The supporting shoulder was gone, but his flailing hand brushed what felt like a naked body behind him. She put a knee in his back and held his head just above water with her arm painfully tight around his neck.

"You must not struggle or I will drown you." Again the voice was calm, as if offering a friendly reminder of a simple cause-and-effect relationship, not a death threat. Happen forced himself to stop moving and breathe. He remembered wanting air and held still, his breath wheezing through a throat constricted by the inside of the naiad's elbow. Somehow, the turbulent river stayed just below his bottom lip.

"That's better." She relaxed her grip, and resumed pulling

him through the water.

"Where are you taking me?"

"Be calm. Breathe easy now. I will not harm you," she sang, as if swimming with his extra weight took no effort at all.

"But I thought . . ."

"You did not enter my home by choice. I will not harm you."

"My cousin—"

"He is safe. I will not harm him. We must go underwater for a moment. Ready yourself." He took a deep breath and closed his eyes. She pulled him under, moved him, released him. He felt her hands on his ankles, and then the rope was gone, and she guided his right foot to a rock. He pushed against it and broke the surface in a shallow pool sheltered from the current by a fallen tree.

Happen dragged himself up onto a large, flat rock to keep his head out of the water. One of his ankles hurt whenever he moved it, and the cut from Osgar's knife burned and tingled in the cool air. He could not make himself look at it, but kept his cheek on the rock where he rested. The rock had a comforting solidity. He stayed still, remembering a time long ago.

His mother's lap was so perfectly made for him, and he drifted effortlessly into the other world of the story she was reading to him; until she sneezed, jarring him back. He held her thumb in one hand, a finger in the other, and she held the book with her other hand. She put the book facedown on her leg, held open to their page, and stretched her hand this way and that. He wondered why the veins in her wrist were blue, but didn't ask because it would delay her from reading more. The story was a scary one, about naiads. His mother wouldn't let the naiads get him. There was a pond for swimming, but he must not go near the river's edge. If a boy went in the river, the naiad would find him—and drown him.

The rock under his cheek was not perfectly made for him, though it had been worn smooth by the river in wetter seasons. Osgar's triumphant whine crept into his mind.

*Ah, the last little elk finds the wolf, eh?*

Happen listened for Davoura or Cor, but the only sounds were from the river, bubbling, gurgling, and lapping at the rocks. He had not been drowned or broken to pieces in the rapids. Somehow, he was here, breathing, and shivering.

Ragged clouds raced past a heavy moon, providing occasional light, enough to see that the river had carried him out of sight of the bridge, and that the cliffs of the gorge had fallen away, leaving a shallow, sparsely forested valley where the river widened and slowed. Though not as high and steep as the gorge, the south side of the valley, shadowed by tall conifers, towered over the river. The river seemed to prefer the gentler north side, and curved gradually toward its low rocky bank, where Happen pushed himself up to sit on his rock.

"Happen?" Cor's call came from the shadows on the south side of the river.

"Cor!" Happen answered.

"Oh, thank goodness. You okay?"

"Yeah, you?"

"I'm scraped up quite a bit, but could be worse. Kind of cold, though."

"Yeah. We need a fire."

"You mean we need two fires."

"Why?"

"I don't know about you, but I feel thundering lucky not to break my neck or meet the naiad, and I don't feel like pushing my luck by swimming across."

"Oh, I assumed she'd fished you out, too."

"What! Who?"

"The naiad."

"You saw the naiad?"

"Not exactly, I mean a little bit. Come over and I'll tell you about it. She said she wouldn't harm you."

"You're sure it's okay?"

"Yes."

"Then you won't mind coming across to my side."

"That's true, I wouldn't mind, but I can't. I hurt my ankle."

"I thought you said you were okay."

"Considering I fell off a bridge and met a naiad, I think I came out okay, but I can't put any weight on my ankle."

The only response was the steady hush of the rapids downstream.

"I'm pretty sure that maniac Osgar went north, so I'd just as soon go south," Cor said finally.

"Yes," Happen said. "We'll go south over the bridge later, but right now, we need a fire. This side gets more sun. More likely to have dry wood. Plus, you're a much better swimmer than I am."

"Oh, all right."

Happen heard a splash, and then got to work dragging himself the rest of the way to shore using his arms and the one leg that, while sore, didn't feel damaged. Osgar's voice followed him from rock to rock.

*Ah, the last little elk finds the wolf, eh?*


"Happen?" Cor's call came from downstream, but not far, and on the right side of the river.

"Up here."

"How bad is it?" Cor worked his way upstream along the rocky riverbed.

"I don't know. It's swollen, and hurts when I put any weight on it." Blood seeped from the cut on his calf when he tested his ankle.

"Tell me about the naiad." Cor arrived. His teeth were chattering, and he stood slightly stooped over and dripping in the fitful moonlight, his curly hair plastered against his forehead. Happen loved him like a brother at that moment. *My cousin is a tough kid.*

"Let's save it for the fire."

"Right. I'll get some wood." Cor disappeared into the shadowed forest, and soon the snapping of dead branches echoed in the valley. Happen hobbled to a sandy place with a half-buried tree trunk they could sit against, a few paces from the river, and arranged some rocks to make a fire ring. Cor reappeared in the moonlight and dropped an armload of sticks next to the half-formed circle.

"Think you'll be able to call another fire?" Cor asked. "If I help?"

Happen had read of people who, with the right tools, could call a morning fire and an evening fire, but he'd never thought a person could call a second fire so soon after their first.

"Don't know, we'll just have to try. Thunder, I wish I had my knife so I could make us a proper bow drill."

"Here, use mine." Cor set his knife on a flat rock.

"What! Why didn't you cut Osgar's rope before the bridge?"

"I wake up slow. I was just about to cut it when I hit that road, and then it was all I could do not to lose it."

Cor hurried off to get more wood. Happen chose a cedar stick from the pile and stripped it down, saving the bark for tinder. He cut the end flat for the spindle. He chose a longer stick of maple with a slight bend in it and notched the ends to tie the bowstring to.

"Oh, hey, I found a wedge so you don't wreck my knife." Cor handed him a rock with a sharp edge on one side. "There's a tree down in that grove over there, I'll get some more branches."

"Thanks. Bring me a maple leaf, too." He poised the wedge onto the thicker end of a broken cedar branch and hammered it with another rock until the branch split to make bearing blocks. He carved shallow holes in the flat sides of each block to hold the spindle. The effort and attention to detail helped quiet the voice that kept repeating, *the wolf, the wolf, finds the wolf*. When his cousin returned with another load of sticks and a couple of torn maple leaves, Happen folded one of the leaves up, pushed it into the hole on the top bearing block, and spit on it. He tied one of his bootlaces to the notches on each end of the bent maple stick, then wrapped the makeshift bowstring around the spindle, placed the spindle in the notches, and drew the bow back and forth several times.

"This'll work, but my ankle's killing me."

"I'll work the bow, you make some tinder."

Happen carved bark and shavings from a cedar branch to make a tinder pile, then limped down to the river and tried soaking his swollen ankle in the cold water, but sitting still made him too cold. *Better do whatever I can to help with the fire.* He soaked his other bootlace in the river and limped back to the sandy place where Cor was working. He formed a circle in the sand with the wet bootlace for a ciorcagnal, then chose three similar-sized rocks for Agnalian stones, and—

"What are you doing?" Cor asked. "I thought you made a bow drill because you didn't think we'd be able to call fire?"

"In this weather, with this wood, I'm not so sure the bow drill will work, either. But if we do both . . ."

"Brilliant."

Happen arranged kindling around the tinder in the center of the ciorcagnal, and then called fire while Cor worked the drill. After the second verse of the fire song, Happen felt the familiar weight from fire-calling, and hesitated, feeling the warm, dry tinder with his hand. Heaviness turned to weakness, and cold sweat rolled down his forehead, then his back, and then he was pulled down into the sand, unable to move or speak. He felt so heavy he thought his body would force its way through the sand, down into where a living body should not go.

Damp sand stuck to his hands, even after he wiped them on his pants. Blinking, he found he couldn't see, but he could hear a fire crackling, and the river rushing by. The alarming weakness had passed, but a tiredness so heavy and thorough kept him still, so he closed his eyes and rested on the sand.

Footsteps approached, then stopped, and cold water dripped into his mouth. He opened his mouth and more water trickled in.

"There you go, cousin. Drink up. I'll get more in a bit."

The trickle stopped.

"Here. I've brought you some food." A finger pushed some small leafy plant into the corner of his mouth. Happen chewed, marveling at the tangy flavor of watercress. He opened his eyes, and saw gray and orange light and motion, but no detail.

"Where'd you go?" Happen said.

"Where did *I* go? You thundering grub! You bug-eaten, burrowing . . . I thought—" Cor took a long, loud breath, then continued in a more casual tone. "I got hungry. Figured I'd let you sleep and went back to this slow creek I'd stepped in earlier, to see if the collachine had left any watercress."

"Sleep?"

"Just after the second verse, the bowstring wore through and snapped off. I *was* going to hand you the tiniest of glowing embers, but no. You decided to take a little nap. Fortunately, the tinder and kindling were so warm and dry they lit up like dead grass in a lightning bolt. Here."

Happen's vision was improving; the warm light of the fire wavered dimly, as if through cloth.

"Here what?"

"What do you mean? Take this."

He wiped some of the sand off his hand and held it out. Cor gave him a handful of watercress, then went back to building the fire, humming a tune at a pace that suggested his equilibrium was eluding him.

"I'm going to have to fetch more wood. Can you feed this till I get back?"

"Sure." Happen shivered and munched watercress, then concentrated on the firelight as the flames grew more distinct. Other shapes formed, but still indistinct, and at first he had to feel for sticks to place over the fire. The growing warmth and light soothed him as he leaned larger and larger sticks onto the fire, and pushed the unburned ends of the kindling into the center. His mind was calm and quiet, and his vision restored, when Cor returned dragging a small tree.

"That's not firewood," Happen said. "That's a tree."

"Thanks. I wasn't sure. But I knew my wise old cousin could tell me what it was." Cor moved a few rocks and set the tree, a young alder uprooted by a shift in the river's course, next to the fire to dry. "It's a little green still, but not too bad."

The fire climbed, snapping hungrily at the cold. The boys undressed and tried to dry out their clothes by hanging them on sticks and holding them near the fire. Happen checked Cor's shoulder. The scrapes were large, but not too deep, and the river had cleaned them pretty well. Cor tied his handkerchief around Happen's cut calf, then took a burning stick with him to find more wood. The stick was merely smoldering when he returned, dropping an armful of broken sticks on the sand.

"This wasn't as much help as I thought it would be." He indicated the burning stick he'd brought. "Light's better by the river, I'll try downstream. Then you owe me a story. Or two."

Cor had been gone only a few waves before returning. He stumbled out of the shadows, landing on his hands and knees, spraying his cousin with sand.

Happen stopped his joking protest when he saw the fear on Cor's face.

"I know." Cor fought to catch his breath. "I know it's been an unbelievable day already. But you're not going to believe what I found."

"Invisible firewood?"

"Downstream. There's—well, first: there's a big cage. On the edge like it was pulled up out of the river—"

"Has it been out long enough that we can burn it?"

"Not just yet. There's a large something moving inside. Can't tell what it is with the moonlight coming and going like it is."

"That's odd." Happen had read about caged animals in zoos. "Maybe it was headed to the zoo in Aeriskenn? And fell off a wagon into the river?"

"No, that's not the odd part. There's a dead woman lying there, with her hand in the cage. I guess I'm not sure she's dead, but she must be, right?"

"Was she breathing?"

"Don't know how she would. She didn't have a mouth or a nose."

*Osgar's strangers! Has to be.* Happen had thought Osgar was lying about them. *Still, everybody has a mouth. Cor's just been knocked off his equilibrium is all.*

Happen took a deep breath. "I'm hoping that's the odd part. Or is there more?"

"No, that's it. I've never seen a dead person. I just dropped my firewood and came back here. What are we going to do?"

"Take a deep breath."

"Will you just come *look*?"

Cor picked out the two longest and strongest sticks from the pile. Happen took one and held onto his cousin's shoulder as they limped their way among the river rocks downstream until they found the sticks Cor had dropped, and looked up.

The cage was made of stout round sticks; sawn, not chopped, and lashed together with rope. *That's a lot of firewood.* The boys advanced slowly until stopped by a growl from the cage. Something large shifted in the shadows inside.

The woman lay awkwardly on her side with her arm reaching into the cage up to her elbow. She wore a long robe, colorless in the gauzy moonlight that oozed through thinning clouds. There wasn't enough light to tell whether she was breathing or, as Cor claimed, incapable of doing so.

"I told you it was creepy." Cor held on to the back of his cousin's shirt with a tight fist.

"We should check and see. Just go touch her ankle and see if she's dead."

"I'm not going near that cage. Why don't you do it?"

"What if I need to get away fast?" A cold damp fog had risen from the river and was spreading through the valley, transforming the taller river rocks into stooped and huddled ghosts crawling against the mist. The dead woman and the shadowed cage held still and silent. The boys shivered.

"You were right, back at the house." Cor sounded tired, defeated. He looked back at their fire. "We should have waited for my father."

"We need some light over here. Go back and bring more burning sticks. I'll make a fire ring."

Together they built a small fire, trying not to think. Finally, Happen sighed, stood up, and turned to look. Cor grabbed his long stick and joined him, and within a few steps the flickering firelight revealed the cage's occupant to be a cougar, and not a particularly large one. Still a formidable foe without the cage, but not the monster they'd been imagining.

The woman hadn't moved. *She has to be dead.* The little fire muttered, snapped, and hissed behind them.

"Cougar's going to eat that hand soon," Happen said. "But he'll, um, run out of . . . food . . . eventually, and starve."

Cor shrugged and turned back to the fire. "Oh, well."

"Yeah, we'll have to let him out of the cage. At some point anyway." Happen stayed still, looking at the cage.

"What! Why?"

"Yes, and whether she's dead or not, we have to get her away from the cage." He shifted his weight gingerly, favoring his left leg. "She should be buried, not eaten by a cougar. And we can't just leave the poor thing to starve. Remember what Odais learned after the Battle on Yonder Peak?"

"Mouth or no mouth, she's creepy, and I'd just as soon make you some crutches and get out of here. If he does eat her, at least he's caged." Cor poked at a rock with the stick in his hands. "Besides, do cougars even eat dead people?"

"Maybe . . . if it's got nothing else? And everybody has a mouth. We just can't see hers from here."

"Okay, then. How are we going to bury her without a shovel?"

"Maybe we'll have to build a funeral pyre like Odais did for his guide at the troll's lair?" Happen said. Cor was right. Even if they had *two* shovels, they weren't in any shape for grave digging.

"Easy for you to say, since I'm the one fetching all the wood."

"Maybe we could use the cougar cage as the pyre."

Cor nodded. "Now that's brilliant. There's plenty of wood there. And it solves the cougar problem, too."

Happen shook his head. "Might as well go over there now and make sure she's dead first."

"Yes, you might as well."

"No, *you* might as well."

After a moment, Happen picked up a twig and broke it into two pieces, a long one and a short one. "Boon or bane," he said, and held them between his thumb and forefinger so Cor couldn't see how long they were. Cor held his breath, and pulled up the long one.

"Okay." Happen sighed. "We both go over with burning sticks. We'll check out the cage to see what's holding it shut, and I'll find out if she's dead."

# NINE

# NOT BREATHING, NOT BITING

By the end of the period of history known as the Age of Doubt, the most commonly held theory about the shape of Grith was that it was a brick, and rocking in a cradle that generated tides. Debates between "moon theorists" and "cradle theorists" were complicated by Grith's smaller second moon's effect on measurements and equations. (Reilly, 2046)

⸻

Cor found some pitch on a wounded fir tree, and the boys advanced toward the cage with furrowed brows and shallow breath, holding pitch torches. The cougar was lying down, licking the woman's hand. It stopped as they approached and watched them, firelight reflecting eerily from its eyes.

"It's okay, cat," Happen said. "We'll get you out of that cage in a moment."

The cougar raised his head and shoulders, more alert, but

still prone. The door to the cage comprised one short wall of the rectangular cage, on the side that was slightly submerged in the lapping river. Two boulders reached into the river there, creating a small eddy and a calm beach, while the bulk of the river crashed through rocky rapids nearby. The door was tied with thick rope at the top and bottom. The knots looked complicated, but Cor's knife would be able to cut the rope. There was enough space for the cougar to reach out through the bars, so they were careful not to get too close.

Happen turned his attention to the woman, bringing his torch closer to her face to see what was covering her nose and mouth. A low growl came from the cougar, and Happen backed off before he could get a good look.

"It's okay, cat, I won't hurt your friend," he said. "Or should I say, 'I won't take your meal'?" The flames on his stick sputtered weakly, so he held it point down for a moment. "Okay, here goes." Happen didn't know why he was whispering. He reached down and tentatively touched her ankle, pulling his hand back as if he might get burned. Then he tried again, more deliberately.

"I just don't know, Cor. It's cold, but not as cold as I thought it would be. Oh. Oh, musical! Check this out. These shoes are amazing."

"Forget the shoes, look at her face."

Happen raised his torch toward her face to get a closer look and again a low warning growl came from the cougar, but he ignored it this time. The woman wore a tan-colored robe, but he couldn't see anything covering her face. Wrinkles of middle age lined her eyes, but the skin below them was smooth down to her subtle chin. He stared. She *wasn't* breathing. *He* wasn't breathing.

Cor moved closer behind him, the light of his torch helping to illuminate the woman's face for a moment before the flame died. "Well?"

"I don't know . . . what . . . she? Not breathing." Happen couldn't comprehend how this person lying in front of him could exist, so his mind shifted, and he returned his attention to the impossibly intricate design on her shoes. "But look at these shoes!"

"H–Hap," Cor said, his voice quavering. "Back away slowly. Now." Happen limped away a few steps, then looked back. The woman's eyes were half open. Happen staggered, grabbed Cor's arm for balance, and stared. She gestured weakly with her left hand.

"She wants us to come back," Happen whispered.

"Thunder and lightning, this is creepier than when she was dead," Cor whispered. None of them moved for a long moment, then Happen raised his burning stick and its flame died. She pointed at the stick in his hand and again waved him to come closer.

"I think she wants . . . Oh! Of course, she's cold." The boys took some burning sticks from the fire and built a new one closer to her. Happen backed away, watching, but she just stared.

"Get some more. She must be freezing." Cor brought more wood over and Happen placed it. Her eyes opened fully in the growing light and seemed to smile. Cor was handing Happen another stick when she took her hand out of the cage and held it up palm out to stop them.

The boys froze. She pointed to herself, then to the larger fire, their first one with the alder tree. "She wants to move over to our fire," Happen said.

"Can she walk?" Cor said. She shook her head no, but sat up and motioned with her arms like she was rocking a baby. She pointed to Cor, made the baby rocking motion, then pointed to herself.

"She wants you to carry her," Happen said in amazement.

"Aww, grubs, why me?" Cor complained. She pointed to Happen's feet.

"She sees me limping. Smart."

Cor approached the woman and put one knee on the ground behind her, but the cougar hissed and snarled so he backed away. She turned to face the cougar and reached back into the cage to pet the side of its neck, scratching it behind an ear while Happen and Cor's jaws dropped. Then, pulling her right arm out of the cage again, she gathered her long robe up against the back of her bent knees and reached up with her left arm toward Cor and waited. He knelt down, glanced nervously at the pacified cougar, then picked her up and carried her to the larger fire. She appeared quite limp, and heavier than Happen would have guessed. Cor leaned her against the fallen tree. She motioned with her hands as if she were casting a spell to make the fire bigger.

Cor went to search for more wood. Alone with the strange woman, Happen kept his focus on the fire. Looking at her made him uncomfortable, but he kept himself in a position to see her movements peripherally. *She seems to be unusually interested in the fire. But then, she might be thinking the same thing about me.* His mind kept returning to her shoes. He'd never seen anything so detailed. The intricate design had appeared to move in the firelight, and now he wondered if it hadn't been moving for real, and wanted to look again.

*Thunder and lightning am I tired! Here I am, with no food or hunting weapons, in the middle of nowhere, having nearly been killed, and I've stumbled upon a person who seems to be different kind of Grithing I've never heard of—and all I can think about is her shoes.* He laughed out loud at himself for a moment, and then his eyes met hers through the firelight. He wasn't sure he could read her expression, but she seemed delighted. Delighted by the fire, and delighted with his sudden laughter. She put her hands over her heart, and then reached them toward him, as if she was pouring something from her heart to him. Happen wasn't sure, but it felt as if she was thanking him, and his fear of her melted away.

"I'm forgetting my manners," he said. "My name is Happen Fell. I hope you'll forgive my surprise at your unusual appearance. I'm guessing that you're not from around here?"

She nodded, and then tried to stand. She wobbled unsteadily, then knelt down and performed a ceremonious bow from her knees. Happen wondered why she couldn't stand.

"Are you hurt?" he asked.

She shook her head and pointed at the fire.

"Oh, just cold," he said. "Good."

Cor returned with more firewood. He set it down next to Happen and muttered. "How are things?"

"Good," Happen said. "She's quite friendly. Remember Balorphemus? Some folks are just born different. Go ahead and introduce yourself." Cor stared at him skeptically for a moment. Balorphemus was a man who Odais had met and befriended early in his first journey. He had been born with a single eye in the middle of his face, instead of two like everyone else.

"Go ahead. She won't bite."

Cor stepped around the fire, and shyly reached out his hand to shake. Happen chided himself for forgetting that part.

"Hello. My name is Cortham Fell. I'm Happen's cousin. You can call me Cor. I'm, um, sorry about your, um . . ." he faltered, and pointed at his mouth.

She shook her head, then repeated her bow from her knees. Cor returned to Happen's side.

"She shook her head at me," he said quietly. "What does that mean?"

"Maybe it means 'don't be sorry'? I'm not sure."

The woman gestured toward the pile of sticks that Cor had brought.

"She wants more fire. Here. Grab that end."

The alder tree had burned through enough for the boys to

break it and bring the bottom end next to the fire to dry, and put the top end on to burn. The strange woman pointed at the sticks again, gesturing like she wanted them.

"She still can't walk," Happen said. "Bring her these sticks." Cor carried some of the sticks around the fire and set them down in front of her. She picked up three and held them up with two touching at the top and spread apart at the bottom, and the third crossing about halfway up the other two. The boys watched, not comprehending. She put the sticks down, then pointed to herself, and then picked up the sticks again in the same formation. Happen thought she was making a mountain with a bridge or something.

"Oh!" said Cor. "Is it the letter 'A'?"

She nodded, put the sticks down, and then pointed to herself again.

"Is that your name?" Cor asked. "A?"

She nodded again and repeated her bow.

"Nice to meet you, A," Happen said.

She pointed at his left ankle.

"Are you wondering what happened to my ankle?"

She nodded. He paused, yawning and wondering where to begin. Leaning against the fallen tree by the warm fire, he felt exhaustion start to overwhelm him.

"My cousin and I were on our way to Aeriskenn for the trade fair. We were camping up by the highway . . ." He started there and told her what happened. He was embarrassed that it seemed like they hadn't taken precautions, so he explained that Osgar wasn't a stranger to the tulls, and that nobody else would have been able to do what he did without them raising an alarm. When he got to the part where Osgar cut the ropes, another yawn interrupted him.

"Oh, pardon me. I'm a bit sleepy, I guess."

A pointed next to him, and he turned and saw that Cor had fallen asleep on what remained of his pile of firewood. Happen turned back and smiled at her. She put her spelling sticks onto the fire, pointed at him, and then put her palms together and placed the back of one hand alongside her head and tilted it.

"You think it's okay if I sleep?"

She nodded. The eastern sky was beginning to glow just a little. *The daylight will come soon and wake me. I shouldn't feel safe sleeping with only this stranger to watch out for me and Cor, but I do.* He lay down in the sand and fell asleep.

## TEN

## 100 YEARS OLD AND STILL SPRINGING

> Two years before the end of the Age of Doubt, the leader of one of the many religious factions in Berythea—Gracarrai—requested a meeting with the king to discuss an imminent natural disaster of global proportions, but was dismissed as an attention-seeking witch. The same endeavor met the same results with the Guild Council. (Reilly, 2046)

T HE CLOUDS BROKE up, letting the midday sun shine down onto Happen's face, and he woke with a start. The fire had burned down and Cor and A weren't there. He pulled himself up, standing gingerly, very sore. The cougar slept in its cage. The river lapped on the shore nearby, and rushed through the rocks downstream. Happen limped to the river to get a drink, soak his ankle in the cold water, and consider his situation.

*Hunt up a little food and make some crutches, then we'll head back to Pury to warn everybody about Osgar. But what about my Summering Task?*

*Thock.* A rock fell, striking another. He turned and saw movement downstream, beyond the cougar cage. He looked down to pick up a throwing rock, and when he looked up, a young woman was running toward him, but looking down to find her steps among the rocks. The cougar snarled.

Happen held his rock as if to throw it at her, and bellowed, "Stop!"

She unsheathed a long hunter's knife that reflected sunlight unnaturally. "Where is she?" the young woman demanded. Happen couldn't tell if she was looking for A to attack her with that knife, or if it was meant for him. The new stranger looked at the ashes from the fire, and then turned back to Happen.

"Tell me!" She advanced slowly, the knife clenched in her fist. She wore sturdy pants with extra pockets, a tan leather jacket, and a dark green backpack. Her long blond hair was tied back, and dark eyeglasses covered her eyes. He had never known anyone who could afford eyeglasses, but he'd read about them in the newspapers from Aeriskenn. The long knife and heartless eyes made him feel like he'd kicked a wasp nest.

"Where is who?" Happen responded coldly.

The young woman slumped, lowering her knife.

"Wasn't there . . ." She faltered. ". . . Wasn't there a woman with this cougar?"

Happen couldn't help himself, and started to laugh. He knew it must be rude, but he couldn't stop. She pocketed her glasses and glared at him.

"I'm sorry," he gasped, trying to quell his laughter. "You . . . you said that as if . . . of course, naturally, *every* time you find a caged cougar by a river, there *has* to be a woman that comes with it."

Her glare softened somewhat.

"Okay, I see your point, but still. My . . . friend is missing, and I've been looking for two days . . ." She replaced the knife into the sheath on her belt and started walking upstream.

"This person you're missing is your friend?" Happen asked. She had paused before using that word, and he still wasn't sure about her.

"She was—is—my guide and teacher here. We're traveling together. She fell in the river," she said as she passed the camp. "I'll have to keep looking. I can't get home without her."

"There was a woman with this cougar," Happen said quickly. "She was here last night, but I don't know where she is now."

"Why not? What happened? Is she okay?" The young woman's voice was suspicious again.

Happen put down his rock, and limped up the bank to sit by the fire ring. "When we found her, we thought she might be dead—"

"Because she wasn't breathing."

"Right. We lit a fire, and were looking at the cougar's cage—"

"Wait, 'we'?"

"My cousin was here, too. They were both here by the fire when I fell asleep near dawn—"

"Oh, thank goodness," the young woman said, as if Happen had taken a boulder off her back.

"What?"

"She had a fire," she said, as if that explained everything. "Thank goodness. It had been days. Then what?" she asked.

"Nothing. I woke up several waves before you arrived, and they were both gone." Happen leaned back against the fallen tree.

"Interesting. I bet they'll be back soon."

"I can't imagine they went far. She couldn't walk last night." He looked at the stranger's shoes, but other than unusually precise stitching, they seemed like normal leather boots.

"Really? I've never seen her like that, but I've heard it can be pretty bad. Your fire probably saved her life. If she let it go out, she's fine now."

"Yeah, I guess she got quite a chill."

"Sure, but the main thing was the firelight, Ariadne is a . . . a bit different."

"Ariadne? She told us her name was A." Happen thought for a moment they might be talking about different people.

"Told you?" Now the young woman looked doubtful, too.

"She held up three sticks to make an A. We asked if that was her name and she nodded."

She breathed a sigh of relief. "She's like that. Always as efficient as possible. She wanted you to have a name for her, but within that context, it didn't need to be any longer than A. Oh, I'm so glad she's okay."


"You were going to say something else about—" His question was interrupted by a shout from Cor, who hurried down the slope with several trimmed maple saplings and sawn and split cedar in his arms.

"Hey! A shot us some rabbits to eat and she cut some saplings to make crutches for you and you're not going to believe the . . . the weapon tool thing she—Oh, hello, who's this?"

The young woman walked past Cor as if he weren't there and greeted Ariadne, who was several paces behind him, with a big hug, which Ariadne tentatively returned. In one hand, she held four large rabbits tied to a string. She disengaged from the hug and pointed to the site of the fire.

"She's A's traveling companion or something," Happen told Cor. "And it turns out A's name is Ariadne."

Ariadne set the rabbits down next to the cold fire ring, and then motioned for the young woman to put something next to her face.

"Oh, yes, of course," she said. "I'm just so excited to see that you are well . . ." She reached inside her jacket and pulled out a thin black box, held it up to her eye, and then poked it a few times.

"Hello all," a voice came from the black box, and the young woman handed it to Ariadne. "Nora, thank you for coming to find me. I made a poor decision and nearly lost my life, and our itinerary has been delayed. From here we will head straight to Aeriskenn, but first we will determine a proper way to thank these two nice boys for saving my life. A Dhaignian scout's life is a heavy balance. This will delay us further, so we must each stick to our tasks. Cor, please introduce yourself to Nora, and then go get the firewood we cut this morning. Nora, I'll need the first-aid kit to tend to the boys' injuries. Happen, please remove your shoe and I will examine your injured ankle."

Happen looked from the box in Ariadne's hand to her face, and tried to understand what was happening.

"Thunder, A," Cor said. "Is that you talking?"

"Yes. There will be time for explanations later. Please remember my instructions." Cor introduced himself to Nora and went to get the firewood. Nora opened her backpack for Ariadne, who handed the talking-box to Happen.

"I left the tulls grazing in a meadow just below the rapids," Nora said. "It's not far. I'll bring them up."

Ariadne bent over Happen's ankle, feeling it with her hands while he gawked at the strange box in his hands. A lightweight, rectangular thing not much larger than his palm, it was made of a smooth, hard material with rounded edges and corners, like sea glass, only lighter.

"How does this work?" he asked.

"It's not broken," the thing said, startling Happen so he nearly dropped it. "I will attempt a lymph drainage to reduce the swelling. I will need to massage your leg in a way that may seem unrelated to your ankle, but you will trust my judgment. Please remain still."

The voice was richly toned in a way that wasn't possible from such a tiny source. It had a curious musical quality, and yet had no particular rhythm or melody, more like random notes. Ariadne rubbed his leg on his inner thigh, and under his knee, and several places on his calf and ankle. Then she cleaned his calf wound, smeared some ointment on it, and bandaged it.

"There," the thing said as Ariadne patted his knee. "Put your ankle in the river for a while, and the swelling will go down. In a bell or so we can tape it. This device lacks a name in your language, but translates roughly as "distance voice." It belongs to Nora, and I'm able to speak to her through it. If you wish to converse with me, you can ask her for it." Ariadne took the device from him, and returned it to Nora, who had returned with two large tulls who'd had their horns removed.

"The boys will have many questions," the distance-voice box said for Ariadne. "As they have taken the trouble to fish me and the cat out of this violent river, and saved my life, I will accept them into my confidence, so please answer them accurately. Give Happen what he needs to prepare three rabbits for eating."

Happen and Cor looked at each other but didn't say anything. Cor handed him his knife, and Nora brought three of the rabbits and a split piece of cedar that worked well for a cutting board. Ariadne took the fourth rabbit to the cougar, who stood lazily and stretched nearly the length of its cage, seeming as if it were accustomed to receiving breakfast this way.

While Happen skinned and cleaned rabbits at the river's edge, Cor brought several loads of firewood, including some sawn logs, and prepared kindling for a fire. *Where did he find sawn logs around* here? The cut ends were charred, just like the sticks used to build the cougar's cage. When the rabbits were ready, Happen brought them to the fire ring. Ariadne appeared to be talking to the cougar somehow, and Nora was watching him and talking at her talking-box.

He had so many questions to ask these strange people, but he couldn't ask them all at once. He felt like Nora might be talking about him, so he started there.

"Are you talking to Ariadne?" he asked.

"No," she said. "I'm taking notes. I can talk to this device, and then later, when I get home, I can read the words that I spoke. It's like writing things down to remember them, only faster."

"Oh. Is Ariadne talking to the cougar?"

"That's something I'd like to know, too. It sure looks like she is, doesn't it? Hey, how's your ankle?"

Happen was surprised to see that the swelling in his ankle had gone down substantially. It still hurt to put weight on it, but it looked a lot more like an ankle should. "It still hurts, but not as much, and it looks a lot better."

Nora sighed. "She has so many talents."

"Let's get this fire going," Cor said. "I'm so hungry I could eat ten rabbits. Hey, Miss Nora, do you have one of those light-beam things like Ariadne? To start the fire?"

"Please, just call me Nora. And no, I don't have one. How did you start the fire last night?"

Cor showed her the bow drill, but before he could explain how it worked, Ariadne returned. From a pocket in her robe she pulled out a tool unlike anything Happen had ever seen. It had a long black handle, like a large knife would, but longer, and where the blade would have been was a short, shiny cylinder with a small hole on the end. She pointed it at the fire ring, and a ghostly green dot appeared in the tinder Cor had arranged. Almost immediately, the tinder began smoking and caught fire.

"Isn't that the most amazing thing you've ever seen?" Cor fed the fire with kindling from the pile. "She can cut logs with that thing."

"How does it work?" Happen wanted to touch it, maybe even

try using it, but it had been put away and Ariadne sat staring into the growing fire. "Ariadne, how does it work?"

But Ariadne appeared to be lost in the fire, or ignoring him.

"Um, she's not going to answer that question," Nora said. "It takes some getting used to. When she's busy, which is almost always, she doesn't respond to anything that distracts from the task at hand. She's maddening that way, though she really does mean well."

"She doesn't look busy."

"I'm remembering now that she asked me to answer your questions. She must have thinking or planning to do, and figures my answers will be good enough."

"Do you know how the light-beam thing works?" Cor asked doubtfully.

"Believe it or not, I do, although it will be challenging to describe in your language." Nora paused to look at her talking-box.

"Its name translates to visual impairment system with enhanced response, which doesn't exactly roll off the tongue, does it? Let's call it a VISER. It uses vibrations to concentrate light. It was originally designed as a nonlethal weapon, used to temporarily blind people, but as the . . . craft developed, it became more . . . versatile. Like all Dhaignians, Ariadne has an innate ability to manipulate tiny radiant airwaves with her mind, so there are no controls on a viser that you or I could use. She can adjust the diameter of the beam, as well as the power output, making the device function as anything from a simple pointing tool to a devastating weapon. Does that answer your question?"

The boys looked at each other. The light-beam thing wasn't fun anymore. They had been around dangerous tools and weapons before, but they had understood how those worked. Happen didn't understand all of what Nora said, but he could tell that this device was something he would probably never be able to use or understand. Something shifted inside him, and he felt small and homesick. Nora saw the looks on the boys' faces, and her expression softened.

"I know it's a lot to take in all at once. I remember when I first learned about the Dhaignians, it was an academic pursuit. To have one suddenly appear on your . . . riverbank must be difficult. But the good news is she likes you and wants to help you. Given her penchant for efficiency, adding you to our team is an unexpected decision. Normally, she only goes out of her way for cats."

They all looked at Ariadne. She added wood to the fire, apparently not listening to them. The flames appeared ghostlike and insubstantial in the bright sunlight. Happen remembered stories about witches who could communicate with cats, or even become cats, and cast spells to start fires or turn boys into toads. But those witches were wicked and dangerous, like naiads.

"Where is Dayg . . ." Happen hadn't ever heard of such a place. Not wanting to pronounce it wrong, he stopped himself.

"Tell you what," Nora said. "You cook the rabbits, and I'll tell you about Dhaignians, because, unlike them, I need to eat food. Deal?"

While Nora talked, Happen roasted the rabbits on a spit over the fire.

Nora settled down in the sand next to Cor and leaned back against the fallen tree. "Before I start, I have to ask you something. What does the word 'planet' mean to you?"

"We learned that in school. It's a star that moves independently of the others," Happen said.

"Oh, dear." Nora took a deep breath, and sighed. "Okay. Beyond the stars that you can see, there are more stars, and also other worlds, some very much like your Grith, and some less so, and many of these places have people living there."

"Dhaigne is a large world with a very old civilization, much older than yours or mine. They're very advanced scientifically, and highly capable at things like space travel and warfare. The average life span of a Dhaignian is about four hundred of your

Grith years. They don't require air for breathing, or food and water. They do require an energy source, however, but this varies. Each Dhaignian biotype requires a specific combination of wavelengths that can only be attained naturally. Members of the most common biotype, almost half the population, require sunlight. Some need moonlight. Seventeen percent of Dhaignians, like our Ariadne here, need firelight. Some islands and coastal areas have people requiring starlight, but Dhaigne is over three-quarters land, so there aren't many star people. Several extremely rare types exist as well, needing things like bioluminescence, thermal radiation from molten rock, polar aurorae . . . I don't know them all." Nora paused to breathe in the aroma of roasting meat.

"So . . . you're saying that Ariadne is from a different grith?" Happen asked.

"Yes."

"And she got here how?"

"We took the bus."

Ariadne's voice broke in from the device in Nora's pocket. "Please don't tease the boys, Nora," she said. "We took the Interstellar Transit Authority's Outer Reach Carrier to the drop-off point over the Irelian Ocean."

Happen wanted to argue, to show that he was not simpleminded enough to believe them, but Nora's story reminded him of that old fable: The Tull, the Monkey, and the Madman. The tull argued with the "seething imagination" of an eccentric bard, and missed his chance at the golden fruit. But the monkey pretended to see the devils named by the bard. Even though the villagers laughed at him, the monkey pretended the bushes were bears, appeasing the strange wanderer, and won the prize. No, Happen wouldn't argue, but he was too proud to let these strangers make a fool of him.

"That's really interesting," he said.

"You mean Grandma interesting, right?" Cor asked.

"Of course."

"Grandma interesting?" asked Nora.

The boys looked at each other. Happen shrugged.

"It's what our Grandma used to say when we told stories that, well, that might not be true," he said.

"Your skepticism is understandable," Ariadne said. She turned to Nora and continued, "It appears that their cosmology remains Grith-centric, and probably their fiction, too."

───  ⎣⌐

After Nora and the boys ate, Ariadne helped Happen and Cor make a pair of crutches, and she asked them questions about their situation and their plans.

"Osgar thought we'd get drowned by the naiad, so he'll probably go to the fair, make our trades, and return with his story of how we fell off the bridge at Davoura Gorge," Cor explained.

"We can meet him in Pury with the sheriff, and I'll take the cart home from there." Happen picked at his bandage. He didn't want to think about the fair, or Osgar.

"Yet you say your. . ." Ariadne paused, looking at the both of them in turn. "You say your Tinker is possibly looking for you on the road to the fair?"

"Yes."

"How many roads are there between Pury and Aeriskenn these days?"

"One. There's only ever been one."

"Hmm. And why did you undertake this journey to begin with?"

"My assigned Summering Task is to go to the fair and make the family's trades." Happen's chest tightened as the consequences of the night's events began to sink in. "This was supposed to be the start of my Summering. I'm going to have to wait a whole other year now."

The shadowy specter that had haunted him since his father

broke his leg returned, oozing from its hidden corner, swallowing hope. "I'm going to have the latest Summering ever. I'll be a hundred years old and still Springing. I'm—" Happen's throat tightened and he couldn't say any more.

Cor tried to fill the space for him. "And *I've* always wanted to go to the trade fair, but couldn't because of school. But Hap needed my help, so . . . I guess I'll probably get in trouble . . ."

"I understand now how I can repay you. I will take you with me. If we don't meet with Tinker on the road, perhaps he will be looking for you at the fair. Nora, the boys may be useful for your research." She cut the end off the stick they'd used to peg the handhold, and Happen's second crutch was finished. "Go for a walk, test our work."

Happen and Cor wandered upstream, Happen swinging his left leg carefully past the rocks.

"Sure goes faster making stuff with that viser thing for cutting and drilling," Cor said.

"Yeah." Happen moved slowly, having to find three places to step for each of Cor's two.

"So what do you think about these folks?" Cor asked.

"If I had a . . . well, I don't know if you'd call it a deformity or what, but if I were as different as Ariadne is, I might make up an explanation for it too, but saying you took a bus from beyond the stars? I don't know. They do things and have things like witches, but they don't seem like any of the witches I've read about. They seem kind of nice, actually."

A yellow butterfly tumbled over the river and settled on a shallow pool shaded by a young maple.

"Yeah. A bit bossy sometimes, but overall pretty nice. You think we should go with them?" Cor picked up a rock.

"No one would blame us for going home."

"I was thinking that, too."

Happen poked at some sand with one of his crutches, not

looking at his cousin. "Though they might put down the Legend of Cortham Fell."

"Does that mean we're going?"

"They might be witches, but if they wanted to hurt us they've had plenty of chances already. I only have four days left to get to the fair, and I can't afford to say no to a ride. At least until we can find your dad. He's got to be looking for us on the road, right?"

"Yeah. Thunder, is he going to be mad at Osgar." Cor turned, stepped, and took a calming breath.

"He doesn't know about Osgar though," Happen said

Cor released the rock. The butterfly rose from the surface of the pool only to be snapped up by a leaping trout as the rock skipped past harmlessly.

"We'll just have to find him before Osgar does," Happen said.

PART TWO

# THE BLACKSMITH
# CONSPIRACY

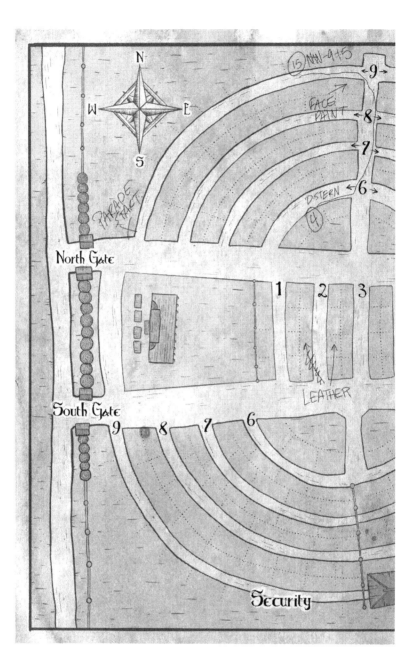

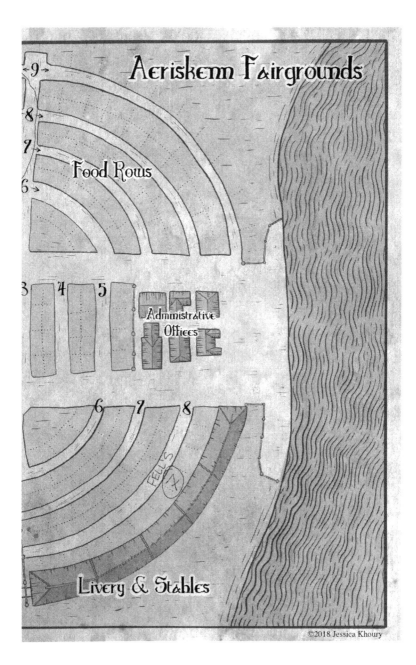

©2018 Jessica Khoury

## ELEVEN
## IT'S NOT MAGIC

 None of the subjects interviewed had actually met a witch personally, but neither did they express any doubt as to their existence. Berythean legends describe a wide range of witches, from the extremely powerful and dangerous, to the friendly neighbor who's quick with a headache cure. While their vocabulary on the topic is limited (for example, the Maithean language has nine words for *witch*), subjects can usually convey the difference using context and tone. (Reilly, 2046)

Nora had hidden their wagon off the road north of the bridge, where the hills west of the highway gave way to a gentle slope down to the river valley. They returned with the cougar's cage on a travois dragged by one tull, and Happen on a travois dragged by the other. Cor, Ariadne, Nora, and the cougar traveled on foot. After cutting up both travois for firewood, Ariadne and Nora set out for the Aeriskenn Trade Fair, the two boys riding in the back of the wagon with the luggage, firewood, and the cougar, who surprised Happen by walking willingly back into its cage, apparently expecting Ariadne to provide more rabbits in time.

Ariadne's wagon had nice new leather thoroughbraces, and the ride was smooth enough for Happen and Cor to catch up on their sleep stretched out in the back. At times Nora talked quietly into her talking-box, and the boys occupied themselves watching the scenery when they rolled through villages or passed slower vehicles. Occasionally they sat on boxes at the front so they could listen to their hosts' strange conversations.

—⌒⌒—

"What's the cougar's name?" Nora asked Ariadne.

"Why must all the animals have people names for you? Her name does not translate to this language. Or yours."

"She's traveling with us. It feels wrong for me to think of her as, well, as just an anonymous pronoun." Nora gestured as if she hated pronouns.

"Well then, if you must. But please make it more dignified than the ones you assigned these poor tulls." Ariadne held the reins loosely, and displayed none of Nora's animated conversation style.

"Oh, come now," Nora said. "Banjo and Lute like their names, don't you boys?" The tulls did not respond. "Anyhow, I would imagine that the cat's name, even if it doesn't translate, must have some meaning, or suggest a possible meaning, that could guide us in choosing a name that I can pronounce."

"No."

Nora laughed and turned away. "Okay, then. Be that way."

They passed a slow cart pulled by two young men. Happen saw Ariadne pull her deep hood farther over her head. *She's probably tired of people staring at her.*

Nora turned back to face Ariadne. "Can't you tell me anything about her at all?"

"Yes. Her mother was killed when she was very young, and she was raised by the people at the inn we engaged near the Irelian peninsula. It's not a great life, but she's old now and not interested in being released to the wild. After our business in Aeriskenn, we'll need to return her to her home."

"How do you know all that?" Nora asked. "Can you talk to animals? Oh, how magical you are!" Happen and Cor looked at each other. Cor seemed surprised, but Happen felt his brow furrow in consternation. He kept forgetting they were traveling with a witch.

"It's not magic," Ariadne said. "After many years of study, I have learned to communicate on a very rudimentary level with some cats. I haven't tried with other animals, though I know some Dhaignians who have. It requires a significant investment of time and energy to learn."

"Oh. Still, it feels magical to me because I couldn't do it even with all that study."

"It's true that it does require a Dhaignian's ability to manipulate radiant waves."

"I've got it!" Nora put her hand on Ariadne's knee. "I will name her Marimba. It's a lovely name, don't you think?"

"We have already established that my thoughts on this topic are irrelevant."

On the afternoon of their second day in the wagon, Nora called the boys to the front, saying she thought she saw something on the road ahead. They knelt on boxes so they could see over the front seat. She held what looked like a connected pair of small black tubes in front of her eyes.

"It's two wagons coming this way, with flags on them."

Shadows reached across the road as if yielding to the western breeze. They were riding through a series of abandoned farms, and the only traffic they had encountered had been heading north like them.

"What's that thing you're looking at, Nora?" Cor asked.

"What? Oh, these? They're called binoculars. They're for seeing things far away. Would you like a try?" She turned around to put a strap around his neck and showed him how to adjust the black tubes. "Perhaps you'll know what those flags are about."

"I don't see anyth—oh. Oh, wow. Hap you have to look at this. Those wagons are really far away. But you can see details that you'd never—this is amazing!"

Happen ignored his cousin. He liked Ariadne and Nora, but he did not like their magical devices like the 'distance-voice' and the viser.

"The flags, Cor," Ariadne said.

"Oh, right. Those are highway patrol wagons. Although . . ." He paused, adjusting the thing. "They don't look like highway patrol wagons. But they do have the flags."

"Could they be fake?" Ariadne asked.

"Oh, I don't know," he said. "If you did that and ran into the real patrol, you'd get arrested. There was a poster up in Pury about that a couple of years ago."

"Let me have a look, please," Ariadne said, and Cor handed her the binoculars. "Yes, I see the flags are tied on with rope. Not a fixture. Could be fake, could be some form of deputization, either way, it's not a good sign." She handed the binoculars to Nora, and pulled the hood on her cloak farther down.

"Oh, hey. It looks like they have a prisoner," Nora said.

"Ooh, can I see?" Cor asked.

"Don't, Cor. Those witch things creep me out." Happen turned away and sat back down.

"But what if it's Osgar?"

"It's not Osgar." *But what if it is? Maybe he's already been caught somehow!*

Cor stood, leaning against Happen's shoulder and the front of the wagon box for balance while looking through the witch thing.

"Oh, thundering maggots," he said. "My dad is tied up in that wagon. Grubs! Ariadne, can you help me get him out?"

"Let's start by finding out what we can about who these men are and why they're holding your father. Has this happened before?" she asked.

"No. We don't always get along with the Pury sheriff, but nothing like this. Maybe he had some trouble with Osgar?"

"Sometimes Berytheans can be reasoned with. Let Nora speak with them, and we'll hope for the best. This is a task that calls for charm as much as anything. We'll stop here and give them plenty of time. Please put the binoculars away, and cover the cage with that tent to hide the cat. You two should stay under the tent as well."

Nora stood in front of the tulls and hailed the approaching wagons. They stopped, and a man hopped out and sauntered past his tulls to stand close to Nora, between her and Banjo. Happen, watching from under the tent in the back of the wagon, thought it was odd that he came so close. Odais always approached a group of strangers cautiously, stopping where he could see all of them.

"Good evening, sir," Nora said. "Thank you for taking time from your journey to speak with a traveler."

"Not at all, little lady," he said. "All part of the job for the highway patrol. What can we do for you?"

"My aunt and I have come a long way to visit the Aeriskenn Trade Fair, and we were supposed to meet our local guide in

Pury, but we missed the meeting time and were hoping to catch up to him on the road, but we haven't found him. By any chance, have you seen a Mr. Tinker Fell along the road to Aeriskenn?"

"Why as a matter of fact, I have." He turned to gesture at the second wagon. "But Mr. Fell won't be doing any guiding today, will he, boys?" The other men laughed. Nora laughed, too. Tinker gaped at her.

"Oh, is that him?" She shielded her eyes from the sun and peered in Tinker's direction.

"Yeah." The patrol man looked her over thoroughly. "We're taking him back to Pury, to the sheriff there."

Nora reached out to put her hand on the man's arm. "Maybe instead you could let him guide us at the fair, and we'll make sure he sees the sheriff in Pury when we're done."

"Uh, no." He scoffed. "That's not how we do things here."

"Well, sure, but you don't want to ride all that way to Pury, do you Mr. umm . . ." Nora said, gently squeezing his arm.

"Marsul, Deputy Marsul now."

"Deputy Marsul," Nora said firmly, somehow making it sound as if she liked the name. "We'd really appreciate having him come with us."

"No, you don't understand. This man needs to face justice. We can't just let him go."

"Oh, dear. Has he committed a crime?"

"Yes, he has. Resisting arrest, and . . . and disturbing the peace. The sheriff knows what to do with his type."

"You tried to arrest him, and he disturbed the peace then?"

"That's right. A real troublemaker this one. Not someone you want as a guide."

"If he disturbed the peace after you tried to arrest him, what were you trying to arrest him for?" Nora asked in a polite tone.

"He was—" The deputy stopped himself, then scowled. "Listen, lady, I don't need to answer to you. I have a prisoner to deliver. Good day." He turned to go back to his wagon.

"Deputy Marsul," Nora said. "If you tried to arrest him before he committed a crime, that's not something you want them to hear about up in Aeriskenn, is it?" The deputy stopped, keeping his back to her.

"What I mean to say is," Nora added quickly, "wouldn't it be easier for us to pay his fine here, and save everybody the trouble of addressing a dubious legal situation? It might be better to handle it less . . . formally."

The deputy turned and walked back. "Oh, I understand you all right." He sneered as he walked past her to Ariadne's wagon. "But I don't think you do. See, honey? You're not going to Aeriskenn to spread lies about me. This here wagon? Not up to official highway standards." He pulled out a knife and sawed through one of the wheel spokes. Happen felt his jaw clench as anger welled up inside him with every rasp of the serrated blade.

"It isn't legal for these roads. We're going to have to . . . well, it's like this . . ." Marsul reached out and ran his finger along the hairline behind Nora's left ear. "We can't have pretty young ladies riding illegal wagons out on the road all by themselves, now can we?"

Without thinking, Happen pushed back the tent and jumped out of the back of the wagon, landing on his good ankle, but needing to grab the wagon to stay upright. He was followed closely by Cor. "They aren't alone!" Happen yelled. "So you just . . . you—"

"Hap! Cor! Thank goodness!" Tinker yelled through the laughter of the deputy and his men.

Marsul raised his right hand and circled his forefinger in the air. Bowmen clambered out of the wagons and spread out to surround Ariadne's wagon.

"Stop!" Nora yelled so forcefully that the men slowed, and looked at her in surprise. "If you continue to advance we will have no choice but to defend ourselves."

The deputy scoffed, and the men moved closer on both sides

of Ariadne's wagon. Ariadne raised the viser and a bright green beam appeared briefly between it and the front foot of the closest bowman on the east side of the road. He yelped and leaped back. The same fate befell the closest bowman on the west side. Another bowman nocked an arrow to shoot but the green beam appeared again, burning a spot on his hand. He dropped his bow, cursing. The deputy reached back to throw his knife toward Ariadne but then jerked his throwing hand away from the green beam. The acrid smell of burning skin hung in the air. He dropped his knife and fell to his knees, holding his charred right hand with his left.

"Halt!" he shouted at the road. "Stand down, men! Avert your eyes."

Nora was already cutting the ropes that bound Tinker to the patrol wagon at his wrists and ankles.

"What is this conjury?" The deputy stared at his hand, and held it as if it might fall off.

"Put some cold water on it," Nora said to him as she picked up his knife, returned to Ariadne's wagon, and swung herself up to the seat. "Honey."

# TWELVE
## WHETHER TO BELIEVE

> Scientists on Earth became aware of Kepler4-71d in 2037, when Dhaigne downloaded an update to UINSA's galactic map. One year later, habitability and language data became available, and by 2041, the IAU-PHL was contacting Dhaigne's Collector Magistration Office about possible expeditions to the planet that became known as Grith. (Reilly, 2046)

—⌒—

"Let's go," Nora said.

"But—" Cor protested.

"Tinker said for you to come with us, and he'll catch up. Hurry."

The boys scrambled onto the back of the wagon. Ariadne goaded the tulls into movement past the stunned bowmen who were all looking down or away from them. Some even had their hands over their eyes. An agitated tull with large saddlebags was tied to the second wagon. Tinker stopped talking to it as they drove by, and gestured to the boys to go.

"I told him we were heading north and asked if he could recommend a place to meet." Nora faced back, looking at Cor. "He looked like he might either trust me or attack me, so I gave him my knife, and he said to tell Cor: 'At the first sea fire, aim to the lee of pine.' He said you'd know what it meant, and to go quickly."

Ariadne set the tulls going at top speed.

Nora put her hand on Ariadne's shoulder. "I'm sorry—"

Ariadne gripped the reins tensely. "They told me young Earthlings sometimes make reckless choices in a difficult situation. *I* should have been more careful. Where are we going, Cor?"

Happen and Cor looked at each other. Nazellen Pyneley was Cor's mother's name, and she lived with her family over the mountains inland, so 'aim to the lee of pine' would mean turn east.

"Sea fire?" Cor scratched his head. Happen shrugged. Cor stood up, balanced against his cousin like before. "I'll have to watch for landmarks. I'm not sure what we're looking for, but I know we'll take a right when we find it."

"I bet he gave us that riddle so those deputies won't know where we're going, and hopes they won't follow us," Nora said.

Happen stood up to look ahead, too, holding on to the cougar cage to keep himself and his cousin steady. "Thunder and lighting, Nora. *I* wouldn't follow us if I were them."

She turned and smiled at him. The wind pushed her blond hair, shining like firelight in the sunset, across her face as she turned, and the smile in her eyes made Happen feel warm inside. The lingering anger and fear and embarrassment of his impulsive stand in front of the deputy melted away.

_ᘓ_

After about a league, a small village appeared and Ariadne slowed the tulls. As they approached the crossroad, muffled shouting and merriment drifted through the dust raised by a caravard that turned onto the highway before them. Ariadne slowed further to let the dust settle. The last rays of sun lit up the sign for a tavern on the corner, the Capering Fiddler.

"The Capering Fiddler, the Capering Fiddler," Cor muttered.

"What?" Happen asked.

"You sure Father knew we were going north, not south?" Cor asked Nora.

"Yes."

"Turn right here!" Cor said the words just in time for Ariadne to turn without having to circle back. The road east dwindled quickly into a weedy lane that entered a young forest. Rock walls showed where fields and pastures had been before the eruption.

"How far should we go?" Nora asked.

Cor shrugged. "I don't know. All Father said was turn east at the first tavern."

"We will see where this lane takes us. Some time away from the main road will help bring calm," Ariadne said.

Ariadne's movements still seemed tense, surprising Happen. It wasn't the poisoned snappiness of an angry person, just tension, but he'd not seen it in her before. She would benefit from Odais's three-step procedure to restore equilibrium, but step one was to take a deep calming breath, and she couldn't do that. Just thinking about it made Happen's chest ache.

The lane took them to an old abandoned farmhouse in a dusky clearing. Crickets, bird calls, and a burbling stream added to the peaceful atmosphere.

"We will camp here. I need a fire."

Tinker still hadn't arrived by the time the tents were staked and fire was burning. Ariadne, sitting close by the fire with her hood up, asked Cor to explain the riddle.

"I've been away all summer, so I'd forgotten until I saw it. Just before I left, Father and I were talking about how odd it was that so many taverns on the Old King's Highway have the initials 'C. F.' There's the Crackling Fire, the Capering Fiddle, the Caravard's Friend . . ."

"And the Cat and Fish, and the Crooked Finger . . ." Tinker arrived, leading his neighbor's tull.

"Father!" Cor jumped up for a hug, Happen close behind.

"Sorry it took me so long. I took a different route, just in case they decided to unhitch a tull from their team and follow me. But I told them after running errands for a few days I'd turn myself in to the sheriff in Pury, so perhaps they'll find something better to do. Tonight, anyway."

After tending to his tull, Tinker sat down at the campfire opposite Ariadne and passed around some bannock his neighbor had given him, as well as some apples he'd brought from home.

"Oh my goodness, Mr. Fell," Nora said. "This bread is amazing!"

"Please, you can call me Tinker. I'll pass your compliment on to my neighbor. I agree he makes a fine bannock."

"I haven't heard that term before—bannock," she said. "What's the difference between bread and bannock?"

"Hmm. I never thought of it as bread. Bannock is what we make for traveling, but it's not that different from bread, I suppose. This one was made at home, but you can bring the mix on the road and make the dough in camp with a little fat from a rabbit or something, and wrap it around a stick to cook over a fire."

Happen was impressed by Tinker's skill at maintaining his

equilibrium—discussing bannock with two witches and a cougar as if it were a regular part of his day.

"It has such wonderful flavors," Nora said. "Rosemary, garlic, and something else. So much better than the boring travel bars I brought. Do you know what's in it?"

"I think it has stuff to help it keep from spoiling: salt, dew of the sea, thyme, garlic. Sometimes, if we can trade for cinnamon, we use that and dried berries."

"There will be time for your research later, Nora," Ariadne said. "Now we will plan for tomorrow. Tinker, do you expect the highway patrol to come looking for us?"

"Under normal conditions, I would expect them to stay on the highway," he replied. "But I don't know why the patrol is using deputies, and I don't know what happened back there. I think you used some kind of magical weapon we aren't familiar with, and I'm not sure how they'll respond to it."

"Listening to your answer, I begin to understand where Cor gets his better traits," Ariadne said. "It takes courage and wisdom to consider the facts that you don't know equally with the ones you do."

"Well, thank you. I have a long history of not knowing stuff, so I've gotten used to it. I do think there is at least a chance they will come after you, and you should probably be prepared for that. They'll head back to the city to improve their armor and weapons first, though, and being deputies, it could take a while, maybe several days."

Happen suddenly realized Tinker couldn't see her face, and maybe hadn't seen her face. The talking-box was resting on Nora's knee, but sound moves in strange ways through a fire so big. *He might not know she's a witch? That could be the key to his easy manner.*

"If there were to be an armed response tonight, would it arrive on the track that we used, or might there be other ways to approach?" Ariadne asked.

"These guys have been the top dog around here for years. They have little need for subtlety. But they won't leave the highway to look for you in the dark."

"Good," Ariadne said. "Now the boys will tell you about their journey."

"Yes, and I want to hear that, but first I'd like to explain to the boys why I wasn't at home when I said I'd be. It's been eating at me, and it'll ease my mind to explain myself."

"If you'd like some privacy, we could—"

"Oh, no, not at all," Tinker said. "I was just—I mean, it's probably not of interest to travelers . . ."

"I understand. A brief clarification is required. My student and I are traveling to Aeriskenn where I have two business contacts to meet with. One of them is likely to be at the trade fair. Since your son and nephew saved my life, and my path coincides with theirs, I will help them regain their belongings and restore their journey as they have restored mine. With your permission, of course. And if your explanation has any bearing on the current situation, it may be helpful for us to listen."

"That's very kind of you," Tinker said. "Normally I'd say that we'd manage our own affairs, but given my current uncertain legal status, it may be wiser to accept any help available. And parts of my story might have some bearing on the current situation, in regard to the deputies and a seasonal employee at my brother's farm."

"We told them about Osgar," Happen said.

"Okay. So, like I said, I don't know why they're deputizing, but I imagine it has something to do with an increase in unusual travelers we've experienced lately. I'd heard a few rumors, but didn't pay them any mind until one night when Osgar knocked on my door, accompanied by a stranger. He'd been asking at the Crackling Fire for a blacksmith.

"Now, I'd never heard that word before, and no one in Pury knew what it was either, but when the stranger described it, they sent him to me, saying I wasn't a blacksmith, but might do in a pinch. Osgar volunteered to bring him over. The man said he had a business proposition for me.

"He had information about how to turn certain rocks into something called 'steel,' which could be made into powerful weapons. These rocks had to be dug up out of the ground, so I said that's not going to be a very popular undertaking in these parts. He said in his travels he'd learned that most Gracarrai scholars and some Gracarrai leaders were changing their views on both mining and rock transformation. He had some pamphlets I could read to learn more about it. I told him I wasn't interested.

"He said craftsmen like myself were going to have to learn how to make and use steel because it's a much stronger metal than copper and good for other things, too, like making tools and starting fires, and if we didn't learn we'd run out of business shortly. He proved his point with an impressive demonstration, but still, us Fells aren't too popular to begin with without me being the first guy in town mixed up in something like this.

"*Osgar*, however, *he* wanted to hear more about powerful weapons. So those two went off talking about swords and battle-axes and the like. I didn't think too much of it at the time, but I'm wondering if old Osgar didn't get himself into some kind of trouble. I'll tell you why in a moment."

Happen saw again the glint of moonlight reflecting off Osgar's knife. "Would a steel knife be shiny?"

"The ones I've seen have been. Did you—? No, wait." Tinker sent Happen a look full of friendly chastising. "Let me finish.

"Now, around that time other odd characters were passing through town, coming in from the coast and heading up north. It put folks on edge around Pury. Then, someone stole one of Bahnsen's tulls, and its head, hide, and offal were found by the road not far from town. Some excitable types said it had been cut up and eaten raw, because there was no evidence of a fire, but I suspect it had been butchered, packaged up, and carried off. Still, who eats tull?

"Anyhow, folks in Pury were downright frightened and anxious after that, and I admit it was a little contagious. So I had Reg's letter, and was expecting you Harvest Mester ninth to full, traveling alone up the inland route, when here comes Osgar, knocking on my door again. This time he's all out of breath like he ran all the way from town, saying I've got to go get young master Happen because the highway patrol won't go and Mr. Fell broke his leg.

"Once I get him calmed down he explains that he was talking with some patrolmen outside the Crackling Fire when this traveler rides up the inland route saying he saw some bandits make off with someone's cart. Says he was camped under some oaks by a creek and there was a nice young man camped there, but bandits came just after nightfall. He tried to help the boy, but they knocked him out with a rock to the head and it wasn't till morning that he felt steady enough to make his way to Pury.

"This traveler had even picked up the boy's staff that had been left behind, and it's got your name on it, Hap. Osgar had it with him to give to me."

"Rrrr," Happen growled. "I had it right up until the night before I was supposed to leave. Osgar showed up that night warning us about strangers on the road. I thought he was exaggerating or maybe lying, but it sounds like that part was true. But he must have taken my staff that night because I couldn't find it the next day."

"Hm," Tinker said. "Well, Osgar tells me this story and of course the highway patrol won't leave the Old King's Highway, and so I figure I'd best go track you down. What really sells it though, is Osgar offers his tull. It's about the only thing he has in the world. I really thought he was worried about you, I mean, for Reg's sake at least.

"So I get down to the camp and there are scuff marks on the

ground that could've been from a fight, and there's a broken sack of oat flour with the Fells's symbol on it, and some of those wild onions Reg sells at the fair like they got knocked out of a bag or something, so off I go down the road as fast as I can. I passed the cart path, and saw that it had been cleared, so I knew, or thought I knew, that you'd come that way as expected."

"But that had to have been before I got there!" Happen pounded on the ground. "Osgar was supposed to give you the message that I would be a day late. I remember now when I came to the cleared path near the road. I thought someone had tried coming up the trail but gave up and turned around."

"It must have been Osgar just making it look cleared. He was very thorough," Tinker said. "I made it out to the Catamount Inn late that night, riding through a terrible storm, and they're all upset because their cougar had been stolen several days previous. For a couple of days after, they'd set a night watch, but they said there wasn't much for traffic, and they gave it up and worked on strengthening their stable locks instead. Some carts had passed through, but they didn't notice anything unusual."

"Wait, they had a cougar? As a pet?" Happen asked.

"Yes. The innkeeper there will talk your ear off about it. They'd raised it from a kitten fifteen years ago, and it was a big draw for them. On the solstice every year they'd put a live deer in its yard and folks would buy tickets for a view from the balcony."

Ariadne raised her hand and rubbed her finger and thumb together. The cougar pushed open the cage door and padded over to the fire to lie down next to Ariadne, who scratched the large cat's neck. Tinker moved his hand to the knife at his belt, but the cougar ignored him.

Happen was dumbfounded. It was too coincidental. It had to be the same cat. How could Ariadne have known Marimba came from an inn? Unless she was the thief?

"We were able to recover the stolen cougar," Ariadne said. "Thanks to the skill and kindness of your son and nephew. After my business in Aeriskenn, we will return her to the inn as soon as possible."

"You should have seen it," Cor said. "Can you imagine? I was looking for firewood by the river—"

"We'll tell that part after," Happen interrupted, throwing a twig at Cor. "Wait your turn." Their story wouldn't fit with Ariadne's belief that they'd fished her and the cougar from the river. It must have been the naiad who had done that, but having Ariadne and her viser helping to get his cart back wasn't something he wanted to give up. He wouldn't claim credit for something he didn't do; it just might be better to avoid that part of the story, and leave the naiad out of it, at least for now, if they could.

Tinker continued. "So the innkeeper at the Catamount recommended that I head out to the inn at Parvukenn, as folks there are known for keeping an eye on things. Next night I reach the coast and ask at the Four Seas Inn, and they hadn't seen you or anyone unusual in the past couple of days, but they suggested I talk with the harbormaster in the morning.

"By that time, I was thinking either those bandits had turned off somewhere I'd missed, or maybe Osgar was being fooled by that traveler for some reason, or even maybe that I was being fooled by Osgar for some reason. But the tull needed rest, and I was there already, so I poked about the harbor and the stables at the inn the next morning before heading back. I was feeling pretty low at that point."

Happen had pulled up some grass and shredded it as he listened.

Tinker's tone changed. "But the day after that, pretty early on my way back, I finally met somebody who'd seen you, and safe and headed in the right direction, after all."

"Was it that farmer I passed before Pury?"

"He went out of his way to tell me how refreshingly polite you were. So, then I had some idea what happened, but for the life of me I couldn't figure out *why*. I got to thinking that Osgar must have wanted me out of Pury, and the only reason I could think of for *that* was so he could do some kind of mischief to you or Cor or both.

"I rode his tull pretty hard that day, poor thing. Limped into Pury about middle of the next day. With no one home and the caravard gone I checked the desk and found your note, Cor, which was very helpful, thank you. Went to my neighbor's and he took on the care of Osgar's tull, and let me borrow his. That night I made it to the gorge camp pretty late, but in the morning I scouted around a bit and found your camp.

"I couldn't guess why you'd left in such a hurry, but I figured it couldn't be good, so I grabbed your bedrolls and knapsacks and set out up the road feeling low again, imagining all kinds of troubles and you boys wondering where I was. I was so relieved when I ran into those fellows from the highway patrol.

"I suppose I can see, if you look at it a certain way, that it could be funny for a man riding a fast tull to be looking for a slow cart that really, really ought to be somewhere but isn't. But at the time, I didn't take kindly to them laughing at me. I also suppose you could say I was rude to them after that, but I did not threaten them in any way. They were just so pleased that I was upset; it irked me. So when they decided to arrest me and take me back to Pury, things got a bit out of hand."

"It's quite understandable to us, having met their leader," Ariadne said. "We were hoping our negotiations would result in a reasonable bribe, but we failed to understand the man's volatile nature in time."

The boys told Tinker about their conversation with Osgar, and how they decided to travel without him. From their years at school together, they'd learned certain cues about storytelling, and Happen was able to silence Cor with a look when they got to the part at the bridge.

"Then Osgar said he was going to inherit our farm. And I

have questions about that, but sometime when I'm not so sleepy," Happen said, and Cor yawned.

"I'm getting tired, too," Cor said. "Maybe we can tell more about this tomorrow."

"Yes, we will plan for tomorrow. Nora and I might be dangerous to travel with going forward, but we also might be the fastest way for you and your boys to get to the fair. Happen believes that you will find your Osgar there. Also, it has been fifty years since I've been to Aeriskenn, and I have never been to this trade fair, so we could benefit from your experience. Will you travel with us?"

"I appreciate the offer," Tinker said. "And I'm sorry I can't think of a more polite way to ask, but it would help me feel better if I could see who I'm talking with."

"I understand. Often the only thing worse than what's real is what we imagine." Ariadne pulled back her hood. "But not always."

Tinker recoiled. Happen had never even seen him flinch before. He didn't have Odais's warrior physique, but he was tough as tull horn just the same. Tinker's whole body winced and shrank, but his eyes stayed fixed on Ariadne through the flames.

"I do not wish to frighten or harm anyone," Ariadne said. "I have come from beyond the stars that you can see, for what is supposed to be a peaceful, scientific research mission."

Tinker took a deep breath, and restored his equilibrium. Happen could see him tapping a rhythm with his fingers, in place of humming for step three. Tinker took another breath and said, "I would also like to know how you ended up on the road with my son, nephew, a steel knife, and a stolen cougar."

It was so good to have his uncle with him again. With all the strangeness that had occurred in the past few days, Happen hadn't thought of asking Ariadne this simple question. Or maybe he'd just been afraid.

"Yes, of course," Ariadne said. "Five days ago, we spent the entire night tracking a rumor of a rare creature, the northern flying hedgehog, for my research, and I wasn't able to feed. By the evening of the next day, it had been almost two days since I'd had a decent fire. But before we could camp, I was surprised to meet an old . . . acquaintance at the bridge over the gorge. We'd had a bitter disagreement ninety-seven years ago, and I hadn't seen him since. Not until that night. Also, by law only two Dhaignian scouts are allowed on listed planets at a time, and I had already seen the other one on the coast. It was like seeing a ghost. For many reasons, he wasn't supposed to be there.

"I was very tired and hungry, and my judgment was clouded by his unexpected reappearance. He had this cat in a cage hanging from a rope tied to the bridge over that river. Once he'd made sure I'd seen it, he cut the rope with his viser. As much as I love cats, I still shouldn't have done what I did. It was irresponsible of me to let a known outlaw scout go free here. I risked the lives of hundreds of thousands of cats trying to save one, and even that attempt was not likely to succeed. Except that it did, thanks to these two boys. They saved my life, the cat's life, and possibly a whole lot more."

Then Nora told about how the rogue Dhaignian had temporarily blinded her with his viser, and by the time she could see again, he was gone. She had used some tools from home to locate a navigable path to the river valley and find Ariadne with the boys.


"Do you have any other questions?" Ariadne asked Tinker.

"Yeah. So . . . you are a Dhaignian scout?"

"Yes."

"And there are two others like you in the vicinity?"

"Yes."

"But only one of them is trying to kill you?"

"Dhaignians do not kill each other. The rogue scout created a situation in which I was liable to do myself harm, possibly resulting in death, and I can only imagine he'll attempt it again if given the chance. I expect he followed me to the Catamount Inn, and stole the cougar, and butchered the tull in Pury to feed her."

"Do Dhaignians kill Berytheans who travel with Dhaignians?"

"I understand your concern. Dhaignians do not engage in violence for its own sake. This rogue scout has some reason for wanting my demise, but unless you threaten him in some way, it's very unlikely he'd attack you or the boys."

"That's a relief. One more for tonight. Have you ever heard of a ventriloquist? One performed at the fair last year and was quite impressive."

"I am not familiar with that term, no," Ariadne said.

"I love it!" said Nora, laughing. "Something I know that Ariadne doesn't!"

"It's unlikely to be particularly relevant." Ariadne added a log to the fire.

"Oh, maybe, but it's fun for me." Nora had been holding her talking-box casually on her knee as she sat by the fire, but now she got up and handed it to Tinker.

"You will see," she said to him. "Ariadne is no ventriloquist, this is not a trick."

To Ariadne she said, "Tinker is curious about your voice."

"Naturally," Ariadne said, her voice emanating from the box in Tinker's hand, startling him. "A Dhaignian's voice is certain to seem quite foreign to a Berythean. As you have noticed, I have no mouth with which to speak. Dhaignians communicate with each other by transmitting and receiving radiant waves, but as this is not a common trait among the intelligent species we've discovered on other planets, we developed a device able to receive our transmissions and articulate them in an oral language, such as yours. We've since learned that some species, of which Nora is a good example, found our device's articulations discordant—"

"Hideous," Nora said.

"Yes, well, fortunately, Nora's mother is a science engineer, and was able to work with us to create an application for her distance-voice which uses the words sung in the songs stored therein to generate the sounds needed to articulate our communication. It doesn't sound much better to me, but I can see a profound improvement in how her people react to my speaking. Since her language and your language use similar sounds to structure words, we were pleased to find that once we integrated the new application with our translation program, we've had the same success here."

"*Very* pleased," added Nora. "Does that help?"

Tinker hadn't been listening to the words as much as he had the sound of Ariadne's voice, while inspecting the box, turning it over, putting it behind his back, and covering it with his hands. "It must be a *tiny* little sprite," he said to himself.

To Ariadne he said, "The box has little breathing holes for your familiar spirit. Very little holes, on one edge where its voice comes out."

"Yes," said Ariadne. "It does. We can decide our paths in the morning. Nora, will you help me place the TMD nodes, please?"

"What are TMD nodes?" Cor asked.

"Part of a motion detection system to protect our camp," Ariadne said as she and Nora went off into the darkness. The cougar raised its head to watch Ariadne go. Tinker and Marimba looked at each other for a moment, her pupils contracting as firelight filled her golden irises. She closed her eyes and settled her chin on her paws.

"What do you think, Tinker?" Happen asked. "Are they witches, or bewitched?"

"It may be," Tinker said slowly, "that there are places in the world where science and discoveries have gotten further than in Berythea, and we just haven't learned about some of these things yet. Or it could be that Ariadne is some kind of witch. People, and probably even witches, sometimes have sensible reasons for saying strange things. Ariadne could have seriously injured or killed someone in that skirmish yesterday, but she didn't. Which is right. Those guys might be disrespectful louts, but that's not enough reason to kill them. And she's been kind, or at least grateful, to you. So we've seen her make some good choices."

"But they really think they're from a different grith," Happen said.

"You know what? I don't think there's any need to worry about that. You can get all worked up about whether to believe someone or something, but what matters is making good decisions. We don't know where she got that weapon, but we do know that we don't want to get in its way. It doesn't matter where it comes from. We don't have anything they can steal from us, and if they wanted to harm us, they could have easily done so already."

"Can we travel with them to the fair, please?" Cor asked. The boys settled down in their bedrolls by the warmth of the fire.

"Sure, why not?" Tinker said. "I can't tell what they're talking about half the time, but I like them. Plus, I'd rather not put all three of us on one tull's back. We've got two or three days of travel left. I'm sure we'll find Osgar at the fair. He's been bugging Reg to bring him for years."

## THIRTEEN
## THE SMILING CREATURE SPOKE

> Until very recently, Grith was considered an uncontacted planet. Visits from Dhaignian scouts were rare, quiet, and conducted for the sole purpose of gathering data. It is possible, however, that these visits inadvertently contributed to the widespread and colorful legends of supernatural activity on Grith. (Reilly, 2046)

The wagon wheels rolled beneath him, the warm sun felt good in the cool morning, and Happen was glad to have his uncle, and his knapsack, with him again. *A clean set of clothes makes a person feel different inside. Never noticed that before.* His bow and arrows were still in the stolen cart, but now he had a change of clothes, his father's hat, two waterskins, his knife, and his sling and tull's horn full of angry rocks. He was forbidden from slinging the angry rocks unless his life was in danger, but he felt safer just having them back. And Tinker would figure out a way to get his cart back. And he was on his way to the fair.

As the rolling wheels took him closer and closer though, familiar nagging thoughts returned. What would the people at the fair be like? Would they try to cheat him? Would he have time to get his trading done once he got his cart back? He'd had enough to worry about before Osgar took his cart.

"What's troubling you, Hap?" Tinker winked at him. Tinker rode behind the wagon sometimes, sometimes he disappeared ahead, and sometimes he kept even with the wagon to talk.

"Thinking about trading. People are going to think they can take advantage of me because I'm just a country kid. I hate that they already think I'm dumb before I even start."

"Aside from being clean and dressing well and knowing your business, there's nothing you can do about that. Even when you're successful, you can just as easily be envied and hated as admired and respected. You can't worry about what folks think of you. Pay attention to business and you'll earn respect. It takes time."

Time was another concern. The fair opened in two days, and they were still far away. He'd read that it was important to have time, time to walk away from a bad trade, time to compare options. And although the two-tull wagon traveled farther in a day than walking, it still seemed unlikely that they'd get to the fair before Osgar had time to start trading. The elk antler powder was worth more than anything else and would sell the fastest, too. Happen didn't know if Osgar knew anything or everything about it. Osgar had at least three tulls to pull the cart and Tinker's caravard, and he'd had a long head start. He pictured Osgar sitting smugly on the caravard's driver's bench and seethed. But then it suddenly dawned on him that *he* wasn't walking either. The back of a wagon wasn't the smoothest ride, but it beat hiking two leagues a day. So at least one good thing resulted from Osgar's meddling. Plus, Cor was there with him, instead of sitting at school resenting him.

After Tinker's harrowing experience looking for the missing boys over the past few days, he preferred to keep Cor with him instead of sending him back home by himself, which they wouldn't be able to do anyway until they reunited with their tulls at the fair. Cor was happily engaged in conversation with Nora. He had taken Tinker's advice to heart, and wasn't concerned at all with her outrageous claims.

Nora claimed to be a university student from another world called Earth. She'd been awarded a prestigious fellowship to become the first Earthling to visit Grith, and the first woman to take an internship away from Earth with a Dhaignian. She said she was working on an ethnography of the people of Grith, which she explained was a study of Grithing customs and ways of living. Happen thought perhaps she was a student from another continent, studying Berytheans, and felt she needed to pretend that she was from a different world in order to achieve the right perspective for her project.

"Let's start with you, Cor. How old are you?"

"Fourteen." Cor sat on a box, leaning forward to talk with Nora, who sat with Ariadne on the driver's bench.

"Goodness. And you said your cousin is a year older, so is only fifteen!"

"Yeah, so?"

"These young boys are truly remarkable for their age, aren't they?" Nora asked Ariadne.

"Don't forget, dear, although Grith is a bit smaller than Earth, it rotates slower. A fifteen-year-old on Grith would be sixteen point nine years old on Earth, so Happen here, unless his birthday was quite recent, is what you would consider a seventeen-year-old."

Happen, sitting on the change of clothes in his knapsack, grimaced. *These people are so weird.*

Nora joined the boys in the back of the wagon so she could interview Cor without having to turn around all the time, and Ariadne called Happen up to the driver's seat.

"Your attempt to provide backup for Nora with the highway patrol was admirable in a way, and very brave, but not especially helpful," Ariadne said. "Please let us handle encounters from now on."

"But how?" Happen asked. "That guy wasn't going to give in to anything but force."

"You don't know that for sure," she said. "In a similar situation last time I was here, I was able to temporarily blind the leader, and convince him I was a witch. He instructed his men to stand down and let me leave. A much less dramatic encounter, one that left no physical scarring or evidence of any kind. It is very important, both for my work and for Nora's research, that we have as little impact on the local culture as possible."

*Fine. See if I stand up for you or Nora again.* Happen was annoyed at what felt like a scolding, but remembered Tinker's wisdom and said nothing, keeping his focus on the free ride they were getting. They had passed a few abandoned farms that morning, but the land here was dry and featureless—Tinker said it was used for grazing cattle—so Happen noticed the riders while they were still quite a ways back. Nora had asked Cor to describe a typical day, and he was listing his chores when Happen interrupted.

Tinker advised them to cover up the cougar cage and keep moving. Nora and Cor took turns looking back with binoculars. The two riders wore the armbands of rank-and-file deputized highway patrolmen, but they were geared for fast travel, not battle. Tinker said he had been expecting the patrol would send more men from Aeriskenn, and not quite so soon. Coming from the south, and without shields, these deputies might not mean trouble after all. He decided to stop and meet them alone. Happen waited tensely as the riders caught up with Tinker; Cor watched through the binoculars.

"Almost there . . ." he said. "They're next to him now, and they're talking. Hey, they're talking like normal, like they're not arresting him or anything. Thank goodness. One of them looks kind of familiar; maybe they know him. Oh, here they come." He handed the binoculars to Nora who put them away. The patrolmen slowed briefly as they passed and wished them a good afternoon, and then they were gone. Tinker was smiling when he caught up with the wagon.

"That turned out well," Nora said.

"Yes," said Tinker. "A pigeon arrived in the Pury sheriff's office this morning asking for men to help put out fires in Aeriskenn. It's quite an event; these are just the first two of several men coming from Pury. It also warned of witches on the road, telling riders not to engage in conflict, but come straight to Aeriskenn. I told them you were relatives of Cor's mother from over the mountains, and that we hadn't seen any witches, and that set them at ease."

"A pigeon said all that?!" Ariadne seemed much more interested in the messenger than the message.

"Uh, no," Tinker said. "This was a courier pigeon carrying a message. It's just how we talk about it, kind of a shortcut, to say 'the pigeon said . . .'"

"Oh," Ariadne said. Excitement drained from her face. The voice coming from the talking-box had very little expression, but sometimes her eyes made her feelings clear, even in Happen's limited experience.

"Do you know about courier pigeons?" Nora asked Ariadne.

"I don't," Ariadne said. "I'm sure it's in the database, if you know about them, but I'm not personally aware of such creatures."

"They're amazing birds," Nora said, proud of her knowledge. "They know where their home is, so you can attach a message to a pigeon's leg, and it will fly hundreds of leagues to get home where it can be read. On Earth we used them to deliver intelligence during wars."

"Of course you did. Were they a special breed of smart pigeons, or just ordinary pigeons with training?"

"I don't know. Do you, Tinker?"

"I just know they only go one way," Tinker said. "Pury sends pigeons by coach, ten each lusk, to Aeriskenn, which takes three days. They release one each day to come home, whether they have a message or not, and it only takes three bells. Then they do it all again the next lusk. Does it matter?"

"If they were a special breed, they might be helpful for Ariadne's research."

"The good news is they advised against engaging in conflict with witches," he said. "We should be able to get to the fair without trouble."

The next day, Cor was playing around with the binoculars. "Uh, Nora? I think you should see this."

Nora took the binoculars, lifting the strap over Cor's head. "Oh. Oh my goodness. Those don't look like Grithings."

Ariadne stopped the wagon and took the binoculars offered by Nora. "Bufonuriads. They're not supposed to be here."

Happen and Cor looked at each other. "What's a Bufonuriad?" they said at the same time.

"Are they dangerous?" Nora asked.

"What's the holdup?" Tinker, who had stopped in a ways back at the Crooked Finger, had just caught up to them.

Everybody looked to Ariadne. Her shoulders slumped. If she could have sighed, she would have.

"There are some people up ahead from a planet called Riasi. I need to find out how they got here and why, but it's very likely that they will run from me—"

"Hold on now." Tinker squinted at her. "That's the second time you've made a reference to planets as if a person could be *on* one or *from* one. Planets are impossibly far away, and very bright. I'm thinking you'd be blinded, or burned up—"

"I'm sorry. We have a situation here that takes precedence over astronomy lessons. Nora will speak to these people with a translator while I hide in the back of the wagon. The rest of you will avoid contact with them. They won't be dangerous if we don't threaten them, but they do represent a potential threat to Grith, so we need to find out what they are doing here."

Ariadne was speaking from out the wrong end of the tull, as the saying goes, and Happen thought Tinker would be angry, but he responded calmly.

"How long will this take?"

"I estimate five or ten waves." Ariadne climbed into the back of the wagon, covered Marimba's cage with a large tent, and hid underneath.

Tinker nodded to the boys, and they hopped up front next to Nora, who took up the reins. They resumed their traveling pace. The landscape flattened, and Happen appreciated Tinker's wisdom. They were approaching the Rillbane, and a significant delay could have them still out on the causeway when night came, making them easy prey for marsh trolls. Instead of getting upset or offended by Ariadne's rudeness, he kept his focus on what mattered most. Ariadne's strangeness was less stressful and more interesting with Tinker around.

"I'm curious," Happen said to Nora. "Where we're going to meet this translator, and what text is he going to translate for us?"

"Well, I'm glad someone's enjoying this." Her expression was grim, and she held the reins too tightly.

"What's the matter?"

"This task is above my pay grade. Translators can be dangerous when you don't know the culture, and I don't know the first thing about Bufonuriads or Riasi. What we need is an interpreter, but we don't have one for that language. They weren't supposed to be here." She kept a fierce concentration on the tulls' backs, even though there were no forks in the road or any other reason why the tulls might do anything other than follow it. "I've heard horror stories about using these translators, it's like a dangerous game of riddles."

"Sometimes you manage to say a lot of words that I know well," Happen said. "And still I have no idea what you're talking about."

She chuckled briefly. "Just like the boys back home."

Banjo and Lute were uneasy as they approached the causeway and the people with the funny name who weren't supposed to be there. They were well onto the bottomlands, and the hills on the other side of the valley appeared blue and indistinct, more an idea than actual hills. The magnitude of the space made Happen feel small and weightless. He pulled his father's hat lower on his forehead and held onto the wagon seat to keep from floating away. Even Tinker, following a short distance behind, seemed uncomfortable. Cor alone was relaxed and eager to meet Bufonuriads.

It was a cool afternoon, not one Happen would consider for swimming, but several very skinny people seemed to be jumping off the causeway into the marsh, and then climbing out and doing it again, occasionally pushing each other playfully. Something wasn't quite right about their proportions, as if their limbs were too long for their bodies. The closer they got, the more Happen felt that Ariadne was right; these people should not be here. The tulls seemed to agree, and Nora had to use the goad that came with the wagon.

One of the strangers saw the wagon approaching, and they all jumped directly in with a splash. None climbed out again. This calmed the tulls somewhat, and they pulled the wagon right up to the foot of the causeway before Nora stopped them. There was no sound beyond a watery burbling coming from the marsh. A mix of bulrushes, sedges, and reedy grasses grew among slowly wandering channels and brackish pools spread over the bottom-lands. Nora took a thick slate out of her pack, held it up to her eye for a blink, then tapped it with her fingers. Its precise shape and the glow that came out of it told Happen it was another of her witch-crafted devices. He turned away.

Nora stood looking out over the marsh. "Hello?" she called out. Not even a bird answered. She called out again using a word Happen did not know.

A Bufonuriad rose out of the water behind a bank of sedges, and kept rising. It was much taller than the ones that had been jumping off the causeway. The tulls snorted and fretted. Happen's muscles all seemed to clench at once, his fingers pressing painfully into the wooden seat. Its head was too big. Its neck was as wide as its body, and its limbs were indeed too long. Wide eyes appraised them, and its mouth spread into a wide, closed-lipped smile, and kept spreading, supported by a prominent jaw as excessively wide as its limbs were long.

Happen wanted to run, or disappear, but couldn't move.

The creature spoke strange words, revealing flat brown teeth, then it smiled again, made what looked like a gesture of introduction with its wide, flat hand with too-long fingers, and bowed slightly. Nora spoke in a language Happen didn't know, holding up the slate for the creature to see, and then different sounds came out of it, just like Nora's talking-box, only this one's voice was very unpleasant, emotionless and pallid. Nora mimicked the greeting gesture and bowed also.

The smiling creature spoke again.

"He's a king from Riasi, and wants to know where we are from," Nora said, reading from her slate, and Happen understood that the slate also contained a tiny sprite familiar, and that was the translator. It displayed the foreign words on the witch-crafted slate in a way that Nora could read. *Why had she said using it was dangerous?*

She answered, and the translator sprite spoke again with its dreadful voice. It wasn't just expressionless in the way her other sprite was, it was entirely devoid of spirit, consisting only of sharp edges and buzzing.

The king responded again, this time with a raised fist instead of a smile. Nora groaned, and responded with a flurry of words, which then spilled from the translator like shards of broken glass. The words seemed to appease the king, and his huge bony hand and arm relaxed. The wide smile returned.

"What was that about?" Cor whispered. Happen still couldn't move.

"The translator insulted him," Nora muttered. "I have no idea what this damn thing is saying to him. I apologized and explained that my intentions were good even though my language skills are limited."

The king pulled up a clump of sedge and took a bite. His eyes regained the curious appraising look from before, and he spoke through the half-chewed stems. The writing on the slate seemed to pierce her like an arrow. She blinked a few times and took a deep breath.

"What did he say?" Cor peered over Nora's shoulder, trying to read the slate.

"I-I can't even interpret this for you. It says, 'Oh, you shout from Earth. I'm so sorry for your loss. I understand the limits now. You must be strong by birth or fortune to escape and be a gift like us.'"

Nora tilted her head, and asked him a question with one short word.

He turned, speaking at the water, and several Bufonuriads of varying sizes rose up out of the water. They all had wide smiles, with mud and limp grass drooling out the corners of their mouths.

"This is his family," Nora said, then made the translator talk again.

The king looked around before answering, providing an unwelcome reminder of Osgar. His answer took some time. In the middle of it, he pulled up a sleeve of the gray robe he was wearing to display some sickly green splotches on his light gray skin.

"It says: 'We saw a Dhaignian predator near the first nutrient bed we ate at, and felt sized like ants, so we kept traveling until we found this one. This rock is strangely underserved by nutrient beds, but the ones they do have are adjacent to the sky. We are thrilled with the quality of the meal. Much better than even the royal nutrient beds back home. It's so adjacent to the sky I'm already turning green again, and I have only been here fourteen days. Our children have never considered green food, since the last royal marsh transferred brown before they were knowing. I own shame to see them so pale, but not for much longer.'"

Nora asked him a short question. The lids on his eyes closed halfway for a moment, and the smile faded. One of the smaller ones, standing in the water behind him, threw a clump of sodden grass at another, who ate it, and they made a happy, burbly sound. His smile returned, and he spoke.

"It says: 'Riasi is expected to be employed after Thujaplid. To spare my children that fate, and currently the royal life on Riasi is too much—always fighting rebellions of the hungry lower classes. We left in search of the mythical green, expecting to die.

Our exporter said Grith might support us, and he hit his nose. Or, he would have, if he had one.'" Nora looked up from the translator, to the back of the wagon. Then, after a brief exchange that she didn't translate, he gave a longer answer, ending by opening his long arms out wide and turning as if to show them the lovely view of the marsh.

"It says: 'The exporter was indeed a Dhaignian, and very expensive, but wasn't either of the two predators. We are settling here. I would gladly pay you to transform my family into a castle right in this place. You could stay and enjoy the view if you kept dry and we would not flog you beyond your requirements.'"

Nora answered him curtly, and he raised a bony knee to step toward them.

"I think we got what we needed." Nora sat and the tulls eagerly pulled away onto the causeway as the Bufonuriads watched.

They traveled without speaking or stopping until they reached the island that supported the south end of the bridge over the main channel of the Rillbane. Nora dropped the reins, jumped down from the wagon seat, and watched Tinker dismount. Cor followed.

"Were those marsh trolls?" Cor asked him.

"Please, Tinker? Do you have any whiskey?" Nora asked him.

They traveled as far as the tulls would go that day and set up their camp by moonlight. Nora drank some of Tinker's whiskey, and crawled into her tent while the fire was still high.

"If those things weren't marsh trolls, why haven't they been eaten by marsh trolls?" Cor wanted to know.

"I don't know." Tinker dug around in his saddlebag, looking

for something. "I have heard that there aren't as many marsh trolls as there used to be."

"Do *you* know why?" Cor looked across the fire to Ariadne.

"Because there is no such thing as a marsh troll."

Happen looked to Tinker, but he just shrugged, shook his head a little, and continued his search. The boys spread their bedrolls near the fire.

Cor set his closer to Happen's than usual. "Will those things come—"

"Marimba assures me that a pack of wolves patrols this area, and they will solve the problem eventually. Please do your best to forget you ever saw a Bufonuriad."

"I wish I could," Happen said.

Tinker found what he was looking for. He gave the boys each an Azmerian stone wrapped in paper. "You've had quite a shock. This will help get you settled down after we eat." He handed out some bannock, then hesitated, glancing at Ariadne. "Will Nora be joining us tonight?"

"No."

"Hm." Tinker's eyes had a hard look, and his jaw muscles flexed under his thin beard. "Can you explain to me why that encounter was necessary? If we should just forget about them, why did we have to see them at all?"

"The outlaw Dhaignian I told you about before is behaving in ways that are endangering my mission here. For me to effectively counter his actions, I need to understand what he is doing here and why. He's always been reckless, but smuggling a royal family from one listed planet to another is a much more serious crime than just visiting out of turn. It also indicates that he's working with others in some fashion to handle rigorous transactions in the fields of travel and finance. If I can convince Nora that the Bufonuriads couldn't possibly have accurate information about Earth, the true information gained will be worth the price."

"Did they give her bad news from home?"

"They rather inelegantly passed on some misinformation."

"Poor thing." Tinker looked over at Nora's tent.

Ariadne gave Tinker a strange look then. Happen wasn't sure if she disapproved of his sympathy, or if something else was bothering her, but Tinker seemed less angry at least.

"Really, you've never had an Azmerian stone?" Cor poked a stick into Ariadne's morning fire. "Really?"

"Yes, really," Nora answered, flustered. "I mean, no, I haven't. I've never even heard of this. Have you, Ariadne?"

"No."

Nora waited a moment to see if she'd add anything else, then asked, "Is Azmer, or Azmeria, a place near here?"

The boys looked at Tinker, wondering if he'd give Nora a different answer than he'd given them.

"It has something to do with an old religion; I don't know the details. Some folks call them Azmerian water stones, or just water stones. Maybe someone at the academy might know more about it." Tinker started packing his bedroll.

"Hmm," said Nora. "What *is* an Azmerian stone?"

"Hard to describe," Tinker said. "We'll get you one at the fair."

"Cor said they were used at city schools," she said.

"Yes," Tinker said. "Excessively."

"But I thought . . . wouldn't using stones taken from Grith be antithetical to Gracarrai teachings?" Nora watched him pack, drinking from her waterskin.

"Sure, but Azmerian stones aren't extracted, they're found. A skilled forager gathers them in riverbeds and at the ocean shore."

"Are they expensive?" Nora huddled closer to the dwindling fire.

"Not at all, but that reminds me. We do have a bit of a

problem with money." Tinker cinched the buckle on his saddlebag.

"We have some local money," Ariadne said. "What do you need?"

"Getting into the fair is expensive, and my money is in my caravard. You have to have a vehicle to enter, and you're allowed two people per vehicle, plus an extra person per axle. But the extra people cost more. If you took the boys in, your entrance fee would be one hundred and forty solani. I could try to get in with another vehicle, but I'll need what's called a 'foster fee,' which is usually around one hundred solani on the first day of the fair, then a little less as time goes on. Fostering is not allowed, so you have to be careful, but it's quite common."

"We only have one hundred and sixty solani," Ariadne said. "But we have some items that we could sell at the fair that will probably yield a significant return. Can we bring some money out for you once we've made some exchanges?"

"That would be very kind of you," Tinker said. "I could pay you back once I've recovered my caravard."

# FOURTEEN
## CELEBRATING THE NIGHT CHEETAH

 According to historical records housed at the academy's library, Grith today is substantially different from pre-Eruption Grith. The Mount Tambis volcanic eruption (known in Berythea as The Eruption) reconfigured a significant portion of the Preathean continent, killing large forests, burying cities with no warning, and coating the Ezid River valley with a thick layer of toxic ash. The catastrophic global cooling that followed The Eruption suggests to Earth geologists (see Appendix C) that fine ash particles and gases (likely sulfur dioxide) reached the stratosphere and spread across the globe, disrupting food production and seasonal weather patterns.

Much of Inirthea, too, was devastated by toxic ash fall, and cold, dark summers led to crop failure, famine, and disease worldwide. But by far the most comprehensive and lasting change to the planet was the rise to prominence of the Gracarrai religion. (Reilly, 2046)

⌐⌐

W hen they arrived at the end of the line of wagons and carts waiting to enter the fair, Tinker covered the cougar's cage with a small tent from Ariadne's gear, and the whole back of the wagon with a large tent, tying it down on the outside corners of the fencelike wagon walls, creating a covered space for the women's gear and luggage, the small amount of firewood left, and the boys. He spoke to the boys through a gap in the tent at the back of the wagon, and handed Cor a pair of dice.

"Remember, when it's their turn at the gate, start rolling these dice like you're playing a game. The idea is to seem unconcerned with inspection. You have to be polite and respectful with these guys. They'll throw you out for the slightest reason these days. Don't try to hide anything from them. The best you can hope for is that they won't be curious enough to search. I have no idea how they'll react to the cougar, but I do know how they react to suspicious behavior. Understand?"

"Yes." Cor rattled the dice in a closed fist.

"And once you're in, stay hidden until they find you a disguise of some sort. We can't take the chance of running into Osgar. Everything will be easier if he doesn't know we're here. Understand?"

"Yes, Father."

"Be careful in there. Don't borrow money, stay away from the stables, and don't talk to fortune-tellers. I'll be in as soon as I can, and we'll take it from there." Tinker headed toward the gate, and the wagon soon followed. Happen and Cor sat on wooden boxes, looking out through the loosely tied tent flaps at the back of the wagon.

"I don't like this," Happen whispered.

"What? Being in the back of a wagon with a cougar, or hiding from the guy who tried to kill us?" Cor whispered back.

"It's just . . ." Happen tried to find the right words. "It's not how I imagined it. Going to the fair, I mean. It was supposed to be . . . different than this." The wagon stopped for a moment, then started rolling again.

"Yeah, but soon we'll be in, and we'll get some kind of disguise like Father said, and we'll get to walk around and . . . and be at the fair."

"Sure, but we have to get our stuff back so I can do my Summering Task."

"Yeah?" Cor shrugged.

"We don't even have a plan or anything," Happen said, still whispering. The wagon stopped.

"Father will figure out something."

"I hope so." The wagon started rolling again.

The usher at the gate asked, "Goods or service?"

"Service," answered Nora. "Tile cutting."

"We've already got one tile cutter. Don't think you'll get much business."

"My aunt is familiar with the work of the Stern family," Nora said. "Our service is complimentary with theirs, not in direct competition. It would be useful for clients if we could be located near them." After a moment, the usher walked around to the back, where the boys had been rolling the dice quietly so they could listen.

"My turn now."

"No, you had two turns last time, so I go again."

"So go then."

"There, see, I got a seven, so I get another turn."

"Now you're making up rules!"

"Don't you know that one?"

"Hello, boys." The usher peeked in though a gap in the tent.

"Sorry to interrupt. Just checking to see if you've got any stowaways hiding out back here."

"No, sir," Cor said, untying the string and holding back the tent flaps. "Just us two." The usher stuck his head under the tent and looked at the boys and the smaller tent covering the cage.

"And Marimba," Happen said. "But she doesn't count, does she?" He pulled back the tent to reveal the sleeping cat. The usher stared for a moment, then pulled his head out of the tent and strode to the front of the wagon.

"Can you explain to me why a tile cutter needs to bring a mountain lion to the fair?" he asked. "Is it part of some kind of entertainment?"

"I know it's strange. I'm sorry," Nora said. "It was not our choice. This is a domesticated animal whose home was destroyed by a fire. We didn't have time to find her a new home before the fair, so we have to keep her with us for now. She has been well fed, and will remain peacefully in her cage."

"Harrumph." The usher shuffled some papers. "We do allow domesticated animals, though this type is irregular. Any complaints and you will be removed from the fairgrounds with no refund. Fair policy."

"That seems reasonable," Nora said.

"The Stern stall is in the artisan row of the northwest quadrant. I'm no tiling expert, but I'm thinking a second cutter is a low priority for the fair. I'll place you in the same quadrant at least, but in the assorted services row, which is furthest from center." The usher made some notes with a scratchy quill, then turned some pages. "Since you've arrived in time for a better site, you can appeal to the site coordinator once you're in, but with that lion it's not likely. Row nine, stall twenty-three."

"Thank you," Nora said.

"You have two extras in back," he said. "You fostering?"

"You mean the boys? They're not um . . . extra? My aunt is

very old and frail. My cousins and I are working to learn her trade, but we're also needed to take care of her."

"I see," he said. "Very well. One hundred and forty solani."

Happen heard the exchange of coins.

"First time here?"

"Yes."

"Here's a map for you. Enter at the north gate. Site coordinator's office is here. Exchange office is here. You'll need to buy script for all transactions. Spending or accepting true currency will get you removed from the fairgrounds with no refund. River's here, washing to the north of this point, waste to the south. Some folks like more privacy, but I recommend staying within the naiad fence. Fires outside of the provided chimineas are not allowed without permit. Here are your flags. These hang on pegs at the top of the poles in front of each stall. The red one signals a need for emergency help, the white one calls a boy who can take your tulls to the stable, sell you firewood, or whatever errands you need. Enjoy the fair. Next!"

The wagon rolled forward to the north gate, then turned onto the loosely graveled lanes of the fairgrounds. The crunch of the wagon wheels on the lane was gradually assimilated by the sound of the fair, a chaotically musical composition of hundreds of voices talking, laughing, singing, and various musicians playing different songs. As they passed, a few specific sounds would slowly separate out and announce a discrete identity— rhythmic drumming came from one direction, a loud voice from another calling, "Waterskins here! Taste before you buy," a brisk melody played on a fife, before incrementally re-engaging until it joined seamlessly into the general clamor.

Happen felt the wagon turn, then lurch as the wheels on one side slid through some softer gravel on the edge of the narrow track. Cor, who had been peering through the gap in the tent, pulled back one of the flaps as he steadied himself, and Happen got his first glimpse of the fairgrounds. They had left a wide road for a narrow one lined with empty stalls. Where they'd turned, the wide road continued but was busy with people. A man wearing stilts and a billowing green and orange shirt stalked over the crowd.

Soft fur pressed against the back of Happen's fingers, and he froze still. Without thinking, he'd grabbed a bar of Marimba's cage to steady himself, and then she'd changed her position, apparently taking no notice of him, and lain against the bars of the cage.

"Cor," he whispered. "I've never touched a cougar before."

Cor gaped. "I want to."

Happen slowly pulled his fingers free. The fair noise was quieter here, the wheels on the gravel louder. "I don't think that's a good idea," he said, but Cor ignored him, reaching toward the cage. The wagon turned again, and Cor hesitated, but then the wagon stopped, and Nora called out, "We're here."

Nora appeared at the back of the wagon, wearing a waxed canvas rain hat pulled low over her forehead and carrying the toolbox Ariadne kept under the wagon seat. She ducked under one of the tent flaps, letting it rest against her back.

"Ariadne has come up with a plan," she said. "And we have to be quick. This place is filling up fast. Of the two of you, Cor is less likely to be recognized by Osgar, so you'll be the first to venture out."

"Great!"

"But not without disguise," she added. "We'll start with your hair." She pushed her hat back and took a pair of scissors from the toolbox.

"Wait, what? My hair?"

"We don't have time to argue. If this works, we'll buy you a very nice hat. The best we can find. And I think short hair will make you look older."

"Can I pick the hat?"

"Sure." Nora, with the dangerous-looking scissors still in hand, moved Cor by his shoulders. "Sit here, and don't move. Oh, but first," she pulled back the pointed weapon to give him room, "take off your boots. Happen, take his boots to Ariadne."

"What are you doing to my shoes?"

"Calm down," Nora said. "She's just going to add insoles to make you a bit taller and change your gait."

"My what?"

"She's going to make you walk different," Happen said. "I read about it in the *Cravey Mysteries*. Inspector Cravey and his assistant, Morgone, were always coming up with different disguises. Only Cravey changed Morgone's gait by putting pebbles in different places in his shoes."

Nora started cutting. "Please get going, Happen. Ariadne has the leather for the insoles up there, and she's going to have to cut it with her viser, so the sooner the better."

He scrambled out the back of the wagon, then hurried to the front and handed the boots to Ariadne. The stall on that side had what appeared to be a tall black tent in it. As he scurried back to cover, Happen wondered who would use such a large and dark tent.

Nora alternated between cutting, evaluating, and combing Cor's remaining hair with her fingers. "Her hooded cloak would just be odd normally, but if you're looking for a Dhaignian, it's a dead giveaway. It's best if she stays in front of the wagon, where she can't be seen from the road. You and Cor don't want to be seen by Osgar, and Ariadne and I don't want to be seen by the Dhaignian guy who's not supposed to be on Grith. If he's here, and hears gossip about someone with such a deep hood, or chances to walk by and see us, we could be in for trouble."

Once inside, Happen carefully turned himself around in the cramped space to avoid bumping Cor.

"Sounds like you're lucky Ariadne's nicer than this Inspector Cravey character," Nora told Cor as she cut, pushing the fallen curls of dark brown hair back behind him so he wouldn't see the growing pile.

"Oh, thunder," Happen said. "How much are you cutting off?" Nora shot him an angry look, but kept the light, cheerful tone in her voice.

"As much as I can get with these scissors."

"Wait, really?" Cor touched Nora's right elbow to stop her cutting.

"Settle down," Nora said, massaging Cor's head with her left hand. "You have a very nice head. And you have strong facial features that are going to work well with short hair. Not everybody would be able to look as good. Turn around now, and sit up straight."

"How did you learn to cut hair?" Happen asked.

Nora tilted Cor's head forward. "Tell me more about Inspector Cravey," she said. "What other things did he do to disguise his assistant?"

"Sometimes he'd use paint to change his skin color, and put wax against his gums to change the shape of his face and the way he talked at the same time. And once, they didn't have much time, so Cravey just broke Morgone's nose with a brick," Happen said.

"Ugh. Well, with this haircut, more height, and a different gait, Osgar won't recognize you from a distance. We don't have time for anything more, and we don't have a brick, so . . ." She stood back, then stepped to each side, looking intently at Cor, murmuring something about making it even, and then returned to snip a little more from the right side before stepping back again. "There. Stay here. I'll get your shoes." She returned the scissors to the toolbox, pulled her hat back down over her forehead, and left. Cor put his hands up to his head tentatively, looking to Happen.

"It'll grow back soon," Happen said.

Nora returned with his boots and Cor put them on and hopped down out of the wagon.

"Oh." Cor took a step and frowned.

"You'll get used to it," Nora said. "It's better than pebbles, right? Hey, you're almost as tall as Happen now."

"No, he isn—" Happen started to say, but Nora interrupted him.

"Take this map. It shows the artisan row here," she said, pointing. "See if you can find Dunkler Stern's tile cutting. Ariadne says his grandfather had a painted wagon with his name on it. If you find his stall, see if you can find out if he's there now. Also, try to figure out the most direct route between here and there. Okay?"

"Got it," Cor said. "Find Dunkler Stern, and the best route to him."

"Also, do this quickly, but don't draw any attention to yourself," Nora said. It sounded so much like a mission from the *Cravey Mysteries*, that Happen wished he could go too, but he stayed in the wagon and tried to see out without being visible from the track. All there was to look at was the empty stall across the way. Graveled wheel tracks led past a tall post on one side. Behind the tracks, a small grassy yard featured a brown clay chiminea holding old coals and ashes in its sooty belly. A thin wooden fence bordered the back, and on each side a length of twine ran from a peg in the fence to short posts at the road.

He pulled one of the tent flaps in, trying to keep his face shaded while expanding his view to one side. A loaded cart waited in the stall next to the empty one across from them. A sign hung on the post by the road, but he couldn't make it out. A caravard arrived and parked in the stall across the way, so he let the tent flap fall back, and waited eagerly to see what service would be provided there, but the driver tended to his tull. Slowly.

After scratching his ankle for a while, and trying to find a way to sit comfortably, he pushed and pulled at the edges of the tent until he discovered a place on the side where it was looser. He found he could push the edge up enough to peer out to the east. All he could see next door was the mysterious black tent. But these folks had two signs on their post, facing to each side, so he could read one. The Amazing Esmerlia, Visionary Seer, the sign read, with a border of rose vines framing the words. The incoherent old fortune-teller from *The Odais Chronicles* had a crystal ball full of swirling fog. Happen bit his knuckle and reminded himself that Osgar was out there somewhere.

The man across the road finally unpacked his caravard by setting out a table and arranging several dark gray bricks on it. They were much thinner than normal bricks though and not exactly rectangular. Happen scooched closer and craned his neck, but he couldn't figure out what they were until the man brought out a sign which read Fierce Edge Sharpening. One of the *Cravey Mysteries* was about a criminal who sold whetstones from a quarry. These ones must have been found at the site of some kind of natural Grith disturbance. Or maybe they had been quarried? Mr. Fierce had a meek, bland look about him, neither fierce nor criminal. Happen yawned and scratched his ankle again.

A boy in a gray uniform came to take Banjo and Lute from Nora, stamping "NW 9-15" on their rumps in red ink. A cart pulled into the stall on his right, but Marimba's cage prevented Happen from pushing up the tent on that side. He leaned back on his knapsack and rolled Tinker's dice several times without looking at the results.

"How can you sleep through this, Marimba? If I have to stay in here five more waves I'm going to explode." The lowering sun cast an orange glow on the Amazing Esmerlia sign, and he sighed. Then Cor walked past. Happen hopped out of the wagon, careful to land on his good ankle, and followed him. With the tulls out of the way the boys could stand in front of the driving seat to talk with Ariadne and Nora, the bulk of the wagon hiding them from people passing by on the road.

"I found Dunkler Stern's caravard, but he's not there. If you've got a quill and ink handy I can mark the route on the map for you."

"Here," Nora said, opening the toolbox. "Use this. It's called a pen." She pulled something off one end of the pen and handed it to Cor.

"Ink?"

"There's ink built in to it," Nora said. "Try it." Cor unfolded the map, held it up against the footboard, and drew a circle where Stern's caravard was, then a line showing the route.

"That's a neat trick," Cor said. Happen imagined a bird with ink for blood, and was going to ask why they cut off the feather vane, but Nora interrupted his thoughts.

"This is three rows away from us," Nora said. "How are we going to disguise you enough to get you there safely?"

"One step at a time," Ariadne answered. To Cor she said, "How do you know he's not there?"

"He's got a bigger stall than ours, and his caravard is set up like a house with these thunderous stepping stones that go up to the door. I was looking at the stones when a boy came by and told me how Mr. Stern had made them from broken tile pieces. So I asked if he thought Mr. Stern was in his caravard, and the boy said no, he'd seen him walking to the food rows. But on the way back here I saw something that might be helpful."

"Yes?" Ariadne said.

"Two stalls down, on the other side, there's a place where they were painting people's faces. I thought maybe, um, maybe they could paint a mouth on you so you could walk around without—"

"What were they painting on people's faces?" Nora interrupted.

"The person I saw being painted looked like a maybe a skull with big dark eyes and extra teeth?"

"With that and a local dress or something, I bet he wouldn't be able to recognize me," Nora said to Ariadne. "We just need some money. I doubt twenty solani will get us face painting, a dress, firewood, and dinner for three."

"Did you see any stalls nearby that sold leather goods, by any chance?" Ariadne asked.

"Yes, I think so," Cor said. "There's a cobbler just on the other side of the seer here, and one row south was another place that said something about leather on the sign. I wasn't looking too carefully at that point."

"How about a dressmaker or someone selling dresses?" Ariadne asked.

"No, I didn't see anything like that," Cor said.

"It sounds like I can try selling the leather and then get my face painted anyway," Nora said. "I'll check back in here before I go searching for a dress. Hopefully it will be dark and crowded enough . . ." She handed her talking-box to Happen and picked something off the floor of the wagon seat.

"That's good, thank you," Ariadne said. "Only take half, though. We will get a better price for the rest when we can access a wider market."

"Can I get my face painted, too?" asked Cor.

"And me, too?" Happen added quickly. Nora hesitated.

"We may have to do something like that pretty soon," Ariadne said. "But not now. Nora will assess the venue first."

Nora took a deep breath as if she were preparing for a long dive into a lake, hopped off the wagon seat, and was gone.

"I understand that you're anxious to explore the fair, but your uncle will be here soon, and we must be patient. We will stay out of sight and wait for him, and wait for Nora." Happen could barely see Ariadne's face under her deep hood.

"Is Nora selling her leather jacket?" Cor asked.

"We're selling some very unusual and high-quality leather. It's from the hide of an animal from . . . far away, much thicker and tougher than leather known in Berythea. We knew we'd need local money, and we expected, based on my previous travels here, there might be challenges selling something a bit more efficient like precious gems or metals."

"Cool!" Cor said. "Can we see?"

The leather was thicker than Happen's thumb and yet folded without a crease. It had a dark, bluish gray color like clouds sometime get near dusk. It was supple, smooth, and felt like leather, but it didn't smell like leather, or anything he could identify. He had read about Inirthean rhinoceroses with skin this color, so maybe this was a clue to where Ariadne came from.

"What did you say the name of this animal was?" he asked.

"I didn't," Ariadne said. "In this language it would perhaps be called an aceros."

"Why is its skin so thick?" Cor asked.

"It's an extremely large animal," Ariadne said.

"And maybe to defend against the horn of its rival when fighting for a mate?" Happen added.

"Ah," said Ariadne. "You are thinking of a rhinoceros, like you have here on Inirthea. This is a different animal, although there are some similarities. It has four legs and eats plants, although the aceros only eats leaves from trees, and your rhinoceros has a more varied diet. Also, the aceros lacks the magnificent horn. The thickness of the skin is proportional. It's the largest animal on Dhaigne. Almost three times the size of a rhinoceros." Happen was annoyed by Ariadne's mention of Dhaigne, and had to remind himself of Tinker's words about not getting worked up about whether to believe someone.

"I wish Tinker would get here," he said.

"Yeah, me too," Cor said. "I can't wait to go see more of the fair."

"You must wait for Tinker to resolve your unfinished business with Osgar, and recover your stolen goods," Ariadne said. "There will be plenty of time for enjoying the fair once that is accomplished. In the meantime, Nora and I will do what we can to help. Cor, tell me about the last time you saw Osgar. I mean, in the daylight."

"He came to my house about six days ago, but we only talked for a few waves."

"Were you standing, or walking, while he was there?"

"No, I don't think so. We were sitting on the porch, and he was in the yard, right?"

"I think so." Happen couldn't remember.

"And the time before that?"

"That would have been, um, maybe in the spring sometime, maybe longer than that," Cor said. "I don't remember. It's been a few years since we were in school together and I would see him a few days every lusk."

"That's good. Your height will make it harder for him to recognize you," she said. "How about you, Happen?" He considered lying for a moment, in case it made it easier for him to go see the fair, but thought better of it.

"I saw him just before I left, eleven days ago. And . . . I saw him almost every day all summer long."

"I see," Ariadne said. "Your gait is changed by the tape on your ankle, but we will still need a very good disguise for you, in addition to different clothes. You will have to be patient. Cor, when Nora returns, put out the flag for firewood. If Nora thinks it's a good business, get some money from her to get your face painted, but don't go until you've handled the firewood transaction and it's dark. I'm not sure which will occur first, but you must wait for both."

Happen could see the excitement in Cor's eyes. *It's not fair.* He knew it was silly of him to begrudge his cousin's freedom, but he had to do something, so he decided that it would be unlikely for Osgar to visit the Amazing Esmerlia at this time. *There must be lots of seers and the like at the fair, since Tinker had gone out of his way to mention them.* It would be quite a coincidence to find Osgar in the very next stall on this quiet assorted services row.

Nora returned and really did look quite different. Her lower eyelashes, and the area below her eye and toward her nose, were painted to match the whites of her eyes, and exaggerated lower eyelashes had been added below the white, making her eyes seem unusually large. The rest of her face, and parts of her neck, were a tawny yellow, with black lines running from the outer ends of her lips up to the inner points of her eyes, like the lines on a cheetah's face, and this, along with black paint covering the horizontal bottom of her nose and the cleft running from her nose to the middle of her upper lip, made her nose appear wide and flat. Her upper lip was white, with fine gray cat whiskers reaching from there across her lower cheeks.

"Did you know, Ariadne, that they have a type of cheetah here that hunts at night?" Nora said while Cor jumped up and down a little. "Oh, right. Of course you do. Well, how do you like it?"

"That's quite stunning, dear," Ariadne said, her voice muffled in Happen's pocket.

"Oh, sorry," he said, handing the talking-box to Nora.

"That's quite stunning, dear," Ariadne said again for Nora's benefit.

"Wow, just . . . oh wow," Cor said.

# FIFTEEN

# THE AMAZING ESMERLIA

 One year before the end of the Age of Doubt, half of the members of the Gracarrai religion embarked upon a coordinated campaign to warn all of Grith of an imminent natural disaster of global proportions. Sailing the four seas and hiking across Berythea, they spread the message of preparation and teamwork, speaking to magistrates, clerics, bards, and thieves. Although their numbers swelled as they traveled, the most influential among their audience scoffed and derided them.

The remaining Gracarrai members worked at home to preserve, store, and safeguard as much food, water, and medicine as possible. They took loans at poor rates, engaging in business as if the future would value staples above luxuries, and safety above comfort. They made sure to describe their concerns to trading partners before deals, when they still had their attention, but most just shook their heads in befuddled pity as they charged twice what the bushels of wheat were worth on the market, or more.

A year later, when the bushels of wheat would be worth ten or twenty times the same price if the currency had kept any value, the same traders shook their heads again, this time for different reasons. (Reilly, 2046)

A rich glow still hung in the western sky, hiding all but the brightest stars. Cor had gone off to get his face painted; he left still trying to decide between a scary death skull and a fierce, snarling wolf. Nora had gone dress shopping. Happen told Ariadne he was going to sit in the back of the wagon and wait for Tinker, but this was not a time for hiding. He put all his weight on one hand on the back of the wagon, hoping that would be enough to mimic the feeling to Ariadne that he had climbed in and sat over the axle. Then, leaping over the gravel wheel track to the grass beyond, he dashed over to the black tent in the next stall.

In his hurry, he burst in through the door, and felt immediately shy and embarrassed about it, but fortunately, no one was there. The tent had an entrance room set off by a black curtain and furnished with a small wooden table and a chair made of wood and rope. On the table a large red candle burned next to a ceramic box with a glazed image of rose vines entwined around it. The air was still and heavy with a scent new to him, like the burning of some fragrant wood or herb from the southern continents.

The back curtain waved and rustled, and then a woman waltzed through, her flowing black skirt, loose red shirt, and multitude of shimmering, jangling necklaces of copper enhanced her curious rhythm as she moved toward the table but then away, and circling Happen, she peeked out through the door, motioning for him to sit in the chair. So he did.

She turned and fixed him with a stare. A wide black scarf tied about her head covered most of her dark, graying hair. A pale scar, several thumbs long, marred her lower jaw. But the most singular thing about her was a false eye, and Happen couldn't help but stare at it, and as she stepped closer to inspect him, she led with it as if it could see. But though the eye kindled a creeping uneasiness inside him, he doubted that it could see. There was no pupil, just a blue marble with some flashing gold that he took to be the flicker of candlelight. She advanced another step and the flicker of gold in her eye reminded him of a scene he'd read about in *The Odais Chronicles*. In the second book, Odais visited a sacred well in a temple on the eastern coast of Maithea, and there he'd found a round pool of blue water, with a single goldfish swimming in it.

"You have a question!" the seer announced.

"Is that a. . . a goldfish? In your eye?" Happen asked timidly.

"Yes, but that is not what you came here to ask."

He could see it quite clearly now, swimming around. "How does it . . . breathe, and eat? How do you feed it?" His fear abated, replaced by curiosity.

"You have come to ask the Amazing Esmerlia a *burning* question. You arrived in desperation!"

"Well, yeah, but can't you just tell me, is that really a live goldfish? And then we'll get to my question?"

"You have no money!" she said in a voice deep and exasperated.

"How do you know that?"

"One should not ask how. When he appeals to the Amazing Esmerlia, one should not ask how," she said dramatically. "*Especially* when you have no money."

"I'm going to get some money soon. I can pay you then."

"Ahh, so you are the one who tells the future!"

"Actually, it's not the future I'm having trouble with, but the present. I need to know about now."

She changed the angle of her head, and seemed to be seeing him with her good eye for the first time. "I see, yes, I see that," she murmured, moving closer again. Her breath smelled of some kind of spice his father had brought home from the fair once. Cinnamon maybe. "I see that you have many questions about things hidden from you. I see that you are a curious soul, with a good heart," she continued. "Maybe, maybe." She straightened, stepped back, and peeked out the front door again. "Yes," she said, returning. "You will be good for Esmerlia . . . for PRAC-TICE!" She emphasized this last word alarmingly.

"You're going to . . . practice . . . on me?" Happen suddenly noticed the time that had passed. He had expected that without money, this would have been a very brief adventure, and then he'd be safely back in the wagon.

"Oh!" She leaned back in surprise, one hand on her chest, the other on his shoulder. "Oh, you darling young man! You take *me* for the Amazing Esmerlia." She paused to sigh. "I suppose I am amazing in some respects, yes, but I am nothing—*nothing*—compared to Esmerlia. Her wisdom and beauty are unsurpassed by mere mortals like you and I. I am just to take the money at the door. But she, she can answer to your heart's desire: the future, the present, anything you want to know. And when you get your money, you can bring some to her. Right now, this very moment, she is looking to the future, parting the veils of time, and she will let us know whether you will pay."

Happen sighed. He had come to see Esmerlia, and so he would wait. The tiny goldfish changed direction with a pulse of its flowing fins.

"While we're waiting, can you tell me about the fish?"

"Can you tell me, young man, how the full moon became so perfectly round? How the tiniest seed becomes a gigantic tree?" Muffled wooden wind chimes plunked and tinkled behind the curtain. "Ah, there it is! You speak the truth. Money will come, later, but now, *now* it is time to discover. You have been wasting precious moments with an old woman who guesses and riddles, but now you will experience the Amazing Esmerlia, who *knows*. All you have to do is pass through that curtain."

Behind the curtain was another, thicker, curtain of rough black canvas. Inside the air was warm and heavy with scented smoke and candlelight. Behind a low table a woman stood facing away from him, her long, wavy black hair mingled with the tasseled ends of a dark purple scarf tied around her forehead and poured down over a red short-sleeved blouse that ended mid-back.

"Please, be seated," she said in a husky voice, which cracked awkwardly on the last word, followed by a quick "ahem." Two long reclining chairs waited on his side of the table, so he sat on the edge of one. The woman turned and faced him, stepping one black leather-booted foot on the table, her black skirt parting to reveal a muscular thigh. She was a lot younger than he'd expected, similar in some ways to the older girls at school, but it was hard to guess her age. She had paint on her face like he'd read about—dark red lips, black lines around her eyes, and heavy black eyelashes and eyebrows.

"What is it that you want to know?" She enunciated this question very deliberately, as if it were an incantation designed to draw the truth from a reluctant speaker.

Happen swallowed. His mind was blank. What was it that he was going to ask? What became of Ariadne's mouth? What does Nora think of him? What should he do now that he's out of school? *No, Ariadne was right, take it one step at a time.*

"Where is Osgar?" he asked in a small voice. It had seemed reasonable in his mind, but as soon as he said it, it sounded ridiculous, and he cringed. She tilted her head with a subtle smile on her painted lips. *She's trying not to laugh. She's thinking,*

*'You came in here with no money to ask me* that *ridiculous question?'* But she didn't laugh. She took her boot off the table, covered her shoulders and belly with a black lace shawl from a shelf behind her, and stepped around the table to approach him. *She's going to escort me off the premises.* But instead, she sat in the chair next to him, took his right hand in both of hers, and looked him in the eye.

"Thank you," she said. "The Amazing Esmerlia has had many visitors; rich and poor, young and old, brash and shy; but never has anyone come in here to ask, 'Where is Osgar?'" I like to have such a different question." She sighed, and looked away for a moment. "When you can tell the future, you are rarely surprised by people's questions. No, wait—" She looked away again with a short laugh. "I didn't say that. I mean, people who come here because they want to know the future, they all tend to ask the same few questions, over and over again. You have a question about the present, one that means so very much to you, and this is a rare challenge for me. I want to help. Tell me about Osgar." These last four words were delivered in the same manner as her first question, powerfully compelling him to answer.

Astonishment made him hesitate. From what he'd read about fortune-tellers, he was expecting an adult, for one thing, and a brief show, just a few moments of something more interesting than the back of the wagon or a lecture from Ariadne. Esmerlia's hands were warm and her eyes were kind and beautiful, and she was asking about him. He wanted to tell her everything, but wasn't sure where to start. When at last he decided to begin with his cart, the story poured out of him, unedited and raw.

"I was supposed to bring the cart to the fair, and sell or trade our harvest goods for what we need for the year. It's my Summering Task, and plus I've always wanted to come to the fair, and this is my first time. I have to get extra lamp oil because I accidentally burned too much reading this year, and I have to get medicine for the kids at the school my mother runs because their parents can't afford it, and I have to get nuts and spices and stuff so we don't have to eat nothing but elk stew all year, and I have to get whiskey for my dad because he can't make it himself, and he broke his leg and drank all he had because it hurt so much and the whiskey helped a little . . ."

As he was talking, Esmerlia moved to sit on his chair next to him, and she took his head in her hands and pulled him toward her, guiding his cheek to her shoulder.

". . . and he's always saying I mess everything up because I don't take it seriously and I don't pay attention to what I'm doing . . ."

She held him and he started to cry. He didn't want to, but he cried anyway and his shoulders began to unclench.

". . . but it's not my fault because I was asleep when Osgar came and dragged us to the bridge and dropped us in the river for the naiad to drown us because he wants to take the farm and . . . and I don't even know if I want it. I didn't think I'd have to decide so soon."

Happen sobbed a little into Esmerlia's shawl, then continued. "But I do know that *I* want to do the selling and the trading and bring all the stuff back for my family, not Osgar. And I want to explore the fair and see things. My Uncle Tinker is supposed to help but he can't even get *into* the fair because his money was in his caravard and Osgar stole that, too." He let out a long shuddering breath, and felt like he'd just set down a huge stack of firewood he'd been carrying.

"There, now," Esmerlia said. "You feel much better." She pushed him up to sit next to her. "You were very tense."

She pulled a red handkerchief out of her pocket and offered it to him. He accepted gratefully.

"Your story is a bit confusing," she said. "May I ask some questions to clarify my understanding?"

"Yes."

"Did Osgar steal your uncle's money, or his whole caravard with the money in it?"

"The caravard with the money in it."

"Was this here on the Aeriskenn River?"

"No, he hung us upside down by our ankles from the bridge over the Davoura River Gorge, and then cut the ropes."

"Us?"

"Me and my cousin, Cor."

"But the naiad did not drown you."

"No, she saved us. She said it wasn't our fault we were in her river."

"That's . . . incredible." Esmerlia was staring at him like he might be a naiad himself. "And how did you get to the fair?"

"My cousin and I met a woman, two women actually, traveling together. One of them had also been rescued by the naiad, the day before, but was very cold and needed a fire, and Cor and I made a bow drill and lit a fire, and she said we saved her life. They brought us to the fair and paid our way and everything, only they didn't have enough money left to get my uncle in, but they are going to try to sell some things and then get money out to him. But they can't just go do that, because there's someone here who tried to kill Ariadne by drowning a cougar in a dangerous river, and so she has to stay hidden because she's very er, unique-looking. And Nora looks like regular folks but the man saw her with Ariadne so she has to get a disguise, too, and it's all taking a long, *long* time."

"I see. Where are these women now?"

"Ariadne is in the stall right next door. Nora got her face painted like a night cheetah, and she's out now shopping for some local clothes so she can fit in here. And somehow, we have to get to Dunkler Stern because he has some information Ariadne needs, and can help her sell things to get money to get my uncle in. But I don't know how—"

Just then they were interrupted by a bell ringing somewhere behind Esmerlia.

"I am sorry. Wait one moment." She stood up and stuck her hand between the curtains where Happen had entered, and then passed through, and he was alone with the candles and black curtains and darkly stained furniture. He cleared his nose again, and Esmerlia returned.

"Is your name Happen?"

"Yes."

"A boy celebrating the wolf was looking for you. Moth—er, my assistant said she hadn't seen you. He seemed quite upset. What would you like to do?"

"That's my cousin. I have to go. I didn't think they would be looking for me already. I have to go back."

"Please, go out by the back door, this way, and watch out for the string when you cross to the next stall. Come back later if you want, by the front door."

"Thanks."

She ushered him through some curtains out into the cool night air, whispered in his ear, "You will find Osgar among the flags of red," and then, with her hand on his arm, steered him in the right direction. The moon was not up yet, and he used slow, shallow steps in the dark until his shin pressed against the twine, then he hurried to the wagon where Ariadne was still waiting. His heart pounded as if he were approaching his parents after getting caught breaking a rule.

# SIXTEEN

## MANIACAL ENTHUSIASM

> Some Berythean customs, based as they are on agrarian life, will seem surprisingly familiar to readers on Earth. The Spirit Moon, for example, has many of the same features as autumnal Earth celebrations known as Halloween, All Souls' Day, Samhain, Food for the Souls, or Dziady, among others. (Reilly, 2046)

"I'm glad you've returned," Ariadne said. "Your cousin is out looking for you, but I asked him to check back here often. Will you build me a fire, please?"

Grateful for something to do, Happen arranged kindling inside the chiminea until Cor returned and joined him.

"Where *were* you, pig bottom?" Cor flopped down on the grass and sighed.

"Not getting my face painted," Happen said. "What's wrong with you?"

"Nora said my face paint is adorable."

"She's like that."

"It's supposed to be fierce."

"It is fierce. It's thunderously fearsome. That's just how she talks. There was a character in Cravey's, Miss Mithey, who talked that way."

"She wouldn't have said that about the scary death skull, though, would she?"

"No, I guess not, but she might have pretended to be scared in a way that was too fakey and didn't feel right anyway. Let's get Ariadne to light this fire, so I can see your face better."

Ariadne wanted to set up her tents before the moon rose, and before they lit the fire. The large tent had door flaps that could be rolled aside to create a three-walled room where they could fit Marimba's cage and the boys' packs and bedrolls. They set the smaller tent next to it at an angle, leaving a narrow path between the two.

Only then did Ariadne light the fire. Marimba stepped out to sit next to her and get her neck scratched while Ariadne fed. Nora went into the smaller tent with a package.

"So, cousin." Cor sat down in the firelight and took off his boots to rub his feet. "Where did you go, anyway?"

Happen could see the details on Cor's face now. His eyebrows had been extended to look like gray fur, and above them, a pair of wolf's ears reached his hairline. There wouldn't have been room for the ears before his haircut. His nose had grown into a furry gray snout. His lips were gray and elongated, with long sharp canine teeth added, giving the appearance of a wide, sinister smile. His jawline was covered, beard-like, in dark gray fur that extended down his neck on either side of a white throat.

Esmerlia had said he was a boy celebrating the wolf. Another item on the long list of questions he wanted to ask her. Part of him wanted to keep his visit to the seer a secret, but he couldn't think of anything else to tell them.

"Yeah, sorry about that," he said. "I couldn't stand the waiting anymore, so I paid a visit to the seer next door. I thought it was unlikely for Osgar to step in there, too."

"I knew you'd go there!" Cor rolled over onto his stomach and picked at the grass. "But I checked and they said you weren't."

"That was risky of you, Happen," Ariadne said. "But it's a good sign that they were discreet about your presence."

Just then Nora came diving out of the tent, let out a squawk of surprise, and sprawled on the grass, landing with her head on Happen's lap.

"Oof. Sorry. Darn this thing. Never worn a dress in a tent before." She stood up brushing and tugging at her dress and laughing. "Grass stains are not going to help this deception!"

Her dress had a dull green bodice, laced on both sides, over a light gray shirt with big sleeves, and a long brown skirt. It reminded Happen of the dress his mother made for Aunt Nazellen for Longest Night dinner one year. Aunt Nazellen wanted bishop sleeves. His mother agreed they looked elegant, but called them "candle catchers," and said they were only practical if you had servants, which evidently Aunt Nazellen was expecting her to be that year.

"Well, what do you think?" Nora asked. "I tried to find something more practical, but I didn't want to take too much time."

"Well done," Ariadne said. "You look much more like a *Berythean* night cheetah now, and ready to search for my adversary."

Someone knocked on the wagon, and everyone froze.

The tents stood at angles to the chiminea, and the wagon blocked the view from the road created by the space between them. The arrangement created an almost private space centered on the fire, but the knock dispelled the illusion.

"Hello?" a boy's voice said after a pause.

"I think it's the firewood guy," Cor whispered.

"I'll see what he wants." Nora stepped out between the tents, returning a moment later with an envelope.

"It's a letter!" she exclaimed, handing it to Cor. "Addressed to the wolf boy in stall twenty-three." Happen's heart and mind raced, trying to imagine who it might be from. *And how does Cor get a* letter? *He wasn't even supposed to be here!* Couldn't be Tinker, because he wouldn't know about the wolf paint. Could Osgar have spotted him somehow? Cor pried up the red wax seal and pulled out a folded piece of paper.

"It's for you," he said, handing it to Happen. "Says so inside."

Happen read the graceful handwriting silently. *When the full moon clears the horizon, there will be a parade celebrating the cattle. A cart full of masks and robes waits at the western end of our row for anyone who wants to join in. The parade route includes the artisan row where Stern is.*

It had to be from Esmerlia. He didn't want Ariadne to know that he had mentioned Dunkler Stern by name, so when he read it to the others, he changed "where Stern is" to "in our quadrant."

"It is not signed?" Ariadne asked.

"No."

"Check the seal."

Cor handed the envelope to his cousin, who brought it closer to the firelight to be sure. An E entwined with roses.

"I believe it's from the Amazing Esmerlia," Happen said. "I told her we needed to find disguises to safely get to the artisan row in our quadrant."

He climbed onto the wagon to look for the moon. A cool, dry breeze blew from the east, full of curious smells and sounds. About a tenth of the moon had risen in the north of east, like one smooth glowing orange mountain rising among the jagged black peaks of the Antler Range. Some passersby, chatting gaily, entered the black tent. He remembered her smell, and the way she held him while he cried. He folded his letter back into its envelope, put it into his pocket, and found that he still had her handkerchief. Very soon it would be too bright to show himself like this, but he paused a moment to watch the moon and feel the laced edge of his secret memento.

"Moonrise has started," Happen said when he returned to the fire.

"Do you trust this Esmerlia person?" Ariadne asked.

"Yes."

"In this matter, we will, too. Nora, let's change plans to take advantage of this opportunity. We will all go and find this parade. Happen and I will 'celebrate the cattle' with costumes. Nora, you and Cor will walk with us if possible or follow somehow. It may be difficult with masks on to see Dunkler Stern's caravard, so please make sure to pull us out of the parade if we miss it. Happen, we will try to stay at the end of the parade, so we can slip away without attracting attention."

Nora lent Happen the floppy rain hat she'd worn earlier, helped Ariadne wrap a thin scarf around her face, and then arranged her hood so it appeared less like something meant to hide a Dhaignian, folding the edges in and pinning them.

With the brightening moon at their backs, they were able to keep their faces in shadow during the walk. The stalls at the western end of their row were still unoccupied, so the cart was easy to find. Already a small crowd of people mingled about wearing white robes and large cattle masks that covered their heads and necks. Nora walked up to the cart with Ariadne and Happen. Cor hung back, leaning on a pole nearby.

"What sizes can I get for you, young lady?" A man without a mask stood by the cart.

"May I have two small, please?" Nora asked him. "For my aunt and cousin here."

He handed her two robes, and then two cow head masks one at a time. "Nice to see a young man taking part in the old traditions," he said to Happen. To Nora he added, "Sure you won't help us celebrate this year's cattle? It's lots of fun . . ."

"No, thank you. Cattle are fine, but I'm more a cat person."

"Suit yourself."

The thin robes were a little short on Ariadne and a little long on Happen, but not enough to matter. The masks were white and gray with black eyes and ears, and made of some kind of lightweight plaster. Several of the masks had impressive golden-brown horns; these were worn by the larger men in the crowd. All of them had ornate patterns painted in thin golden lines on the white cheeks and the gray nose. Nora helped them put on the bulky masks. Small eyeholes in the bridge of the cow's nose provided limited vision, mostly forward. The mask smelled like hay, and he thought he might sneeze. He could not see his feet or the ground in front of him at all.

"It's almost time," someone in the crowd squealed, and Happen tilted his head back, trying to see the moon. Nora laughed.

"What's funny?" His voice filled the small space inside the mask. She responded, but he couldn't hear her through the mask and the crowd noise. Everything seemed far away. Nora put her arm around his shoulders, and spoke directly into a hole near his ear, and it felt then as if she were the only other person in the world, and very close to him.

"When that person said 'it's almost time,' I saw about forty cows all face east and lean back, and I was imagining them howling, or moo-howling, at the moon. No such luck, though."

"Moo-howling?"

"Never mind." Then she said something he couldn't hear again.

"What?"

"Oh, it's up all the way now, Happen. Your moon is so pretty, so amazing. It's much bigger than—"

"Celebrants!" a booming voice overcame the crowd noise.

Nora squeezed his shoulder gently and was gone. "Parades can get a bit chaotic in the busier parts of the fair. If you get confused, listen for the bells. If you get lost, look for a cart like this one at the beginning of row nine in the southwest quadrant where we'll gather the costumes at the end of the parade. Any questions?"

Happen couldn't see the speaker, but guessed the man was standing on the cart where the costumes had been.

"Celebrants! With gratitude and respect we are here to honor and celebrate the cattle chosen for this year's harvest!" A muffled cheer erupted from the people in the parade. "We humbly request the Spirit Moon to shepherd their souls to the winter grazing fields, as we thank them for their service in life, and for their bodies that will help sustain us until the growing returns."

Another muffled cheer, followed by a loud moo, and laughter. "Hurrah for the cattle! Hurrah, hurrah!" Wooden bells made *thok, thok, thok* sounds, and the crowd shuffled off then settled into a regular walking pace.

Happen followed, trying to imagine why Nora would think of cattle howling at the moon. He could still feel where she'd squeezed his shoulder. Someone bumped into his other shoulder, and he realized he didn't know which cow was Ariadne; he was surrounded by strangers. The wooden bell sounded off to his left now, and ahead, but those in front of him hadn't turned yet. Angling his big plaster nose, he could see the parade had thinned as it left the main road, white robes and masks were dimly lit like ghosts in the low moon. In this thinner line and ghastly light, the cattle people looked more like grim specters than a celebration.

One of the horned bulls stood at the turn, making sure everyone went the right direction. The bull masks weren't all the same, like the cows were. This one had a wide grin with uneven teeth; it leered at Happen with a maniacal enthusiasm. Unsettled, he stumbled, stepping on the grass between the gravel ruts, but a strong arm steadied him, and feeling with his feet he found the gravel rut on the left side of the track and followed it.

Applause, and shouts of "Hurrah for the cows!" and "Thanking you!" filled the air as they neared the busy middle section of the fair. Someone wandered through the cattle blowing into a wooden pipe with finger holes to make notes, but Happen couldn't follow the tune. The parade slowed, and the crowd along the road thickened.

As his feet told him they were turning onto a road like the one they'd started on, the smell of roast chicken and onions seeped under the mask, along with some spice he couldn't name. It seemed like ages since the elk jerky and bannock lunch he'd had in the wagon before entering the fairgrounds. After several more steps he smelled sugar and cinnamon, and something baking. His mouth watered. Sweat rolled down his neck as heat built up under the mask. *I'm baking, too. This is all Osgar's fault.*

They turned again quickly, and the aromas relented. He couldn't decide whether he missed them or was glad to be free of their tantalizing scent, but the next row was even more crowded than the first, slowing their pace. He tripped and banged his plaster cow nose into the person ahead. Laughter behind and cursing ahead made him flush and wish again for escape. But these big masks weren't exactly going to melt into the crowd. He doubted they could just walk away once they reached the artisan row. There was no *away* to walk to. Maybe Ariadne thought she had a plan, but he had forgotten to watch for Dunkler Stern's caravard, and now couldn't remember what they'd said it looked like. Cor had mentioned stepping stones in a path, but he wouldn't be able to see those.

After another turn they entered a wide row with gravel all across instead of just in the wheel tracks like the others. The wooden bells ahead started up a frantic clamor, and everyone stopped. A plaster nose bumped into him from behind. He was trapped in the middle of a dammed river of cows, and the banks were lined with the faces of strangers. *We've probably passed the artisan row by now anyway.* Three shrill notes pierced the crowd noise, and the bells started a rhythm. The shrill notes were from a wooden pipe like he'd heard earlier, but this one trilled a simple tune, cheerful and bouncy, working with the rhythm from the bells. Cow heads bobbed up and down as the parade started up again, dancing with the music. Cows ahead of him weaved back and forth, heads swaying and bobbing in time, and spread out in the wide row. He tried to fit in by weaving a little, but was afraid to lose his footing again. He was sure the audience was laughing at him, saying he was the silliest cow in the history of cow parades.

A tall bull stood in the middle, rotating warily, its dark eyebrows angled down to form an angry glare that defied anyone to dance away with one his cows. Happen felt sure now: they weren't going to get out of this parade—or these stifling masks— until its end, when Ariadne would be farther away from Dunkler Stern than ever with no hope for disguise. And he would be farther from those delicious smells at the food row, easy prey for Osgar, who could be anywhere, even watching right now. The applause from the parade watchers built in intensity as they danced along. A few revelers joined the parade, clapping in time with the bells and dancing artfully among the slower moving cattle.

Suddenly, the name Dunkler Stern flashed past his eyes, some-where ahead and off to his left. He swayed his head that way again, scanning, and found it. A nearby torch cast a wavering light onto a tall caravard, painted purple and blue with a moon and some stars, just visible above the crowd. Fancy white letters read Dunkler Stern's Magical Tileworks.

Happen turned all the way around to see what was behind him, hoping to see a way out, and added some tentative weaving, hoping to make his turn look like dancing. There was only one cow behind him, but then a solid wall of singing, dancing people followed close behind. The bull with the angry glare was on his right now, but there wasn't any way to get past the crowd lining the parade route or the dancers behind them. Happen edged to the left as they neared their tall purple target, turning his head back and forth, heart pounding in his plaster cave, trying to find Nora or Cor.

And then he heard Nora, singing somewhere behind him. Now they were passing Dunkler Stern's caravard, but he kept on, not sure what else to do. Nora twirled past him, singing "wheeeeee!" her long blond braid swinging about her head, and she swerved and careened into him, knocking him into and then through the crowd on the left side, shouting, "Sorry!" and "Look out!"

# SEVENTEEN
# DUNKLER STERN'S MAGICAL
# TILEWORKS

 At the same time as the Gracarrai were pressing their message, another group of people, this one geographically diverse, but connected through the scientific community, were also facing ridicule for radical notions in the field of geology. These folks were convinced that Grith was actually round like a ball, not something flat rocking in a celestial cradle.

The fact that they were better at predicting tidal behavior than cradle theorists was not considered proof, partially because they still weren't perfect and partially because their mathematical arguments were incomprehensible to most people. Fortunately for the moon theorists of Grith, unlike our own Giordano Bruno, there was no dominant religion at the time, and so no Inquisition to face at a perilous trial for heresy. (Reilly, 2046)

appen staggered, and some bystanders tried to catch him, but Nora kept pushing and apologizing, and he fell onto some grass with Nora landing on top of him, saying, "tripped over a cow, oh dear, I'm so sorry." He tried to stand but a hand held him down. Nora was up already saying, "Oh, no thanks. We're together, actually. No, go ahead, we'll catch up soon." Then Cor's voice was right in his ear, whispering, "Get up like you're hurt, limp and lean on me." Happen's mask sat askew on his head and he couldn't see, but he followed Cor's lead. They stopped and Cor talked him through stepping over a twine stall-separator that he couldn't see, then continued a bit farther.

"Sit here," Cor said. "And let's get this thing off."

As they wrestled with the mask and robe, Happen heard Nora saying, "We have important tileworks business to discuss with Dunkler Stern." The cool night air refreshed his sweaty head, and Happen closed his eyes and breathed. *Maybe this tileworks person will offer us some food.*

"What is the nature of your business?" a cranky voice from the caravard said.

"Please, sir," Nora said. "May we come inside? Our business is of a private nature."

"Of course it is," the voice said. Nora and Ariadne stood before a door on the side of the caravard, waiting for it to open, but no further response came. Ariadne's cattle robe and mask were gone, and her deep hood covered her face in shadow. She extended two fingers in a subtle gesture.

"Please, sir," Nora said. "My aunt was a friend of your grand-father's."

"He's not here. He's been dead for twenty-one years."

"And a friend of your great-grandfather's."

"He has also d—so . . . then this is a social call?"

"No, sir," Nora said. "It is as I said, important tileworks business." There was another pause. Happen noticed Ariadne's cow head mask looking at him from out of the shadows under the purple caravard, so he put his next to it, with the robe stuffed inside.

"Stand back a moment." The voice lost its cranky edge, and now sounded resigned to the fact of unwanted visitors. The bottom third of the door was covered by a short ladder on a hinge, pulled up to prevent entry. The ladder was released and swung down on a cord, allowing the door to open out. A small, bent old man stood at the doorway, with a thin, gray beard that reached his waist. He peered at his callers over round eyeglasses, as if evaluating how much of a threat they were. He looked so frightened that Happen felt bad for him, and gave a little friendly wave and smile. But the man cringed and sank back a little.

"Please, sir?" Nora asked.

"Very well, you may come inside."


After negotiating the rickety ladder, they stood in a dim lamplit workshop, with various tiles and tile pieces stacked or piled in woven baskets on the worn wooden floor. Dunkler Stern stood fidgeting with a broken quill by a dusty desk, behind which several stone hammers and a chipped stone axe hung on the wall. He looked at the floor and waited until all were in and Cor had shut the door.

"Is there something I can do for you?"

Ariadne pulled off her deep hood, but the old man just looked at the floor and rubbed one of his long gray eyebrows. Nora pulled the talking-box from her pocket.

"Dunkler Stern," Ariadne announced. "It is time to fulfill and renew your great-grandfather's contract with the Dhaignian scout."

Stern looked up and stifled a gasp. With fear and wonder in his eyes, he crept around his desk to approach Ariadne, and

Happen was reminded of when Odais watched Jenb'lla as she approached Dunlcoh's unicorn for the first time. Since she'd been a little girl Jenb'lla had yearned for the old legends to be true, but everyone had always said they were just make-believe. She knew that wild horses were dangerous, but still, she had to get closer, she had to be sure.

"Could it be?" Stern whispered, leaning on his desk and gripping it for support.

"Yes, it is I. You may call me Ariadne."

"But, but, I was told to"—he pushed his glasses up his nose a bit and stared—"to expect a mouthless woman with . . . with a terrifying voice."

"This visit will be somewhat different from my previous visits."

"But how can I be sure that you are the one?"

"Because of what I know. Your great-grandmother's name was Dodelia, and she was particularly fond of blueberries. In a locked chest hidden somewhere in this wagon, you have a tile cutting machine unlike any other, with heavy-stone scoring wheels that need replenishing."

"Oh, thank goodness," Dunkler Stern said. He let out a deep breath, his brow unfurrowed, and he seemed to grow taller right there before Happen's eyes. "You are most welcome, Ariadne." He took another deep breath, and then seemed to remember something. "Welcome! Right. I will put on some . . ." He hesitated, glancing at Nora.

"Forgive me," Ariadne said. "This is my assistant, Nora, and our companions Happen and Cor."

"Very happy to meet you, sir," Nora said. "And yes, the rest of us would love some tea."

"May we please sit down?" Ariadne asked.

"Oh, yes, of course," Dunkler Stern said. "I'm sorry, I'm quite flustered. I had assumed that "mouthless" was metaphorical somehow. But the moon can't see a thing until it rises. Please understand. I will arrange some seating." He brought a couple of chairs from a back closet, banging them on both sides of the door frame in turn as he came through, and cleared a bench along the wall for the boys to sit on, spilling a basket of broken tile pieces.

"Is there any refreshment I might offer you?" he asked Ariadne.

"You could leave the stove door ajar," Ariadne said. "So that I may enjoy the firelight."

"Oh, yes, that's right! He *did* say you had an affinity for fire-light that rivaled Dodie's for blueberries. I will have to order some extra wood first, though. Down to just hot coals in there now. I've had to be thrifty for so long. But this is most definitely a special occasion."

He turned up the lamp wick to brighten the room, then attached a white flag to a rope on a pulley and gave the rope a quick tug so that the flag shot through a hole in the wall. As the whirring pulley slowed, Happen noticed a red flag hanging from a peg next to it. *Among the flags of red! Had Osgar been here?* But this was a single flag. He looked for others but saw none. Then Happen remembered the signaling system described by the usher at the gate—white flag for errands, red flag for emergency. Esmerlia must have meant a different kind of flag.

Dunkler Stern fussed with a waterskin and a ceramic kettle and set the latter on the small masonry stove. Then he perched on a stool, bent forward with legs crossed, and sighed and chuckled.

"I have been looking forward to your visit for a long, long time." As he spoke he absentmindedly twirled his beard into a coil on his thigh. "According to our family legend, I would have to live a long life to have another chance to meet you. My wife and son don't believe the old tales, and even my father was skeptical, but I knew you would come, and I have prepared well."

Happen caught himself staring. He'd never seen a beard even half that long.

Nora turned to Ariadne. "But weren't you just here, wasn't it only fifty years ago?"

"Yes, yes," Stern said. "I was but nine years of age at the time, but I remember missing the visit. My father and I had been in Eyrakenn buying a new tile cutter. We'd heard of some new labor-saving design invented there, and for almost a year my grandfather had been saying our mysterious benefactor would come back with sharp scoring wheels any day, but my father had given up. We spent the last of our savings and went all that way for a trifle: a cutter that might save three days a year at best. When we returned disappointed—oh, I remember the smile on eldpa's face like it was yesterday. He said you'd come at last. And still my father did not believe!"

Stern's eyes were glassy and bright, and Happen thought the old man might start leaking tears of joy at any moment.

"That is a fond memory for you," Ariadne said.

"Well, it is *now*!" Dunkler Stern gave a laugh that sounded mightier than would be expected from his frail body. "Right. Ahem. Do you have, er, would you like to hear my report?"

At that moment, a knock came on the door in a short, repeated pattern.

"That will be the firewood." Stern crossed to the door and opened it.

"Got your wood here, Mr. Stern," an errand boy said. "I apologize, sir, but the boss says you've got to pay up front."

"Yes, of course." Stern's face reddened. He pulled a small purse from his pocket and knelt down to hand the boy some coins. "With a little something for you. You've always treated me with respect, when others would not."

"Oh! Thank you, sir. Having a good fair so far, then, Mr. Stern?" The boy handed several small bundles of split firewood up to the caravard.

"Yes, actually. Luck visits the hopeful on a sunny day." Stern carried one of the bundles to the stove and built up the fire.

Happen didn't think Stern would have gotten tea that evening without buying wood or burning furniture.

"Before we get to your report," Ariadne said. "We need to show you something."

Nora took the deputy's knife from her bag and presented it to Stern handle first.

"We found this knife being wielded by a highway patrol deputy on the road south of Aeriskenn," Ariadne said. "Have you ever seen anything like it?"

Stern accepted the knife and took it to the lamp on his desk to study it.

"I have not. I have heard about bronze weapons, and I wouldn't be too surprised to learn there were some among the officers of the highway patrol, although they were described to me as having a coppery tint, which this one lacks. Such items are controversial, however, and I would not expect them to be wielded openly."

"The markings on the handle?"

Stern pushed his glasses up and reexamined the leather handle. "Ah, there. These markings are quite mysterious to me. There are only four languages still in use on Grith and, although I cannot read any but Berythean, I would at least recognize the others. This is either very old, or else from some new culture not known to the Royal Academy of Aeriskenn."

"The markings identify the weapon as issued by the armed forces of another planet named Thujaplid," Ariadne said. Happen watched intently, curious to see the old man's reaction to Ariadne's bizarre ideas about planets.

"I see," Stern said grimly, handing the knife back carefully. "That does not sound like good news."

The kettle whistled mournfully on the stove, and he got up to prepare tea. Happen was disappointed by Stern's noncommittal response, but at least there would be tea. *Tea and . . . Cookies? Cake? Stale bread would be great right about now.*

"It is not," Ariadne agreed. "But the fact that the blade or the mark of Thujaplid is not common here is a relief. You may proceed now with your prepared report."

"Ah, yes. I was instructed that you would want to hear about significant advances over the past fifty years in the fields of mining, metallurgy, zoology, and politics. Which would you like first?"

"Unfortunately, we have some pressing issues to take care of. I only have time for a brief overview, and we can cover more detail later. Let's start with metallurgy. When last I was here the only knives were made of bone or flint."

Happen had never heard of metallurgy. *Knives are* still *made of bone or flint.*

"Very well." Stern searched through some bare cupboards as he spoke. "According to my grandfather's research, copper was discovered forty-six years ago in eastern Berythea. Grith-thunder disrupted the land in the Anabelis Hills, exposing a wide band of greenish rock. Some travelers passing through built a fire ring with rocks at just the right place, and noticed an interesting change . . ."

Happen stopped listening. He was too hungry and thirsty for a long history lesson. If there wasn't food with the tea, he would have to devise a plan to escape.

"I am sorry to interrupt," Ariadne said. "I do appreciate your thoroughness, but, for the present, I only need to know which technological advances occurred, not how they occurred."

He remembered what Nora had said about Ariadne being efficient, so perhaps this wouldn't take as long as it first appeared.

"That's quite all right," Stern said. "I am eager, myself, to return to work with sharp tools."

"Excellent. Please proceed with what happened after copper was understood."

"Very well. As you can imagine, Gracarrai priests were quite alarmed by copper, and sent representatives to investigate the source. It was determined that Grith had provided this resource of its own volition, and so it was not technically forbidden, but the acceptable use of it was limited—"

"I see, so Gracarrai is still the dominant religion in Berythea? Is that still true on the other continents, as well?"

"Goodness, yes. Truer than ever."

Stern found what he had been looking for, but it wasn't food, just a fourth mug. He handed steaming mugs of tea to Nora and the boys, then poured one for himself. *No bread, no cookies.*

"Fascinating. And the bronze weapons you've heard of, how long have they been in production?"

"Only about fifteen years, but as this use of bronze is strictly forbidden under Gracarrai law, most people are still unaware of this development."

The tea was thin and tasted of fennel root and dandelion. Happen caught Cor's eye and nodded at the door. Cor tapped his mug. They would finish their tea and then try to get out.

"Have there been efforts to mine the resources needed?"

"Since the discovery of tin, there have been prospectors who travel about looking for unusual rocks and testing them. Some of them share information with the academy, and my sources there suspect that illicit mining is occurring in very small-scale operations. The Church investigates any apparent sources of ore, and Gracarrai inspectors are respected and feared, so you just don't see these things around. However, just yesterday, I heard rumor of some who say the Church is considering a change in mining policy."

"Mining policy? Do you refer to the six-foot rule?"

"Yes, but only in certain places. Word is, proponents argue that since the root of the six-foot rule lies in the need to avoid disturbing buried souls, unlikely burial places should be exempt, which would open up many rocky, boggy, or sloped places available for mining. But this would also make enforcement extremely difficult."

Happen tried to imagine how that would work. Once something had been extracted from Grith, how could you know what place it had been taken from?

"What do your sources in the Church say about this?"

"I just heard of this possibility in line outside the fair and haven't had the opportunity to pursue more information. It may just be gossip, but I've never heard the like."

"Such a recent development. Interesting," Ariadne said. "This could be the comet's tail that leads to my adversary. Have there been any other major changes in Berythea, or on Grith as a whole, since my last visit?"

"I'm not sure what you'd consider major. The population is gradually recovering from the Great Eruption, but is still much lower than it used to be. The guilds and the kings have formed alliances that have been mostly peaceful and prosperous. Balance of trade among the four nations has been improving. Our recent affairs have been blessedly stable compared to your last visit."

"Very good," Ariadne said. "Now, I must ask your assistance with a few matters related to our immediate situation."

"However I can help," Stern said.

"We have reason to believe that there are persons here at the fair who wish us harm, and this has prevented us from being able to show ourselves publicly. Happen and I arrived at your door disguised within a costumed parade, but we won't be able to use those costumes again. Also, we need local money. We have some unusual leather to sell, and are hoping you can recommend a buyer. And, finally, a legal question for you. If a cart was stolen on the highway, and then taken into the fair, which authority would the cart owner appeal to, the highway patrol, or the fair security?"

Happen had begun to drift off, soothed by Stern's gentle voice, but hearing his name caught his attention, and the legal question inspired him to listen.

"Oh, dear. Well, one tile at a time, my father used to say. I don't know the answer to your legal question, but if you like I can ask a man I know who works in security here. I should be able to find him in the morning."

"Yes, thank you."

"About the leather. The best price would come from one of the premium dealers on row three east. Then there was something else . . ."

"Disguises."

"Ah, yes. Let's see . . . the face paint is not unusual during the Spirit Moon festivities, but it will become increasingly so after tomorrow morning. My son's family will be able to help with this, once I explain the situation." Stern sat behind his desk, used his lamp to light a thick red candle, and began to write. "I need my grandson Helter to help me in the shop tonight anyway, and he can bring some helpful clothes for the young men. For you, however, your hooded cloak is not that unusual, though, so long as you are careful near light sources. I am sure your appearance would create quite a stir."

"Yes, this cloak hides my face well enough, but it is also exactly what my adversary would be looking for," Ariadne said. Happen remembered a *Cravey Mysteries* episode where a thief was able to steal the king's only white riding horse. The thief had entered the king's bailey with a cart drawn by one white horse, then left with a cart drawn by two white horses. When the loss was noticed at the stable, the sheriff and his men went looking for a single white riding horse, and no one remembered the team of two white draft horses, because it wasn't what they were looking for.

"He'd be on the lookout for a single hooded cloak. What if Nora wore a hooded cloak, too?" Happen asked. "And you walked together." The room was silent for a moment.

"Should I see if my grandson can borrow a hooded cloak as well?"

"Yes, please, Mr. Stern," Ariadne said. "Thank you, Happen. Although it's not a solution, I think it's the best we can do for now." Stern finished his letter, then sealed the envelope with wax from the candle. Using the white flag to call an errand boy, he sent the letter on its way.

"My son sells tile from a stall in the next row," Stern said. "This won't take long." He returned to his desk, humming, and looked at Ariadne. "I am so glad that you have come. I hope you'll let me introduce you to my son tomorrow so I can see the look on his face. He didn't even name his son Dunkler! Oh, er, did you bring the scoring wheels with you tonight?"

"I brought you three tonight," Ariadne said, pulling her hand from a pocket and handing him three small gray wheels with sharp edges. "The rest are in a box which I will bring at a safer time." Dunkler Stern sighed as he accepted the little discs with shaking hands.

"The Gracarrai priests talk about the beauty of copper and bronze, but for me they can't compare to some of your heavy-stone with a sharp edge. At the academy they speak in grandiose terms about the potential for bronze tools, and I hold my tongue that wants to call them soft."

Happen wanted to ask Dunkler Stern if he really believed that these tools came from a different grith. He also wanted to ask for more tea.

# EIGHTEEN

## AMONG THE FLAGS OF RED

> The religion of Gracarrai is described by a set of twelve documents, three of which comprise the origin covenant, which is only available to a select few. The rest, known as the nine articles of the open circle covenant, are familiar to nearly everyone, as they are taught in schools.
>
> Article eight led to the apparently disorganized governing structure in Berythea. At its core it holds all people responsible for keeping three kinds of power from exerting authority above the others: economic control, military force, and religious influence. (Reilly, 2046)

With help from the Stern family, Happen was fed and dressed in a cap and a double-breasted jerkin common among young men in the city. With black and white paint, his face was transformed into a skull with large dark eye sockets and a wide toothy grin.

Dunkler Stern's grandson Helter, who was a year younger than Cor, took a liking to him immediately, and joined him in celebrating the wolf. The three boys were given a half solan each to spend and let out to enjoy the moonlit fair while Ariadne and Nora visited with Dunkler Stern.

Happen, Cor, and Helter bought fried dough covered with butter, cinnamon, and sugar, and wandered through the food rows. Happen mentioned that his cart had been stolen on the way to the fair, and Helter said that anything stolen is bound to make its way to the red flag district, over by the stables. *Among the flags of red! This must be what she meant.*

"Didn't Tinker say something about the stables?" Happen asked Cor.

"Yeah, something. What's the red flag district?"

"It's where the bad people go," Helter said. "Boys my age aren't allowed there. There's robbers and stuff."

"Ha! We're not afraid of robbers," Cor said. "All our stuff has been stolen already."

"Take us there," Happen said. He didn't feel as bold as he sounded, but he didn't want to seem timid compared to his younger cousin.

"Oh, no, I can't do that." Helter shook his head. "I'll get in trouble!"

"You won't need to go in," Happen said. "Just show us where it is. Dunkler said for you to show us around, right?"

"I'm not sure that's what he had in mind."

Helter led them to the south gate road, then east toward the river. People on this road moved quickly, not browsing but on their way to or from somewhere, and they flowed around the boys' tentative pace in both directions. Laughter and singing and face paint compliments trailed in everyone's wake, mingling and fading. "Oh, look at the darling wolves and spirit!"

When they got to row seven, Helter looked around nervously, then nodded toward it.

"It's this row and the next."

All along the row, every stall had their red signal flag out, indicating a need for emergency help. There were plenty of people about, but no one seemed either aware or concerned about any emergency.

"Are you fellows really going in?"

"Sure. Why not come with us? You won't get in trouble. How many people know you got painted like a wolf?" Cor asked.

"Yeah, but still. They say calls for help in there are not heeded. I'll wait out here."

At row eight, which seemed less crowded than seven, Happen and Cor turned off the south gate road and entered the red flag district. The first stall had a tall black tent similar to Esmerlia's, but the door flaps were tied back. Sitting at the door, a woman with dark painted shadows around her eyes smiled at Happen, curled fingers with impossibly long red nails to beckon him, and parted her long skirt, revealing a pale upper thigh. He turned away, steering Cor to the other side of the row. They passed an apothecary, then looked over a display table of serrated obsidian blades.

A large man celebrating the tiger approached them with a flabby smile. "Come right this way! The Sorcelege Treasure Shop has amazements and wonders just for you!" The man's high-pitched cackle sounded like it should belong to someone else.

"N-no thanks," Happen said, veering away from the man to the other side of the gravel track, where rough-throated curses and the rattle of coins and dice filtered through a large shuddering tent with a sign that read Rumbling Jiggs's Cards Dice. The feeling of being watched followed him. *There's no place to just stand and breathe.*

"Hey now, boys, come celebrate the Spirit Moon with a nice massage from Monissa," said a woman's voice behind them as a hand caressed Happen's back, making him jump and turn.

"No thanks," Happen said, angling back across the track. And there it was. His cart. The stall was dark and empty. The boys stopped, and Monissa sauntered past them, swinging her hips. Happen grabbed Cor's elbow.

"Don't look at it," he muttered, "Let's see if we can find Tinker's, too." They recrossed the track to where a distillery was offering samples of whiskey. From there they could see Tinker's caravard in the stall next to Happen's. A light burned inside.

Helter led them back toward the fair's center, eager to move on, but Happen and Cor dragged behind.

"Osgar's in Tinker's caravard," Cor said.

"Yes," said Happen. "I'd sure like to know what he's doing in there. It looks like he hasn't even touched my cart."

"Me too. If we could hide under the caravard, we'd be able to hear what's going on inside."

"Are you sure? Sounds risky."

"I've done it before. We'll just listen for a little while, and then get out. No big deal."

"But how would we get there? We can't just walk over and crawl under it. Someone will see us."

"We'll just explain to them that it's my father's stolen caravard."

Happen laughed, and Helter slowed down to hear what they were talking about.

"How would Cravey do it?" Cor asked.

"Cravey?" Helter said. "You fellows read Cravey, too? He's my favorite."

"Great!" Cor said. "So you'll know how to do this sort of thing and be able to help, right?"

Helter's fur-fringed eyes grew large. "You're going to catch the thief who stole your cart?"

"No, we just want to spy on him," Happen said. "Cravey

would either have Morgone create a diversion, or he'd approach from an unexpected direction or something like that . . ."

They stopped and looked at Helter. Crowd flowed around them in a stream of noise and motion.

"Oh, no," Helter backed away a step. "I'm not creating a diversion to get the attention of everybody in the red flag district. Are you daft?"

"No, you're right. That wouldn't work," Cor said. "It would get Osgar's attention, too, and we don't want that. You're good at this, Helter."

"I am?"

"We need an unexpected direction then."

"Well, that's the last row in the quadrant, right?" Cor said. "What's behind that fence?"

"The stables, but it costs money to . . ." Helter trailed off.

"Costs money?" Cor asked. "To get in the stables?"

Helter sighed. "I'm not supposed to tell anyone, but you fellows wouldn't rat on me, would you?"

"Not a chance."

"Okay," he said. "There is a way to get through the fence from the stables. I've never done it, but my sister has. She and her friends go in sometimes early in the morning and look around for dropped coins and stuff. But you have to pay the guy at the gate."

"That's fine, we can pay you back double tomorrow," Happen said. "No problem."

Helter Stern led the way through the darkness and the thick smell of tull dung behind the fence, counting posts as he walked.

"Okay," he whispered. "It's this one. There should be knot holes for lifting the board." Cor lifted the fence board and moved it aside, and the ruckus from the cards and dice room tumbled through the gap. He stuck his head through, then pulled it back.

"Ugh," he whispered. "Smells like piss. There's a bush right there, so I can't tell for sure if it's safe to go, but it looks dark and empty in the backyards."

"We'd have to be sure, though," Happen whispered. "Maybe we better go back."

"Right. I'll go out and check." Cor stepped between the fence rails, then stuck his head back in a moment later.

"It's clear and dark along the fence to the caravard, and no one's about back here. But remember, you have to be silent under the caravard. We can hear him, but he can hear us, too."

"You're really going," Helter said. "If we get caught, you guys owe me thunders."

"We already owe you thunders," Happen said. "If we all get caught, we owe you thunders and lightnings. But if only Cor and I get caught, you'll be fine, we're not rats."

"My sister's not going to believe you went through at night," Helter said as Happen stepped through the fence.

"Remember, if something goes wrong, whistle twice if we should come back here, whistle once if we should just run for it."

Each stall had a scrubby bush in the back corner of its yard, and Happen and Cor crept from one to the other till they reached the shadows under Tinker's caravard, crawling on the grass between the gravel wheel ruts.

". . . away from that girl. One is always underfoot, getting on my nerves."

"You must admit he's been useful. That gorge he suggested was perfect. And he seems eager to continue your work here after we leave." The words were Berythean, but they were delivered by a voice very similar to the broken-glass voice of Nora's translator. It was unnerving to hear their own language in that hideous voice, but the boys kept still.

"Yes, great find, he's just making me look forward to leaving."

This came from the other voice, which sounded normal, other than being oddly deep.

"How many of the Gracarrai pamphlets did you and Osgar distribute today?" said the glass voice. Happen looked at Cor, but they couldn't see each other in the darkness. *It said Osgar! This voice in Tinker's caravard talking. It had to mean* their *Osgar.*

"Not many," said the deep voice. "Best to be subtle at first. Big announcement would be investigated. Rumor is just rumor. Tomorrow, it will gradually become true rumor, and then some day or two after that before investigation."

"These investigators, what will they do to your helper?"

"Don't know. Jail time at least."

"Why jail time? The bog ore doesn't break the six-foot rule."

"Ours doesn't, but they don't know that, and they'll hold him while figuring it out. I'm hoping they learn all about that iron your miner scout found in Faddich Bog, but it's least among Osgar's worries."

"Oh?"

"Gracarrai inspectors won't be happy about us using their seal of approval on pamphlets."

There was a moment of silence. *We've been noticed.* Happen stopped breathing and listened for footsteps or a whistle from Helter. A bright torch burned on a tall pole in front of the next stall, and the full moon filled the yard and road with enough light that he'd been sure they couldn't be seen in the dark shadows under the caravard.

"The penalty for this heresy on Dhaigne would be a gradual starvation," the glass voice said.

"Similar on Thujaplid: several days of torture before death," said the deep voice.

Happen breathed again. It had just been a thoughtful pause in the conversation. But he'd heard those names before, Dhaigne and Thujaplid, from Ariadne and Nora.

"Perhaps we could bring him with us?"

"Who knows how long he'll be able to continue my work after we leave? Just keep me safe and leave my plans alone. We have one day to get people at this fair excited about steel before we move on to Maithea. I cannot risk my planet for one or two Grithings. Besides, if we took him with us, we'd have to take her too, and they are both insufferable."

"What if—" A strange sound interrupted them. It was similar to the glass voice, but like a birdcall translated by glass. It repeated three times, then stopped in the middle of a fourth.

"Time for my argon already," the deep voice said. "Stupid weak atmosphere."

Someone scuffled about above them, then a sharp hiss startled Happen. The deep-voiced man gasped, coughed, and grumbled.

"I support your complaint," the glass voice said. "The sunlight here is different. It's close enough for me to live on, but I tire easily."

"I keep forgetting about that. Dhaigne! Say, how can you do gradual starvation for people who don't eat?"

"It's quite simple. Just close their cell window a little more each day. With the fire people, you just give them fewer candles each night."

"Can they live on candles?"

"No, but it . . . extends things somewhat."

This had to be the same Dhaigne Nora had told them about, where Ariadne was supposed to be from. Happen had been sure it wasn't something other people knew about.

"How can starvation be used for punishment if Dhaignians don't kill each other?"

"In these situations the heretic is provided with a drug that will end their life quickly and painlessly. Some last longer than others, but invariably they self-administer the drug that takes their own life. That is what will happen to me if I get caught helping you."

"Say, *is* there any chance they'll catch you?"

"There is always a small chance, but it's much more likely if we fail to raise Grith's listing rank above Thujaplid's."

"What if some other planet was to be . . . what was it? Harvested?"

"Employed."

"Right. Employed. Dhaigne!"

"Most likely, Thujaplid or Grith will rank highest. Slightly higher chance, at this moment, for Thujaplid."

"But these people have no defense!" The deep voice sounded frustrated. "We would at least put up some fight. Resistance must have some impact on ranking?"

"Thujaplid also has a productive mining industry with substantial identified reserves. Once the Dhaignian miners come to employ a place, it's not long until it's uninhabitable, whether you're prepared to fight or not. Your mind is cycling again."

"I better get some rest. You going to sleep in here? I'll arrange tenting."

"Good. I'm working on a plan to buy Osgar some more time, but I will be resting soon as well. I'll set up the TMD system now, though, so you are not disturbed."

Movement in the caravard made enough noise that the boys could scurry back out through the yard without being heard.

They found Dunkler Stern humming at his desk, surrounded by stacks of tile. He stood to greet them, and a fine cloud of dust billowed up from his apron.

"Boys! Thanks for returning so soon. I have more boxes that you can move for me. I had forgotten how fast this goes with a sharp cutter."

"Eldpa," Helter said. "They found their stolen caravard, and hid underneath and heard men talking about a huge apple lid coming to make Grith unhabitable."

"Whoa, there. Slow down. Who did you hear talking?"

"The two men in there," Helter said. "In Cor's caravard that was stolen. They found it and hid underneath, listening."

"You rascals!"

"No, not me. These fellows did. I told them, but they didn't care about the rules."

"I see, and what were these men saying?" Stern looked over his glasses at Happen and Cor.

"They were talking about a contest between Thujaplid and Grith, and an army will make the loser uninhabitable," Cor said.

"Oh. Oh, dear. Well, blessings and troubles can spill from the same basket." Stern untied his apron, folded it over a box, and pulled his beard up out of his vest. "At least we know why Helter was worried about a 'huge apple lid,' right?" He ruffled Helter's hair fondly.

"Where *is* Thujaplid?" Happen had never seen that name on the atlas at school, but he remembered from studying pre-Eruption history that there had been chaotic times when people fought about religions, cities, countries—even whole continents attacked each other, and places would have different names afterward. Since the post-Eruption famine, there'd been peace and stability throughout Grith. But maybe that was going to change.

"I don't know," Stern said. "But I know someone who does."

"She's going to say it's on a different grith."

"I know it seems unnatural, but I'm inclined to take Ariadne at her word."

"But—"

"And, in fact the very first thing she asked me about was a knife from Thujaplid, a place I've never heard of. Well! I think we should take this news to her right away!"

.  .  .

Dunkler Stern ushered the boys out of his caravard, and walked with them to the assorted services row, Helter bouncing ahead. They found Ariadne sitting by the fire with Nora and Marimba.

"Hello." Ariadne's voice came from Nora, confusing Happen, but then Nora tossed her the talking-box. "You bring me news."

"The boys have been doing some eavesdropping," Dunkler Stern said. "And they heard men talking about Thujaplid, so I thought you would want to know."

"Yes, thank you."

"One of the men had a weird scary voice, and he talked about Dhaigne," Cor said quickly, wanting to be the one to tell her.

"What did he say?"

"He said Osgar was helping them but he's going to get charged with heresy, and on Dhaigne the punishment is starvation, and he was risking that to help the other man and—"

"They said an army was going to come make Grith inhatibable," Helter said.

Dunkler Stern put his hands on Helter's shoulders, pulling him back a step. "Please don't interrupt, Helter."

Ariadne looked back to Cor.

"They said either Thujaplid or Grith would get—"

"It wasn't an army." Happen winced, remembering the strange voice. "The scary voice guy said miners. Dhaignian miners."

"Tell me about the other man," Ariadne said. "Where is he from?"

"He's from Thujaplid," Cor said.

"Are you sure? This is very important. What did he say?"

"It just seemed like he was from there, from what he said." Happen hadn't thought about it, he'd just assumed the deep-voiced man was from Thujaplid. He tried to recall his exact words. "He complained about Osgar being annoying, so we know it's the right Osgar. And they said something about going to Maithea."

"I know!" Cor jumped. "The man said they torture people on Thujaplid for heresy. So he must be from there, right?"

"It certainly adds to the case."

"They were distributing Gracarrai pamphlets," Happen said.

"Yes, and he said the Gracarrai guys weren't going to be happy about it, and they had to get people excited about stealing."

"I think he meant steel, the metal," Happen said. The knife they'd taken from the deputy was steel. The knife Osgar had cut him with was steel. Happen had only just heard about it from Tinker two days ago. Saying the word out loud for the first time left a sour taste in his mouth. "Like the guy back in Pury who tried to get Tinker to make steel weapons . . . oh. That's probably how Osgar got into this."

"Yes, Happen," Ariadne said. "I think you are correct. I just hope it's the same man. This is very helpful information. Can you remember anything else?"

"What's 'miargon'?" Cor asked. "The man said it was time for miargon."

"Oh." Ariadne froze, staring at Cor. "That's the proof right there."

"It is?"

"Of what?" asked Dunkler Stern.

"Well done, Cor," Ariadne said. "You may have helped save the lives of every person and animal on Grith. You've given us a fighting chance anyhow." Cor beamed, and he and Nora did the little celebration ritual she taught him where they each put a hand up in the air and clapped them together. Happen felt ill and confused. Nora, Cor, and even Helter Stern were acting like this was some Spirit Moon prank, like in the haunted house episode in the *Cravey Mysteries*. And if Ariadne was just a crazy witch, then perhaps there was nothing to worry about. But what if she were from another grith, like Dunkler Stern seemed to believe?

"Miargon?" Dunkler Stern asked.

"Based on what I've heard so far, this man could have just been someone familiar with Thujaplid's customs. But because he called it 'my' argon, he must be using it. Thujaplid's air has a higher percentage of a gas called argon. He could survive for a few days here, but he certainly wouldn't enjoy it. He has to supplement somehow . . . Last time I was there, they didn't have the technology to build a portable argon concentrator, although they might by now. Otherwise, he'd have to bring compressed argon in canisters."

"But why? Why are they here?" Dunkler Stern had absent-mindedly gripped Helter's shoulders tight enough to make the boy squirm away.

Ariadne held up a finger. "I must first ask the boys. Where did you hear this conversation? Where are these men right now?"

"They're in row eight of the . . . southeast quadrant, in Tinker's caravard," Happen said. "It sounded like they were settling in for the night."

"Good. I have time for planning. Nora can answer your question, Dunkler."

"I can?"

"I could say that the Dhaignian is trying to help Thujaplid by raising Grith's list ranking, he's brought one of them here, and they are traveling the four continents trying to encourage mining and blacksmithing. But I have planning to do, and I think you will explain it just fine."

"Oh, so they're . . . I get it. They're trying to undo what you did with Gra—er, undo the Gracarrai canon's protective work here. Yes, I can explain that."

"Carefully though, please, Nora." Ariadne turned away from the group and stared into the fire.

Everyone else turned to Nora, and she sighed.

"I'm about ready to turn in, so I'll keep it short. What you need to know is that Ariadne is working to save Grith from the Dhaignians—yes, her own people. The Dhaignians have been around for ages and used up all their own resources, so they travel to other planets, other worlds like Grith, to extract resources to bring home. It's an expensive and lengthy process, so when they choose their next source, it's important they get it right. Apparently, there's no shortage of candidates."

Happen frowned at her 'other griths' nonsense.

She noticed his look and said, "I know, right? Who knew?" which didn't help.

"Anyway," she continued. "They have two main political factions; Ariadne says the names translate roughly into the Berythean terms 'miners' and 'collectors.' The miners, quite sensibly, want to choose planets they know are rich in resources, and are easy to access. But the collectors want to preserve some planets based on other features that might be rare or even unique—within the extent of Dhaignian knowledge, at least. To choose the next place to . . . oh, God, they have some awful word for what they do . . ."

Happen looked up from his boots. "Employ?"

"That's it. You heard him say it, I bet. Picking a planet to 'employ' used to require super long debates, but now they have a system that involves sending scouts to gather local data to feed into a ranking system. The candidate with the highest ranking gets 'employed,' and then they add the next nearest one to the list and rerank them."

"Where does Grith stand in all this?" Dunkler Stern asked.

"Grith's lack of mining activities adds a lot of uncertainty to its resources score. It's mainly what keeps Grith's ranking down, which is why Thujaplid wants to encourage mining here. Personally, I think Grith will survive this round, but if these men succeed in changing Grith's culture without getting caught, maybe not."

"Young lady," he said. "Even beyond the outlandish situation you're describing, the contrast between your relaxed attitude and your alarming words is baffling. Are you not frightened for the future of our home?"

"I'm sorry, Mr. Stern. I am very concerned. Grith is so beautiful. It reminds me of the descriptions of how my home used to be. But Grith is not my home. I'm from another world called Earth, and I feel more optimistic about Grith's future right now than I do about Earth's."

"Oh, my goodness," Stern said. "Is Earth going to be 'employed' by Dhaigne as well?"

"No. Dhaigne is not particularly interested in Earth. Please don't be too alarmed. By tomorrow Ariadne will have a plan. We should all get some rest in case she needs help."

# NINETEEN
## WHEN DEATH ASKS NICELY

> Since the beginning of the Proven Age, the popularity of fortune-tellers has risen dramatically in Berythea. (Reilly, 2046)

Cor thought he was funny, and circled three times on his bedroll like a wolf before going to sleep. Happen wasn't able to take Nora's advice about sleeping. He had so many questions, but Nora was in her tent, Ariadne was planning, and Dunkler Stern had gone back to work.

He parted the black canvas door tentatively, unsure if it was too late, if the Amazing Esmerlia would see him. The large red candle on the table had burned low, but still glowed, so he sat on the chair by the table to wait.

"Come in, Happen," Esmerlia said from the back room. He pushed through the curtains into the warm, smoky room where she stood with her back to him, like before.

"Please, be seated." Her voice didn't crack this time.

"How did you know it was me? Where's the lady with the eye?"

She turned and placed her boot on the low table. "Those are not the questions you came here to ask." The manner with which she said this made Happen feel that if it hadn't already been true, it would have become so upon her saying it.

"No, you're right. I have a new question. I need to know where Ariadne is from."

"Ariadne is one of the women you are traveling with?"

"Yes."

"Happen. You do not want to know if the price of wheat is going to go up, or go down. You do not want to know if the girl at the tavern will ever love you. I *like* your questions. I will help you, and you will pay me tomorrow, or the next day."

"I will. Thanks."

"If you can bring me a hair from this woman's head, I will tell you where she is from."

He slumped. Even if he could quietly borrow her scissors, he doubted that he'd be able to sneak up on Ariadne. "I don't know how I could do that. Is that the only way to find out?"

Esmerlia's dark eyebrows arched. "This woman, she is bald?"

"Oh, no. It's just that she's always wearing this cloak with a big, deep hood. I can't imagine how I could ..."

"Is she awake?"

"Yes, but she's probably busy."

"I see. I understand what it is like to be afraid of someone. But your question is very important, and your fear is not. You must go to her right now, and ask nicely for one hair."

"Right now?" A wave of pressure passed through his head. *Maybe tomorrow?*

"Yes, now. Think of it this way: if someone who looked like death itself asked you for something, you would be glad it was only for a hair."

Happen smiled. He had forgotten about his face paint.

Ariadne sat cross-legged before the fire as if she hadn't moved, but the snapping of a fresh log on the fire proved she was awake. As Happen approached her, something large moved in the shadows behind the chiminea. Large, and low to the ground. He froze. But it was just Marimba prowling about the small yard. He continued over to the fire and sat next to Ariadne, facing the fire.

She set Nora's talking-box on her knee. "You have been to the seer again."

"Yes."

"You returned very quickly. Do you need money?"

"No, that's not it." He took a deep breath. This whole thing would be easier if she wasn't so nice. "I asked her about you."

Ariadne pushed her hood back enough that he could see her face. The stunning blank smoothness below her cheeks glowed in the flickering light, and he caught his breath and looked away, back to the fire. He would never get used to that. Her eyes seemed so kind and familiar, but somehow her lack of a mouth and nose prevented Happen from breathing when he looked at her.

"She provided helpful information about the parade, but I would be surprised if she knows much about me."

"Me too. But I have to try."

"I understand."

Happen felt himself growing tired. He wanted someone else to ask Ariadne for a hair—and then give it to him. Even if Cor were just with him, it would be easier. Maybe.

Tinker had said that it didn't matter if you believed someone's story or not, what mattered was making good decisions. But now Happen needed to know. If Ariadne and Nora were telling the truth, the men in Tinker's caravard had to be stopped somehow. If not, then he just wanted to get his cart and it wouldn't matter what those men were up to. It could be they were playing a joke on the kids they knew were listening. It could be something else he didn't understand, and Tinker would clear it all up tomorrow.

But Esmerlia had said she could tell him where Ariadne was from, and that would make all the difference. He had to ask her for a hair. He had to do it now, she said. Then he remembered again his face paint. He was scary and mysterious. He could do this.

"Ariadne," he said. "May I please have a hair of yours? To give to the seer?"

She turned and faced him then, a hint of amusement in her eyes.

"Yes." She reached into the darkness under her hood. "Why does she want a hair?"

"I asked her where you were from and she said she could answer if she had a hair from you." His hands were shaking as he accepted the shining strand of hair.

"Thank you," he said before hurrying off.

Moonlight illuminated a sign hanging across the front of the tent reading Closed. Had he taken too long? He ducked under the sign, and the curtain parted for him as before, but his passing disturbed wooden wind chimes whose clinking song was muffled as if resting on the canvas wall. The sound was subtle, but very close to his ear, so he startled, spun around, and lost his balance. Only the tiny glowing ember from the wick of the spent candle reoriented him in the darkness of the front room.

"Esmerlia?"

Something rustled in the back of the tent. A moment passed when his breath was the only sound.

"Yes, please come in."

He pushed through to the back room and was surprised by cool, fresh air. Also, Esmerlia had removed her face paint, and changed into trousers and a work shirt. She seemed younger now, close to his age probably.

"I brought the hair," he said, holding it out.

"Great!" She laid it on the table next to an ornately carved wooden box, then carefully placed the corner of the box on the hair, keeping it in place. "Now sit quietly, and I will tell you about Bealsio."

"What's bealsio?"

"*Who* is Bealsio, is the question. And please, I'm trying to recite this story from memory, so just listen, okay?" She took a deep breath and opened the fancy box to reveal a large ball that looked like polished glass on the outside, and ice on the inside.

"Bealsio lived hundreds of years ago among the evergreens of the Anabelis Hills until one day, with an unspeakable act, she incurred a great debt to my family, a debt that remains to this day. The ragged bones of her story have been passed down through many generations, losing clarity, but we know that she died on a day when grith-thunder came to her village.

"Some say she caused the troublesome grith-thunder, and that was how she earned her debt, but others say Grith itself was angry with her, and took her life without harming others in the village. What we do know is that my ancestors began having dreams instructing them to bring her home from a cave near the village and when they found the cave, inside was Bealsio, in the form of a crystal."

The ball sat nestled in a purple velvet pillow. Parts of it were milky, but some parts were clear, with cracks and facets that reflected candlelight deep inside. Happen tried to imagine it lying casually among dirt and rocks in a cave somewhere.

"For generations she served my family, speaking to us through dreams. Then about one hundred years ago now, the religion of Gracarrai took shape and grew. And after Gracarrai foretold the Great Eruption and became the primary religion, we found that it was not safe to advertise, or even own, a crystal formed by Grith.

"We commissioned magnificent glass crystals from a glass-blower in Aeriskenn, and convinced the Gracarrai inspectors that our honest depth-seer business was merely a stage performance based on intuition and the careful observation and manipulation of clients. You can see the Gracarrai seal on this crystal, proving that it is artificial." She turned the ball, and Happen could see the red mark on the smooth surface.

"Oh, okay. So this is not Bealsio," he said, and Esmerlia shook her head. "Why are you telling me this?"

"The night is old, and we have much to do. And look, it is almost time." She took a small sandglass out from under the table. Together they watched the final grains fall into the lower half. "Wait here one moment." She left through the back door.

Happen watched the candle flame weave and jump, dupli-cated in reflection by the sandglass and the fake crystal. She returned with a plain wooden box, her eyes smiling.

"*I* knew you were trustworthy, but Mother required Bealsio's estimation before going any further. And you must give me your word that you will not share our secret with anyone, for any reason. Yes?"

"Uh, which secret?"

"The one I am about to tell you."

"Okay. I will not tell anyone, for any reason."

"We know your intentions are good, but you must also be careful if this subject arises through circumstance. If you were to accidentally lead the Gracarrai to reinvestigate my family, you would be discredited unpleasantly, and I don't want to see that.

"Now. What I told you is true." She put her hand on the plain box, watching him. "And here . . . is Bealsio. My mother was asleep with her and the question of whether we could trust you. We do not use this kind of knowledge for all of our clients, only when we are especially interested in a question. The sleep with Bealsio is . . . not restful."

She closed the fancy box with the fake crystal, put it under the table, then opened the plain box. On a bed of crumpled black fabric sat a translucent green rock clutched in a nest of milky gray rock with many small shiny facets. The green rock reached up out of its nest like a sawn tree stump, but with six precisely edged facets instead of a tree's normal round shape. Candlelight penetrated deep, making the rock glow with a pale, sickly bluish green, and highlighting a set of rich dark green veins like bolt lightning frozen in time.

"It's—she's . . .beautiful."

Esmerlia seemed pleased with his reaction. "Now comes the dangerous part. We have seen your Ariadne, and feel that this is not a question to be taken lightly. Bealsio knows and remembers many things, but for certain kinds of questions, she needs to communicate with other spirits. For this, we must lower her into Grith. Six feet into Grith, for true depth-sight. In the morning, I will know your Ariadne's whole family's history."

*Depth-sight!* Happen didn't know what it was; he only knew it was forbidden under Gracarrai law.

The black canvas floor of the tent was not connected to the walls, but overlapped them, as they were long enough to reach the ground then fold toward the middle of the room. Happen helped Esmerlia move the chairs, then she folded back the floor. There, on the flattened grass, lay a half solan coin.

She unfolded a large piece of gray canvas that revealed a thick bone knife and two pairs of leather gloves. She cut a circle of sod around the coin, and started lifting it out, tearing roots.

Happen was flabbergasted. "We have to dig six feet down here? Now?"

"No, silly, we dug this ages ago. We use several sites at the fair, and we didn't use this one last year, so the grass roots will be a bit of a chore, but the rest is already done."

Still, he hesitated. She looked up at him with a measuring gaze. Her dark wavy hair, freed from the scarf she'd worn earlier, had fallen over one eye, and she tried unsuccessfully to push it back with her elbow before giving in and taking off one of the dirty gloves to push the hair back behind her ear. This small gesture seemed so normal and comfortable that it charmed him and made him want to help her.

"Will you help me dig one foot down, please?" she asked. "It's the only way I can help you."

Happen put on the other pair of gloves and helped her lift out the turf onto the gray canvas. They covered the rest of the canvas with dirt until they found two coiled ropes. Esmerlia handed one of the ropes to Happen.

"Stand like this," she said. "Lean forward, to the right just a bit. Bend your legs." They stood close together over the hole, chins over each other's left shoulders. She smelled like soil, cedar, and something else, something magical he couldn't identify. "Okay, now lift," she whispered in his ear, sending a chill down his spine. They pulled, and after a brief moment of resistance, a section of peeled cedar tree came up past Happen's knee.

"And again. . . Now." As the tree rose, a damp, grithy smell filled the tent, which worried Happen until he remembered that the scented smoke would mask that smell tomorrow.

"Now, it is Bealsio's turn." She wrapped Ariadne's hair around the green rock, and lowered Bealsio down slowly with a length of twine. She unfolded the floor material to cover the hole, and together they replaced the chairs, which Happen noticed would prevent a person from stepping in the hole when positioned just right.

"There. Thanks for your help. I'll send for you in the morning. It will not be early. You may not even consider it morning."

"I—"

"No," she interrupted. "You have many questions, but I must

rest now, while I can. Remember, do not tell anyone, not even your cousin."

Happen tried to sleep. Part of him felt good that Bealsio had said he was trustworthy, and that Esmerlia had said she'd already known it. And that part felt excited about Bealsio being six feet under Grith's surface communicating with other spirits about Ariadne, and wondered what would be discovered about her family history. Another part of him scoffed at his excitement, scorned him for believing Esmerlia's performance, and shamed him for committing heresy. *Thunder! How did it come to that?* He hadn't had time to think enough about what he was doing. But all he'd done was help pull up a buried tree. *Does that count?*

# TWENTY
## NO REENTRY ALLOWED

 Although many aspects of life on Grith seem commensurate with the Middle Ages in Europe, gender roles are much less rigid than one might expect, especially in Berythea. Wage disparity for the same work is rare, though in general, occupations considered "men's work" pay more, and a review of the prominent positions in politics and military forces in one Berythean city (Aeriskenn) listed a majority of men. Prominent positions in health, business, and religion, however, were dominated by women.

Article three of the open circle covenant describes the importance of human variability and warns of the harm resulting from social imposition of binary gender stereotypes upon the human spirit. The idea that the soul is not gendered, and that the temporary assignment of physical sex characteristics during a given lifetime should not impact basic human rights or dignity was not disputed, but seemed to make subjects uncomfortable when queried. (Reilly, 2046)

**W**hen Cor folded back the tent doors, letting in bright light and cooler air, the sun was well above the horizon.

"I got us some breakfast." He handed Happen half a loaf of bread and some cheese wrapped in paper.

"Did you go somewhere last night?" Cor asked through the bread in his mouth.

"Went over to the seer again—but didn't learn anything new."

"Don't you have to have money to even get in there?"

"Told them I'd pay later." Happen bit off a chunk of bread. It was made from wheat, not oats like at home, and was very good.

"Father said not to do that." Cor drank from his waterskin, then wiped his mouth with the back of his hand and frowned at the gray paint smudge that resulted.

Last night's mysteries were rebuilding in Happen's mind, but he focused instead on Tinker. Tinker would know what to do. "Does Nora have enough money to get Tinker in yet?"

Nora, Happen, and Cor approached a security guard at the gate. He held a spear in one hand and the other was idly spinning a short section of rope with a knot and two loops in it. Happen recognized it from an episode of the *Cravey Mysteries* as a hand-cuff knot.

"Just the man I was hoping to find here. Is there some token or pass we can use to get back in, if we go out for a moment?" Nora said.

"No, ma'am. New rule this year. No reentry allowed." His sullen tone countered her cheerfulness.

"Please sir? We just need to deliver a quick message and we'll be right back."

"No, ma'am. A messenger service is available. Addresses in Aeriskenn are free. Elsewhere for a small fee."

"We're just meeting our friend outside the gates."

"No, ma'am. That sort of activity has been abused by the criminal element."

"I assure you we have no criminal intent. Can we just send one of the boys?"

"The boy would not be allowed to reenter. And I assure *you* we don't believe everything said by strangers still wearing Spirit Moon paint."

Happen spoke up. "They just let a man in the other gate."

The guard squinted toward where Happen was pointing. "He's with the textile guild. Don't you recognize the jacket? That's different."

"So . . ." Nora said jingling her coin purse in her pocket. "If we could offer something else . . ."

"No, ma'am," he repeated slowly, as if she were having trouble understanding his words. "The textile guild has an arrangement."

As soon as they were out of earshot, Nora said, "Ugh. They can't all be that pig-headed. Let's try another one." The guard at the south gate was a little nicer about it, but still wouldn't help, even after she jingled her coin purse at him.

"Not from around here, are you?" he asked as if he knew the answer.

"Can you let us look out the gate? If we see our friend we can use the messenger service?"

"Sorry ma'am. Security policy. Can't open the gate unless

you're going out." The guard spun his rope handcuffs around his finger idly.

"Do you have any idea how ridiculous that sounds?" Nora crossed her arms, clenched her fists, and glared at the man.

The guard yawned and glanced up at the sun. "Pretty soon now, my shift will be over."

"What is that supposed to mean?"

"Just saying, is all." He looked at her with an awkward smile.

Nora led the boys away from the gate. "Okay. They're all pig-headed. But still, let's try one more. Third time's the charm, they say. Do they say that here?"

"Who?"

"Never mind. Here he comes."

They returned to find the new guard reprimanding the old one.

". . . I know it's the end of your shift, Garsidge, but you've got to keep sharp, man."

"Sorry, sir," Garsidge said, flustered. "Was a commotion by the north gate. Drew my attention, sir."

"Well, it's been handled. As you should have expected, while you took care of business here. Don't let me find you distracted from your post again or you'll lose it! Dismissed."

Happen didn't think they'd be asking this new guard anything.


"Thank you, sir. Young lady here was wanting directions," Garsidge explained. "Ma'am if you'll follow me, I'll show you the way you were asking about."

Nora hesitated briefly, then followed him down the main road heading east into the fairgrounds, and the boys hurried after. They turned south, down row seven.

"Have to watch out for that one," he said, gesturing back toward the gate. "A real stickler."

"You can show me the way out so I can get—"

He cut her off with furtive gesture, then drew closer and whispered, "Listen, there's a side door I can take you to, but you have to be quiet about it. It costs five solani. You have that?"

She nodded.

"Good. It goes through a red flag row, so you have to leave those two. Can't be seen taking kids that way."

Happen was curious to see if he could find the side door. "They'll have to get to the outer fence somehow. Let's go down to row nine and see if we can watch them go by from there."

The boys weaved impatiently through the crowd on the main road, sauntered casually past the south gate, and headed down row nine, of which only the first three stalls were occupied. Someone crossed near the end of the row, by some caravards. Happen stopped, grabbed Cor's shoulders, and turned to face him.

"What?"

"I think I saw them. Look around me, down at the end of the row. Can you see them?"

"Lower your left shoulder a bit. There, yeah. Looks like they're arguing. He's holding up one finger. And now they've gone behind where I can't see."

"Nice work, Morgone. Let's go." About two thirds of the way down the row, a sign hung on a length of twine strung across the road which read Security. Keep Out. Past the sign, all the stalls were full of large caravards, none of which had signs or labels of any kind.

The boys dashed along the inner fence for the rest of the row until they reached the twine, then slowed, checking each stall before darting across to the next.

"Aaah! Help! Hel—" Nora's voice rang out, and the boys froze.

"Thunder," Happen said. "Go get Ariadne. We need her viser."

"What are you going to do?"

"I don't know, just go! Run!"

Cor ran, hurdling the twine stall separators. A door slammed. Peering around the edge of a caravard, he could see the one at the end of the row shake violently for a moment.

He stepped across the packed gravel in the lane as quietly as he could, and knelt in the grass where he could see down the row, hoping that Cor and Ariadne would come running. Nora's cry for help echoed in his mind. *Why did no one else come?* They were right up against the edge of the southeast quadrant. *Which is the red flag quadrant. That's why.*

He heard some commotion inside the caravard, and Garsidge's voice.

"Now what's a nice young lady like you doing with a steel knife like this, huh? Brought it as a gift, how nice." He chuckled. "It's good to have a spare. Actually, this one's better than mine. Where'd you get this?"

Cor appeared at the end of the row, running back toward Happen, alone.

Without Ariadne's help, Happen couldn't overpower the guard, but he had to help Nora somehow. He looked around for some kind of weapon or some way to distract Garsidge. Maybe Ariadne was just delayed, and would come soon.

A box of tinder and a stack of kindling on the ground next to the chiminea in the yard gave him an idea. He knocked the chiminea aside to expose the bare dirt underneath, took the spare bootlace from his pocket, found three rocks, and formed a ciorcagnal. Cor skidded to a stop as Happen was quietly singing the first verse. He knelt, and joined the song without hesitation. Soon the kindling was crackling.

Happen put his finger to his lips to keep Cor quiet, then motioned to the caravard. He put one burning stick on the edge of a stair on the short ladder below the door. They held other sticks under the floorboards. Nora's voice sounded above, smothered and inarticulate. *She must be gagged, but at least she's alive.*

The floor above them shook, followed by a groan and a growl, then a low whistle and the jingle of coins.

"Lot more than five solani. I'll get a nice ransom for you this time of year." The vehicle shook again, followed by another loud groan. "Gonna have to tie your legs, too. A woman with sleeves like that shouldn't be so strong!"

The flames sputtered on Happen's kindling sticks, so he dashed back to the fire to add more wood and trade his smoldering pieces for burning ones.

"Hold still you burrowing little—" Garsidge said, grunting with exertion. "Thunder! That smoke is . . . grubs and maggots, my caravard!"

Time was running out, so Happen tried to weaken the burning ladder rail by carving it with his knife. A thin piece of the rail came off, but it wasn't enough. He'd pictured Garsidge stepping on the rail and falling through, but what if he didn't? Should he use his knife on the man, or just run for it? Neither seemed like the right thing to do.

Garsidge doused the burning floorboards, causing angry hissing and more smoke. Happen's stomach clenched. He'd be out any moment. In the *Cravey Mysteries*, the villains would get knocked out by a hammer or a falling potted plant or something. He looked for a blunt weapon, maybe a stick of firewood? No, it was split thin to fit into the small chiminea.

But the chiminea itself was a thick, sturdy ceramic. He carried it over by the ladder, on the side where the door opened out, hoping it would screen him from the man's view and give him the second of surprise he'd need.

Cor started a third fire under the floor. Another loud hiss

indicated the guard had doused the second fire. Happen's heart raced. Garsidge would come to the door next. He hoisted the chiminea up to his waist, and supported it with his thigh as cold coals and damp ashes spilled out onto his boots. Angry footsteps stomped inside. The stairs were still burning. He hoped Garsidge would stomp on that top stair and fall through.

The door whipped out, slamming against the caravard wall, and Happen jerked the chiminea up over his head with a grunt. The burning ladder held up under Garsidge's first step and he paused there, scanning the yard. When their eyes met, Garsidge's fierce glare stopped Happen's heart and fixed him in place.

Two quick footsteps hit the floor, and one of Nora's boots caught the guard at the base of his skull. He yelped and fell face-down in the yard, dropping his waterskin. He pushed himself up, bending a knee and shaking his head. Freed from the guard's petrifying glare, Happen stepped forward and swung the chiminea down onto Garsidge's head.

It sounded like dropping a rotten apple on the kitchen floor.

He let go of the chiminea and it rolled away. A gratifying feeling of power surged up through his arms and shoulders. He and Cor stared at the collapsed man for a moment. *What have I done?* His action felt terribly excessive, and the fading physical contentment was appalling. The prone body at his feet refused to stir.

"You okay?" Cor asked.

Happen tried to clear his mind, but a bad feeling followed him closely, like a bee that would not go away.

"Get his waterskin, put out the fire." Happen jumped up into the caravard, burning his left hand on the top of the stairs.

Nora was looking at a pamphlet on a shelf next to her knife and coin purse. One of her boots lay on the wet floor by some rope. Happen picked up the knife and she turned, presenting her bound wrists. As soon as he'd cut the rope, she grunted urgently, pulling at a knot at the back of her neck.

"Oh, got it. Hold still." He cut into the knot, and she tore it off and gasped.

Charred wood hissed as Cor poured water on the smoldering doorway. Nora put her other boot back on and took her knife from Happen's hand.

"You okay? Look like you just saw a ghost." She pocketed her coin purse not waiting for him to answer. "And this," she continued, folding and pocketing the pamphlet she'd been looking at, "could be useful evidence for us. It's what Osgar's helping to distribute."

They jumped down and stepped around the body. A steel knife like the one from Thujaplid lay next to Garsidge's motionless hand.

"Oh, look, Happen! A gift for me." Nora bent down to pick up the knife. "How nice."

Out of the corner of his eye, he saw some movement across the road.

"Can't move legsss," moaned Garsidge, drawing Happen's eyes back, relieved the man wasn't dead. Garsidge drooled bloody spittle, slurring half-formed words. A sense of panic rose inside Happen, as the responsibility for what he had done buzzed spastically inside him, like a bee trapped under a drinking glass. He looked up, but the row was empty and still.

Nora led the boys toward the gap in the fence leading to row eight, but just before they reached it, a singsong voice called out:

"Hap-pen, I'm tell-ing!" It was a young woman's voice with a childish tone, taunting. "I saw what you did, Happen."

It was Mistine's voice, saying words he'd heard her say many times before, but years ago, as children.

# TWENTY-ONE

# A CHANCE IN THE SUN

 According to Gracarrai, every being on Grith has three spiritual components roughly akin to what Earth-folk would call mind, body, and spirit. All living beings engage in a cycle wherein each of these components gradually gains prominence over the others. Peoples' cycle takes them further from balance than animals, so that the mind and body gain a much higher degree of prominence during lifetime, and the spirit dominates more in between lifetimes. For this reason, artistic representations of animal souls retain roughly the same appearance whether alive or dead, but people souls adopt a much more featureless appearance, often represented in art by skulls or skeletons. (Reilly, 2046)

E verything was dark and buzzing except for the fence post Happen had just vomited on.

"That's Osgar's sister's voice," Cor said quietly to Nora.

Dark, buzzing, and the fence post pushed into his forehead as he leaned into it.

Cor pulled at him. "Come on, Hap. We have to get out of here."

They kept to the fence, passing rows until they reached the south gate road that ran through the fairgrounds and down to the river. Happen followed Nora and Cor through the busy crowd in a daze. He couldn't think about what he'd done, or what it meant that he'd been seen doing it. His mind filled with a protective fog that prevented connections from being made. The falling rotten apple sound replayed sporadically in his mind, causing him to flinch every once in a while for no apparent reason. People stared as he passed.

At the river they turned upstream to the bathing area to wash off their face paint. On the way back to camp, they stopped at a food row where Nora bought bread, cheese, and apples.

Ariadne still hadn't returned, but Tinker was sleeping on Cor's bedroll in the big tent. Just seeing Tinker helped Happen feel like there might be a chance for him to survive the day, somehow.

"Oh, god, after all that," Nora said when she saw him. "Well, don't let's wake him. I bet he needs the sleep."

Happen found a note from Esmerlia on his bedroll, saying he should come see her, but he was shaking and tired and wanted to eat first. Even before eating, he wanted to put his own clothes back on. Now that Osgar knew he was here, there was no point in the disguise. And, though it probably wouldn't matter, he wanted to look as different as possible from how he'd looked that morning.

It would be best to leave the fair before they came to arrest him, but then what would he do? He did feel a bit better in his own clothes, and folded up the borrowed clothes to hide under his bedroll. He should at least talk to Tinker before going anywhere. Sitting down with Cor and Nora by the cold chiminea, he ate. The wheat bread was warm and he savored each bite. Whether he ended up a fugitive or in the work prison, he would miss good food.

"Did you try shouting, or calling for her?" Nora asked Cor. She was still trying to figure out why Cor hadn't been able to bring Ariadne when they'd needed her.

"I called some, but I didn't want to . . . I didn't want anyone calling security," Cor answered. "I didn't know what to do."

"I hope she's okay. I'll ask the neighbors if they've seen her."

"Did she tell you what her plan was for today?" Cor asked.

"Yes," Nora said. "She had Dunkler Stern send a message to the Gracarrai authority in Aeriskenn, saying that Osgar is helping someone distribute heretic pamphlets using a forged seal. Oh, why didn't I think of it before? She must be with Stern. But still it's odd she didn't leave a message. I'll go check there."

Happen parted the black canvas tent door as he entered the front room of Esmerlia's tent. Squinting against the light pouring in around Happen, her mouth full of scrambled eggs, she motioned for him to be quiet. She wore a plain frock, not her seer outfit, and looked pale and tired, like a campfire under a bright sun.

"Mother's working," she whispered, once she could speak again. "But I wanted to tell you what I learned. Soon as I'm done eating, we can sit outside and talk."

She motioned for him to take a chair out, and she soon followed, carrying the other chair and a black ceramic goblet that produced a wisp of steam and a spicy aroma. Once outside, she reached under the tent and pulled out two strings, a thick red one and a thin black one, and wrapped each around a different finger.

"Bealsio had quite a night trying to track down your mysterious friend." She patted his knee. "We could not find any trace of her history anywhere at all." She sipped from her goblet, her dark brown eyes peering over its rim. In the sunlight he noticed the freckles strewn across her face from cheek to cheek like a band of clustered stars.

"Does that mean she's lying when she says she's been to Berythea before?" *I knew it!*

"Maybe." Her voice sounded pale and tired as well, a little rough, and unadorned with the drama of a seer. "But you should know that Bealsio is not limited by rivers and oceans. She communicates with all of the spirits who have ever been. She communicates with every mountain and island on Grith. Every spirit exists outside of time and only rarely is given a body that lives in a time, when they rise up from Grith for their chance in the sun, and this body is unique."

"I know about spirits."

She frowned at him. "Not everybody does. What you probably don't know is everything that comes from or through this body is marked with that uniqueness. And using an example of that mark, such as a hair, Bealsio can know not just the story of how that body is related in families, but also where the body has lived. It can take mesters for a body to discernibly mark its place with the dust of dry skin, fallen hairs, and dripped sweat; but as food and water move through a person's digestive system, it's only a matter of days in one place before the spirits can know the person is there. And we found no trace at all." She gestured with her free hand to show the nothingness they found.

"So, she's not from Inirthea?" Happen felt bewildered by Esmerlia's speech. He had always suspected that Ariadne was from Inirthea because it was the most remote and exotic place he could think of.

"According to Bealsio, not only is she not from Inirthea, she's not from *Grith*. And even if she magically appeared out of a cloudless sky, she's never stayed in one place long enough to leave a mark, either that or she always poops in rivers, if she even exists at all."

"You don't think she *exists*?"

"Shhhh. Settle down, I didn't say that, Bealsio did. I've seen her. I know she exists. I also know that Bealsio has never been wrong. She's found missing people on other continents. She's found minute tin deposits on the far side of the Antlers." She emptied her goblet, then set it down. "Did this Ariadne say she was from Inirthea?"

"No, that was my guess. She says she's from a different world called Dhaigne, and she doesn't poop in rivers or anywhere else because all she eats is firelight."

Esmerlia gaped at him. "Bury me in dreams, you're serious."

"That's not even the troublesome part."

"Oh, thunder. There goes the black string. You have to go right now. Can you come back in five waves?"

"Maybe. My uncle arrived today. He was—"

She interrupted him with a hand on his arm.

"Go, quick. Come back when you can."


Happen dashed over to the back of Ariadne's wagon, where he took out a coil of thin rope and tied it onto a rail to look busy, sneaking glances at Esmerlia's tent, curious to see why he was sent away. Esmerlia took one of the chairs when she went in. He untied the rope slowly. Maybe Bealsio's report proved Ariadne was telling the truth about a different world. *But if that was true, that would mean the other—*

An older man stepped out of the tent, looked left and right up the road as Happen tied and untied another knot. He was dressed in the beige linen and dark green leather uniform of the fair security, with four purple stripes on his shoulder. He looked up and down the row as if he owned it, then headed east with a purpose.

Tinker's rowdy laugh echoed off the fence, and Happen found him and Cor talking in the tent.

"Well, Hap it sounds like you've had an eventful fair so far?" Tinker said. "You've been a cow, a skeleton, a hero . . ."

"I wasn't a hero."

"But you had the idea to burn the caravard," Cor said. "I don't think I've read *that* in any *Cravey* mystery."

"No." He'd been so upset about hurting that man and hearing Mistine's voice, he'd forgotten about burning the caravard. "I guess that was a good idea I had."

"It was. And Cor said he'd never seen a fire called so quickly."

"How did you get in?" Happen asked. "Did Ariadne get you the money somehow?" He was hoping maybe Ariadne could keep him from going to prison, like she had for Tinker.

"No, I haven't seen her. I heard about some folks whose wagon broke down, and rode out to help them fix it, and in return they got me in. I saved some money, but didn't get a lot of sleep, so let's go get some coffee. This is the one time of the year I get to drink coffee." He turned to leave.

"Wait," Happen said. "I guess Cor didn't tell you. Mistine's going to tell security that I attacked one of the guards. I can't just go walk around." Telling Tinker about it, he felt the panic rising again. "I was wearing different clothes and the face paint, but she or Osgar will point me out. I . . . I don't want to go to the work prison."

"Whoa, there, Hap." Tinker put a hand on Happen's shoulder. "Take a deep breath. No one's coming for you. Based on what Cor tells me, Osgar is in no position to accuse anyone of anything. If he did, we'd explain that he's working for the heretics, and because you know he's working for the heretics, he's trying to frame you. It sounds complicated, I know, but the important thing is that you're going to be fine."

"Really?" Happen searched Tinker's face. There was no doubt in his expression.

"Yes. I know you feel bad about hurting that man, but you have to remember, *he* created the situation. Normally, we'd prefer you stop a crime by alerting the authorities instead of burning things and hurting people, but when the authorities are the ones committing the crime, you're kind of on your own there, and you do what you have to do. It's not your fault he got hurt." Tinker ruffled Happen's hair playfully. "Let's go get some coffee. It's time for you to start enjoying the fair."

Before they could leave camp, Ariadne and Nora returned.

"Hello, Tinker," Ariadne said. "I was so glad to hear that you'd arrived."

"Me too," Tinker replied with a grin.

"I have arranged a meeting for you with a security official, a friend of my contact, Dunkler Stern. We have evidence for you to present to incriminate the man who stole your vehicles. The meeting should result in fair security restoring your caravard and cart back to your family. There may even be time to get them moved to stalls in a more suitable location within the fair."

"Thank you, Ariadne. That was fast. When is this meeting?"

"Dunkler Stern awaits you at his wagon now, but I need to speak with you about a couple of complicating details you should be aware of before you go."

"Oh, well, that sounds pleasant," Tinker said. "Can you tell me about it over a cup of coffee and something like breakfast?"

Happen had no appetite for either breakfast or complicating details. He wasn't going to the work prison, and Tinker was there to take care of getting his cart back.

A sign hanging across the front of Esmerlia's tent read Closed. She'd told him to come back, but that had been a while ago. Had he taken too long? He ducked under the sign, and parted the black canvas door, and his passing disturbed the wind chimes that clinked in their muffled way against the canvas. The front room was empty except for the table and one chair.

"Esmerlia?" he called, but there was no answer. He stood there a moment, then decided to enjoy the fair, as Tinker had suggested. He headed toward the food rows to look for Cor and Helter, but at the crossroad Nora caught up to him, grabbed his elbow, and steered him down row eight.

"I want to show you something," she said in a grim voice he could barely hear above the surrounding bustle. She held on to his left arm with both hands, a little too hard, and he allowed himself to be led to the stall of a seamstress. An elderly woman was hunched over a treadle-driven sewing machine, but stopped her work to speak to them.

"Are you needing some alterations? Something made special?" She smiled, accentuating the deep wrinkles on her face. "A wedding dress perhaps?"

"Oh, no thank you, ma'am," Nora said. "I just wanted to show my friend the wonderful kittens you have here."

"Oh, yes, that's fine." She gestured past her cart to the yard behind it. "Darling creatures they are. Last litter of the season. You won't find so many this young, as late in the year as it is." A short fence made of wooden stakes and canvas set off a section of the yard, with several kittens cuddled in a heap in the corner. "The little dears are sleeping now. Someone was here playing with them earlier, tired them out, poor things."

"Yes, that was my aunt."

"I thought you looked familiar. Did you change your hair?"

"I did," Nora said, as if excited that someone noticed. "You're very observant. Which reminds me, I wanted to ask you earlier, but didn't get a chance. My aunt was supposed to be resting, by doctor's orders, and she snuck out when my back was turned. Do you remember how long she was here? I need to know how long she'd been gone, approximately."

"Oh, yes, I remember her. Very quiet, shy. And generous, too. Left me a solan even though she didn't have to. Guess she felt she ought because she was here so long. About two bells, I'd guess, maybe a bit more."

"Thank you for your help," Nora said. "We won't keep you from your work any longer."

"That's quite all right, young lady. What do you think, young sir? Your girl might like a kitten of her own? Or perhaps to gain the favor of her aunt?"

"Maybe on the way out. I'll consider it and let you know."

"Don't wait too long, every moment is precious now. More than you know." The old woman cackled. Nora pulled him away and farther along row eight.

"Thanks for coming with me," she said, holding his arm with one hand now. "I wanted you to know that when I went to Dunkler Stern's to find Ariadne, she wasn't there. I asked the neighbors and eventually found her playing with those kittens." Nora said this as if he would find it devastating. It was unfortunate that Ariadne hadn't been available to help when Nora had been taken by Garsidge, but Happen didn't want to think about that anymore. Tinker was in, Nora was okay, and Osgar couldn't turn him in. He wanted to forget about all that now.

"It was all I could do not to strangle her," Nora continued when Happen didn't respond. "She's supposed to be looking out for me. Her cat fascination is a serious problem. She even had her viser out when she thought no one was looking, making them chase after a glowing red dot on the ground!"

She seemed to want something from him, but he didn't know

what. "I'm sorry, Nora. I don't want to think about what happened this morning anymore. I don't know what else to say."

"Well think about this then, mister," Nora said with an anger that Happen didn't understand. "That eccentric old lady is all that stands between Grith and total destruction." She turned and stomped off, leaving Happen standing agape.

# TWENTY-TWO

# FIXING HIS HUNGRY GAZE

> In contrast to the rugged adventure tales popular in Berythean literature, or the intricately plotted romantic comedies from Maithea, Berythean drama is more realistic and humorous, often satirical in tone. It portrays a broad range of characters, each of whom exhibits one or more defining traits that provide their motivation and perspective. (Reilly, 2046)

Happen wandered the rows in the northwest quadrant, too wrapped up in his thoughts to pay much attention to the fair. Idly perusing a tailor's wares, he passed a mirror and remembered he was wearing his own clothes again. He put his hands in his pockets and there was Esmerlia's handkerchief. The feel of it filled him with a curious warmth and longing.

He reversed direction and strode back the way he'd come to see if Esmerlia had returned, but after a few steps he stopped, stunned motionless. Mistine was standing next to a puppet-maker's signpost, looking right at him. Close enough he could have knocked a quince off her shoulder with a slung rock like Odais did at the Trial of the Green Princess.

He hadn't seen her in over a year, but she hadn't changed much. Still skinny, sharp featured, and confident. She wore a gloating smirk that said, "*I got here before you.*"

She said something to the security guard standing next to her, and they both started walking toward him.

Happen's mother always said Tinker's optimism was going to get somebody in trouble.

He spun and hurried off, skipping laterally to pass small groups of fair-browsers, scattering gravel. Heart racing, he looked over his shoulder. They were walking after him, not running, and he'd already gained some distance—wham! He was stopped as if he'd walked into a tree. He expected a security guard, but it was just a large man who snarled at him to watch his step, so he took a deep breath and walked. It was too crowded for running anyway. He didn't know if Tinker would still be at Stern's, or if Ariadne might have returned to camp. Ariadne had the viser. He would go there.

Turning right at the crossroad, a lane opened in the crowd allowing him to trot ahead, so he stopped at row six to look back. His pursuers turned also, but the lane had been filled by a slow cart, and they would have to go around against the traffic or wait. A strange sound rose up out of the general clamor then, across the busy road beyond his sight. He'd never heard the sound before, but somehow knew exactly what it was—a couple hundred people all laughing at the same time. His mother had said there was a theater group that put on plays. There must be a stage nearby with a comedy. It turned out he'd been correct when he told her he wouldn't have the time or inclination to watch a play.

Resuming his way along the north gate road, he dodged past

a boy carrying a live goose, then looked ahead and saw Osgar for the first time since the Davoura Gorge bridge. He stood in the lane, about two rows away, with a stack of pamphlets in one hand and gesturing with the other as he talked to someone wearing a hat. Osgar hadn't seen him, though. Happen could turn onto row seven before reaching him. He slowed his walk to blend in.

A thin whistle sliced through him. It was Mistine doing that thing with her thumbs and a blade of grass. Just about everyone except Happen could do it, so it could have been anyone, but he just knew it was her. His heart clenched for a moment. That had been the exact phrase she used, that last time they met behind the school's barn. "It could have been anyone."

Sure enough, Osgar looked up and scanned the road in front of him, fixing his hungry gaze on Happen. Arriving at row seven, Happen found a tull and cart had stopped in the way, and people crowded around it, trying to get by in both directions. He wouldn't be able to get through in time, even if he pushed rudely. He thought about crawling underneath the cart, but he remembered his father saying to never go behind a stranger's tull.

The crowd on the south side of the road was thick, but penetrable. *Better than a hoof to the head—barely.* At least they were laughing again. Happen went that way.

He found spaces between groups of people, all facing west toward a large stage, but progress was slow. He turned and saw a disturbance in the crowd behind him as Osgar pushed his way in, but Happen thought he had enough of a head start that he could make it across the crowd to the south gate road before Osgar caught up with him. What would Osgar do if he caught up? Maybe since he was going to be charged with heresy, a murder charge wouldn't matter now? More likely, Tinker was just wrong, and Osgar would turn him in. That's why Mistine had the security guard with her. They would arrest him and send him to the work prison. Unless he could get away somehow.

Once off the road, Happen heard a loud voice coming from the stage.

". . . and the farmer said, 'I'd pay three geese for that!'" The audience roared in laughter. Hurrying anxiously through the crowd, Happen bumped into a small child he hadn't seen, and apologized to her angry mother.

"The very next day the farmer was taken to the library . . ."

"Pardon me," Happen said as he passed in front of a short man, blocking his view.

"Get your ass out of my way," the man hissed at him, spiking Happen's heart rate for a few blinks as he hurried on.

". . . with a loud shout of surprise, the farmer said, 'This place would feed my goats for a year.'"

Again the audience laughed at the farmer's expense. Happen found a narrow aisle behind a tall family, and scooted along quickly for a moment, passing through the center of the crowd.

"The librarian offered to find him a book about feeding goats instead, and the farmer said, 'I'd pay three geese for that!' Thank you, thank you. I'm Sivver the Storyteller, thanks for listening."

Osgar cut in front of the surly short man, gaining ground. Happen's politeness and discomfort with people made him slower. He could hear people cursing Osgar behind him, and see the movement of people ahead on the road. *Almost there.* The uniform of a security guard drew his eye, and there was Mistine, talking to a guard on the side of the road, right in his path. At a slim opening to his right Happen plunged into the thicker crowd in the direction of the stage. He took off his father's hat and crouched low, hoping Osgar wouldn't see he had changed directions.

"Please give a warm welcome to . . . Yularkan the Miraculous!"

Sweat and perfume mingled with applause and muttered curses as Happen squeezed his way through and around people, uncomfortably close. He tried to be small and thin and quick. Osgar was behind him, generating louder curses. A security guard at the front of the stage on the near side scanned the crowd, noticing the disturbance. Happen veered toward the center.

"Thank you, thank you. Prepare to be amazed as I show you that what you see . . . cannot be believed, and what you know . . . is merely illusion. I will perform stunning feats with no hidden accomplices, no trained tricksters, only volunteers just like you."

The security guard paced slowly along between the stage and the crowd, moving toward the center, looking in Happen's direction. Happen glanced back, and all the faces were looking up at the stage except for Osgar, who was just about ten steps back and looking right at him with the satisfied smile of a hunter who's cornered his prey.

"For my first miracle, I will make a person disappear before your open and astonished eyes! Are there any doubters out there? Who among you would like to volunteer?"

Since it was almost as tall as he was, Happen thought he might be able to duck under the stage, but he'd have to get closer see if it was an accessible option. He could probably lose the tall guard that way. He stepped around a large man who smelled of ale and sweat, and saw another security guard at the other side of the stage. But if he could go under . . .

"You there, working your way up to the front. Excellent, let the brave young man through . . ." People turned to look for the volunteer and Happen stepped through a narrow aisle that appeared, but then stopped abruptly at the edge of the crowd. The front of the stage was blocked by stout planks. There was no escape.

.  .  .

A hand gripped his shoulder, fingers digging in.

"Hey, kid," Osgar said. "Let's talk."

"Hey there, unhand my volunteer! Security!" The performer hopped down off the stage, glaring over Happen's shoulder. The grip released. The security guard glared over Happen's other shoulder. He tried to squeeze between the two men. The performer turned his bushy eyebrows down to peer hungrily at him and grabbed him by the arm, and Happen understood then that *he* was the volunteer.

Desperately, he considered calling out for Osgar, but it was too late. Yularkan the Miraculous dragged him up a narrow stair to the stage, then turned him and held him firmly on display. Hundreds of faces gawked at him.

Beads of sweat rolled down his back, then something important drained out of him and his knees buckled, but Yularkan pinned him against his body with his right arm, and stuck a waterskin in his mouth with his other hand. A sweet liquid filled his mouth and he swallowed. It tasted a bit like the way coffee smelled, and although it was cool, it made a warm sensation in his stomach. After another mouthful, the draining sensation stopped, and he was standing again.

"Look at me, not them, it's easier," Yularkan muttered. He wore a ridiculously tall top hat that seemed like it ought to fall off and a ruffled collar that covered his neck and throat. An impossibly long mustache stuck out in two elaborate curls.

"What's your name, son?" Yularkan's voice boomed out toward the audience. He took his arm from around Happen's shoulder, holding Happen's forearm instead, and pulled him back a step away from the audience.

"Hap—" he said, but stopped himself. He shouldn't tell his real name. He started to say instead "it happens that my name is Odais," but the performer was already booming at the crowd.

"Hap here has bravely stepped up before all of you for an

encounter with the Miraculous magic of Yularkan. Who knows where he'll go from here?"

A security guard's head snapped toward the stage when Happen's name was spoken.

"Tell me, Hap," Yularkan said, keeping his firm grip on Happen's forearm. "Tell me why you were so excited to come up here to volunteer. Do you aim to disprove my miraculous magical powers?" Hundreds of people stared at him, waiting for him to say something, wondering what kind of idiot would volunteer at a magic show. Should he point out Osgar now? Say he was trying to escape from a heretic who was trying to kill him?

"I didn't actually intend to volunteer," Happen said, searching for Osgar's face among the strangers. Osgar was gone, and both guards watched Happen intently. *They're thinking about their pal Garsidge.* There wasn't going to be any way to escape what he'd done. "But I don't think I'd mind disappearing right about now."

Some people in the front row started laughing. Yularkan repeated Happen's words with his booming voice, and the whole audience roared with laughter.

"And you think I'm just the man for the job?"

"If you could do a quick and thorough job of it," Happen said. "I'd pay three geese for that."

The audience roared again, clapping and whistling, when Yularkan repeated Happen's request for their benefit.

"Very well, then!" Yularkan went on. "I'll get right to it. I wish to demonstrate that I take good care of my volunteers."

"Onna coun' o' three, follow the yellow chalk line," Yularkan murmured without moving his lips. A line of pale yellow powder angled away from him to the back of the stage, where a narrow gap split the wall. On the other side of the gap the wall had what looked like part of the floor painted on it at an angle, making it look farther back than it was. The painted part looked wrong from where Happen stood, but he hadn't noticed it at all when standing in the audience. He could not see what awaited him beyond the gap.

"And now!" Yularkan boomed, waving his left arm. "Walk sideways," he murmured. The w's sounded funny, but Happen knew what to do.

"With a little help from my handkerchief . . . One!" Yularkan pulled a white handkerchief out of his pocket, but it just kept coming out until it was a long sheet that he waved about with a flourish while the audience laughed.

"And my other handkerchief . . . Two!" he shook his right arm and a green cloth appeared in his hand, but when he pulled it with his left hand it just kept coming out of his sleeve.

"And my other other handkerchief . . . Three!" Happen started walking sideways toward the gap as Yularkan pulled a long blue sheet out of his hat. The performer danced about, waving his sheets in front of Happen as he walked sideways along the yellow line, until finally all those staring faces were gone, and he was standing on a ledge behind the wall. A steep and narrow stairway led to the ground, hidden from the road by a large tent, the first in a row of four standing behind the stage. Happen didn't see anyone at the bottom of the stairs. He was free.

He hurried down the rickety steps, ready to run, but hoping to just saunter across the thirty feet of trampled grass, then blend into the crowd on the road. The traffic was thick enough to hide him, but not so busy he couldn't hurry through back to camp, back to Ariadne. Or maybe Esmerlia could hide him. All he had to do was get to the road without being seen. He peeked cautiously around the edge of the tent.

## TWENTY-THREE
## I WILL SURVIVE THIS

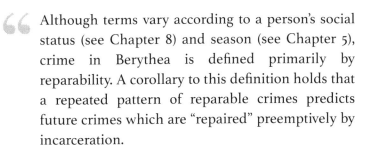 Although terms vary according to a person's social status (see Chapter 8) and season (see Chapter 5), crime in Berythea is defined primarily by reparability. A corollary to this definition holds that a repeated pattern of reparable crimes predicts future crimes which are "repaired" preemptively by incarceration.

The punishment for minor irreparable crimes is a temporary assignment to work for the community and is usually administered by the local church. Major crimes result in permanent assignment to work for the king. (Reilly, 2046)

The side of the tent was clear, but he was being watched, he felt it on the back of his neck. Peripherally, he'd noticed the space under the stage as he reached the bottom of the stair, but now he ducked and shaded his eyes with a hand to get a better look. But for posts and some litter, it seemed clear, until a slight movement in the deeper shadow by the front of the stage drew his eye. A shoulder, moving like it was attached to someone breathing heavily, leaned on a post. Then the shoulder moved, and Osgar peered around the post, facing Happen, and their eyes met.

Osgar raised a finger to his lips, signaling him to be quiet, then glanced fearfully toward the open south side of the stage. Happen only gradually understood that Osgar was not waiting to ambush him, and was no longer chasing him, but was himself hiding.

Happen sank into a crouch, matching Osgar's posture.

Three security guards, with their tall black boots and tan pants, stopped at the side of the shoulder-high stage, apparently looking through a stack of papers.

A crash and a shout from the north side of the stage flushed Happen with fear.

Another shout: "He's under the stage!"

Osgar sprang toward him. Happen sprinted to the road. A cry of pain from Osgar told Happen they'd caught him. He didn't look back.

A whistle shrilled behind him, and dashing left and then quickly right he passed two large groups of people that would surely block the lane for a while. Some space opened up before him and he gathered momentum as he neared the crossroad. Two guards on either side saw him too late, and he tumbled under a passing wagon and popped out the other side triumphantly in stride, entering his camp's row in the northwest quadrant when a guard he hadn't seen tackled him. The force of the blow from the stout man's shoulder stopped him from breathing for a moment, and he collapsed in the gravel, gasping and dizzy.

"It's not safe, running like that in the fair," the guard said amiably. "Makes me curious to find out what's chasing you."

Happen, still trying to catch his breath, spit out some dirt. After the wagon finished rolling through the intersection, the other guards surrounded him. Passersby glared at him reproachfully.

"Happen Fell?" A portly guard said as he caught up, breathing hard.

Coming from this man, here, his name sounded out of place, as if it could belong to someone else.

"Happen Fell. You're wanted at the commissioner's office for questioning." He took a document from his messenger bag, handed it to Happen. "Here's your summons."

"But I haven't done anything wrong."

"You're not accused of anything. We just need to talk to you."

"You always say that when . . ." Happen couldn't finish what he was saying. He didn't want to work for the king, never to be seen again.

"Look, I don't know what kind of lurid crime serials find their way to whatever miserable backwater you're from, but you've got the wrong idea. Still, I have a job to do, so we can cuff you and drag you screaming through the fair, or you can walk quietly with us, and no one will think anything of it. It's up to you."

Happen needed time to think. He stood up and walked with them. They headed south, back past the stage. He looked for Osgar behind the stage, but he wasn't there.

"If you're looking for your friend hiding under the stage, we've already caught him and brought him in."

"Good," Happen said. "He's not my friend."


They turned east on the south gate road, walking at an almost leisurely pace.

He considered trying to call out for Ariadne. With her viser, she could get him out of this. The guard had implied that he'd allow Happen to scream, and if he called for Ariadne while being dragged through the fairgrounds, she might hear him, or Cor or Nora or one of the Sterns might hear him. *But what if all that other stuff was true?* The whole preposterous 'Thujaplid against Grith with Dhaignian miners to destroy the losers' tale would be entirely dismissible if it weren't for Esmerlia and her possibly broken crystal, and the fact that he hadn't seen Ariadne eat, or even seen any way for her to eat, and Marimba's docility, and the viser, and that voice in Tinker's caravard . . .

*What if it were true?* If it was true and Ariadne attempted to rescue him, then her Dhaignian adversary with the awful voice would find out where she was, as would everybody else. Ariadne had said earlier that they couldn't risk another public attack.

Yet Ariadne seemed like the sort of person who might do what was needed to save him, or any stray cat, for that matter, and worry about the consequences for Grith after. Not exactly the person he wanted to rely upon to save the world. Nora had said as much.

But it wasn't like he could send a pigeon to Dhaigne requesting a replacement scout. What would he say?

 Dear Dhaigne (if you even exist), The scout you sent seems dedicated to saving Grith. She cares about the animals especially, and even individual ones, not just animals in general. But supposedly all of Grith is in danger now, and she's been distracted by one cougar, and then by two boys, and then by a box of kittens in a seamstress's stall. She loses sight of the big picture. Please send a replacement at your earliest convenience. Sincerely, Happen Fell

Wouldn't his father be amused by the idea of Happen requesting a less distractible scout to represent their interests? But would a different scout even do that? Ariadne said that she was drawn to Grith by the large population of wild cats. Another scout might not care enough to risk interfering with the meddling of a rogue scout or desperate rival world.

Happen walked with his head down, kicking at the occasional weed growing up through the gravel. A numbness kept his mind from panicking, but also from doing anything but wandering aimlessly imagining courier pigeons flying beyond the stars. *This is not how you're supposed to feel when you are being taken away to die. You're never going to see your family again.* An image in his mind of his mother's sadness harnessed his purpose to the proverbial tull. Odais wouldn't just walk along peacefully to the work prison. Odais got captured at least once in every book; so often, in fact, he developed a protocol that Happen could follow: attitude, vigilance, assessment, plan, execute. First, he needed a better attitude. *I will survive this, I'm just not sure how yet.* Second, he started walking with his head up. Maybe he would see something or someone that could help. Then he assessed the obstacles: four guards surrounded him, the one with the messenger bag in front setting the pace, one following, and one on either side. Time remaining: maybe five waves or so? The flags atop the commissioner's office building were visible, but still a way off along a crowded road.

Before he finished the assessment routine, however, the guard behind him grabbed his right arm and wrenched it up behind his back, and the guard on his left cinched his wrists together with rope.

"Happen Fell, I'm issuing you a citation for resisting summons." The guard behind him spoke in his ear. "Bugs like you get stupider the closer we get to the office, so I'm taking precautions."

The guard on his right held a knotted canvas scarf like the one Garsidge had used to gag Nora.

"You want this, or will you take care of it yourself?"

Happen did not respond. The guard behind pushed him, and

he stepped forward automatically. He decided that he'd walk after the next push, though. The protocol would be easier if he wasn't being dragged, vigilance especially. *I will survive this.* The guard behind pushed again, and Happen walked with his head up, and began his reassessment.

At a large single-story building, they led him through a hallway to a large room, where a man with two purple stripes on his shoulder sat behind a desk reading through a stack of documents. At another, smaller desk by a door on the east wall, two young men sat with quills, ink jars, and stacks of paper.

"This that kid with the stolen cart?" the older man asked the guards. He had thin gray hair and oval eyeglasses.

"Yes, sir."

He shuffled through his stack until he found the one he was looking for, and then frowned at it.

"Your uncle says the defendant attacked you on the road and stole your cart. Is that true?" Happen expected the man to be angry, but this man seemed bored. Also, he was talking about Osgar, not Garsidge.

"Yes," Happen answered. "Sir."

"Do you have any evidence of the alleged attack?"

Happen's mind spun. *Maybe this isn't about Garsidge?* The man was asking about Osgar's attack at the Davoura Gorge. Could a sprained ankle be evidence? The colorful bruising was mostly covered with that stuff Ariadne called "adhesive tape." How could he explain that?

"Look we don't have all day, either you have evidence or you don't."

"My cousin was there, too."

"We've heard his testimony. You need to provide something tangible: a wound that matches your story, some information you wouldn't otherwise have if you hadn't been attacked, something of that nature."

"I guess not." He couldn't show them the tape without exposing Ariadne.

"In the absence of physical evidence, we consider the word of status. Do you own property?"

"My family has a farm on the Irelian peninsula. Does that count?"

"What is your season?"

Happen hesitated, looking at his feet. "Springing, sir."

"Do you have a third-party employer?"

"What's a third—"

"Someone not related to you."

"No."

"No evidence, no plaintiff status. Case dismissed."

TWENTY-FOUR

## ENTERING THE FAIR

> "Springing" children's earnings belong to their parents. "Summerings" are expected to begin saving for a home by learning a trade, although often apprenticeships start with a person's Summering Task. (Reilly, 2046)

⌐

"But it's *my* cart!" Happen protested.

The man sighed and raised his eyebrows at the guard standing behind Happen, who was removing the handcuff rope.

"Sorry, sir. Someone put a spoke in his wheel and spun it. Had to cite and restrain him just to get him here."

"He's a friend of Stern's. Give him to Macel for release assistance."

One of the young men at the side desk stood up, wincing as his wooden chair scraped loudly on the floor. "Thank you, sir," he said briskly. "Right this way, Mr. Fell." He smiled at Happen. Happen hesitated. He'd been ready to argue, but the man's comment about being a friend of Stern's, and Macel's manner, confused him, and so he let himself be led out the side door.

Macel was the youngest security guard he'd met. He led Happen out into the bright sunlight and past an irrigated lawn on a path of raked gravel.

"I imagine you are eager to get to your cart. I must apologize for the disarray you'll find it in. Given the circumstances, the Gracarrai inspectors had to give it a thorough search. This is your first trade fair, isn't it?"

"Y-yes." Happen felt an odd mixture of relief and embarrassment, and still wasn't sure what his legal status was. "Do you know where my uncle is?"

"He is assisting the Gracarrai inspectors with their ongoing investigation." Macel led him onto the south gate road. "But if there's anything you need, Mr. Fell, I can help. It's my first fair, too, but I've learned quite a lot about how things are done around here."

Happen couldn't imagine any of them calling him 'Mr. Fell' if they knew what he'd done to Garsidge. "Do you know how long that will take, I mean how long till he'll be done helping them?"

"Well, assuming he's not actually connected with the Blacksmith Conspiracy, and was just an unlucky victim, it shouldn't take long at all."

"The Blacksmith Conspiracy?"

"Oh, that's not anything real, I mean official. It's just what we clerks have been calling the troubles we've been having in Aeriskenn lately. The Gracarrai inspectors think there's a connection between the fires in the city and the activity here of the heretics that were using your uncle's caravard. Ah! Here's your row. Southeast quadrant, row eight. We've added your name to the wait list for a spot in one of the more reputable quadrants, but it's not likely one will become available soon."

"You're really taking me to my cart," Happen said. "I thought . . . it felt like I'd lost my trial?"

"Your trial? Oh! That. That wasn't about you. That trial was for a man named Osgar Tallowey. You knew him, didn't you?"

"Oh. Yes, I . . ." Happen trailed off. *'Knew him'?* "That was his trial? It seemed short. Was there more to it before I got there? Trials I've read about—"

"There wasn't a lot more to it," Macel said. "The fair administration has more pressing concerns right now than a stolen cart. The highway patrol would take it more seriously, but the trade fair is its own jurisdiction. Besides, from what I've heard, the evidence against Mr. Tallowey is much stronger in his other case, and though technically that's not supposed to matter, sometimes it does."

"What other case?"

"I can't talk about the details. All I can say is that he is assisting the Gracarrai inspectors with their ongoing investigation of the Blacksmith Conspiracy. I can say that my personal opinion is that he is likely to be involved with that for a considerably longer time than your uncle. I don't think you'll have any more trouble from him."

They arrived at Happen's cart in stall seven. A security guard was posted between stall seven and stall nine next door, where Tinker's caravard was parked. Macel greeted him cheerfully, and introduced Happen, but the older man just said, "Proceed."

Half of Happen's wares had been tossed in a pile next to his cart. He looked at the mess and sighed happily, his body beginning to relax. It seemed that he wasn't going to the work prison after all, and here was his cart. He figured he'd better start with an inventory to find out what was missing.

"Boy, they weren't all that careful, were they?" Macel said. "Would you like help putting things back to rights? You should probably start with an inventory to see if anything's missing."

"Don't you have to go back to work?"

"Not if I'm helping a vendor," Macel said, sounding like he'd rather not return to that dim office just yet. "Here. I'll sort the things on the ground into organized piles for you. Okay?"

"Sure, thanks." Happen was starting to breathe easier. He was a vendor, not a criminal. Someone a person might call 'mister' and hold the door for. It straightened his back a bit. He looked into the cart and found that the floorboard over the hidden compartment was askew, but the bag of coins was still there. The inspectors hadn't moved everything.

He rearranged oat flour bags until he found the one with the single yellow thread at the top. It was on the left side, over the axle, where he'd put it. When he picked it up and held it right, he could feel the two glass phials of elk antler powder inside with the flour. He'd expected to be either devastated or intensely relieved, but he just felt tired and a little glad. He wasn't surprised after that when his inventory revealed that nothing was missing. Perhaps Osgar was getting paid to distribute pamphlets, and hadn't had time to sell oat flour and wild onions.

Once they'd returned everything to the cart, Macel took his leave, assuring Happen that the guard would remain in place until Tinker returned. Happen felt as if he needed to start trading right away, to make sure everything got done. But standing there looking at his packed cart he realized he had no idea how to get started. Did he need to make a sign? What would it say?

His wares didn't really fit in any particular category, although most of it was food, it wasn't the sort of food like in the food row, that you could eat right away, except for the elk jerky. He frowned, dug a piece of elk jerky out of a bag, and slouched against the cart. He chewed off a bite and the sharp flavor awoke his senses. He was famished.

He'd have to eat before doing anything else. When he stopped worrying about trading or making a sign, he realized that he could go, just walk to the food row, without disguise or fear, and buy some food. The bag of coins, though, was in the secret box covered with all that stuff he'd just put back in the cart. His fair money! He'd been so concerned about the wares that he'd forgotten all about it. He opened the bow cabinet, and his bow and quiver were still there, and there, at the bottom of the quiver, was his leather wallet. He had thirty-five solani in Berythean bank notes.

Ariadne had spent one hundred solani getting him and Cor into the fair, because of the high price of having extra people in the wagon. He couldn't pay that back, not now anyway, so he might as well pick up a *Sirreltis Seasonal* to start catching up on the *Cravey Mysteries*. And get some food. Maybe he'd find Cor in the food rows.

He was a vendor now, and he had money in his pocket. Turning onto the south gate road, he felt like he was entering the fair for the first time.

PART THREE

# THE BEGINNING OF THE STORY

# TWENTY-FIVE
## LOUDER THAN TEN FIDDLES

> Gracarrai teaches that spirits return to life as Grithings, not as people of a specific nation, and this seems to have reduced feelings of nationalism and xenophobia. With few exceptions, the most notable being the dark green hair prevalent in Eastern Inirthea, visible racial characteristics are subtle, and immigrants are usually well-tolerated in Berythea.
>
> Other nations occasionally exhibit resentment toward Berythea at varying levels of intensity. Some Maithean scholars predict that increase in international trade will lead to more conflict in the future. (Reilly, 2046)

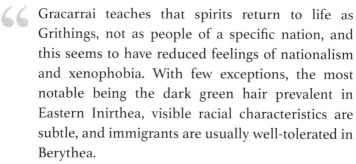

Happen walked through the administrative offices on his way to the food rows, hoping to see Tinker. The purple, tan, and pale green flag of the fair tossed in a fitful breeze atop each building, just above the simpler blue and green Berythean flag. Messenger boys and girls in gray uniforms dashed along the loose gravel paths that led through the green lawns to the doors of each office, but Tinker was not among them. He stopped at the exchange office to trade his solani in for fair script, and wondered what to eat as he set out on the north gate road. A woman with a covered basket and hair like his mother caught his gaze as she passed by and smiled. Happen circled a juggler working in the middle of the road, and paused to watch as a ball of string, a tull's horn, an apple, and a knife looped in a weaving pattern, the horn and knife spinning hypnotically. The juggler winked at Happen and took a bite of the apple as it looped by. It was time to eat.

He chose a food row that he hadn't been down yet, and approached a seafood vendor. Remembering his mother's wishes, he asked for lusks boiled in wine.

"Green or red wine? Is this a late lunch or an early dinner?"

"Um, this isn't—I mean, I don't want to get drunk . . ."

"Oh, no need to worry about that, young man," the vendor said with a lilting Maithean accent. "The lusks are boiled alive, so they get a little drunk on their way, but you will not, I am sure."

"I'll try whatever you recommend."

"Here, try the red. It's my favorite. If you don't like it, come back and I will give you the green for free. But you will like it, I think."

Nearby, a few tables and benches were arranged by a small stage. He was disappointed, after circling them, to find no open spaces for him to sit. With so many people walking up and down the row, sitting on the ground seemed a poor choice. At the end of the last bench, he felt the stare of a grim-looking burly man with painted arms and copper rings in his ears, and started away down the row, when he heard a shout behind him.

"Make room! Every one of you push right just a cheek! Arrrr, you aren't that skinny!" A small space appeared on the end of the bench next to the man, and Happen sat.

"Thank you, sir."

"I was a country lad at my first fair once, too, you know."

He was about to ask the man how he could tell, but was distracted by a yelp of pain coming from the stage. A woman carried a small bowl from one musician to the next, while another bandaged a bloody cut on the ear of one. Each musician spat into the bowl, then its bearer poured something into it from a small pouch and used a pestle to mash it up.

"What are they doing?" Happen asked his neighbor.

"It was loud here last night," the man said as if it explained everything, but he seemed to notice that Happen was still confused. "It was a different sort of band, and I guess they didn't care, or couldn't pay to amplify."

Happen watched, still mystified, as the woman took the mortar and pestle to each of the musicians, dipped her finger into the bowl, and smeared a dark brown paste onto the bridge of each fiddle. With the pestle, she dabbed a bit into each of their mouths. Happen didn't want to seem ignorant, but somehow people seemed to know it was his first fair anyway, so he asked quietly, "What do you mean, amplify?"

"Oh, sorry—I thought . . ." The man looked almost as embarrassed as Happen felt. "Doesn't your town have a mayor speech?"

Happen knew that Pury's mayor gave a speech at the end of the harvest each year, and town school children would be expected to attend like everyone else, but the connection to music eluded him. "Y-yes, Pury does," he stammered. "But I don't go to the town school."

"Of course. That makes sense. If you've never seen it, it's probably a bit confusing. There's three parts to it. First they take something from each member of the band, and one of them has to give a tiny piece of ear. Second they have to buy powdered carpina tree root. I've heard endless debates about which of these two steps is most expensive."

The musicians tuned their instruments as the woman with

the mortar and pestle in her hands stood on the stage with eyes closed and spoke inaudible words.

"And third they have to have someone who knows what they're doing mix it up right and apply it right and all that."

Happen was about to ask the man how it worked, but then the music started, much louder than Tinker's fiddle. Louder than ten fiddles.

A simple melody came from a fiddle played by a tall woman with the impossibly straight, dark green hair of an Inirthean. Another fiddler joined her, also Inirthean, providing a background rhythm. The third player held a larger fiddle cradled in his bushy gray beard. This one had a deeper tone, adding depth and a melancholy feel to the rhythm. A skinny young woman not much older than Happen sat behind what looked like an even larger fiddle, but it stood on its end on the low stage and she played it vertically. She touched a string with her bow and pulled out a rich, deep note that Happen could feel in his stomach.

She increased the tempo then, and the others stopped. Happen closed his eyes. He felt the young woman's instrument build a world of rolling hills, then the others began anew, joining with an intricately interwoven melody. He listened to the first fiddle, following the notes until he felt like a swallow flying over the rolling hills; traveling, but thrilling in flight, not progress. The second fiddle flew alongside, sparkling, exuberant, and their paths tangled like ivy, then separated and soared, rising and falling over the hills as if they dared not stray too high. The third instrument followed the upright one more closely, but occasionally leaped after the dashing swallows, frolicsome and coltish.

When the song ended, he opened his eyes and sat stunned for a moment.

"Don't forget to eat," the man next to him said with a knowing grin.

Even in their open seashells, the pale, quarter-moon shaped lusks looked more like dumplings than sea creatures, resting among chopped carrots and celery, and awash in a thin red broth speckled with bits of some green plant. It was hard to imagine them as either alive or drunk. They felt strange in his mouth, but tasted wonderful.

The music continued, and reached inside him, and led his heart into movement: sometimes soaring like a bird, other times leaping and resting in turns like a salmon climbing rapids upstream. After a few lively tunes, they played a slower, sad song that coaxed the sun languidly down for the night. Although Happen was enjoying the music, the westering sun reminded him that he was running out of reading time. When the song ended, he asked the man next to him where he could buy *The Sirreltis Seasonal.*

The stationers' row was choked with traffic, and Happen hopped from foot to foot, trying to find openings between the slow-moving people in front of him. Bumping up against the wide backs of three large men with tall hats and suspenders, he accepted the pace, and looked about as he walked. A carved wooden sign depicting a tiger and a raven reading a book together caught his attention, and he stopped at U. Paraceltiga, Bookseller.

The bookseller's caravard was in a wide stall, like Dunkler Stern's, with a bench and a stepping-stone path. Each stone featured a mosaic of tile pieces, colored like tiger stripes, and the caravard wall had a painted tiger reading a large book. The door was ajar, so he ventured in. Indirect light soaked in through hidden openings in the top of the room, revealing walls lined with bookshelves, and more books than he'd ever seen. A raven croaked as he stepped into the room. It perched on the gnarled and weathered stump of a small tree in a corner. Happen stopped, and he and the raven looked at each other.

"Hello," Happen said.

The raven cocked its head. A bookshelf at the back rolled slowly into the room, rumbling on low wheels, and a woman stepped out from behind it.

"Welcome." She had short black hair and wore a long yellow shirt over black pants and boots. "Can I help you find something?"

"I . . ." He hadn't planned what to say. He didn't expect that he'd be able to buy anything. The truth was that he loved books and wanted to be near them, but he couldn't just say that, could he? "Do you have any books about Odais?"

"Oh, yes," she said. "I have just the thing for a young man interested in adventure." She led him to a shelf where she pulled out a book and handed it to him. It was covered in leather, not hard paper like the books at home, and smelled like new boots. The writing on the cover was stamped into the leather, then painted with copper: *The Odais Chronicles*, book one, *Youth into Adventure*. He opened it gently. On the first page of chapter one he found an intricately drawn picture of Odais as a young man standing on a ridge overlooking his home city, Eldgya. The text was clear and elegant:

*One.*

*"Where are you going, little one?" Oldis said to his only son Odais. "That axe is much too big for you."*

Happen sighed. "It's beautiful," he said, handing it back to the woman. "Much nicer than mine."

"I see," she said. "Which *Odais Chronicles* books do you already have?"

"I have all four," he admitted. "But I was wondering if there were other books about him, or other books that might be similar," he added quickly.

"All four?" She smiled. "Did someone tell you that the series ends after book four?"

"After the Troll War he gets married and has children. My parents said that meant no more adventures."

"It is a common misconception. After the first four books came out every other year, and the author didn't publish another for fourteen years, most people assume the series ended. But there is a new book." She took one off the shelf and handed it to him. *The Odais Chronicles*, book five, *Knowledge into Wisdom*. It had a hard paper cover like his books. He opened it gently. A small picture before chapter one showed a bearded man holding a staff with a curiously shaped rock affixed to its top.

*One.*

*From the first day that Oddiver started learning to play the trollbone flute his father had carved for him, strange feelings seeped into his mind like an unwholesome mist. He killed a toad for no reason. He tripped his brother on the cobblestone street and laughed at the younger boy's bloodied knees.*

Happen tore his mind from the page. This book was not his. *Yet.* "How much does this cost?" he asked hopelessly.

"Twenty-nine solani," the bookseller said.

"Oh!" He had expected it would be more. He actually had thirty-two at that very moment. "I have that."

"Great. Would you like a nice bookmark to go with it?"

"Hold on a moment," he said. If he bought this book with his fair money, he wouldn't be able to pay Ariadne for getting him into the fair. Tinker would say that he couldn't be expected to pay the extra cost of a fair guest—that was Ariadne's decision. But he should at least reimburse her the amount that he would have paid if his cart had not been stolen—twenty solani.

If she was really from another world, though, Berythean money would mean nothing to her. Surely, she wouldn't care about Happen's twenty solani. But then the story about Dhaignian miners possibly coming to Grith to destroy it could be true. He sighed, looking at the beautiful book in his hands, and tapped its spine a few times. He did not know what to believe.

He also wanted to pay Esmerlia, to show himself worthy of her trust. She had been right after all, when she foretold that Happen would pay her in the next day or two.

"I see in your eyes that this will become a goal for you," the bookseller said, gently removing the book from his hands and returning it to the shelf. "As for similar books, there is nothing recent that compares. There are some older stories. Long, grim tales told in old-fashioned language, that probably inspired the Odais works, but those would be more expensive, not less. Feel free to browse, though. Please excuse me to light the lamp for the evening." She procured a short stepladder from under a table and climbed up to light one of the oil lamps hanging from the ceiling.

Frustrated, he shoved his hands in his pockets, and took a last look at *Knowledge into Wisdom*, snug in its place next to the familiar title of book four, *Conflict into Confluence*. Oddiver was Odais's oldest son. *What was that troll-bone flute doing to him?* The raven croaked as Happen descended the stair to the twilit stepping stones below.

With his hands in his pockets, he found Tinker's dice on one side, and Esmerlia's handkerchief on the other. The stationers' row was still slow-moving, so he brought the handkerchief to his nose as he walked. Breathing her scent from the dark red cloth, he felt certain that he wanted to pay her as soon as possible, so he headed that way, thinking again how nice it was not to be worried about being seen. Osgar was going to the work prison, not him. That thought alone made him hum a cheerful tune. He stopped at a newsstand to pick up a *Sirreltis Seasonal*. He wanted to read the Cravey series in order, so he asked for last winter's edition, and got all four for a discount.

As he approached stall fifteen on row nine in the northwest quadrant, he looked at the cover of the winter edition, glancing up now and then to make sure he didn't bump into anyone or walk too far. Headlines about a trade dispute with Maithea, a shipwreck off Eyrakenn, and something about Aeriskenn tax policy . . . *There!* In the lower left corner, in small letters: *Cravey Mysteries*: "A Spandrel's Luck", page 59.

"Eyes up, kid."

Happen stopped uncomfortably close to a security guard, and saw that he was just about to pass NW 9-15.

"Right." Happen smiled sheepishly and backed up a step. "Thank you, sir." He turned and stepped quickly past the cart and into the big tent to get his gear. The camp was empty except for the cat, sleeping in her cage. He added his new reading material to his pack, and rolled up his bedroll. The borrowed clothes lay, folded untidily, on the flattened grass where his bedroll had been. *Ugh. What do I do with those?* He stared at them, feeling accused all over again by their presence. He couldn't decide between returning them now, or stuffing them into his pack to either hide them somewhere or return them later. He ended up doing what he wanted to do all along, which was pretend he hadn't seen them.

As he left the camp, hoping a visit to Esmerlia would restore his good spirits, he stopped short next to the wagon. That same guard, the one he'd almost bumped into, was still there, looking straight at him as if he hadn't moved the whole time Happen was packing.

## TWENTY-SIX

## SUMMONED A THUNDERING DEMON

> Powerful witches and clerics have a duty to expel demons, although occasionally they become inhabited by demons themselves, and then are likely to summon more. Berythean demons are spirits that can inhabit the mind or the body of a living person. When an illness lingers, medical care is deemed insufficient, and a patient will seek spiritual aid.
>
> Legends tell of witches who could conjure a temporary body for a demon to effect harm to living people (see Appendix D). (Reilly, 2046)

The security guard looked up and down the row, and then back at Happen, but stayed in place, as if posted to keep an eye on their stall. He watched a group of people as they walked by. Happen's frozen indecision was interrupted by the arrival of two figures in deeply hooded cloaks. Happen figured he could spare a few moments to trade news with them. Before he followed them back into the camp, he looked back into the lane, but the guard was gone.

Ariadne pulled her hood back and lit the fire she'd prepared earlier in the chiminea. Nora pulled her hood off, and ushered Happen back into the tent.

"Do you know anything about that guard that was out there?" she whispered.

"No. Just that he'd been there a while, and he left right after you got here."

"Ariadne totally bought into your silly idea that two hooded cloaks are a reasonable disguise, but it makes me nervous. What was he doing?"

Boots stomped on gravel, and several bowmen appeared in the rising firelight on both sides of the camp, arrows nocked. The older man Happen had seen leaving Esmerlia's that afternoon, the one with four purple stripes on his shoulder, stepped in between the tents, another bowman at his side.

"All right, everyone stay calm and you won't get hurt." He puffed out his chest, put his hands on his hips, and surveyed the camp with a sneer. Nothing else moved except the fire behind Ariadne noisily consuming kindling as it grew. "I'm Commander Hagadier. Which one of you is the witch who carries her voice in her pocket?"

Ariadne and Nora looked at each other. It took Happen a few blinks to realize that the firelight behind her was keeping the commander from seeing Ariadne's face. Why won't she tell him? Happen wanted this trouble to end quickly and quietly so he could get back to his cart and start the new Cravey episode.

"We can't shoot you until you resist, but we can shoot your little pet here, if you don't come clean."

Nora took a tentative step toward Ariadne, and Happen saw the talking-box in Nora's hand. If Ariadne said anything, they'd think it was Nora speaking.

"Uh-uh. Don't, missy. Stay right where you are," Hagadier

commanded. The bowman next to him was very close to Nora, and drew his bow. She froze, and the image of that sharp arrowhead ripping through Nora ripped through Happen's mind too fast for him to stop his imagination. He winced and forced his eyes from the point, back to the talking-box.

"Venacer!" The commander barked. "The cat. On my order. Last chance ladies."

One of the other bowmen drew and took aim at Marimba, who had awoken and was watching calmly. Happen saw his last chance to help before Ariadne got out her viser and deep-Grith opened up. Keeping his movements calm, he quickly took the talking-box from Nora and carried it to Ariadne.

"Hey, kid! No, hold fire! Kid, stop right—"

Happen could feel Ariadne's voice as it boomed from his hand, louder than he'd ever heard it, speaking as he reached toward her.

"I am . . ." As soon as she saw she had their attention, she used her normal sound level. " . . . the witch who carries my voice. But sometimes it gets away from me for a moment. I apologize for the delayed response."

"You're under arrest for various crimes committed at Anfelis Printers of Aeriskenn on Harvest Mester 3rd to full, and for printing and distributing material to promote the heresies of mining and blacksmithing."

While the commander was speaking, Happen slunk slowly back toward the big tent, hoping to fade unnoticed into a dark corner.

Ariadne responded forcefully. "I was sixteen leagues south of Aeriskenn on the morning of 3rd to full."

The commander, however, was not conversing with her, but giving orders to his captain. "Take those two into custody, dispose of the cat, clear the stall for reissue."

Happen and Nora both dove into the big tent and hid behind Marimba's cage, where they watched Ariadne through the bars.

Venacer drew his bow and released an arrow but Ariadne had her viser in hand and shot the arrow out of the air in mid-flight with a flash of unnatural green light. More arrows flew, and thin beams of green light stabbed the night like lightning bolts. Marimba hissed and snarled as a ball of red light scorched the grass in the yard, then hit the pile of firewood next to the chiminea. Smoke billowed up. Then, Ariadne stepped forward through the smoke brandishing a long varanid skeleton with glowing green eyes and red teeth, and everything stopped. *Oh dear Grith, she summoned a demon.*

All was quiet and still, except for the drifting smoke and some firelight.

"Please, Commander," Ariadne said. "Please stop attacking us. I'll be happy to answer any questions you have, if we can agree on a few things first."

A few remaining wisps of smoke trailed through the camp. The green eyes of the varanid skull dimmed, and the red light in the teeth faded out entirely, as if the demon was trying to appear less threatening.

"Sir?" Ariadne called.

Commander Hagadier appeared at the front of the wagon looking pale, and Happen marveled at his bravery. "W-we can't have this, uh, this kind of commotion," he stammered. "People will be too frightened to stay. I must make a very public arrest."

"Yes, I understand, but we have to agree on three conditions first."

The commander shifted his weight awkwardly. "I will consider your terms."

"The first," she said. "Concerns your men. Any whose vision has been impaired will improve with time and rest, but those with burns need immediate medical treatment. You must see to that right away. If you do not attack again, there will be no further injuries."

She paused and waited for him to understand that he'd been

issued an order. Once he'd called his captain and passed the order on, she continued.

"Part of my responsibility here is to protect this cat and my assistant, Nora. Like me, they are not dangerous if you leave them alone. See to it that no one is allowed to enter this site except for Nora and the boy named Happen Fell."

"And the third?"

"I must speak privately with the highest-ranking Gracarrai official on site as soon as possible."

Hagadier appeared to consider the terms, and although Happen imagined he must be quite relieved, he did not show it. "If I can arrange these things, you'll confess to the charges and come to trial peacefully?"

"I am eager to begin."

Ariadne shook the skeleton and it seemed to get sucked up into its skull, bones rattling as it folded itself up and disappeared under her robe. She walked to the tent, handed Nora a brown canvas bag, told her and Marimba to take care of each other, and said she'd be back soon. Then she was gone.

Happen leaned against the cage and breathed. The fire burned cheerfully in the chiminea as if the yard hadn't just been full of flying arrows and witch spells and a thundering varanid demon. As his heart slowed down, Happen felt again the desire to be with his cart and his uncle, maybe sit by the fire and read for a while. But the cage was shaking.

Nora shouted angrily in some other language and cried, collapsed against the cage. He remembered now that she had been angry last time he'd seen her, and Ariadne's arrest hadn't helped. Marimba padded over to her and reached a paw through the bars of the cage to rest it on Nora's lap.

Happen knew he should comfort her somehow, too, but he didn't want to stay in a tent with an angry woman. He remembered Aunt Nazellen and cringed. She had been angry quite often when he was young. She could be nice and warm sometimes, but was mostly angry and scary. He shouldered his pack with his new quarterlies, and turned to go, but stopped first and glanced over at Nora.

She was still crying softly, and Marimba was watching him. It looked as if Marimba had one eyebrow cocked at him, as if asking him a question, asking if he was really going to leave Nora while she was crying. *That's just my imagination, cats don't have eyebrows. Or do they?* He couldn't tell in this light.

"Do cats have eyebrows?" he said out loud.

"What?"

"Do cats have eyebrows. The way Marimba was looking at me, I thought maybe she did, but I can't really—"

"Happen," Nora interrupted. "Eyebrows?" She said this in such a sad voice. He remembered their time traveling together, and how she cut Cor's hair, and how she crashed into him to get him out of the cow parade. If he left now he might not ever see her again. In the books a man in this situation would offer a handkerchief. The only one he had was Esmerlia's, but it smelled like her and he didn't want to give it up.

"Are you . . . okay?" he asked. She looked up then, over at him. He half expected she would tell him to go away. It *was* a dumb question he'd asked, now that he thought about it.

"We were so close," she said, sniffling. "Stern hired a kid to keep track of the other scout. He and his friend are leaving tonight. She was going to get the Gracarrai to deal with it or something. We'd be safe. But now she's been arrested . . ." She moved Marimba's paw from her lap and pulled a handkerchief out of her pocket. "And I know, I know she practically invented Gracarrai, and they'll listen to her eventually, but still, I'm . . . I'm scared. If she doesn't come back . . ."

Happen turned back to face her, and knelt by the cage. "She . . . invented? . . .Gracarrai?"

Nora looked at him as if she'd forgotten he was there. "If something goes wrong and she doesn't come back, I'm...I don't know how I'll get back. Just when I thought the bastard was gone and we could forget about him."

"Nora, we are safer now. You can't deny now that she's a witch. She may be an eccentric old lady, but she's also dangerous."

"Wait. You've seen her fight before. What's different now?"

"Oh, I don't know." He put his hands on his hips and glared at her. "Maybe summoning a demon in the middle of a trade fair!"

Nora actually smiled for a moment. "Oh, that. She showed it to me once when you and Cor weren't around, said she might have to scare the locals if things got out of hand . . . wanted me to know about it." She leaned against the cage and patted Marimba's arm where it reached through the bars.

"She *showed it* to you?"

"She called it her staff. She has a skull of some kind of burrowing lizard they're supposed to be afraid of."

"A varanid. Ugh. She's been carrying around a real varanid skull?"

"Yes, and the staff part is this telescoping tube. She sticks it on the end of the viser and fits it into the skull to make the lights. The tube is only a foot long, but she pushed a button and shook it and it opened up to be taller than her, and one of the sections had these things that splayed out like ribs. She mentioned some witch legend—"

"I know that one! There's a traveler in *The Odais Chronicles* who tells about that witch. She goes around with a varanid skeleton blinding people. Mother said it was a character taken from older stories, which is one of the things she likes about the Odais books. There's a new one that just came out. I saw it at—"

"Happen."

"Sorry. It's a fake, not a demon. I get it."

"Happen, do you realize you and Cor are the only Grithings

who know anything about me, who even know that I'm here? Can you even imagine what that might be like? This 'rogue scout' character with his argon-huffing friend has broken Dhaignian law already, how do I know he won't break it again and kill Ariadne, and maybe me, too? I knew coming to Grith wouldn't be easy the whole time, but not like this. This is not what it was supposed to be like." She was working herself up to crying again, and Marimba raised her head and nuzzled Nora's arm.

"Oh, you silly cat," she said affectionately, patting Marimba more. "Can you believe this? Marimba is taking Ariadne's instructions very seriously. She's never given me the time of day before."

"The time of day?"

"Oh, sorry. It's an idiomatic expression from Earth. It means she hasn't paid attention to me."

"Do you miss . . . Earth?"

"No, not really. Earth isn't all that nice anymore. Grith is much nicer actually. But I do miss my family, and going to college. I miss the feeling of belonging I get with my people." She sighed. "But for now, you and Cor and Marimba and my Dhaignian mentor who can't stay out of trouble; you're my people."

"Okay. Good. Speaking of our people, I'm thinking that Tinker and Cor are probably worried about me. I haven't been back to our new site for a couple bells now, and I haven't seen either of them since Tinker's breakfast."

"Oh, right. You got your cart back. That's wonderful."

It did not sound like she thought it was wonderful, but Happen decided it was just because she was distraught and confused. She even said Ariadne invented Gracarrai, even though it had been around for over a hundred years. She probably meant that Ariadne had a strong affinity for Gracarrai or something. He felt like there was something else he should do for her before leaving, but he didn't know what it was, and he really wanted to see Tinker and Cor. "I'll come back. Yes. I'll come see you tomorrow morning. Okay?"

"Yes, thanks. And thanks for talking with me. It really does help a lot."

"Sure. Bye."


Happen walked past several guards and Esmerlia's tent. He would have liked to stop and see her but what he'd told Nora was true, he needed to see his people. He continued past the cacophonous bustle of the food rows, and then past the quiet administration buildings, only some of which were dark. A damp, cool breeze came up from the river. It smelled like frogs and face paint, and he shivered and hoped that Tinker and Cor had a fire going.

But Tinker's caravard was dark, the yard and chiminea were dark, and the guard was a different one from the one who had been there before. He had not seen Tinker, and didn't even know who Cor was.

# TWENTY-SEVEN

## THE TROUBLESOME PART

> While many Berytheans continue to ranch and
> farm, the economy increasingly revolves around
> newer technological endeavors created by advances
> in ceramic engineering. Ceramics serve many
> purposes that would be fulfilled by steel on Earth,
> such as knives and ball bearings. Aeriskenn in
> particular is known as the global leader in
> innovation and excellence in the field, likely as a
> result of proximity to Tascretis Lake, the site of a
> large secondary clay deposit. (Reilly, 2046)

H appen decided to look for Cor, starting with Dunkler
Stern's caravard. He returned to the northwest quadrant, found the purple caravard of Dunkler Stern's
Magical Tileworks, and knocked on the door. The ladder was
already down, and Stern answered with none of the reticence he
displayed at their first visit.

"Come in, young worthy! How are you? Would you like some

tea?" The old man wobbled and weaved as he puttered about, preparing a tray with tea and cookies. Happen hadn't planned on staying, but Stern was so excited to have company that it was hard to say no. The warm stove and the smell of cookies made it even harder, but Happen tried.

"Actually, sir, I'm just looking for my cousin. I think he might be with your grandson Helter . . ."

"Yes, yes, of course. I'll send for him. Sit down. Will you put out the white flag? There's a good man. I have been eager for news. One hears rumors throughout a workday at the fair, but I've been too busy to pursue actual information. Have you and your uncle been restored to your belongings?"

"Yes, sir, at least I have. Uncle Tinker is still assisting the Gracarrai inspectors with their investigation."

"Oh dear, at this late bell? They must have themselves quite a puzzle. I'm quite sure, though, that he'll be joining you shortly. There you are. A little whiskey in your tea?"

"No, thank you. Also, I should tell—"

"Well, I don't mind if I do. What a blissfully productive day I've had." A knock came on the door in a short, repeated pattern. "Oh, bother. Would you . . ."

"Sure, I'll get it." Happen opened the door to see the boy in the gray uniform.

"Oh, hello," the errand boy said. "I've a message for Mr. Stern."

"Come in, young worthy! How are you? Would you like some tea?"

"Brought you this message, sir," the boy said, bringing in an envelope for Stern. "And what can I get for you, sir?"

"For me?" Stern stared at the boy.

"Your white flag is out, sir."

"Oh, yes, yes," Stern said, looking at Happen. "Oh, yes. Fetch Helter for me, please. Tell him that his friend, um . . ."

"Cor," Happen said.

"Yes, tell him we want his friend Cor."

"Yes, sir."

"Well, then," Stern said, once Happen had settled down with his tea. "Where were we?"

"I can wait quietly, sir, if you'd like to read your message. And then I really should tell you—"

"Oh, yes. Thank you." Stern adjusted his eyeglasses, and slid the lamp closer. Happen helped himself to a cookie. It was still a little warm in the middle, and delicious, with lots of cinnamon and small chunks of apple. Stern sighed and chuckled over his note.

"Oh, my goodness, such a wonderful day this is. You've no idea the difference." Stern sat back, then leaned over the note on his desk like a hungry man with a plate of food. "Here, listen to this: 'Dear Mr. Stern, blah, blah, we appreciate the fast tilework, much faster than previous years, blah, blah, blah, every edge perfect, almost no damage. It really does seem magical. Yours truly, etcetera.'"

"That's very nice, sir."

"You have no idea what I'm talking about, do you?"

"I guess not, sir."

"Let me show you." Stern tucked his beard under his vest, and motioned Happen to his desk. "This . . ." He held up a sharp piece of flint and a straight edge made of bone. ". . . is how other tile cutters work."

He took a square blue tile from a stack on his desk, scored a straight line on it, then scored the line again, and a third time, each pass making a grating screech that hurt Happen's teeth. He placed the tile over a thin dowel in a wooden tray, and pushed down on it until the tile snapped. Stern showed Happen the two pieces of tile, and a slight chip missing from one corner.

"That's a good cut, with those tools, because the flint is sharp.

As it dulls, each cut will take longer and have more faults. Now this," he said proudly, lifting the lid of the trunk he used as a bench and pulling out a device unlike anything Happen had ever seen. "Is why my customers call my work magical." He placed a new tile on a tray inside the device, pulled a handle that dragged something across the tile, making a solid scratching noise that left Happen's teeth alone, and then he pushed down on the handle, snapping the tile. He showed Happen the flawless cut.

"Much faster, a perfect cut almost every time to a premeasured size, and most importantly, the scoring wheel will stay sharp for two lusks of solid work. Your friend Ariadne gave this little machine to my great-grandfather Dunkler Stern the First one hundred years ago, along with a box of sharp scoring wheels made from an exotic metal combination we Sterns call heavy-stone. About fifty years ago, as promised, she brought a box of replacement scoring wheels to Dunkler Stern the Second, my grandfather. We've been reluctant to change our names, wanting to make sure she could find us.

"Really, she's given us two tremendous gifts. This machine provides a technological advantage which, when used wisely, provides a life free from need, but also, her price for the machine has been a gift as well. We've learned so much while gathering information for her. Otherwise I fear the leisure afforded to us might have led to time poorly spent. Idle hands spill the tea, as they say. And, come to find out, all that information gathering is for the purpose of helping her do her job, which is basically to prevent the destruction of Grith. A worthy activity for its own sake."

*He said she'd been here a* hundred *years ago. People don't live that long.* Happen recalled Tinker's advice, and didn't argue. Stern would help him find Cor. Plus, he had good cookies. "You don't sound too worried about Grith, sir."

"Ariadne will take care of it. She's remarkably competent."

"I'm not so sure about that . . ."

Stern looked angry for a moment, then his face softened again.

"Oh, yes. I was forgetting. She did say something about you saving her life. Surely a once-in-a-lifetime opportunity for a young man to do such a deed. But events like that don't necessarily define a person. I think it's much more telling that she traveled from beyond the stars to fulfill a fifty-year-old promise. Twice!"

"I see your point, sir, I guess. But I also think that if this . . . um, situation is real, then maybe as the only Grithings aware of it we should try to do something about it? To help her somehow? Especially because she's been—"

"I think we both already have. And you are young and I am old, and these things are best left to the professionals. You have your own important work to do here, do you not?"

"Well, yes."

"And quite recently you were frustrated because you were unable to do that work, were you not?"

"Yes."

"There. It is a joy to be able to work and have success. There is no need to get distracted by things beyond your control. I plan to enjoy myself, what little self there is left before my time is done. I recommend you do the same."

Happen saw the man's logic and wanted to accept the comforting conclusion, though something about it didn't feel quite right. Before he could finally tell him Ariadne had been arrested, Helter and Cor entered without knocking.

"Ah, yes." Stern smiled broadly. "Come in, young worthies! How are you? Would you like some tea?"

"Where have you been?" Cor said, ignoring Dunkler Stern and glaring at Happen.

"Well, let's see . . . I've been running through crowds to get away from Osgar, I've been dragged onto a stage in front of hundreds of people and laughed at, I've been chased, tackled, and arrested by security guards, I've been dismissed from Osgar's trial, I've had to repack my entire cart because it got ransacked by Gracarrai inspectors, I saw what I thought was a demon, I had to cheer up Nora because she was crying, and I've been looking for Tinker and looking for you. Where have *you* been?"

Cor just gawked at him. "Really?"

"Really," Happen said. "I also got some food and stopped in at a bookseller's for a bit. But that was a while ago."

"I couldn't find you and I'm worried about Tinker. I looked all over then went back to ask Ariadne for help but they wouldn't let me near the stall. I went to your cart even though Tinker said not to go to the red flag district, but you weren't there. Esmerlia said she hadn't seen you, and she was worried about you, too. I didn't know what to do."

Cor's anger was too much for Happen. With all he'd been through that day, with Tinker's brief appearance and disappearance, with Nora's anger and sadness, with Ariadne's arrest, even with Marimba's questioning eyebrow, he couldn't have one more person needing him to be strong. He'd been looking for Cor hoping to find someone who felt stable—a respite from the doubt and madness of the day. But as much as he was upset by Cor's anger, he recognized that he couldn't respond in kind.

When overwhelmed by situations like this, Odais had learned to focus on a mundane aspect of the present until he had time to restore his equilibrium.

Happen took a deep breath, and tried. "I don't know what to do either. Have one of these cookies. They're amazing. Mr. Stern says Tinker will be out soon."

Cor looked at him like he'd grown a tull's horn.

"They won't keep him overnight, son," Dunkler Stern said. "Your friend's right. Have a cookie. Can I pour you some tea? Tell me, who are 'they' and why wouldn't they let you near Ariadne's stall?"

"That's what I was trying to tell you!" Happen tapped his head with his fist. "Ariadne got arrested."

"Oh, dear." Dunkler Stern set down his tea, and drank from his waterskin. "Perhaps you were right after all, and we should pay a visit to the commissioner's office and see if there's anything we can do to help."

"Cor and I have something to do first, and then we'll go to the commissioner's office."

"Cor needs his dinner even first-er," Cor said once they'd left the tile cutter's shop.

Happen gave his cousin some script to buy himself dinner, and promised to meet him in half a bell at the seafood vendor. He hurried to Esmerlia's tent, brashly ducking under the Closed sign and rankling the chimes. After all, Cor said she was worried about him.

"Are you unable to read, or merely unwilling?"

Happen recognized the voice of the seer with the false eye. "I know, I'm sorry. I was hoping to speak with Esmerlia. She left a note for me to come see her."

"Ah, you are the young man of whom she chattered all day. You may wait in the front room, or take a chair out to enjoy the moonrise, and I will send for her."

Happen sat in the dark front room. *Of whom she chattered all day?* Esmerlia didn't seem like someone who chattered. Her mother was exaggerating because Esmerlia was interested in the puzzle of Ariadne's identity, and when they'd been interrupted this morning, he'd just told her there was another piece she hadn't heard yet. The troublesome part.

"You left him in the front room by himself?"

"He might be out front with a chair. At least I gave him something to think about."

"What? You meddling witch!"

The older woman's laughter followed Esmerlia through the curtains. She set a bright candle down on the table, smiled at him, and sat in the other chair. He was glad that she wasn't dressed and painted for work. "Pay no attention to that old troublemaker, Happen. Thanks for coming to see me, I was worried. How are you?"

He looked at her and swallowed. This beautiful girl asking him how he was, especially after her mother's hints, was yet another demand for him to be strong. Her eyes tugged at his heart. *I am a vendor. I can do this.* He opened his mouth to mention some mundane aspect of the present, but she stopped him.

"No, don't speak." She stood and brought her chair to his side of the table, and sat facing him, leaning closer. "You have the most expressive eyes I have ever seen. Everyone else is veiled in deceit, but not you, Happen Fell. I can see that you've had a day of extremes, both good and bad, and you are tired, but you have persevered, even succeeded at times. Yet trouble remains. Are you in danger?"

"No. Not tonight, anyway."

"That's a relief. I can see that you did not intend, with your cryptic words this morning, to give me a mysterious locked box and take the key away all day, and yet that is what you have done."

"I'm sorry, I—"

Again she stopped him, this time with her hand on his knee.

"Please. Do not defend. I understand. Just tell me, if you can, about 'the troublesome part.'"

Happen told her that he went looking for Osgar among the flags of red, about the conversation he heard from under Tinker's caravard, and Nora's explanation of what it meant for Grith. He told her about Dunkler Stern's claims of Ariadne's previous visits, but he left out the details about his special tile cutter, because it felt like something you don't tell, like about Bealsio. And he told her about Ariadne's arrest. Esmerlia nodded at times, so Happen surmised that she had heard the event first-hand.

"Oh, what a day. At last I have the key to open the box, and inside is another locked box."

Happen got up his nerve, and put his hand on her knee. "I am sorry I don't have the key to this one." It felt magical to touch her for the moment before she stood.

"We don't have the key, but it might help to see what others do with such a box. The fair hasn't had a witch arrest in a long time, but it's a story every seer, clairvoyant, and small-beer fortune-teller at the fair knows. The Gracarrai inspectors will have an immediate trial. I'm sure it's started already. Wait out front, I'll grab my shawl."

# TWENTY-EIGHT

# THE WARDSHIP COUNCIL

> Most lunisolar calendars on Earth use intercalary periods to account for the difference between lunar and solar years, and enforce a whole number of months into a year. Berytheans divide the solar year into nine lunar based "mesters," and the ninth mester of each year has some days in one year, and some in another.
>
> The year begins on the day after the longest night (winter solstice) and the first mester begins on the first day with a new moon. The mesters are named from the perspective of an agrarian society in the northern hemisphere. (Reilly, 2046)

Esmerlia emerged from the tent still wrapping a black shawl over her shoulders, took Happen's hand, and they headed toward the commissioner's office. Happen's senses all shut down, providing full attention to his left hand, leaving just enough awareness to prevent him from walking into a signpost. He occasionally allowed himself a quick glance at Esmerlia. Her eyes smiled, confident and bright above the starry field of freckles on her cheeks. She told him about the last witch trial at the fair, but he wasn't listening. Had the moon been any higher, he wouldn't have noticed it, the fullness and blush from its daily feast already fading, but still swollen, bountiful, and gold-faced.

Esmerlia let go of Happen's hand as they entered the meeting hall. "You'd think it would be more crowded" she said. "People are such cowards when it comes to witches."

Tables had been arranged to form a rectangle with one side open to several disheveled rows of benches with a crooked aisle through the middle. The table on the left was crowded with two groups of security personnel, one group wearing the red stripes and seal of Gracarrai. The table on the right had a plainly dressed man sitting alone next to an empty chair. The center table had three large chairs with tall, ornately carved backs. Two men sat there, but the chair between them was empty. The seating area was half full, and murmured with conversation. Happen thought perhaps the trial hadn't started yet. He spotted Dunkler Stern sitting with a younger man near the back of the hall.

Stern saw them approaching and stood. "Hello, young worthy. I hope you and your friend will join me and my son here."

After introductions were made with Dunkler Stern the Fifth, Esmerlia asked the elder Stern where the First Chair was, and whether they had missed much of the trial.

"I'm not sure, but I think aside from sentencing, you've missed the trial. I myself missed it, though my son was here and filled me in. Even Ariadne missed the beginning. She arrived only moments before I did. Apparently it took a while to locate the proper transport to publicly display an arrested witch through the fairgrounds."

Esmerlia grimaced. "Oh, that sounds awful. Is she okay?"

"She was most gracious and understanding about the ordeal. By the time I arrived, the Gracarrai prosecutor had already accused her of kidnapping an Aeriskenn printer's family and forcing him to print the heretical pamphlets. One of the pamphlet distributors had testified how she'd provided himself and another with contraband for dissemination yesterday morning. Then the security prosecutor described some alarming behavior involving a varanid demon and flashing lights of unnatural color. I find it impossible to believe, but they claim to have secured a full confession in the field, so there was no rebuttal from her appointed representative."

"Where is she now?"

"In the kitchen behind those doors there. After she arrived the security commissioner announced that one of the conditions of the witch's confession was that she have a private audience with the First Chair. That caused an uproar, as the First Chair is quite popular, and the people feared for her safety, but she assured the audience that Grith and wisdom would protect her from witches."

The doors opened, and Ariadne and the Gracarrai leader returned to their seats. The three people at the center table put their heads together in whispered conversation.

"Who are those people?" Happen asked Esmerlia.

"The wardship council. The First Chair is the highest-ranking Gracarrai cleric here. The man on her right is the Second Chair, and the man on her left is the security commissioner. Oh, they've decided already."

The First Chair stood and addressed the hall.

"By a vote of two to one, the wardship council has accepted the defendant's revocation of confession for the charge of heresy. The confession stands for the charges of witchcraft and resisting arrest. The earlier finding for the heresy charge has been rescinded, and the trial will resume with rebuttal. Advocates approach, please."

Dunkler Stern's expression brightened. "Ah, see? I knew it."

A brief meeting resulted in the group of Gracarrai prosecutors switching sides to join Ariadne's table amid much moving of chairs and grumbling.

"Before we hear the rebuttal," the First Chair announced. "We have a few items of business to address. First, the defendant claims to have been at a different location at the time the pamphlet distributor claimed he was meeting with her. Please send a summons to the seamstress at northwest eight nineteen."

One of the men at the prosecutor's table left the room, and the grumbling in the crowd increased.

"Second, fair security has been operating under temporary authorization concerning the alleged witch's fair stall. Official orders are hereby issued to surround and protect northwest nine twenty-three with members of the Gracarrai inspection force that arrived this morning, relieving fair security of the extra duty. Site protection includes one domesticated cougar, a person answering to the name of Nora Reilly and identified by the good will of the cougar, and all personal belongings present. The only person to be allowed access to the site answers to the name of Happen Fell. He can be identified by an unusual adhesive cloth tightly wrapped around his left ankle."

"You're famous," Esmerlia whispered conspiratorially. Happen felt a growing satisfaction at the apparent change in Ariadne's fortunes. She *was* a witch, but he liked her anyway.

"Third, one of the council votes was conditional, so we'll hear from that member now."

The Second Chair stood, and the First Chair sat with a yielding gesture.

"With all due respect your honor, it seems as if the witch may have put a spell on you, causing you to pursue her, er, unusual agenda . . . quite freely."

The grumbling in the room stopped. All movement stopped except for a smile slowly building on the security commissioner's face. *You could hear a tull blink in here.*

The First Chair considered the accusation for a long moment in the silence. "I understand how it might appear so, and I appreciate your courage in challenging my course of action. I imagine that you are speaking the thoughts of many in the room. However, the witch has shared some information that I am not able to share with you. She knows the three foundations of the origin covenant as well as if she'd written them herself, if you can pardon the expression. She knows the nine articles of the open circle covenant in the original translation. I can appreciate how unhelpful it is for me to ask this court to take my word alone on this matter, so I will send for the Oracle of Aeriskenn, to provide a second opinion. The Oracle will communicate with the defendant, in writing at first, in front of witnesses, so if *she* agrees with our course of action, there will be no suspicion of us being manipulated by anything other than our own abiding faith and duty."

One of the men at the defendant's table left the room, along with several of the audience, and the people spoke in awed whispers.

"The thundering *Oracle* is coming. Here."

Excitement gripped Happen's chest. The Oracle of Aeriskenn was the highest-ranking Gracarrai cleric in all Berythea.

Two guards ushered in an old lady whom Happen recognized as the seamstress with the kittens. She was given a seat facing the audience, to the left of the council's table, and described a quiet old woman in a deeply hooded cloak playing with kittens in her stall during the time the distributor claimed Ariadne was in the red flag district.

"Will you raise a dispute, sir?" The First Chair asked the prosecutor.

"Indeed. It could have been anyone in that cloak."

She turned to her left. "Have you a counter, sir?"

After a brief conference, Ariadne's new advocate stood. "For reasons that will be made clear in a moment, the defendant expected an attempt to deflect suspicion and entangle her with the local authorities, so she carved the letter 'A' on a coin she gave the seamstress. Defense requests the witness's purse be entered into evidence."

"I beg your pardon!" The old seamstress covered the purse at her belt with both hands.

"If you please, ma'am." The First Chair signaled to a guard. "We will return it with all contents in short order."

The purse was delivered to the Second Chair, who found a solan coin with the letter 'A' added to its standard markings. He was pleased to note, he said, that the witch was considerate enough to mark the Berythean side, not the Gracarrai side. The coin was passed among the members of the council. Happen was stunned. Nora had made it seem like Ariadne had been distracted by those kittens, but now it seemed like part of a plan.

"Will you raise a dispute, sir?"

"Indeed. The witch has an accomplice who could have been in that cloak and given the coin to the seamstress."

"Have you a counter, sir?"

"During the time the defendant was at the seamstress's stall, her assistant was seen by a guard at the north gate. She would probably be identified in the gate log as a young woman still having the appearance of celebrating the night cheetah from the previous evening's festivities and requesting temporary egress."

A runner was sent to check the gate log.


"The defense requests to present mitigating factors to the charge of practicing witchcraft on fair grounds. Having established doubt about the identity of the heretic, the defendant wishes to address the council about the urgent matter of the actual heretic who is still at large and causing harm."

The council put their heads together for a whispered meeting. Happen wondered if she was going to tell them about the men he and Cor overheard in Tinker's caravard.

"We'll allow it," the First Chair said when they'd finished. "With the understanding that if the matter is found to be either untrue or not urgent, a contempt charge will be added to the record."

"Thank you." Ariadne stood facing the council. "First let me apologize for disrupting your trade fair. This regrettable situation is the direct result of an extremely unusual witch and his accomplice, who have come to the fair to spread confusion about Gracarrai's position on mining and blacksmithing, and inspire excitement about the potential benefits of steel weapons, so that people will be tempted to disregard the Gracarrai covenant with Grith.

"It is imperative that the effect of this witch's actions be mitigated at once. First, we must find and quarantine the printed materials, knives, and bog ore samples that have been distributed. Second, publicly affirm Gracarrai's position on the matter. And finally, we have to know where he's going, because he's likely to continue elsewhere what he and his accomplice started here." She turned and faced the audience. "He is far too dangerous to confront with force, but if we can follow him and oppose his deeds, Gracarrai and Grith will be protected."

People in the audience were grumbling about the Blacksmith Conspiracy, when the Second Chair asked how Ariadne expected them to find this alleged witch.

"Monitor everyone leaving the fair. I have reason to believe the witch planned to leave tonight to engage a ship, possibly headed for Maithea. Once he's identified, allow him to leave, but follow him. Knowing which ship he's on will help us to negate his agenda abroad in a timely manner."

"We are already stopping departing parties at the gate to tell them reentry is no longer allowed," the security commissioner said. "We don't have time to search every vehicle or check for disguises. Notifying everyone of the new rules has already stretched our resources too thin."

"The witch will disguise his appearance, but not his voice. His accomplice will attempt to do all the talking. If you can make sure that every individual person leaving speaks to you, it will be easy to identify him."

"We don't have time to question every single person."

"All it will take is one word. He has a very distinctive voice."

"Ha! That's preposterous." The security commissioner threw up his hands. "No one has such a voice."

Ariadne switched Nora's talking-box to her left hand, and took a different device from her pocket.

"He sounds like this. Do you think you won't notice?" All of the council members, the people at the prosecutor's table, and everyone in the audience cringed at the sound. Happen recognized that voice from the other night when he hid under Tinker's caravard. It was exactly the same. *Could Ariadne have been there, conspiring with the deep-voiced man in the red flag district?* He wanted Cor to hear this.

The next thought hit Happen over the head like a falling chiminea. He'd forgotten to meet Cor. He broke out in a sweat, and stood unsteadily. *How could I let my cousin down like this?*

"Are you okay?" Esmerlia put her hand on his arm. "Have you heard that voice before? You look like you've just seen a varanid."

"I have to go. Supposed to meet Cor." Happen took a deep breath, steadied himself, and walked out of the room. As he left, he heard the First Chair speaking.

"The Church wishes to uproot the cause of this heresy, and will finance and help staff the additional effort at the gates."

. . .

Happen felt awful as he hustled to the food rows. Ariadne may or may not have been in Tinker's caravard. Esmerlia may or may not be able to talk to a spirit in a crystal. Nora may or may not be from a world beyond the stars. But he carried no doubts at all about his cousin.

The seafood vendor said he had noticed a boy hanging around, fidgeting and looking at the moon a lot, but he'd left a while ago. He hadn't noticed which direction the boy went.

Happen stood and gazed, unsure where to look, trying to imagine how his cousin felt and where he might go. This wouldn't feel so bad if Cor wasn't already upset with him. He bought some water and a couple of fried dough rings, and headed back toward Esmerlia's tent, figuring Cor might look for him there. Before he reached their row, someone shoved him hard on the shoulder.

"How was your tryst, you conniving weasel!" Cor said.

"I did not plan that! Honest!"

"Yeah, right."

Happen gave him one of the dough rings. "I'm sorry I wasn't where I said I'd be. Did you wait long?"

"No, I saw you two go by holding hands, and I figured you'd be late." Cor didn't look at him. "You walked right past me."

# TWENTY-NINE

## AZMERIAN WATER STONES

> Azmer was the god of water, sound, and meditation in the ancient Bandu religion. Agnal was the god of fire. Although these deities have faded from memory, their names remain in words for certain items. These items were not only associated with past rituals, but were also used by common people every day, and so their names survived. (Reilly, 2046)

⌐⌐

Happen told Cor about Ariadne's trial as they headed back to the commissioner's office, but the trial had ended, so they went to see if Tinker was back at his caravard, and found him arranging kindling in the chiminea.

After exclamations, hugs, and questions, they settled by the fire and Tinker related the story of his arrest, questioning, and imprisonment.

"They told us that you were assisting Gracarrai inspectors with their investigation."

"I was, at first. I had a series of meetings with fair security and several Gracarrai inspectors, and they had me wait in an office in between. After many bells of that, though, the tone of their questions suddenly changed, and then I was arrested. Stuck me in a cell and told me Ariadne had confessed to heresy, said her trial would be quick, and they'd get to me right after. I couldn't figure out why Ariadne had set me up like that. But then they released me. The inspector referred to Ariadne as their 'good witch' and said she had spoken to them on my behalf."

The next morning Tinker brought breakfast and coffee and lit a fire in the chiminea before waking the boys. While they ate, a runner came from the fair administration to tell them a stall would be opening up soon, so they could move one of their vehicles if they chose.

"A little out of the way, but better for a tinker than here," he said. "Assorted services row. Northwest quadrant."

"Thanks, but I'd rather send my nephew's cart over there and get these kids out of the red flags," Tinker said.

"I understand, sir. They'll send someone in a few bells to facilitate the move."

"Thanks. Hey, just curious. Do you know the number of the stall?"

"Nine fifteen, sir."

"Thunder and lightning," Tinker said when the runner had left.

"What's the matter?" Cor asked.

"I was hoping to travel south with them. Having Ariadne and her viser around would be nice in case . . ." He set down his mug and stood up to stretch.

"In case what?"

"Oh, bandits or anything. But we'll be fine."

"Are they even going south?" Happen said. "At the trial it sounded like they'd be following the witch to Maithea."

"Hmm. She also said she was going to return the cougar after the fair. Whichever path they cut, we should get over there before they leave and pay them for getting you into the fair."

Three guards stopped them at NW 9-15, but allowed them in when Happen introduced himself. Ariadne and Nora were sitting with Marimba by the fire.

"Oh, I'm so glad to see you!" Nora jumped up to greet them. "Guess what I bought this morning."

"Coffee?"

"Well, yes, but that's not what I'm excited about. Azmerian stones! I told them it was my first time and they became very upset. Complete strangers were actually angry with my parents for not giving me at least one every holiday. Once they calmed down enough to tell me about them I chose an ocean one. They said about two percent of the time a stone turns out 'quiet,' and they wanted to make sure I wasn't disappointed, and gave me two extra for free: a river one and another ocean one. I wanted to unwrap one right there, but they said I should go be with my people . . . if I could."

"We have time to stay a while, right Tinker?" Happen asked.

"Is it all right, Ariadne?" Nora asked.

Tinker and Ariadne assented.

"Is there any, um, special procedure . . . ?" Nora asked Tinker.

"No, just unwrap the stone and hold it," he said. "Some of them are nice to look at. Or you might want to look at the fire, or close your eyes . . . whatever feels comfortable."

Nora unfolded a white piece of paper to reveal a smooth gray rock with brown speckles, and turned it around between her thumb and forefinger. Then she closed her fist over it, shut her eyes, and reclined against Marimba's back, her golden hair bright against the tawny fur in the morning sun. The boys looked at each other, anticipating Nora's delight.

Happen wasn't sure how he felt about Nora. Her enthusiasm and warmth were exciting to be around, but she was quick with a lie when it suited her, which made him wary. Still, he felt connected with her somehow, and it felt surprisingly odd that she would be leaving soon.

"I think this must be a quiet one," she said sadly after a long moment. "I don't feel anything."

"Thunder," Happen said.

"Should I throw it away?"

"No," Tinker said. "Even the quiet ones have to be returned. Remember which ones go back to the ocean, and which one goes to the river."

Nora tried the river stone next, and then the other ocean stone, both with the same results as the first.

"Do they just not work for some people?" Nora rewrapped the stones wistfully. "Or could I have gotten three quiet ones?"

"I've never met anyone your age that couldn't enjoy an Azmerian stone," Tinker said. "But we might as well find out if these are quiet. Can the boys have the ocean stones? We don't get those very often."

"Sure. Would you like the river stone?"

"No, thanks," Tinker said. "They don't do much for me anymore."


The boys thanked Nora and sat down to unwrap their stones. It had been several years since Happen had an ocean stone. Inside the refolded paper was a smooth gray stone with a white band around it on one side. He rolled it around in his palm, admiring the white band. The ambient sounds coalesced, building into waves of liquid whispering, each wave built to a peak with tantalizing precision before spilling over, collapsing, and rolling through him as a cheerful chaos of gentle sounds. After spending its momentum it returned to its source to rebuild, like an inhalation, and Happen's breathing slowed to meet the pace. A scattering of tingles developed on his scalp and crept back from his hairline to cover the top of his head, and he filled with a deep sense of well-being and connectedness with Grith. He and Cor looked at each other. Cor's was not a quiet one, either. After a few more waves, the tingles on his scalp faded away like stars before the dawn, and the whispering sounds gradually took different shapes in his mind, forming the actual noises audible at the fairgrounds: distant conversations, music, a cart rolling by on the gravel.

"Well, since I can't experience this myself, can you at least tell me what it's about?" Nora asked.

Happen described his experience with the ocean stone. "And the river stone is the same, only with a steadier watery sound, and random and subtle tapping sounds like stones being rolled down a rocky river bottom, but the feeling is the same. We usually get the river stones, because they're so much easier for us to return."

"We don't have stones like this on Earth. Ariadne, could it be unique to Grith?"

"I suppose it could be, though it would be considered of little value unless it works for Dhaignians. I'll give the river stone a try, if you don't mind."

Nora gave her the rewrapped stone, and then crossed her fingers on both hands.

"Why are you doing that?" Cor asked. "With your fingers."

"Oh, you don't do that here? It's for good luck. If the Azmerian stones work for Dhaignians, it could save Grith from the miners. And maybe I wouldn't have to spend my semester abroad chasing a dangerous criminal."

After a moment, Ariadne opened her eyes.

"I'm sorry, dear. This might be something special, but if we can't demonstrate it, it won't help our cause. I can take it back and have it analyzed, and see if the special properties can be detected another way, but I wouldn't count on it."

"Oh, no, please don't do that," Cor said. "You have to return that to a river."

"Why?"

"It's a gift from Grith, but not one that's meant to be kept."

"And what if I did not return it?"

"After about a year, Grith would get angry with you. Your crops might fail, or your cow might get sick, or the foundation of your house might crack. It could be anything, but it would not be good."

"How interesting. I would like to test that, but now isn't the appropriate time. Will you return the stone for me? Will that suffice, or must I do it myself?"

"I will, gladly," Cor said. "Yes, it will work."


"Oh, hey," Happen said. "I still owe you my entrance fee, twenty solani."

"Yeah, me, too," Cor said.

"Of course you would view it that way. Although I appreciate your integrity, I must insist that you consider this to be a part of my work here, and allow the Dhaignian government to cover the cost. Given the amount the stress caused to you by the current Dhaignian presence here, it's the very least they could do. In addition, if you're willing, I'd like to hire you to transport the cat back to its home at the inn. My allies in the Gracarrai investigation force have provided me with ample resources to compensate delivery services, and the cat and I would both be grateful to have a familiar and trusted caretaker for the journey."

It meant two extra days of travel before arriving home, but more importantly, it meant that Ariadne trusted him with something very important to her, and bringing home extra money would make his parents proud.

"I would be willing," Happen said. "And honored."

A runner, escorted by a security guard, knocked on their wagon, just like he'd done two days ago with a note from Esmerlia about the cow parade. This time he brought word that the Oracle's convoy had left the administration buildings, and Ariadne had about five waves to get ready.

Nora started toward them, hesitated, then rushed over, hugging Cor and thanking him. Then she hugged Happen with such sincerity that he hugged her back. Breathing in the smell of her hair, a new feeling came over him, and for that moment, he believed them. He thought about the directions they were heading; what they had to do, and what he had to do.

"I have to know," he whispered in Nora's ear. She pulled back from him slowly, and looked at him, searching.

"Oh, right," she said quietly. "She owes you that. I'll take care of it." She looked him in the eye with purpose. "I have an idea. You'll see before we go."

The boys and Tinker helped with the rest of the packing, and five waves later, the runner returned saying that it if they left now they'd meet the Oracle on the north gate road in time. Happen watched them climb up into the wagon seat, leaving the cat in its cage under the large tent, and he felt the weight of responsibility for another being for the first time.

As Banjo and Lute pulled Ariadne and Nora's wagon away, Nora threw a small leather pouch to Happen, and waved. By the time he'd picked it up and looked again, she was facing west and south, rolling away around the curved road.

THIRTY

# A SHIMMERING PATH

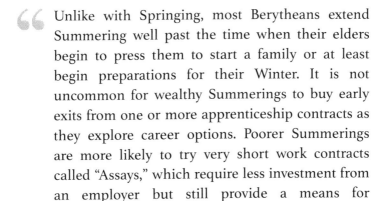

Unlike with Springing, most Berytheans extend Summering well past the time when their elders begin to press them to start a family or at least begin preparations for their Winter. It is not uncommon for wealthy Summerings to buy early exits from one or more apprenticeship contracts as they explore career options. Poorer Summerings are more likely to try very short work contracts called "Assays," which require less investment from an employer but still provide a means for experiencing a potential occupation.

Summerings are discouraged from taking on responsibilities. If they have pets, others will undertake care and feeding. If family members are ill, elders or Springings will be asked to provide for them. A Gracarrai elder expressed it this way, "A Summering's job is to make sure she has no regrets come Winter." (Reilly, 2046)

H appen was surprised by the intensity of his emotions as he watched Ariadne and Nora's wagon leaving the fair. He'd felt safer with Ariadne around, but there was more to it than that. He pocketed the leather pouch, not wanting to open it just yet. It felt like a part of them stayed with him, but somehow opening the pouch would change that.

"I hope Dunkler Stern is right about her," he said to Cor, as they turned away and headed to the river to return Ariadne's Azmerian stone. Just before Cor cast it in, standing on a grassy bluff upstream of the washing area, Happen realized that it probably wasn't Ariadne's Azmerian stone.

"Hey, don't throw that yet." He'd been wanting to tell Cor about Bealsio, even though he had promised not to, but then he realized that the Azmerian stones were telling the same story.

"Listen," he continued. "The stones that didn't work for Nora, *did* work for us, just as if we were the first to unwrap them—"

"Oh, right," Cor interrupted. "So this one could be good, too."

"Yes, but don't you see what it means?"

"Um, Nora was lying about not having had—wait, no, that wouldn't work."

Happen let him puzzle it through for a moment, to see if Cor reached the same conclusion.

"I give up," Cor said. "What does it mean?"

"Maybe, the Azmerian stones didn't recognize Nora as a person," Happen said. "And if this river stone is still good, then the same goes for Ariadne. And if they're not people according to Azmerian stones . . . maybe all that really means is they're just not Grithings."

"Maybe," Cor said. "And maybe they're just both witches, like people are saying. Maybe they bewitched the Oracle of Aeriskenn and Dunkler Stern, and maybe even us."

"Why would they do that?"

"I don't know." Cor pondered his ocean stone as if it might

have the answer. "I don't actually know much of anything about witches."

"Me neither."

Cor held up the wrapped river stone. "Boon or bane?"

"No, thanks. You go ahead. I owe you one for last night."

The boys sat on the grassy bluff overlooking the river, and while Cor enjoyed his river stone, Happen looked to the sky and wondered whether he could ever really believe that people from beyond the stars could visit Grith.

Over the next several bells Happen learned about buying, selling, and trading from Tinker. People still avoided the stall at NW 9-15, but it didn't matter since it wasn't the right location for his wares anyway. Tinker borrowed a handcart which Happen and Cor used to bring oat flour, onions, and elk jerky to the wholesale food row along the outer edge of the northeast quadrant.

That first evening, after working most of the day, Happen stopped in at the seer's tent next door to bring money to the Amazing Esmerlia, and she asked him to come back in half a bell and join her for dinner.

Happen washed up at the river and put on the cleaner of his two sets of clothes. They smelled a little like the river they'd been washed in, but then so did everyone else's. Cor and Tinker teased him, but also helped straighten his shirt collar.

He was nervous, but once dinner started, he was able to relax as they talked about Ariadne, Nora, and Marimba. Esmerlia wanted to hear all about how Happen met them, and everything he'd learned about them since. She agreed emphatically with Dunkler Stern's assessment that Happen should leave the bad witch to Ariadne, and that returning Marimba should be the end of his involvement with the strangers.

.   .   .

After dinner they walked by the river, heading upstream to where the moon peeked over the distant mountains, glowing but still pale in the twilit sky, and the river reflected the sky in that strange color of Nora's knife blade. A cool gusty breeze carried some falling leaves in a wide arc over the river then down where they caught, stilled abruptly by the darkening water.

They found they had some things in common. Esmerlia was expected to carry on the traditional family occupation of seer, but she wasn't sure she wanted to. After many years of study, and a year of observation, she was just beginning her first apprentice year, but she didn't like it. When it wasn't too repetitive it felt creepy and dangerous.

"Beginning your apprenticeship?" Happen watched his boots shyly. "Have you completed your Summering Task?"

"Working this fair is my Summering Task."

"Wow, that's so musical! It's mine, also."

In years past, Esmerlia's family had set up their tent in the red flag district, but they wanted her to start taking fair clients in a safer location. That first day, her mother had sent in a few people paid to act like clients, but Happen had been her first real client. She'd enjoyed meeting and helping him so much, she'd begun to think becoming a seer might not be so bad after all, but she knew most clients wouldn't be like him.

One thing they didn't have in common was their vision for the future. Happen wanted to move to Aeriskenn and become a private detective like Inspector Cravey. Esmerlia was hoping to get out of Aeriskenn and travel the world. Unfortunately, her only skill was fortune-telling, and without her family's protection and Bealsio for depth-sight, it would be too dangerous for one person, so she felt stuck, and was considering attending the academy.

Happen was looking forward to seeing the city and the ocean, but wasn't sure how long he'd be stuck working at home now that Osgar wouldn't be there. He hoped they could find someone else to work on the farm. As they talked and his comfort with Esmerlia grew, the present moment itself grew, crowding out the frustrating past and the uncertain future. The moonlit path along the river narrowed, bringing them closer together.

"Our futures may be clouded with uncertainty," Esmerlia said in her seer's voice, then continued in her real one. "But it's nice to be here now, walking with you." She took Happen's arm, and then held his hand.

Happen's mind emptied at the thrill of her touch, but he knew he had to say something.

"I'm . . . I'm really glad you think so," he stammered, and she squeezed his hand. They walked in silence for a while, and came around a bend where the moon was high enough to shine on the river, casting a shimmering path of light across into shadow. She stopped him there, turning him to face her.

"We should head back now, but you will take me to the dance tomorrow night, won't you?" she asked. Her words had a playful tone that included only the tiniest hint of doubt about his answer. She turned back and forth slightly, as if a little bit of dance had already begun inside her, and the moonlight showed the curve of her cheek with its scattered freckles, as she swung his hand. He couldn't think about tomorrow night, or anything really, but a small voice in the back of his mind reminded him that an affirmative response was required.

"Yes, yes of course. I'd love to."

# THIRTY-ONE

# A WORDLESS QUESTION

 With exceptions for community-oriented holidays like Spirit Moon, or when solar event-based holidays such as Longest Night coincide with lunar phases, at every quarter phase of the moon, called "luskday" after the half-moon shape of a common marine bivalve, Berytheans have a day of rest with family. Following that is a day of recreation, a time for sports, games, music, and dancing.

Berythean courtship centers around community line dances. Summerings often pair up and walk home from dances to share a bed. During Spirit Mester when Grithing women are ovulating, a contraceptive tea (known as Summering Tea) is made available, not just at dances but many sites, and childbirth during Summering is very rare. Although family members are often involved with the process of spouse selection, Gracarrai marriage is only sanctioned between consenting adults who have completed their Autumnal Quest. (Reilly, 2046)

⌒⌐

The next day passed in a blur. Happen tried to concentrate and learn from Tinker, but he just kept thinking about the feel of Esmerlia's hand in his, and the moonlight in her hair, and the playful look in her eyes. Even so, with help from Cor he sold most of his wares that day, and had purchased everything on his list except the fabrics and leather. He was hoping to get Esmerlia's help the next day picking out some nice fabrics for his mother.

He felt he owed his mother a significant apology for shouting at her the night before he left, and he was hoping nice fabrics would help. He also owed her a debt of gratitude for the breadth of his education. In his last two years at school, she'd forced him to learn the basics of dancing. He had protested vehemently, not the least because he was made to dance with Mistine, but even the next year, after Mistine had left the school, he still would rather have been doing anything else. But now, he had to admit, he was very glad to know the basics, just like his mother had said he would be.

Esmerlia wore a plain blue dress, and it was the first time Happen had seen her long auburn hair when it wasn't tied back. There was a charming brightness to her that made him worry he'd seem rude for staring.

The band had two fiddles, and a few other stringed instruments played by strumming or picking the strings. One was so big the musician had to stand behind it to play. He stood on one side and faced the dancers at an angle, possibly to hide his bandaged ear. The music was lively and fun, and to Happen's relief, the dances were simple. With the caller's help he was able to follow along with few mistakes.

Some of the other couples in the line made him uneasy, either because they looked at him strangely, or smelled of something unrecognizable, or because they moved to the music in unexpected ways that felt awkward to Happen, but coming back around to his beautiful partner was a such a thrill, and she was laughing and smiling so much, he lost himself in the music and forgot about worries like Osgar, Mistine, Garsidge, and Dhaignian miners, for quite some time. Esmerlia moved beautifully, and made him feel graceful when they touched. Through some miracle her hair and dress smelled a bit like vanilla beans and maybe apples; not like the river at all. She looked at him like she really wanted him to be there with her, and be who he was.

At the intermission, she tugged down on his arm with two hands, pulling him to a seat on the edge of the trampled dance area, and breathlessly thanked him. Someone had set up a cider mill near the stage and they waited in line for fresh cider.

"I like dancing with you, Happen Fell. You're not show-offy like the boys from the city."

After the dance was over they walked and Happen told her about collachine and cougars. Esmerlia told him about koi ponds and kennlifts. Happen was beginning to think that maybe he might know what love felt like. Odais's story identified several different kinds of love. His mother said the author was wrong, and that they were just parts of one thing. Either way, Happen was feeling the first kind, which in Odais's case led almost immediately to tragedy, but Happen felt sure that he and Esmerlia were different from Odais and Jenb'lla.

"What is going on in that thoughtful head of yours?" she asked. He must have lapsed into a pensive silence as they walked through the fairgrounds, drifting toward the path by the river upstream.

"Oh, sorry, I was just . . ." Happen hesitated. *I should be brave and tell the truth.* "I was just thinking about . . . Odais and Jenb'lla."

"Oh!" Then it was Esmerlia's turn to hesitate. "I read that book." He thought she might be blushing, but there wasn't enough light to know. They had reached the path, away from other people, and the moon above the trees on the far bank of the river would not show him the color of her face. She seemed to reach some sort of conclusion, and took his hand.

"I hope we don't end up like them," she said in a serious tone.

They continued on the narrowing path, talking about *The Odais Chronicles* and how Esmerlia thought that the fortune-teller in book three was too much of a caricature, and Happen hadn't noticed because he'd never met a real fortune-teller until then, and she still didn't think he had yet because she was just an apprentice and even though he'd met her mother briefly, he hadn't seen her perform. And her mother was the *real* Amazing Esmerlia.

"Then, is Esmerlia not your name?"

"Oh, yes, it is, but only because it has to be. It's part of the . . . situation . . . with Bealsio. The oldest daughter of each generation must always be named Esmerlia."

They reached the bend in the river where they could see the path of moonlight cross to the other side, shimmering silver and yellow on the now black water. They slowed, then stopped.

"But I don't like the name at all," she continued. "I'd rather you call me Em."

"I'd like to, Em."

The sibilant murmuring of the river was the only sound. The moonlight on her face revealed a wordless question. He took a small step toward her, his mind bursting with wonder at the beauty of the moment. She put her other hand on his shoulder, and they kissed awkwardly, Happen feeling the softness of her

lips so intensely that he lost his balance. Then they were
hugging, and he could feel his heart pounding in his hands on
her back.

Happen had a hard time sleeping that night. Ariadne had left
him the large tent to keep Marimba from drawing attention, so
he was trying to sleep next to Cor and a mountain lion, both of
whom were breathing as if deep in sleep already. He thought
about lighting a candle and reading, but he knew that he'd stay
up too late if he did that, and he wanted to be awake tomorrow, to
be with Esmerlia. *Em*, he corrected himself. She was right there
in the next stall. She might be awake also. He could creep over
there, and call her name.

But instead he contented himself with remembering the way
the back of her neck smelled, the touch of her hand on his hip,
and the keen way she looked at him when the dance brought
them back together. He loved the way he felt when she looked at
him that way. It was more comforting than Azmerian stones,
more satisfying than shooting an arrow through the bullseye,
more uniquely for him than the first rays of sunshine in spring.

That was the main thing right there—she looked that way at
him because of who he was, because of the way they had
connected when they talked deep into the night—he couldn't
have been "just anyone." The first rays of sunshine in spring were
full of beauty and significance, too, but they shined whether he
was there or not. That Em looked only at him this way; it made
him feel like he could do anything. He would gladly trade all
those other good feelings to be with her.

Once he'd decided that Tinker and Cor could take his cart
and Marimba south for him so he could stay in Aeriskenn to be
with Em, he felt contented and fell into a deep, restful sleep.

The next day Happen was tired and distracted, but happy. Esmerlia took a long lunch break to help him choose fabrics. He'd decided to wait till they were alone that evening to surprise her with his decision to stay in Aeriskenn. He bought the new Odais book from the bookseller with the raven, but he didn't have time to read it. Not yet.

By afternoon, he'd purchased or traded for everything on his list, and sold everything he'd brought to sell, except for two baskets of elk antlers. He tried carrying some around the artisan rows, and ended up giving one away to calm an angry man whom he'd accidentally speared. Tinker had given him a price under which it would be better to haul them home and try again the following year, and he'd had some offers below that price, but nothing close, so he decided to give up and go see Esmerlia.

Then he passed a man selling deer antlers who asked if Happen would join him at his stall, saying together they could offer customers a better selection, and perhaps garner more interest. Happen agreed to try it for half a bell. The man had a just a few antlers left, and said he was in the same situation as Happen, just trying to finish the last of his trading.

"It will be quite a relief to have all the trading done so we can enjoy the last evening here, won't it?"

"Yes, sir, it will." Happen was surprised with the way the stranger said 'we,' but didn't see the point in arguing.

It wasn't long till a wealthy-looking man came by and offered to buy the whole lot, Happen's elk and the other vendor's deer antlers. He was on his way home, and had already traded in all his fair script, so all he had to offer was Maithean money, but said they could change it at the script office on their way out, or any bank in Aeriskenn. Happen said he was told to only accept script or trade, so the man offered to pay extra for the hassle of bank exchange. *If I agree to this, I can go see Em now.*

The deer antler vendor haggled with the man about the exchange rate, and came out with something very close to what he asked for at the beginning, so Happen figured they'd gotten a good deal. And it worked out to a fine-looking stack of crisp bills. When counting out Happen's share, the deer antler vendor explained that Maithean money was worth less than Berythean money for two reasons: first, the bank would charge a fee for exchange, and second, there had been some economic inflation over there; but he assured Happen that they'd been lucky to get such a good deal. They were also lucky that he had some spare canvas sacks so Happen could carry his money hidden safe from thieves.

Heading back to his cart Happen felt a puzzling mix of satisfaction and regret. Now that his trading was done, he didn't have a list to work from, and he felt lost in the forest without a path to follow. Tomorrow he'd need to find his way to Aeriskenn to look for a job and a boardinghouse. It felt great when he thought about it the night before, but somehow in the light of day the idea seemed insubstantial, almost dreamlike. At the same time, he couldn't stand the thought of not seeing Esmerlia until next year's fair.

The last night of the fair, most folks had finished their trade for the season, and the place had the celebratory air of the night of the Spirit Moon, although without the costumes and face paint. Happen and Esmerlia wandered about, watched a juggling act, a magic show, and a Preathean musical band that played drums made of wood and Gracarrai-certified bronze.

"We need to talk," Esmerlia said. "Let's go walk by the river again."

"Great," Happen said. "I've got a surprise for you."

Once free from the noisy crowds and walking on the moonlit path, she took his hand and turned to face him.

"I hope you don't mind . . . I consulted Bealsio about your future. I . . . I want you to be safe."

"I don't think I mind. I . . . uh, how much did you find out?"

"Not much. Bealsio is better at knowing what is than what will be. But we do know that there's danger awaiting you on the road. South of here. I'm not sure of the details, but I believe Osgar will try to prevent you from returning home."

"Osgar was convicted of heresy by the Gracarrai and sent to work for the king."

Esmerlia looked skeptical. "How do you know that?"

Happen tried to remember how he knew that. That security guard, Macel, had said they had a strong case against Osgar, but Happen couldn't recall the details. Tinker was acting as if Osgar was no longer a threat, but hadn't mentioned him at all.

"I guess I don't know for sure. But I do know that he was arrested, and then we haven't seen him since. And Macel said that even though he wasn't found guilty of theft by fair security, he thought the heresy charge prosecuted by the Gracarrai inspectors would be the last we heard of him."

"But if he got out of that somehow, he'd be in the fair without a cart, so they'd send him away," Esmerlia said. "Without a hair or something, we can't know for sure, but Bealsio thinks he went south, and the work prison is east."

"Oh. Oh, thunder." They started walking back toward the fair, still holding hands. "Tinker would have told me this if he knew Osgar was free," he continued. "I'll have to find someone from the Gracarrai investigation . . . maybe Macel will be able to tell me."

"Why does it matter? It won't hurt to be prepared for trouble on the road, will it?"

. . .

"That was what I was going to tell you," he said, stopping to face her again. "I was going to have Tinker return the cart. I want to stay in Aeriskenn and find a job. We could still see each other." He watched her face, but his words weren't having the effect he had hoped for. "We could go dancing again."

She looked at him like one might look at a puppy that had been left out in the rain.

"Oh," he said. "You wouldn't want that."

"This is why I'll never be the Amazing Esmerlia. I'm so easy to read. It's supposed to be the other way around." They started walking again.

One winter long ago, when an unusual cold snap had frozen the swimming pond, Happen's father tied some sharpened elk bones to his boots, and sent him out on the ice with his staff. At first, he felt awkward and tentative, but he learned quickly how to push from the side and glide straight, and he built up so much speed it seemed he might lift off the ice into the sky. But he fell on the far side of the pond, and the ice which had supported his near-flight cracked and let him through into the coldest water he'd ever known.

"Listen, Hap, I think you're very sweet, and I really would like to get to know you better, but we've met at the fair. It's a special time. Life in the real world is different. You and I would also be different." She paused a moment. Happen was surprised by how different she looked. "I've really enjoyed the time we've spent together the last couple of days, but it's a fond memory, maybe a possibility of something more someday, but it's not something you . . . alter your course about."

Torchlights and voices filtered through the trees near the wood's end. Esmerlia stopped him.

"You've had a big trouble you thought was gone come back to you. And you've got a big journey ahead of you. Let's make a nice memory for you to take along." She handed him an envelope.

"This has my address and a note for you. Don't read it now, save it for a long day on the road."

She kissed him, much less awkwardly this time. It felt nice, but his heart was cold.

When he got back to his tent and lay down, it was late, but he felt like reading. Somehow though, the idea of reading the new *Odais* book didn't appeal to him. Even the new *Sirreltis Seasonal* wasn't what he wanted. It was the first *Odais* book that called to him, just like it had so often before. He considered getting up to dig it out of the cart where he'd stowed it, but it just wasn't the same without his Springing blanket. The familiar yearning made him feel like nothing had changed except his location. He wasn't a vendor, he wasn't a lover, and he wasn't free of Osgar. He felt very tired, and very much alone in the world, here at the trade fair surrounded by more people than he could imagine.

He closed his eyes and an immensity of space surrounded him, a growing but featureless immensity that made him smaller and smaller until he became merely an idea in the dark. And it was there, where he'd been reduced by disappointment, disillusionment, and this strange sense of space that bloomed in his awareness, there in the darkness he turned his question toward himself. If he wasn't those other things, who was he? The mere idea of his self then took shape as a desire. He was hungry for story as if it were food. But not a story in a book, not Odais or Cravey or the like, he hungered for his own story; his story which hadn't even begun yet. That thought echoed in the vast darkness. His story hadn't even begun yet.

It wouldn't begin until he left home for real, and he couldn't do that from here.

And that thought broke the spell, dissipating the sense of space back to the world's usual proportions, and returning him to his body lying in the tent, which was now hungry for an apple from the bag he bought for the trip home, so he grabbed one and crunched into it with gusto, savoring the sweet juice and cool, firm flesh. Happen knew now that he needed to bring the cart home, and then leave on his own terms, with the money he'd earned from Ariadne. From there he would find his story.

# THIRTY-TWO

# A SPELL OF EMPTY SADNESS

" The Irelian peninsula is the last unmapped place in Berythea. Around the time the Fells started bringing their harvest to market, the nearby towns of Parvukenn and Pury were growing. Local woodcutters and elk hunters worked at the edges of the forest. The Eruption reversed the trend. Many Berytheans involved in the relief efforts abroad did not return, either settling overseas or succumbing to the hazards of post-Eruption life on Grith. (Reilly, 2046)

⌇

The morning light crept, dissipating and dispersing, through a thick misty fog. Each caravard, wagon, or cart that rolled over the gravel and away left a spell of empty sadness in its stall, along with damp ashes in the chimineas, scattered pamphlets, torn sacks, and broken pottery. A gray rat nuzzled through some trash left in the edge sharpener's stall. Esmerlia's stall was quiet, the tall black tent becoming more and more prominent as the row emptied around it. Happen felt like the flattened grass left behind when a tent has been packed up.

Tinker arrived, leading Abernathy, Hendrin, and his neighbor's tull, and parked his caravard and the tulls in a vacated stall.

"Come on, you slugs, let's get going." Tinker carried a loaf of bread, a ceramic coffee pot, and three unglazed clay mugs to the space in front of their tent. "No time for a fire. We need an early start to make sure we can cross the Rillbane before dark." They ate and sipped coffee in silence, watching the occasional departing vehicles roll by, each set of four wheels sounding like eight in the foggy quiet.

"Will she get up to say goodbye?" Tinker asked Happen, with a nod to the black tent.

"Naw. It's all right."

Tinker looked at Happen thoughtfully for a moment, then nodded.

"Oh, hey Tinker," Happen said. "Where did Osgar end up? I was thinking he would be sent to the work prison, but . . ." He could see the answer on Tinker's face before he looked away.

"I've been meaning to talk to you boys about that. I knew he wouldn't be able to get back in, so I was hoping you could forget about him and relax for a while."

"How'd he get out?" Cor asked.

"Somebody spoke on his behalf, corroborated his story that he had been manipulated by the witch who carried her voice in her pocket. Then someone planted some stolen goods in Ariadne's wagon and accused her of theft and witchcraft. Once they found the stolen goods and she demonstrated witchcraft, they considered Osgar a victim, and let him go."

"Will they find him?"

"I don't think they're looking. I think everyone's more worried about Ariadne's 'bad witch.'"

"Where will he go?" Happen asked. "He can't go home."

Tinker got up and prepared to leave.

"Wait," Happen said. "He can't go home, can he? We've got to warn my parents!"

"I sent a message three days ago. There's nothing else we can do."

"But you could ride there faster than the post! Cor and I can bring the cart and caravard back."

"I can't do that. We don't know where he is. What if he attacked you on the road at night again? Reg and Darlem can handle themselves pretty well, you know."

"But he's got a broken leg!"

"I know that. But he can still shoot arrows and sling rocks. Listen, the best thing we can do right now is get going. So let's do that."

Happen split an apple with Abernathy and hugged him sadly while Tinker hitched him to the cart. "It's not your fault, old boy," he said.

They moved some of Happen's trade goods into Tinker's caravard to spread the weight evenly between the two vehicles and make room for Marimba's cage in the cart.

"Okay," Tinker called back over his shoulder from atop the borrowed tull. "Everybody ready?"

"Yes," Cor and Happen said from the caravard's driver's bench.

"Good. We'll rotate the tulls between hauling me and the heavier loads, and try to make twelve or fourteen leagues a day."

On the way out they stopped at the busy exchange office to sell their script for solani. Then Happen nervously hoisted his bag of Maithean bills up onto the counter. He didn't want to have to go to a bank in Aeriskenn. The agent thumbed through a stack, frowning.

"Hey Bren, look. These are real! This kid has a fortune."

Happen felt like a golden loaf of bread fresh from the oven, and grabbed Tinker's arm.

Bren sidled over to look and said, "Yeah, real worthless. Don't you read the mail?" He reached over his co-worker's back and pulled a sheet of paper from a shelf.

"Grubs. Sorry, kid." He read aloud, "'Due to civil unrest overseas, we cannot accept Maithean currency at any exchange rate.'" He stuffed the stack of bills back in the canvas bag and pushed it toward Happen, who's heart was collapsing as the meaning of the words sunk in.

"But I could exchange it at a bank in Aeriskenn, right?"

"Maybe? Who knows? Next!"

The long ride reminded Happen of a section of Odais's first big journey. After meeting Balorphemus and the Sage of Dunleoh Forest, the three of them continued on through the flatlands to the sea, knowing all the time that Tormenc's servant would attack them, but not knowing where.

Crossing the Rillbane, Happen looked for the Bufonuriads, and was relieved to see no sign of them.

At first, they traveled with some vendors Tinker had met, and Happen felt pretty safe. But the group grew smaller and smaller the farther south they went, until, by the morning of the third day of travel, they were alone. It was likely to be the longest day on the road, but he kept putting off opening the envelope from Esmerlia, and eventually decided to wait until he got home.

But he did open the pouch from Nora on this day. It had a folded piece of paper, several oddly shaped pieces of some heavy material that looked like tiny steel wheels, and a large coin. He'd seen something like these wheels recently, but couldn't recall where.

The coin was almost two thumbs in diameter, and felt heavier than it should have for its size. It was blacker than charred wood, and the precision and intricacy of the carvings on it were impossible. One side had a crescent moon, several stars, and some complicated symbols, and the other side had lots of tiny symbols arranged in lines as if they were words.

Fortunately, the note had words he could read, though the meaning of some of them could only be guessed at. Nora wrote that Ariadne had a molecular resonance detection system that could detect the approximate location of elements in heavy-stone from many leagues away. So *that's* where he'd seen these things before—Dunkler Stern's workbench. They were heavy-stone scoring wheels dulled and misshapen from overuse. Happen was supposed to keep the old scoring wheels with him wherever he went so Ariadne could find him before she left Grith, to tell him whether she'd been successful.

It was Nora's idea to include the coin, just to give him something nicer that a handful of scrap metal to remember them by. She said it wasn't worth much on Dhaigne, and even less on Grith, so he'd be wise to keep it to himself. He returned the note, the old scoring wheels, and the coin to the pouch, tied it carefully, and carried it in his pocket.

On the fourth day of travel they crossed the Davoura Gorge, and Happen could hardly eat anymore; the fewer leagues that remained ahead, the more likely an attack became.

But still they had seen no trace of Osgar as they pulled into Tinker's lane just north of Pury. Tinker walked the lane, slowly leading his tull, looking for signs of anything unusual, and the boys followed on foot, leading their tulls with their burdens. Crickets chirped as the sun set, lighting up the tall trees with an orange glow.

It had been seventeen days, almost half a moon, since Happen last walked this lane, and the trees had transformed from late summer's mottled green to a glorious autumnal flourish, with vibrant yellows, oranges, and reds splashed among the green and brown. His home and the surrounding hills were covered with a variety of coniferous trees. They had a few maples and alders that changed color in the fall, but nothing like this. On his first visit he hadn't even noticed that he'd been surrounded by a mix of deciduous trees, some kinds he'd never seen before. He strayed off the lane and stepped on a fallen branch that snapped under his boot, and Cor jumped.

"Sorry," Happen whispered. "It's just so beautiful here."

Tinker searched the entire house, knife drawn, and then the barn, before letting the boys unpack and light a fire in the stove, while he went into town to buy meat for them and the cat. None of them referred to her as Marimba anymore, just "the cat." It was late when Tinker returned, and said the only news was that it was a good year for hopvines.

"Oh, and, uh, down at the Crackling Fire, they got all excited when they saw me, and asked me to deliver these." He slapped two letters onto the table.

They were marked urgent and addressed to Reginall Fell. Happen recognized Tinker's handwriting. "But . . . these are . . . from you?"

"I sent them from the fair," Tinker said. "The man who would normally deliver an urgent letter went to Aeriskenn to fight fires and hasn't returned yet. So here they are."

## THIRTY-THREE
## ANGRY AS THUNDER

 After the Great Eruption, famine, disease, and civil unrest reduced the population drastically throughout all of Grith's four continents, although Berythea suffered less than the others. Estimates of the death tolls were not available.

It took two years for the weather to return to normal and eight years for the violence to subside enough for a new geopolitical map to take shape. With economic assistance from Berythea, and spiritual guidance from the suddenly respected Gracarrai leaders, most of Grith's old borders were forgotten, and each continent became a single nation.

Grith's vast oceans had received many more improperly buried soldiers than the lands, and the people feared these borders more than any before or since, due to the belief in danger from sea creatures fattened on (and maddened by) human remains. Generations passed before the lure of trade riches and seafood led to the gradual conversion of warships to peacetime pursuits. (Reilly, 2046)

‹‑

"**D**epending on the angle, the distance, the sharpness of the point, and the strength of the bowman, you can still get badly injured, but this could save your life if someone shoots at you. Turn your head, a bit farther . . . there." Tinker lowered the boiled leather vest over Happen's head.

Happen scrunched his nose. "It smells awful."

"Yes." Tinker reached through the arm holes to straighten the padded lining. "Old Bahnsen said it was made seventy years ago, just after the eruption. It's amazing he still had it. There." Tinker knocked on Happen's chest, and it sounded like a door.

"Do they really boil it? It seems like that would make it soft, not stronger."

"They don't boil it, but they do soak it in hot water, and you're right, that softens it so they can form it into the shape they want. When it dries it shrinks and stiffens. Then they paint it with a lacquer made with sap from a Maithean sumac and a special ceramic powder that makes it even harder."

"It's too big."

"Yes, but you *can* walk, right?"

"I guess so."

"You sure you wouldn't rather try a disguise?"

"I'm sure."

"So why are you complaining?"

"Sorry. I forgot the rule."

"It's not just a rule."

"I know," Happen said with his repeat-after-me voice. "It makes things worse for everybody else."

"Yes. Here's your helmet." The helmet was a boiled leather bowl, with worn and cracked straps connected to plates that protected the back of the wearer's neck. "Remember, this armor doesn't make you invincible, or even keep you from getting hurt if attacked. It just increases your chance of surviving. Right? So if we see Osgar, what are you going to do?"

"Be angry as grith-thunder."

Tinker sighed. "Then what are you going to do?" he said.

"Be calm and smart." *And then I'll be angry as grith-thunder again.*

"Good. And if you need to take this off, you have to turn your head to the side, like you did to get it on."

Tinker put on his leather armor, which was even bigger and older and smelled worse than Happen's. In all of Pury, these were the only two sets of armor he could find to borrow, but Tinker didn't want Cor to come with them anyway. Happen could tell Cor had mixed feelings about it, but he did ask his father if he could please come with them. 'It's not your time,' Tinker had said, and left him to work for their neighbor for a few days.

Since Happen's cart couldn't carry all his stuff and the cat, and Tinker's caravard was both slow and easily recognizable to Osgar, they rented a wagon in Pury. They covered the cart with an old tarp and hitched it to the back of the wagon. When they left Cor and rode through Pury, Happen knew that he looked ridiculous in his old-fashioned armor, but he no longer cared what the people of Pury thought. Tinker didn't seem to care, either. They sat at the front of the open wagon, hauling his family's trade goods and a stolen cougar through town as if they did it all the time.

The wide-open fields west of Pury, lacking cover for a potential ambush, rolled by pleasantly. The wind picked up a little after lunch, as if trying to push them back to Pury, but with both Hendrin and Abernathy pulling, they kept up a good pace. Waves of wind flowed through the tall dry grass, dull gold in the gray light of the overcast day. Each gust raised a whispered hiss from rubbing stalks and rattling seed pods. By midafternoon, the grove of oaks that marked his first camping spot crested a low hill. When they crossed the old stone bridge over the creek that crawled out from the oaks, an uneasy feeling came over him.

"We're not camping here tonight, are we?"

"No," Tinker said. "We've got another two leagues to go today. But our camping place won't have water, so we'll stop here to refill."

"Do we have to? My waterskin's nearly full still." He shook his waterskin, which wasn't quite half full.

"As much as I enjoyed the Crackling Fire's ale last night, I've had to drink extra water today, plus the tulls' fighting this wind is thirsty work. What's it matter? Got something against oak trees?"

Happen couldn't think of a way to explain how he had felt here, that stormy night.

"I had a bad dream here, is all," he said.

Tinker looked at him thoughtfully.

"Okay. We'll park in the turn out, and leave the tulls hitched. Fill their bucket and the cat's with what you've got left. I'll run over and refill the jugs. Then we'll be on our way."


Happen watered the animals, then returned to the wagon seat to watch and wait for Tinker. Some of the leaves on the oak trees had a jaundiced hue, but most were just brown, nothing like the splendor by the lane in front of Tinker's house. Tinker kicked playfully through some drift piles on his way to the creek, but the uneasy feeling continued to gnaw at Happen and soured his stomach.

At the creek, Tinker took off his quiver and set down his bow, then leaned over the bank with one of the empty water jugs. The cat lapped at her water, and a gust of wind shivered the cart. Happen's attention drifted among the tottering oak branches. A sudden movement by the creek drew his eye. Tinker jumped convulsively, scooted backward on his knees, grabbed his bow and quiver and rolled away from the creek. Standing by a tree, he shouted.

"Hap, he's shooting at me. Stay there, I'll be back soon."

Happen grabbed his bow and quiver and ran toward the creek. Tinker was gone, but if he was chasing Osgar, Happen wanted to help. Before he reached the grove, someone appeared on the road, back by the bridge. Happen slowed to look. The person was carrying a small round shield, and jogging toward the cart and wagon. That person moved like Osgar. Happen stopped. Tinker must be chasing someone else, and Osgar must have been hiding up the road somewhere.

*He wants the cart.* Happen was about to complete his Summering Task and bring the cart home with extra money from delivering the cat. He imagined them welcoming him home, with a fire in the hearth, and his favorite barley soup. And maybe, just maybe, his parents might speak to him with a little more respect. That would be worth more to him than everything in the cart.

But if Osgar took the cart he'd take both tulls and the wagon, leaving Happen and Tinker to walk, and he'd arrive at the farm long before them. Long before they could warn Reg not to trust him.

And Osgar was running for the cart. Straight toward the back of the cart.

Happen shouted for Tinker, then sprinted back to his cart, shouting Tinker's name as he ran. Happen was closer, a lot closer, but slowed by his oversized armor. Also, Osgar was on the hard-packed road, and Happen was running through tall grass.

Two wide bands of steel circled Osgar's shield. His other hand held the blade of a sheathed sword. Happen considered trying to shoot Osgar, but he'd have to stop running, and if he missed, and Osgar reached the cart, he'd lose access to his best weapon, and the cat could be in danger. Also, moving targets were something he rarely practiced. Dropping his bow and quiver, he drew his knife as he ran, planning what to do, and trying to remember the order of things.

Happen arrived at the cart a few waves ahead of Osgar, skidded on the gravel, and banged into a wheel as he cut the twine holding the old tarp down to get access to the cabinet with the crossbow arrows. With shaking hands he rolled them onto the tray. The fourth and fifth ones jammed because he was rushing, but he didn't think he'd need them, so he dove under the front hitch to the get to the other side of the cart.

Scrambling to his feet, he cut the twine holding the tarp on that side, and pushed the trigger back to the load the arrow. While reaching under the armored vest to dig the crank wrench out of the pouch on his belt, he glanced up at the road. Osgar was close enough now that Happen could see the grim expression on his face and the sweaty hair plastered to his skin. He wouldn't have time to open the back cover, but at this distance it shouldn't matter. He dropped his knife and fiddled with the wrench with shaking hands, got the square peg into the slot, and then stopped. *Which way to turn it?*

Osgar's footsteps pounded the road, closer and closer. Happen turned the crank to the rear of the cart, and it clicked, but it didn't grab after two turns, so he tried the other way. After three clicks he felt the resistance and drew the bow. He reached for the trigger and looked up, but Osgar was now on the side of the lane. The aiming lever was under the back cover.

There wasn't time to unlatch both sides and then get in position to aim. Osgar was too close now, sword drawn, his steps slower, grinding into the loose gravel on the road's edge.

Happen pulled out his sling and angry rocks, shaking a few into his hand and dropping the tull's horn. He had time for one slow deep breath, and then another, because Osgar stopped when he saw what Happen was doing. A sneer seeped onto Osgar's face, and he turned his body to present a slimmer target and raised his shield to his shoulder.

Happen breathed, then stepped forward and swung, aiming at Osgar's yellow teeth. The small rock struck the shield and it shattered into splintered pieces of wood and warped steel that fell at Osgar's feet. The scoff was gone as he gaped at the shield handle in his hand, letting it fall to the road with the rest. Then he raised his sword and regained his pace. Happen had another rock ready, and he stepped forward and swung, but his second cast missed.

Osgar sprinted ahead and before Happen could cast a third rock he spun around to build momentum for a mighty back-handed swing with the sword, striking Happen in the chest. The blade was turned by the armor, but Happen was knocked back against the cart, stumbling and dropping his sling and rocks. By the time he'd righted himself, the tip of Osgar's steel blade was embedded in his armor, about a thumb and a half from his sternum. Osgar leaned on the sword, pinning Happen against the back of the cart, right in the center, with the loaded crossbow thumbs away, pointed at his spine.

Trapped. Part of the armor had cracked inward against Happen's ribs, but it held.

Happen kept his head up, watching his assailant carefully. *Obstacles: my armor vest is held against the cart by a stout and sharp sword. Time remaining: unknown. Assets?* He'd dropped all his weapons. There was only the crossbow, which pointed at both of them now.

The cat growled from her cage in the wagon, but she stayed in it.

"Come on out, mouser, and I'll slay you, too." Osgar laughed as if he'd played a great prank on Marimba and Happen both.

"Leave the cat alone."

Osgar looked back down at Happen. "Like my sword, kid? If I can't inherit your farm, I might have to just take it." He pushed on the hilt, forcing the blade deeper into the armored vest. "I saw the look on your face when Reg gave me your seat at the table. I enjoyed that better than the ale. But that's not the seat I want—not anymore."

Happen kicked as hard as he could, but Osgar dodged just out of reach, and smacked Happen on the side of the head. Most of his strength was holding the sword, so the blow only knocked Happen's helmet off.

"You know when I get there, old Reginall, he'll be real interested in this sword. Real interested, until he feels my new steel knife in his back. I gave you Fells every chance to do something, anything more than own me."

Happen squirmed. He felt tiny and helpless. Captured. *Do Odais's protocol. The whole thing, not just assessment. Attitude. I will survive this.*

"But I'm not going to kill Darlem. I'm going to save her for things you know nothing about. Yeah, things they don't write about in your hero books." Again Osgar laughed as if he'd said something funny.

*Vigilance. Don't listen to him. Watch.* Happen scanned Osgar's stance, looking for an opening.

"But you." Osgar looked to each side of the road, as if checking to see who was watching him use his shiny new sword. "You wouldn't even make a decent slave."

*Plan.* Seeing Osgar's annoying habit, Happen remembered turning his head to get into his armor, and thought of an idea.

With both hands Osgar pushed harder on the hilt, forcing the blade farther through the hard leather. If he got any closer, Happen might be able to reach his face, but the tip of the blade was now pricking his skin through the padded shirt. Osgar gathered himself for a final push.

*Execute.* Happen pulled his arms into the vest like a turtle, then turned his head and dropped down through the pinned armor, the tip of the sword slicing a straight line up his chest and left cheek. On the ground, he rolled to the side of the cart, lunged for the trigger, and pushed.

# THIRTY-FOUR

## A NICE MESS

> Some aspects of Gracarrai teachings were inspired
> by, or adopted directly from, an ancient Maithean
> civilization known as Bandu. Most of Berytheans'
> beliefs about death and the treatment of dead
> bodies is described in Bandu literature, translations
> of which are found in the academy's library, but not
> in typical bookstores. (Reilly, 2046)

T he back cover board snapped. Happen sprawled on the
gravel by the wheel, then looked back through the
spokes and the dust he'd kicked up.

Osgar was still standing. His pants were wet below the knee.
*Must have been hiding under the bridge.* It sounded like he was
reaching for something in the cart, searching for something, but
not finding it. Then his knees buckled, and he groaned and fell,
crying out as he hit the road. The armored vest, with the tip of
the sword poking out the back, bounced twice and landed several
feet away.

Happen crawled to where his knife lay on the ground next to the cart, grabbed it, and stopped to listen. All was quiet but for a strange wheezing sound. His tull's horn lay on the ground between him and Osgar. He didn't know if Osgar even knew about angry rocks. He stood and approached the back of the cart cautiously, leading with the knife. Osgar tried to raise himself but cried out again and kept still after that.

"Kid," he called weakly.

Osgar's right hand lay empty, motionless, half curled up like a dead spider, but it wasn't far from the knife in his belt. Happen knelt to pick up his tull's horn, keeping his eye on Osgar's hand. He found one angry rock still inside the hollowed-out horn and breathed a sigh of relief. He stood up tall and approached Osgar confidently now and still Osgar did not move. He wheezed through a trickle of blood that pulsed from his mouth. Happen verified that his left hand was empty and motionless as well.

"Osgar." He was surprised to find that he wasn't angry anymore.

Osgar tried to check the field next to the road to see if someone there might overhear what he was about to say, but he stopped himself. It was clear that any movement caused Osgar intense pain, so Happen returned the angry rock to the tull's horn. He didn't feel sorry for Osgar, or sickened like when he hurt the security guard at the fair.

"I just . . . I just wanted a home of my own," Osgar said.

"That doesn't seem like the right way."

"You don't know. Everything's just there for you. But you don't deserve it, never worked a day in your life." Osgar's breath was quick and shallow.

"That's not true."

"It is though. You don't know what work is. It's a different thing when you can choose what to do."

· · ·

Happen kicked at the gravel and wondered what was taking Tinker so long. He watched, with increasing worry, for any movement near the place by the stream where he'd last seen him. If Tinker's not chasing Osgar, he should be back by now.

Osgar coughed, spattering blood on Happen's boots. *Work is a different thing when you can choose what to do . . . Was he talking about that uncertain feeling of not knowing what you want, or of wanting to go in contradictory directions; that feeling was supposed to help?*

Finally, Tinker appeared near the creek, limping toward the cart. Happen waved, and Tinker waved back as he continued. *Why is he limping?*

"Kid," Osgar said. "Happen. I need a favor. Two favors."

"Tinker's coming."

"Happen, please. Promise me. Look out for Mistine, okay? She's a good kid, just needs a little help now and then. She never meant you any harm, it was all me. Promise me." He coughed again, and his voice weakened. "Say it."

"I'll look out for her, sure."

"She's hiding out at a secret cave. Be there for a couple of days. Ask at the Fire. Maybe put a little something on her account there . . ."

"Yeah, sure. Hey, Tinker's coming. He'll know what to do. Get you to the doctor in Pury or something."

"Other favor. Get the sword. End the pain. Please."

Happen didn't answer. He couldn't find his anger toward Osgar. Nor could he find enough pity to end his pain. Tinker would know what to do.

"Please."

Happen kept still and watched Tinker arrive and take in the scene.

"You okay, Hap?"

"Yeah. He said hasn't been up to see my folks yet. Was going there next. You okay?"

"Slipped and banged my knee on a rock. I'll be all right. Nice mess you've made here."

He stood over Osgar, then, with his boot, lifted Osgar's left hip a little. Osgar cried out, then coughed.

"Two favors, kid," he croaked, and a fresh surge of blood drained from the corner of his mouth.

Tinker looked at Happen.

"He wants us to kill him with this." Happen stepped on the armor and yanked the sword out.

"Please," Osgar whispered.

"Want to?" Tinker asked Happen.

Happen hesitated. The image unfolded in his mind as if he were picturing an event as he read it in a book. He gagged, dropped the sword, and stepped back, trying to shake the numb horror out of his hands. *How did Odais do such things?*

"I might as well. What a maggot of a day." Tinker picked up the sword. His shoulders slumped with a heavy, tired sigh. "Say the prayer, Osgar."

Happen stepped around to the far side of the tulls. Osgar whispered something.

"Say it with everything you've got left," Tinker demanded. "Or I won't do it. I'll not have you haunting this road."

"I, Osgar T—"

"Louder!" Tinker's voice was angry now.

"I, Osgar Tallowey, shun life this day. Tonight may I dine with my ancestors; tomorrow to retake my place in the wheel."

Tinker raised the sword, and Happen buried his face in Abernathy's mane.

⌐⌐

When Happen returned from fetching and filling the water jugs he found Tinker had removed his ill-fitting armor and rolled Osgar's body up in the tarp they'd brought for the cat.

"I expect they'll be glad enough to get their cat back they won't mind if she's a little wet. From the inn, we can find somebody to carry the body back to Pury," Tinker said as they each took an end and hoisted it up into the wagon next to the cage.

Happen poked around in the gravel by the cart and found most of the angry rocks he'd dropped. His father said if they weren't stored properly, they gradually lost their unique properties, otherwise it would be irresponsible to leave any out where a kid might pick one up. He replaced the stopper at the base of the horn, packed it away, and climbed into the wagon.

Tinker flicked the reins, and they set out on the inland route, heading west toward a darkening sky and the beginning of a light rain. Happen ruminated fruitlessly about work and choices until Tinker interrupted.

"What was the other favor?"

"Other favor?"

"He said, 'Two favors.' What was the other one?"

"Oh, right. He wanted me to look out for Mistine, put some money in her account at the Crackling Fire on occasion."

"Got you covered on that one as well."

"What do you mean?"

The rain was too light to make a sound, but the sand-colored gravel darkened, the grass drooped, and the air chilled.

"I'm filling a water jug at the creek, right? And thud. An arrow sticks in the bank near me. I know Osgar's not a great shot, and who else would be shooting at me? So I got angry as grith-thunder and set out in the direction I think it came from. Soon enough I hear I'm gaining on him, and he hears me, panics, and makes even more noise than before, leading me on through the scrub toward those woods out that way. We cross a creek, and I was going too fast and hurt my knee, which just made me angrier. Then he trips and falls, and I get close enough to risk a shot, and I tell him to stop or I'll kill him. He didn't stop, so I shot him in the back. At which point I was able to catch up."

"Oh. Oh, thunder."

"Yeah. Lucky shot, for me and her, got her in the heart, and it was over pretty quick. She fell just a few steps short of what looks like a hideout cave they'd stocked with food and weapons. Even had a door I could drag shut to keep her from getting eaten. But aside from the lucky shot, and you being okay when I got back, it hasn't been a great day." Tinker had a small whiskey jug on the seat next to him, and took a drink before continuing. "It's funny, when you get into your Harvesting years, and things go well, it's just fine, just okay. But when things go badly, it cuts you up cruel inside. It doesn't seem right, somehow. Maybe it's just how men are, or fathers anyway. Or, just how Fells are." He took another drink from the jug, offered it to Happen, who declined. "Or, grubs. Maybe it's just how Tinkers are."

# THIRTY-FIVE

# ANCIENT BATTLES AND ANGRY ROCKS

> Collachine are small, gray-skinned humanoids with spoken language that remains unstudied by linguists (either local or galactic). The concept of collachine intelligence is controversial among Berythean academics. Those who scoff at the notion point out their taste for slugs and their fear of fire. Others describe a remarkable adaptability and call for further study. (Reilly, 2046)

They camped that night where the cart path to the school left the inland route. The next morning's weather was cool and overcast but dry.

"Listen," Tinker said. "I've been thinking about your parents. If there's an inkling that things aren't right with their child, they won't be able to rest, and since they didn't get my messages, Cor's absence at school won't feel right to them. Now that we know Osgar hasn't been there, and won't be, I think it's time you go home. I know two leagues uphill on soft track is a long, hard day with a loaded cart, but if you'll do that, I'd be willing to return the cat to the inn for you."

"I was hoping to earn that money from Ariadne."

"You will. I'm asking you to put in an extra hard day of travel for my peace of mind, to check in with my brother for me. In exchange, I'll return the cat for you. You're still earning it. When you're hiking that last half league, you'll understand."

"That doesn't feel right to me. How about if you go up there, and I'll take the cat?" As soon as he said it, he knew that wouldn't feel right, either. He had to be the one to bring the cart home.

"I appreciate that you want to follow through on this, but sometimes things can be okay even if they don't all fit together the way you'd like them to."

"All right. I guess."

"Your parents need to see you, not me. Plus, you need to get that cut cleaned out."

Tinker took out his knife and cut the knots from a few of the ropes holding Marimba's cage together, unlashed one of the walls, and then tied the ropes together to make a longer rope, while Happen and Marimba watched and wondered.

"Here. You may need to help Abernathy pull the cart."

"Oh."

Happen walked along next to Abernathy, stepping over the bent and broken stems of weeds poking up from the cleared trail like skeletal knees of slain soldiers on an old battleground. The more he thought about it, the better he felt about Tinker's idea to send him home. He didn't really want to explain to some stranger how he ended up with their stolen cougar. *Plus, this is my Summering Task. I should probably do* some *walking.*

The school looked smaller than he remembered. The little

building was quiet, windows staring blankly. A sudden loneliness compelled him to open Esmerlia's note.

 Dear Happen,

Thank you for making my Summering Task so much fun, and for providing my finneswyn. I've been hoping the world was more than what I've been told, and meeting you made me believe in that hope. I'll be offering Ariadne's hair, because it provides proof of more. It's the only thing I've ever even heard of with no history. When you get to Aeriskenn, ask for Mr. Boonesen at the Boon or Bane Tavern on Lower Commerce Street. If I'm still in the city, they'll have my address.

Thanks for being yourself. When winter comes I hope you'll dream of me in your home among the trees. Till we meet again, much love, Em

Happen tried to remember what she looked like. He thought it might help him sort out his feelings, but they spun away and returned with a different face like dancers in the line, and he didn't know them. *The finneswyn, though!* To Summer, you had to offer an item of unique value to prove that you completed your task. The finneswyn hadn't been on his list and he'd forgotten all about it. He'd have to think of something, at some point. But he still had another league to go, and it was well past midday. He split an apple with Abernathy, and plunged into the dark woods.

The school sat at the ragged edge of the forest, where the scattered trees and groves grew together into a dense congregation as the elevation rose west and north. Ages ago great battles, glacially paced and quiet, but deadly all the same, were fought here among the trees as each raced to overreach, repress, and smother its neighbor. These trees here that Happen and Abernathy trudged through, these were the victors, joined now in apparent peace, with varied layers of communion among them: intertwined underground; interlaced atop, where they shared the glorious openness and light at the extent of their grandeur; and, especially on windy days, at the ends of branches, where the drooping hemlocks dragged their feathery fingertips along and tickled the uplifted limbs of the firs.

Happen had never thought of the trees or the forest this way before. On this day he felt their vitality, and was aware of it consciously for the first time. The road, which he'd always taken for granted, now felt like an affront barely tolerated by the trees. Someone had spread gravel about six feet wide for the entire two leagues between his home and the inland route. *What weary work that must have been under the stifling disapproval of the forest! Why not live closer to town?*

A hundred years ago Bartholofew Fell built a house and established a farm where people said it couldn't be done. He cut trees for building and dug rocks from the ground to shape a foundation and hearth. His brother Harlind joined him and then his aunt and uncle. Happen's grandfather had hinted that Bartholofew had chosen such isolation to escape a scandalous history. At the time, Happen had been in the middle of his first reading of *The Odais Chronicles*, and hadn't thought to ask his grandfather to tell him more.

He hadn't walked under the trees for long before the sounds of rain began to slowly build. A light breeze brought the smell of his favorite time of year. Some mysterious combination of decay, damp fungi, and wandering mists reached ideal proportions between the Spirit Moon and the Windy Moon, and Happen loved to be out on the trails and deer paths in the forest breathing it, surrounded by it, absorbing it. He took a long, deep breath and felt like the dried apples in his mother's oatmeal when she poured hot water into the bowl: expanding, softening, relaxing. Abernathy seemed to be doing the same thing.

"It's good to be back, Aber," he said. "But still, it's going to get dark soon, can you keep the pace, please?" The brighter clouds were dimming behind the western peaks, leaving a dull gray twilight that would last for some time, but there was a long way to go yet, and Abernathy wasn't slowing down to enjoy the air, he was tiring. Abernathy stopped, turned to look at Happen, and waggled his ears in a tired way.

"All right, time for a carrot."

But Abernathy would not eat the carrot.

Happen sighed. "I suppose you're right, it's time for the rope, too." He unpacked the rope Tinker had fashioned from the cage lashings. It felt strangely smooth in his hands, but he put on his elkhide gloves anyway, after tying the rope to the cart's hitch. Then he tried giving Abernathy the carrot again, and it disappeared in a few quick crunches. Happen took his place ahead of Abernathy, trying to keep centered to avoid pulling the cart off the road.

Happen passed the time trying to spot collachine in the forest. Fortunately, there were no cougars in the area, so he could hear the collachine breaking seed scales off fir cones with sharp rocks for their breakfast. In the spring he would trade with them for maple sugar, but this time of year they ate conifer seeds, grubs, and slugs; certainly nothing he wanted, so he was surprised to find some young collachine running alongside him, grunting and pointing.

He'd been struggling to find a reasonably comfortable way to pull the rope when he noticed them. The work aggravated the long cut from Osgar's sword, making it sting and ache. The combination of the growing discomfort of the rope and the impertinent behavior of the collachine irked him enough that he stopped and confronted them with too much temper.

"What's so thundering funny!" he demanded, and they scattered silently, disappearing among the trees in seconds. Happen

was immediately sorry for yelling at them, and took a water and
carrot break, hoping to restore the good mood he'd had earlier.
While he filled the bucket for Abernathy, an older collachin
approached, holding a large stick with the bark removed, and
stopped at a safe distance. He grunted softly and raised his hand
in the friendly gesture. Happen put down the bucket slowly and
returned the greeting.

The collachin put the stick down by the end of the rope that
Happen had thrown down in frustration. He untied the rope
from the cart's hitch, and reaching as high as his long, nimble
fingers could, tied it to Abernathy's collar at the front of the trace.
Grunting softly as he worked, he brought the ends of the rope
together to find its midpoint, tied a clove hitch there on either
end of the stick, then tied the other end of the rope to the far side
of Abernathy's collar.

Then Happen understood that the collachin had fashioned a
tandem hitch with a yoke of sorts for a boy to push. Happen
bowed to thank him. He didn't have anything to offer that he
knew the collachin would want, but he tried offering an apple
just to show appreciation. The collachin declined payment,
bowed politely, and silently faded into the woods.

Happen positioned the stick and pushed his chest into it. It hurt
his cut, but placing his gloves on either side of the wound kept
the stick from rubbing it. Once Abernathy joined in the effort,
they moved forward, faster and more comfortably than before.
Twilight deepened as they trudged on, leather boots and worn
hooves striving against the duff-covered gravel. He guessed they
must be about half a league away, because he was starting to
wish he'd taken the cat to the inn. He also wished the collachin
had taken the apple, anything to lighten the burden, even a small
amount. Could anything be left by the road, to be retrieved later?
He listed his inventory. He wanted to arrive with all of the money

and trade goods. The only other options were clothing, kitchen gear, two books, the worthless Maithean money, a small bag of apples, two carrots, some bannock, and some firewood. They stopped again, drank some water, ate the bannock, and then he left the firewood in a neat pile on the road, with the kitchen gear, a pair of pants, and the bag of apples on top.

He wasn't sure what was heavier, the Maithean money, or the shame he felt about accepting it as payment. Somehow, leaving it behind seemed to add to the weight of the shame, so he kept it. He also considered leaving Esmerlia's note and handkerchief, but that didn't feel right either. His mixed feelings for her weren't much of a burden, but then neither were the reminders.

The cart didn't feel any lighter. It became too dark to look for collachine. Happen's legs and back ached, and the yoke chafed his skin where it had worn through his linen shirt. He felt like Odais in the work prison. When he wasn't busy planning his escape, Odais had to tell stories to pass the time and keep from dwelling on the pain. Happen told Abernathy the story of angry rocks.

"Here's the story as my grandfather told it to me, Aber. On the fine early summer day when Bartholofew Fell came to the Irelian peninsula, he set up a tent in a grassy clearing, the site of our current homestead, left his tull with some water, and set out exploring on foot. After lunch at the High Fells, he wanted to refill his waterskin, and soon found a spring feeding a small creek. It was a warm afternoon, and he drank deeply before filling his waterskin. But when he stood up to hike back down to camp, he felt ill and dizzy. He took one step before weakness buckled his knees, and he fell to the ground, vomiting and feverish. After a time, he fell asleep.

"Bartholofew awoke during the night, parched from sweating out the fever, but otherwise feeling somewhat better. After another long drink at the spring, though, the illness came over him again, worse the second time. Again, he fell asleep. He was awakened in the morning by a wolf pulling at a leg of his trousers, and shouted to scare the wolf off. But his shout was weak, and the wolf did not go far. In fact, he found that he was surrounded by a pack of them, less than three rods away. He had a knife, but was too weak to stand and fight. He needed water, but was afraid to drink from the spring, thinking that might be what was poisoning him."

Happen paused to drink from his waterskin. Night reached farther over the forest, and it became too dark for Happen to see his way. The old trees stood close to the road, and branches joined above it to form a dark ceiling. Starting forward again, Happen felt the ragged right edge of the road with his feet and steered back to the center.

"The wolves, seeing Bartholofew's slow movements, grew bolder, and took turns badgering him. Bartholofew knew he needed to try something else to defend himself, so he dragged himself closer to the spring, and found some stones in the water to throw. He didn't have the strength to hurt the wolves, but hoped it might keep them at a distance long enough for him to think of something else. The first stone he threw missed, but the wolves paused, concerned by his new tactic. He leaned up against a fallen log to get into better position to throw, and the next time a wolf came near, he tried again. This time he hit the wolf near its hip. He expected the wolf to bound away, if it reacted at all to his weak throw, but instead, the wolf yowled in pain, and dragged its leg on the ground as it limped away whimpering.

"The other wolves gave Bartholofew no time to ponder the strange occurrence. One came at him from behind, and he slashed at it with the knife in his left hand. As he turned, another dashed in from the front, aiming to bite a leg, so he threw another stone. His aim was true, and he hit the wolf between the eyes. He couldn't get much speed on the throw, and the stones weren't particularly large or sharp, so he was shocked to see the wolf fall dead as if its skull was broken.

"Bartholofew threw one more stone, wounding a wolf who complained loudly enough to convince the pack to move on. Exhausted, he lay still for a long time pondering the mystery of the stones from the spring that had made him sick. He crawled to his rucksack and found an apple and some elk jerky, and eating them soon found the strength to return to camp. But before he left, he marked the spring and took note of the way. Also, he picked up a pocketful of stones from the spring to bring with him.

"And that, dear Abernathy, is how the Fells discovered the angry rocks, which you mustn't tell anyone about, or we'll end up with a slew of haunters, mendicants, and scroungers traipsing through our hills drinking in all the springs. Is what my grandfather always said anyway."

Happen sighed, and kept pushing, forcing his heavy legs forward as his wound throbbed.

"And we're still not home yet."

But then he felt a dip in the road, followed by a slight, but still painful, rise; and then his left foot found the edge of the road. He knew a place in the road with a dip before a curve to the right, and it wasn't that far from home. He and Abernathy ate the last two carrots, and he poured the last of the water into the tull's bucket. *Almost there.*

At home his parents would be glad to see him, say he did well, and give him warm food. At home he could stop pushing against this stupid stick and talking to a tull in the dark. At home there'd be a warm fire, a soft dry bed. His Summering Task would be done. That would make it all worthwhile.

THIRTY-SIX

A LIGHTER DARKNESS

> Summerings typically wear a wristband braided from their mother's hair, and most leave home soon after their ceremony. (Reilly, 2046)

*·ᘿ·*

As the night wore on, Happen alternated between doubting his memory about the dip and curve to the right, and wondering if his parents had moved the house. The road just kept going and going. *Should be there by now. It must be close to morning.* But the cold, dark road and the rain continued step after tired step.

"I need more stories to tell, Aber. I can't do this." He slowed his pace a little and found himself standing still, holding the yoke up with his hands, rain dripping off the brim of his hat. Abernathy stepped up behind him and nuzzled his neck. He looked up and saw the hint of a vaguely shaped area of lighter darkness, floating above the road ahead in the distance. *That could be it.*

He leaned into the yoke again, stumbled, then strove forward, and sure enough, the area grew larger. It was the clearing where he lived.

"Halloooo," he called as he entered the clearing and collapsed into a puddle. It wasn't deep, and he lifted his face from the water onto his forearm and closed his eyes. He thought for sure he would fall asleep, but he didn't. The cold water felt good where the skin had rubbed off from his shoulders and chest. Rain pattered. Then another sound mingled with the rain, a subtle gravelly whisper came up from the solid stillness of Grith especially for him. The whisper solidified into a grinding sound like that made by the grindstone when they ground oats at the mill.

"You are all right now. You are home, and everything is right now."

Happen took a deep breath and felt the weight of his limbs press into the ground. Happiness created a place for him separate from the cold and pain in his body, and he breathed easily and listened.

"You are home, and everything is right. You may not leave."

The back door opened and banged against the railing. A light came with footsteps. Heavy footsteps hurrying.

"What under thundering Grith . . ." His father's voice. "Happen?"

Happen could barely stay awake as his father washed his wounds and applied a salve. Reginall had tried asking questions like, "where's that good-for-nothing Tinker?" and "how'd you get a cut like that?" but his first question was puzzling and annoying. He asked if his cousin was okay, as if that was the most important thing. He asked it as if Cor had been stolen and Happen had gone to Aeriskenn to get him. He asked it as if he hadn't been worried about Happen the way Tinker said he would be. Happen was too tired and annoyed to answer any of his questions, and his father stopped asking.

Happen woke up wrapped in a blanket and sleeping on the braided rug by the fire with his mother trying to feed him some broth. She said something about ruining a shirt, but she smiled, and it was nice to see her smile.

"I'm sorry," he croaked, his mouth dry. The broth felt like the rain on the fields of Nerrinen after Odais ended the drought curse. This feeling continued all the way from his mouth to his stomach, and spread out from there. He turned his head and saw the special jug they used only for water from the healing spring. He accepted another mouthful.

"Shhhh," she whispered. "It's okay. Just a shirt. Eat and rest." The sound of her voice slid through his mind and lifted, swirling like dry autumn leaves in a playful wind.

"No. 'Bout yelling."

She smiled. "It's okay. I'm glad you're home safe. I love you."

Another spoonful swallowed. He closed his eyes. "Love—"

"Shhhh," she whispered. She'd cooked an Azmerian stone in the broth. "You're going to be fine." A slow wave of tingling seemed to call attention to each hair on his head individually— briefly, but without hurry—and his mother's voice spun like a dancer then settled gently down. "Shhhh."

Sometime later Happen woke in bed, and he could tell by the dim gray light outside that it was still very early in the morning, so he stayed in bed, enjoying the smell of his home and the weight of his blanket. All of his muscles ached, and his shoulders hurt under their bandages, but if he held still it wasn't too bad. Next to his bed, two books waited on the little table, the beat up old first book of *The Odais Chronicles*, and the nice new fifth one.

A bowl of cold broth and a spoon waited next to the books.

He ignored the spoon and drank the broth straight from the bowl. The window grew darker. It had been dusk falling, not the rising dawn. He fell back asleep.

A few years back a Windy Mester storm blew a tree into the mill's waterwheel, so Father and Tinker dug a diversion channel to drain the mill pond so they could repair the damage, and they left just a thin section of the turfed edge of the pond so that Happen could finish the channel. When they lowered the gate sluice to block the mill race, and the pond level rose, that thin section of turf held back what would become, once Happen struck it with the adze, a powerful flow of energy.

Something in him was somehow both that pent up energy *and* the thin membrane holding it back.

Perhaps that was the meaning of the dream voices, if that's what they were. He could not leave. He was still Springing. The Summering ritual made sense to him now. There *was* something holding him back, and he wouldn't be able to take that with him. It was time.

The water in the mill pond cared not where it went, it just went, and it would find out what awaited it once it got there. It was time for his story to begin.

The next morning it was raining, and Happen went downstairs hungry for breakfast. His parents were up and cooking. He didn't feel like answering questions, but wanted to get it over with, so he sat at the table and waited.

"Good morning, Happen." His father brought him a steaming bowl of oatmeal with nuts and dried apples. "What should we do today?"

That was not the question Happen expected, and he choked on his first bite of oatmeal. After coughing into his napkin and signaling to his concerned parents that he was okay, he took some time to restore his equilibrium. He explored the way the divinity of the wood grain overcame the randomness of the nicks and scratches time had inflicted upon the kitchen table. He set his goal to construct a thoughtful answer to his father's question. He'd always been told what to do; or, when he wasn't needed immediately, he'd taken off before being assigned to some task or other. Now they were asking him.

"Unpack the cart?"

"Done. Tinker was here yesterday and helped us unload it. Also unloaded an outrageously fanciful concoction of a tale that my mother would have found merely 'interesting.' I was surprised he didn't need a few more tulls and a bigger wagon to haul it up here, but he was always was one prone to exaggeration."

"Oh, good. I don't want to spend all day talking. I need to build a bonfire for my blanket. Also, I have some things to learn. Do we have any books about witches or naiads?"

"What are you offering for finneswyn?"

Happen and his parents stood by the unlit fire he'd prepared. A makeshift canopy kept the light but steady rain from soaking his blanket and the carefully arranged pyre of kindling and firewood beneath it. Close by, the Fell family ciorcagnal, formed on a bare circle of ground and soaked, awaited the dry tinder in Happen's pocket..

Happen held up his staff hopefully. "See the green stains? Still there from when I had to hack my way from the school to the inland route. It gave me quite a bit more than 'a little trouble.'" He could tell from their stillness that he needed to try again. The staff wasn't unique. It had clear value, but only proved that he'd been to the inland route, not the trade fair. He had the note from Esmerlia, but it only had value to him, and he still wasn't sure how he felt about her. He had the fifth book in *The Odais Chronicles*, but he hadn't read it yet.

"Please don't offer the book," Darlem said. "I don't want to keep that from you."

"If you had something related to the more outlandish parts of Tinker's . . ." Reg didn't know how much of Tinker's story was exaggeration, and how much was untrue.

*I don't know how much to believe, either. But I do know I have to offer Ariadne's coin, because it hurts to part with it. While they fuss over the bewildering impossibility of the thing, I place dry tinder in the circle and call the fire.*

# ACKNOWLEDGMENTS

Thanks to friends who suffered through early versions of the book to help make it better: Audrey, Todd, Corey, Sara, Tamara, Andrew, Mark, Lindsay, and Daisha. Thanks to Jessica Khoury at Lizard Ink Maps for the helpful map of Aeriskenn Fairgrounds, and to Matt Samson for helping with the map of Berythea. Thanks to Jeff Brown at Jeff Brown Graphics for the inspiring front cover. Thanks to Kat Betts at Element Editing Services. If you find a mistake it's because I tinkered with stuff after she worked on it. Thanks to Jennifer Crain at Pearl and Ink for help with cover copy, the hardest 150 words in the project.

Thanks to Joy and the rest of my family for the support. Thanks to Beethoven for continuing to work on the symphonies, and the Grateful Dead for Dark Star and the rest. And all the rock and roll musicians and authors who made me think I might be on the right planet after all, so that I could be here to meet Dave, Kevin, Charlie, Paul, Johnny Shoes, the Emerson's, Doug, Cathy, Emmett, Spawn, Che, O'School, Happen, Tristessa, Sherrie, Colsen, and Case.

# AUTHOR'S NOTE

Thanks for reading my first (published) novel. I would appreciate the chance to learn from your experience with this book, so please post a review at your retailer of choice, or your favorite discussion forum, or here: facebook.com/IWFerguson. Also, please tell your friends if you liked it. It's not every day that a few minutes of your time can help launch a career.

If you're not sure what to put in a book review, here's a handy list of ideas: www.happen.net/br.html

Please sign up for my newsletter to receive updates about my progress with the next book in the series. Also, newsletter folks will get notified in time to get the Book Two ebook pre-order at a special low price. To sign up, visit my site at www.happen.net.

If you're on Instagram, stop by and say hello at instagram.com/i.w.ferguson/

## About the Author

I've always believed there's more to the story than we know, and I read and write to explore possibilities.

I attended The Evergreen State College in Olympia, WA and still live in the Pacific Northwest where I enjoy hiking in the mountains, playing ultimate Frisbee, and being a member of the Olympia Writers Group. I'm a night owl who is most comfortable in the company of cats, fire, strong coffee, dark chocolate, and interesting weather.

Made in the USA
San Bernardino, CA
01 December 2018